Last of an Exceptional Breed

The Legend of Draconis

Draconis Closes Its Doors

In

Book III

By

Janet Taylor-Perry

Last of an Exceptional Breed

The Legend of Draconis

Draconis Closes Its Doors

In

Book III

By

Janet Taylor-Perry

ISBN: 978-0-9990692-8-8

**Dragon Breath Press
Ridgeland, Mississippi**

Other books by Janet Taylor-Perry

The Raiford Chronicles:

Lucky Thirteen
http://amzn.to/1ld8grm
Heartless
http://amzn.to/1iWuYmP
Broken
http://goo.gl/6YTwyz
Whatever It Takes
http://goo.gl/1eLv66
The Legend of Draconis:

King Satin's Realm
http://goo.gl/wf7UbM
Spirits' Desire
Winner: Preditors and Editors Award
2017, Best "Other" Novel
goo.gl/H9St2K
April Chastain Intrigues:

Wilted Magnolias
https://goo.gl/2oJOjc

3

Hillbilly Hijinks

Homegrown Healer
https://www.amazon.com/dp/0999069233
Laura Beth Copeland Misadventures

Head Count
https://amzn.to/2msMt9z
Gods and Children

Ain't No Mountain
http://amazon.com/dp/0999069276

Disclaimer

All entities in the following story are fictional. Any resemblance to any person living or dead is coincidence.

Dedication

For Dr. Willard Boggan, a man who was beyond doubt the last of an exceptional breed. Mr. Willard was born in Memphis in 1921. During World War II, he joined the Navy, and he became a Reservist after active duty in 1949. He began private medical practice in 1959. In 1981, he established River Oaks Hospital (Now a part of Merit), where he practiced the rest of his career. He spearheaded the beginning of Charter Hospital (for psychiatric needs). He retired in 1992 at the age of seventy-two. But these are just facts, public record.

Who was Willard Boggan? He was a devoted husband to Lottie Brent Boggan. He was a stalwart father of four. He was a doctor who made house-calls when they had become obsolete. He was a healer for whom eggs or potholders were acceptable payment. He was an athlete—football (semi-pro), tennis, golf. He was a gentleman who still opened doors for women and stood to give them chairs when all seats were taken. He was a philanthropist, opening his home to those in need. He was a dog-lover. He went to his Heavenly reward on Valentine's Day, 2015, but will be forever in the hearts of those he touched.

Dr. Willard Boggan was the last of an exceptional breed.

Acknowledgements

Thank You, Lord, for giving me the gift of painting with words. Help me to use this gift to further Your Kingdom.

Appreciation to Guns and Roses for their song, "Sweet Child 'o Mine." My visualization of eyes of the deepest blue inspired Renée's eyes.

As always, my editor, Lottie Boggan, deserves a great round of applause.

Gratitude goes to my daughter, Mary Catherine Perry, for reading this in its infancy as I typed it and to the rest of my family for putting up with the strangeness of an author.

I have to thank Nidia Hernandez, aka Barbra Best, for being a beta reader. Check out her work in *The Rock Star Records*, available on Amazon. Also, thanks for lending me the use of Bujold Vineyards from your entertaining series.

Great appreciation to many fellow authors who continually offer me encouragement: Melanie, Patricia, Terry, Glen, Darden, Philip, John F., Dot, Marty, Mike, Joss, Leslie, Apryl, Gemma, Susan M., Jeanne, Cathy, Sol, Rebecca, Hazel, Reni, Gerald, Reva, James, Vivian, Judy, Wynne, Mary, Carlene, Graeme, Rhiannon, Dena, Tammy, Bill, Randall, Linda, John R., Patti, David, Susan S., Forest, Melissa, Jazmine, Mark, Janet F., Johnny, Carole, Janice, Charna, Lydia, Edrie, CC, Luna, Patricia N-D., Malcolm, Diana, Michael, Chuck G., Chuck M., Diana, Ann, Dirk, T Cat, DelSheree, NancyKay, Charlotte, Bonnie, Linda R., Linda Kay, Janet R. Please forgive me if I've forgotten anyone.

Merci and gracias to my proofreaders. With three of them, if there are any mistakes left, well, we're only human.

Last, I can never express my gratefulness to Christopher Chambers (juroddesigns.com) for another masterpiece in cover design.

Ye shall do no unrighteousness in judgment: thou shalt not respect the person of the poor, nor honor the person of the mighty: but in righteousness shalt thou judge thy neighbour.

Leviticus 19:15

Contents

Prologue

As the small sailing yacht approached the coordinates on the map, Rennin looked around him. Perplexed lines etched his brow. Behind him, the sun blazed brilliantly in the azure sky. A hundred yards in front of him, rose a thick cloud of fog. His vision could not penetrate it.

He gazed at Rebekah as she lay sleeping on the chaise lounge. He recalled the words his sister, Catherine, had spoken when she first met Rebekah. "This woman will take you places you only dreamed of…She is the magic that once was lost." Marie LeVeau had prophesied the same thing during a chance encounter, and his own mother, Caitlin, had repeated the exact words.

Rennin brushed away tears as he thought, *My magic is fading quickly, being eaten away by an invisible enemy.* He knelt by his wife and roused her. "Rebekah, honey, can you sit for a bit? I need your advice."

She leaned heavily on his arm as he helped her up. He said, "I've followed the map from the back of the old book precisely. All I see is a fogbank. What should I do?"

"Sail into the fog, Rennin, for it is not fog, but a curtain of mist. Once inside, you will see what we have sought."

"Whatever you say," he acknowledged. The woman relaxed her weakened, diseased body back onto the chair, but she stayed awake with anticipation.

As the ship slid silently through the haze, the sun once again showered the couple. They glanced behind them and saw clearly the ocean with no sign of the smoky curtain. Ahead in the distance, they spotted a silhouette.

Shortly, the sun was eclipsed, and Rennin and Rebekah O'Rourke turned their eyes skyward. Above them, hovered a glistening gargantuan pearly beast.

Before he could stop himself, Rennin blurted, "Draco."

The beast replied, "You *do* know me. Might I inquire your identity, though I'm sure I know the answer already?"

Rebekah sat up with more energy and strength than she had displayed in months. Rennin clasped her hand and spoke. "I am Rennin Aidan O'Rourke, also known as Friend of Dragons, and the descendent of Alexander, Duncan, Aidan, and Rennin the First. This is my wife, Rebekah. We have come in search of Draconis."

"And you have found it," replied the massive beast jovially. "Just as Rennin predicted, one of his descendants has come home. Welcome, Rennin and Rebekah O'Rourke." Draco sniffed Rebekah. "She is ill. Come. Let me take you to our doctor."

Rennin said quietly, "She's dying."

"Not so soon as you have thought," said Draco. "Rennin, you have found your spirits' desire."

Part One

Rites of Passage

1
Fairy Dust

As the U-Haul truck pulled into the shabby trailer park on that sultry Sunday afternoon in July, five-year-old Troy Tomerson stopped playing in the dirt by his front door. He pushed his curly chestnut locks from his emerald eyes to watch his new neighbors begin to unload their paltry belongings. The first thing he saw was a fragile-looking little girl being handed down from the front seat. He gasped at the sight he beheld. The little girl turned her sapphire eyes toward him and smiled. Her short blonde pixie haircut and fluffy pink dress made her a fairy picture. Slowly, Troy walked toward the truck, but he stopped short with a snap from his mother. "Troy! Where are you going?"

"To say hi."

The beleaguered woman gazed from her wilted tomato plants she was trying to salvage toward the new neighbors. The fetching face of the angelic child calmed her discomfort. "Well, all right, but be careful of that truck."

Troy marched boldly toward the moving van once he had his mother's approval. "Hello. My name is Troy Tomerson. Who are you?"

The little girl giggled. "Renée Peyton." Then, she threw a handful of confetti mixed with glitter on the boy.

He sputtered, "Why did you do that?"

"It's fairy dust," replied Renée delightfully. "Now, you can fly. I'm a pixie. I'm magic, like in *Peter Pan*. Only in my world, we don't have to fight pirates and Indians, but we do get to ride on dragons and soar above the earth."

"Oh. Okay," said Troy, brow etched in bewilderment.

"Don't you believe in magic?" asked the little girl, her blue eyes stretched wide.

Troy looked around the dingy little trailer park. With a wrinkled nose and a sigh, he said, "It'll take a lot more than fairy dust to make this place magic."

"Then, you should be happy I've moved here." Renée giggled. "I will show you magic."

A scruffy, burly, ruddy man came around the truck. Gruffly he questioned, "Renée, whom have you met?"

"This is Troy. He lives next door."

Through heavily knitted eyebrows, the man surveyed the small dark-haired, green-eyed boy. "Hmmm. He looks harmless." The man extended a bear-like hand to the little boy. "I'm Eugene Peyton, Renée's father."

Timidly, the boy shook the giant paw. "Welcome to the neighborhood," said Troy, trying to sound sincere.

The man laughed heartily, showing that his ursine façade was an act. "I can think of better places to be but thank you. We'll call you our first new friend."

Troy liked the sound of that. "Thank you," he replied proudly. "Can Renée play in my yard? Mom might have some cookies and milk inside."

"Very well," permitted Eugene, "but don't get into any trouble, young lady."

"I won't," assured Renée as the two children scampered off to find chocolate chip cookies.

While the Peytons unloaded their things from the moving van into the double-wide trailer that was next door to the Tomersons' small single-wide trailer, the two children became fast friends. The grounded, somber little boy fell under the spell of the would-be fairy. Soon, he, too, found himself pretending to live in a fairy world where he could be a knight in shining armor and rescue the damsel, Renée, from some wicked witch or greedy dragon. Of course, Renée's fascination with dragons went much further. She insisted all the stories that dragons were evil were lies. She believed that they were magical creatures meant to be friends. Troy reluctantly played her game. After all, it was fun.

At one point, Renée place a paper crown on Troy's head. She laughed and pinched his ear.

"Ow!" He clapped a hand over his ear. "Why'd you do that?"

"You have points. You can be an Elf prince this time."

"Fine. Just don't pinch me again."

The adults laughed at the exchange.

Mrs. Eva Tomerson, a widow who had borne a child late in life, prepared meatloaf, new potatoes and sweet peas in white sauce, and a pear salad that evening and invited her new neighbors, Eugene, Agnes, and Renée Peyton, to dine with her and her son. The tired newcomers readily accepted the invitation. Eva laughed at the vivid imagination of the little girl. "She will be a breath of fresh air for Troy," she confided. "He's always so serious. I often worry about him. When he was not quite two years old, my husband was killed in an Ameri-Rail derailment. Miraculously, Troy and I were unharmed. Many people died all around us. He hasn't been carefree since. He seems to have a great deal of sadness and anger buried in his heart. I'm glad to see a ray of sunshine affect him."

Eugene, who was twelve years older than his wife, chuckled. "Renée is my little fairy. She *does* bring magic into my life, just like her mother," he added as he patted his wife's hand. "I read some stories years ago about a land where men and dragons were friends. I've read her those stories at bedtime all her life. She has internalized them. Sometimes I think she needs a small dose of reality. Maybe Troy can give her that. They seem to play well together." Agnes, who was quiet, just nodded in agreement.

Renée pouted as her parents took her home to bed. She didn't want to go to bed—the day had been too exciting. Troy assured her he would play with her the next day, so she gave in with a frown. Troy yawned widely as soon as his company closed the door. "Mom," he said, "Renée has too much energy."

Eva burst into laughter. "You need some of it. Borrow a little. I would like to see you laugh like she does."

Troy furrowed his eyebrows. "I'll try," he agreed, nonplussed, "but she wears me out. I'm sleepy."

Eva bathed her son and tucked him into bed with a kiss and a prayer. Troy fell immediately to sleep, but the fairy dust was far from finished with its work.

That night Troy's dreams were filled with visions of dragons, witches, fairies, and heroes. One dragon in particular, a great glistening gray beast, came to him and spoke. "Hello. I'm Smoke, but you're not who you think you are. You belong here. One day you'll come. Trust Renée. She'll lead you where you need to go. From this day forward, she will be your guide. She truly is magic, but it will take much sorrow for you to believe it. You will, indeed, be her knight, and she will be your salvation. You'll need each other more than you can fathom right now. When you're confused, call for me, and I will send you wisdom, but you must believe. This land is incomplete without you. We need you here to finish the work your ancestors began. The name O'Rourke will change you forever when the time is right. Be warned. It will be a battle, and you're still a child, but with the proper guidance, you'll grow into a fine man, just like the first Rennin O'Rourke."

Troy awoke the next morning, dazed and confused. He felt as if he had not slept at all. At the breakfast table, Eva noticed the dark circles under his eyes. "What's the matter, honey?" she asked with her mother's heart.

"Who is Rennin O'Rourke?" he asked honestly.

Dropping the spatula she held and sucking in a great gasp, Eva replied, "I don't know. I never heard of him. Now, eat your breakfast. I have to get to work, and Sally will be here to take care of you. Did you forget that you start your karate classes today?"

"No, ma'am, but now I don't know if I should take the kind with the tiger or the dragon. Renée would like the kind with the dragon."

Unaware of her reply, Eva said, "Do both."

That is exactly what Troy did over the next several years, finding that in competition, Tae Kwon Do katas produced flair and show and first place finishes while Shotokan produced power and strength in sparring; and when he fought, the eye of the tiger pierced the darkness and the cunning of lions came to the forefront while the hearts of dragons reared their heads, often resulting in first blood and stern warnings and a few disqualifications when actual blood was drawn.

2
Profound Sadness

For the rest of the summer, Troy and Renée were inseparable; and Troy did, indeed, learn to laugh in her presence. The little girl's imaginary worlds offered endless entertainment. Alas, all good things must come to an end, and first grade loomed like a mammoth monster ahead of the two children. Troy tuned six the day before school started, and Renée turned six one day before the cut off day to enter first grade. Each day of school Eva and Agnes walked the two children to the entrance of the trailer park to catch the bus, and Sally met the children there in the afternoon since both mothers worked.

The first afternoon, Renée was in a tizzy. She fumed that she and Troy were not in the same class. It took an entire week for her to settle in and accept the fact that for seven hours a day she and Troy would be separated; but she finally did, and both began a successful school career.

Christmas holidays came. Since school was only a half day, Sally ran late meeting the bus.

Renée had an arm load of gifts from her friends, and she was preoccupied with contemplating how to magically bring snow to Florida for Christmas. As she rounded the front of the bus, she fell. The little troupe of students walked away toward home.

The bus began to pull away from the bus stop as Troy turned to tell Renée to walk faster. Unaware of the danger, she gathered her strewn items into her arms.

Taking in the scene in absolute terror, Troy bolted toward the moving bus to snatch Renée to safety.

He grabbed her arm with a jerk.

Her treasures covered the asphalt.

Troy sprawled to the ground.
The bus driver felt a bump.
Renée's scream shattered the air.

Eva Tomerson clutched the cold, limp hand of the little boy she loved with all her being as the respirator forced oxygen into his lungs and the electrocardiogram beeped a faint pulse. Her tear-stained face punctuated the nearly breathless prayer, "Please, God, don't take him from me again. He's all I have. Please."

Outside in the lounge of the pediatric intensive care unit, the Peyton family, Sally, the bus driver, and school officials waited in tense silence. Renée sobbed softly onto her father's shoulder. She had not stopped crying since the accident twelve hours earlier, half of which Troy had spent in surgery. He had his spleen removed, seven broken ribs, a shattered left arm, a collapsed lung, and a cerebral hematoma. The doctors described his condition as critical.

As Eva held her son's hand, a nurse padded into the cubicle. She checked Troy's vital signs and pulled out a hypodermic.

"What is that?" questioned Eva.

"Just an antibiotic. Nothing to worry about. It's routine after surgery to administer antibiotics," assured the nurse.

Eva nodded wearily. The nurse injected the penicillin into the child's I.V. and left the room. Immediately, Troy's tiny body began to convulse. Eva screamed. Emergency personnel scurried into action, forcing Eva from the room.

An hour later, Dr. Patel emerged from Troy's cubicle, wiping his brow. He smiled wanly at Eva. "That boy is stronger than all of us put together. Did you not know that he is severely allergic to penicillin? We almost lost him."

"No," whispered Eva. "He's never sick," she continued as the room began to spin, and she saw visions of a charred child's arm with a medical alert bracelet. Eva fainted.

Dr. Patel prescribed a medical alert bracelet with instructions that Troy should wear it every day for the rest of his life and had the still unconscious boy moved to a private room. Renée begged to put a little Christmas tree in Troy's room so that Santa wouldn't forget him. Eva allowed her to decorate a small artificial tree and place the gift she had bought for Troy beneath it. The girl hugged Eva. With her child's faith, Renée reassured the adult, "Troy will be fine. Just wait and see. He won't leave me."

In the darkness of the hospital room, Eva brooded. Her mind wandered back four years to an Ameri-Rail wreck. The past had come back to haunt her, and she had almost lost the one thing of any importance to her twice in one day. She spoke aloud to the darkness, "Why didn't I read that damned bracelet?" Eva lifted Troy's hand and kissed his fingers. "Mommy is so sorry, baby. I hope one day you'll understand and forgive me. I love you so much."

Christmas morning arrived quietly in the subdued hospital room. Eva stroked Troy's forehead and touched the bandage around his head, knowing that all his lovely curls were somewhere in a dumpster. Eva sighed, "Santa, where are you now? We could use a Christmas miracle." She kissed the little boy's pale cheek. A soft knock at the door startled her.

"May we come in?" asked Eugene.

"Of course," replied Eva. "He's still asleep."

Renée tiptoed to Troy's bed. Gently, she touched his cheek. She glanced up at Eva. "Maybe I should pinch his pointy ears."

Troy soared above the earth. He laughed gleefully as the voluminous creature dipped and rose at breakneck speed. Peering down, he saw Draco, a pearly shimmering beast, on the crystalline beach. Draco bellowed, "Just like the first Rennin, eh, Smoke?"

"Almost," replied the dragon on whose back Troy was perched. "Not as carefree or adventurous. He would never sneak out at dusk and return at dawn just to see a woman."

Draco laughed raucously. "He will when he realizes it's the right woman. Yea, he'll do much more than that." The white dragon sighed. "Although some of what he must do will not be happy and carefree; death shadows him."

Troy heard a soft, sweet, familiar voice.

"No! I want to stay here," Troy shouted as he opened his eyes to the starkness of his hospital room. By his bed, stood his best friend. Just a few feet away, were his mother and Mr. and Mrs. Peyton. "Where am I?" he demanded. "I want to go back. Smoke, come and get me!"

Somewhere in his subconscious, Troy heard the words, "All in good time, Rennin. Be patient."

Troy came home from the hospital but spent the next several weeks in bed. Renée no longer played the fairy games but became somber. She blamed herself for Troy's accident. She was still sweet and thoughtful, but she put away her magic. Eugene regretted wishing his daughter would get a dose of reality. It seemed in some way that Troy and Renée changed lives. Troy now desired to talk about dragons and be a knight. Renée doused his enthusiasm when she told him that her silly magic is what got him hurt in the first place.

Troy recovered completely from the accident, but Renée maintained her new demeanor. The next several years did not heal her shattered dreams. On the contrary, they became more splintered as the years wore on. Both children excelled in their studies and other endeavors; but Renée never asserted herself to a place of prominence as Troy did, ranking to black belt in Tae

Kwon Do at the age of ten, but having to wait until he was thirteen for Shotokan; and in playing peewee football taking command of the field. Renée studied and read unusual literature, old and obscure authors on subjects of questionable matter such as Druids and Celtic magic. Although she outwardly abandoned her belief in magic, she sought knowledge about true mystical practices.

One Friday evening when the children were ten, Eugene knocked on the Tomersons' door and asked Eva if she would let Renée stay the night. Eva agreed without hesitation although Eugene had a grim expression on his face. Eva asked if everything was all right, and Eugene silently shook his head. He looked toward his trailer and motioned for her to come outside. He explained when they were out of range to be overheard. "Agnes has left. You know I lost my job a few weeks ago, and she has decided it's time to move on with someone else. I simply cannot explain to Renée right now. How do I tell a ten-year-old little girl that her mother wants neither of us?"

Eva placed her hand over her mouth and spoke through her fingers. "I'm so sorry, Eugene. Agnes never indicated to me that she was unhappy."

Eugene laughed a soft but bitter laugh. "She never told me either until today. She didn't even have the courage to say it to my face. She left a note and divorce papers. When I got back from the employment agency, all her things were gone. I'm headed to the nearest bar to drown my sorrows."

"Eugene, getting drunk is no answer to the problem." Eva tried to comfort the man. "Please don't do that to Renée. She has lost enough."

The normally jovial man nodded, waved, and walked inside his trailer, closing the door behind him, but he did not visit a bar.

Renée accepted the turn of events as one more sign that happiness did not exist. She plodded on her course, made good grades, and kept to herself except for Troy. Eugene found another job although it paid far less than the one he lost. He provided for his only child. Eva continued her secretarial position at the law firm, and Troy became immensely popular as he took on more athletic endeavors and maintained excellent grades.

Adolescence descended with a vengeance. Troy turned many heads and never lacked for female companionship. As an accomplished athlete, he dated frequently. Still, Troy managed to spend time with Renée, who tried in every way she could think of to hide her beauty and her femininity. She kept her hair cropped short, always wore jeans and tee shirts, and never put makeup on her face. No matter how hard Troy tried, he could not persuade the girl to date. Except for the rare occasion when Troy hoodwinked, finagled, or blackmailed Renée into having fun, such as competing in a dance contest with him, the girl seemed to keep herself shrouded in a perpetual state of profound sadness.

3
Flights of Fancy

Both Troy and Renée were able students. Not long after the incident with the school bus, both children were placed in a class for gifted children. Both excelled at their studies, but Renée conformed to all that was expected of her while Troy constantly challenged authority and became notorious for doing things his own way. Troy's reputation in school made his teachers either dread and loathe having him in class or anticipate and relish his keen mind and sharp wit, although it could be caustic at times.

In addition to being bright and athletic, Troy showed great artistic and musical ability. While he found an outlet in painting and playing the guitar when he needed solitude and relaxation, Renée read ravenously and participated in debate and academic challenge meets.

Although tremendously talented, Troy's artistic endeavors did not always please his teachers, especially when he took flights of fancy when he was supposed to be doing serious paintings; for example, painting a smiling worm in his fruit still-life and arguing that a worm in a bowl of fruit would be extremely happy. Another incident that got him into trouble was drawing flying pigs when told to do a pen-and-ink of farm animals. The drawing itself was not what caused so much trouble, but the comment he made about the art teacher only having any imagination when pigs did fly.

However, neither the smiling worm nor the flying pigs caused as much trouble for Troy as did his beloved dragons. Mrs. Spencer, the sixth-grade art teacher, assigned an oil painting of the students' happiest memory. For days, Troy diligently and lovingly worked on his project. He surveyed his work with pride. He felt it was the best thing he had ever created. When Mrs. Spencer came to Troy's painting, she shrieked, "What is that garbage? I told you to paint a memory, not a fantasy."

Deflated, Troy eyed his painting of a glistening gray dragon with a small dark-haired boy on its back. The two soared through the air against an azure sky while a pearly white dragon looked up at them from a pristine crystal beach as aqua waves lapped at his feet. Troy defended his work, "It is not *garbage*. It's my memory. I did it when I was six years old. Smoke and Draco are real."

Mrs. Spencer glared at the boy. "You will redo this or receive a zero. I am tired of your flights of fancy. You will do exactly what you're told from now on."

"I will not!" defied Troy. "You can't tell me what my memories are. You weren't there, you wicked old witch!"

Having a student teacher in the classroom, Mrs. Spencer grabbed Troy by the collar with one hand and the painting with the other. She dragged the boy to the principal's office and threw the painting on Mr. Stiles's desk as she demanded, "Do something about this brat, now! He is rude, arrogant, disrespectful, and disobedient. He was supposed to have painted a memory. Look at that! It's a blasted dragon, no *two* dragons. And he refuses to redo it. Besides that, he called me a wicked old witch."

Troy retaliated, "I was wrong! It should've rhymed with witch!"

"Troy!" Mr. Stiles scolded. The principal calmly tried to defuse the situation. "Mrs. Spencer, other than being a bit imaginative, what's wrong with Troy's painting?"

"It's not what I assigned. I asked for a memory." She snapped her hands to her hips and tilted her chin upward.

"It *is* a memory!" Troy shouted. "It happened to me when I was run over by the school bus!"

Mr. Stiles turned to the student. "Troy, when you were unconscious, did you dream about dragons? Is this the memory of a dream?"

Troy folded his arms. "It was real. It was not a dream. The old bat said to paint our happiest memory." He pointed. "*That's* the happiest I've ever been."

Mr. Stiles rubbed his temples. Troy Tomerson was one of his favorite students, and Mrs. Spencer was rigidly old-school. He hated to discipline the boy for being creative and inventive. When given the chance, Troy was easy to love, but at the moment, Troy was showing his obstinate side. Mr. Stiles had to be a principal. Shaking his head, he said, "Troy, I will *not* allow you to call Mrs. Spencer names. Apologize immediately."

"No," said Troy decidedly. "I wouldn't mean it if I did. And I am not redoing my memory."

Mr. Stiles looked at the painting and sighed. He flipped through his rolodex and dialed Eva Tomerson at work.

"Mrs. Tomerson, I'm afraid I need you to come to pick Troy up," he said reluctantly. Mr. Stiles told Eva what was happening and hung up the receiver. He turned back to Troy.

"Last chance, Troy. Apologize and you'll only receive after-school detention for five days."

Troy glowered at Mrs. Spencer. "I-I-I. No. I can't."

"Very well. I'll miss you, Troy." Mr. Stiles set his lips in a fine line.

"I won't!" snapped Mrs. Spencer. "I want him out of my art class."

Mr. Stiles looked at the painting again. "You want to get rid of a kid with this much talent? Why, it looks just like..." Mr. Stiles stopped in mid-thought.

"It looks just like what?" Troy jumped on the principal's Freudian slip.

"Nothing," denied the principal. "Troy, you leave me no room. I'm taking you out of art, but don't stop painting. You are gifted."

Mrs. Spencer smirked triumphantly as she started out the door. "I'll send your things," she gloated.

After Mrs. Spencer left, Mr. Stiles said softly, "May I keep the painting, Troy? It looks just like my flight of fancy. His name was Smoke. What do you call yours?"

"Smoke. Yes, you may keep him."

Student and principal locked eyes just as Eva Tomerson came into the office with a look of exasperation on her face.

Troy preempted her wrath. "I'm sorry, Mom, but I can't apologize to Mrs. Spencer. It's a matter of principle. She called me a liar, and I don't lie. Besides, she's thwarting my creativity."

Eva spoke softly, "Do it for me, Troy. Apologize for calling her names."

"Mom," Troy said in a pleading tone, his lip quivering.

Eva shook her head. "Write it if you must, but I don't want a suspension on your record. Honey, there are times for flights of fancy, but sometimes you just have to suck it up and deal with it. You're *different*. Not everybody can accept that."

Because he loved his mother, Troy wrote an apology to Mrs. Spencer, but he did not mean a word of it. As a matter of fact, he worded it so that it made Mrs. Spencer sound as if she were to blame and should be writing an apology to him:

Mrs. Spencer,

I apologize if you were offended by my words. You caused me to become angry. I am sorry that you could not believe me. I hope all goes well with your class now that your troublemaker is gone.

Troy

Troy received five days of after-school detention, but Eva grounded him for two weeks. He was not even allowed to play with Renée, the worst punishment he could have ever received. However, nothing could keep Smoke from coming to him. Troy whispered to his dragon, "I guess I need to keep you a secret. Nobody believes in you but me, not even Renée anymore. Thanks for being my friend even if you are a flight of fancy."

Troy opened his guitar case and retrieved his rather expensive acoustic guitar that Eva had found at a pawn shop. Troy had made it truly his as he had painted Smoke on the back. He lovingly stroked the work of art before he leaned back on his bed and began to play and sing the heaviest, hardest metal tune he knew, AC/DC's "Highway to Hell."

4
Blown Away

A frustrating year passed for Troy before Eugene Peyton pounded on Eva's door. She opened to the frantic knock, and Eugene handed her a suitcase and a box of canned goods. Renée trembled behind her father. Eugene commanded with authority, "Eva, take the children and get as far inland as you can. I don't care what the authorities say; Andrew is headed straight for us. I have to stay because of my job with public works, but you and the children get to safety. If anything happens to me, take care of Renée."

Eugene knelt in front of his terrified daughter, "Renée, you go with Miss Eva. Do whatever she tells you. I love you."

Renée flung her arms around her father's neck and sobbed, "Daddy, please don't die. I can't lose you, too. I just can't."

Eugene realized his fear had spilled over and comforted his only child. "I'll be fine, but I still want you to go with Miss Eva and Troy. You know that they love you, too. They would never let anything happen to you. Now, be brave and obey me."

Renée nodded and went inside the home of her best friend. Eugene spoke once more to his neighbor and friend. "Seriously, Eva, this storm is bad whether the weather service has said so yet or not. Pack as quickly as you can and leave."

Eva knew Eugene did not scare easily. If he was so concerned about the approaching tropical storm, she felt certain his warning carried merit. She packed for her and her son, and she, Troy, and Renée left at noon.

As Eva drove inland, it was obvious Eugene was not the only one who was concerned. Evacuation traffic was high. Interstate movement was bumper-to-bumper. Hours longer than it would have taken under normal circumstances, Eva stopped at a motel in Tallahassee only to find there were no vacancies at that motel or any other.

Listening to the radio, the trio learned Eugene had been right. Hurricane Andrew appeared to be headed straight for South Florida and Miami. They also heard that Florida State University had opened its facilities to evacuees. They at least found a dry safe place to await news from home.

In South Florida on August 4, 1992, 175-mile-per-hour winds and torrential rains pounded the coast in a natural disaster. Because of his job with public works in Miami, Eugene rode out the fury of the storm and assisted with rescue and immediate maintenance. It was an experience he never forgot.

Neither did Troy forget the graciousness of those associated with Florida State. It was then that he decided that was where he would attend college. The football players took the five-foot-nine twelve-year-old under their wing while he was there. They even let him run some plays in practice with them. Troy found an outlet for his energy.

On the other hand, even with the distraction of being on a college campus with a law school, which Renée intended to attend, the girl could not focus on much except what was happening back home. They had not heard a word from Eugene and could only see what was reported on the news. They heard Dade County emergency management director Kate Hale exclaim at a nationally televised news conference, "Where in the hell is the cavalry on this one? They keep saying we're going to get supplies. For God's sake, where are they?"

After almost two weeks away from home, Eva cautiously made her way back. From all she had heard and seen in the news, she was terrified of what she might find, and they still had not had communication with Eugene. The trek back home showed the three Miamians immeasurable damage. Living in a mobile home, Eva feared the absolute worst as she approached the mobile home park.

Sure enough, as they entered the area where they lived, they saw many of the mobile homes were completely destroyed while others had major damage. Driving toward the center of the park where their homes were located, Eva wanted to close her eyes. Suddenly, Troy shouted, "Mom, look! It doesn't appear our house was touched. How? Renée, yours doesn't look very bad either, but I don't think there's any electricity. Your dad is sitting on the steps with a hand fan and the grill going."

Troy realized that Renée had closed her eyes because she was afraid of what she would find. Once they were out of the Nissan Sentra, Eugene met his daughter and his friends in a run. He engulfed them all and explained, "I had no idea how to contact you or even where you were. We got off easy here. You should see just a little farther south. Our electricity came back on about fifteen minutes ago, but we still don't have phone service. Eva, I knew you would be fine. Tell me where you ended up."

"Florida State," piped Troy. "I got to play football with the team. I'm gonna to play there after high school."

"Well, that sounds like a fine plan." Eugene chuckled and rumpled the boy's hair. "Just don't get blown away too soon like we did around here. This is the first day I haven't worked since I last saw you. I really needed some rest. I'm cooking some hotdogs that the government gave out. Are you hungry?"

They all agreed they were starved and ate hotdogs and chips. They decided to sleep outside because the sweltering Florida heat inside their homes was unbearable, and the electricity kept blipping on and off, never giving the air conditioning time to cool the metal boxes they called home.

The next day Eugene showed them some of the areas that had been hit really hard. The children were flabbergasted but talked constantly about each area. Eva was devastated by the loss she saw for she understood the time and energy and funds that would be used to rebuild after what would become the fourth most intense hurricane to hit the mainland United States.

As time progressed and school was still out, the children became more and more aware of the impact of the storm. They volunteered their time with a Red Cross group and prepared meals for those who had lost everything. The dingy little trailer park took on a new light in their eyes, and their station in life was lifted. They began to understand that the Power who had created all things was just as strong to destroy all things. Although their possessions were meager, they still had a home and those they loved. They began to appreciate what they had, and for the first time, they felt blessed to be poor with all the looting. They had nothing anybody wanted. Troy and Renée were grateful their entire lives had not been blown away.

5
First Blood

If ever there should be a question of original sin, one only needs to watch the actions of children, who can be extremely cruel and cold. Such was the plight of Renée as she withdrew more into herself after her mother left. While other teenage girls flaunted their entrance into womanhood, Renée did all she could to hide her beauty. Nonetheless, Troy saw her for who she truly was, especially after having survived Hurricane Andrew together. Troy often caught her looking at herself when she thought she was alone. He asked her, "Renée, why don't you dress like the other girls? You're just as pretty as they are, but you won't show it. If you acted like the other girls, they wouldn't make fun of you."

She responded, "I'm not trying to impress anyone. I am who I am. Take me or leave me."

Feeling as if he were fighting a losing battle, Troy let the argument lie until ninth grade. Seniors rarely accept freshmen as equals; therefore, when the senior quarterback invited Troy to a beach party, he could not refuse the invitation even if he wanted to. Troy did not want to refuse the invitation. On the other hand, he did want his best friend to go to the party with him.

After much wheedling and pleading, Renée gave in and went to the party with Troy. There were very few freshmen present. The exceptions were people such as Celina Ortiz whose brother, Raphael, was a senior. In addition, there were no other students from the dingy little trailer park where Troy and Renée lived. The crowd at the party was simply not in the same social circle. Renée paid more attention to this than Troy did because when several seniors started the hazing routine on Troy, Alfonso Gibbs, the quarterback, rescued the kid that he knew would one day have his position. Troy had talent, so money did not matter where he was concerned.

At fourteen, Troy already stood nearly six feet and weighed in at a hundred seventy pounds. He was the junior varsity starting quarterback. Since Troy was Alfonso's guest, the uppity seniors backed off quickly. Nonetheless, many of the boys continued covert conversations regarding the girl the upstart freshmen had brought with him.

Troy's attentions wandered to the bikini-clad females. Renée had consented to wearing her one-piece bathing suit with a pair of cut off jean shorts. Troy looked from his friend to the other girls and could not fathom why she thought herself unattractive. She was far prettier than most of the other girls Troy saw. Then, he spied a buxom girl who was in his algebra class. He recognized her as Celina Ortiz. Not knowing the definition of the word shy, Troy asked her to dance with him. Celina gave him a look of utter contempt and told him she only danced with men, not boys. Troy walked away determined that sooner or later that girl would go out with him.

Meanwhile, Renée found a quiet spot, if one existed, and sipped the Coke some boy had given her. It tasted strange to her, sweeter. She did not realize that she was drinking rum and Coke.

Troy found the drinks at the party to his liking and consumed several before realizing he was tipsy. Alfonso Gibbs good-naturedly clapped Troy on the shoulder, and exclaimed to the other football players, "Tomerson can hold his liquor, boys! This is my protégé. Don't bother him or his friends."

It was at that time Troy realized Renée was not around. Raphael Ortiz, who had given Renée her first drink, had found her sitting alone and had given her a second and a third. With the alcohol having loosened her inhibitions, Renée had been dancing with Raphael while three of his friends gathered to watch how the little freshmen, who could be stunning when she was not self-conscious, moved. Raphael heard his sister call his name and excused himself with the promise to return shortly.

In the absence of Raphael, Colton Johns decided to take up the slack and danced with Renée. Colton was well inebriated as he put his hands atop Renée's shoulders and commented, "This is a beach party. I think you wore too many clothes for a beach party." He slipped the straps of Renée's bathing suit off her shoulders.

Renée sobered instantly. "Stop that," she insisted.

"Come on now, baby. Show us what you've got." Colton pulled the strap hard enough that it broke and passed Renée off to Quincy Talbot, who in turn passed her to Glen Thomas, who tried to kiss her. Renée pushed herself away from Glen and slapped him.

"Whoa!" shouted Glen. "This is a little tiger. Grrrrr." He tried to kiss her again, but when she raised her hand to hit him, he hit her and threw her to the ground. "No little upstart freshmen is gonna get away with that. You came to play with the big boys— let's rumble." Glen ripped the button off Renée's cut-offs as she struggled beneath his weight.

When Troy noticed he did not see his best friend, he went in search of her. Hearing the commotion down the beach, his heart told him to follow it. For some reason, Alfonso Gibbs trailed Troy. As they approached the little gathering and heard two voices encouraging their friend in whatever he was doing, Troy heard the voice that he lived to hear scream, "Get off me!"

To the spectators, it seemed as if Glen Thomas flew into the air at Renée's command. In the moonlight, Troy saw Renée's torn bathing suit and a trickle of blood from her lip. Something inside him exploded, and he picked up Glen, a senior football player, from the ground where he had already thrown him and punched Renée's attacker in the face, breaking his nose.

Colton and Quincy, both senior football players, felt the obligation to support their friend, and each came at Troy. As the crowd gathered, Alfonso Gibbs kept everyone else back, saying, "I wanna see what this kid is made of."

Roundhouse and flying kicks, palm-heel and ridge-hand strikes, back fists and elbows to ribs found their targets as if unhindered and without resistance. Twenty minutes later, three senior football players lay crumpled on the beach while one angry, green-eyed freshman quarterback authoritatively dared them to move from a front stance poised to strike again if they did. Troy took off his shirt and covered Renée as he glared at the entire crowd. The only person who dared to speak was Alfonso, and he spoke to his classmates. "You should've listened to me. I told you not to bother Tomerson or his friends. I would say you got your asses royally kicked."

Colton groaned from the ground, "Yeah, well let's see how the little prick likes jail. I think I'll file assault charges."

"Do it," threatened Alfonso, "and that little girl will file attempted rape charges." He pointed toward Renée. "Since you just turned eighteen, I would suggest you keep your frigging mouth shut. I would also suggest that none of you ever talk about the fact that a freshman kicked your ass. What happened here tonight stays here. Troy, agreed?"

"Ask Renée," snarled Troy, still enraged.

Alfonso spoke gently to the girl, "Renée, do you agree?"

Renée looked at Troy. "Do you see why I hide? Take me home, Troy. For *you*, I will say nothing, but only for you."

The two friends walked home in silence. Finally, at their dingy little haven, Troy said mournfully, "I'm sorry, Renée. Please forgive me."

She said, "It wasn't your fault. They drew first blood, but I would say you finished it. Where did that come from, Troy?" She laid a hand on his arm. "I've never seen you like that. Honestly, it was a little scary. You were so angry."

"I don't know where it came from, Renée. All I know is when I saw what that asshole had done to you, something snapped. Sensei Spell says I have a killer instinct. I think it showed itself. I would never let anyone hurt you. You know that, don't you? You're my very best friend."

"Yes, Troy, I do. And you're my best friend, too. Good night."

Renée went inside, and Troy walked across the lot toward his own home. A voice that he had not heard in a while whispered, "Why didn't you kiss her, you dummy?"

Troy answered the voice, "Renée is my best friend, not my girlfriend."

"Right," said a dream dragon's voice. "That's why you beat the hell out of three guys."

"Be quiet, Smoke. You're only a figment of my imagination anyway."

"Is that what you think? Time will tell, but don't wait too long to realize Renée is real. Your enemy has already drawn first blood."

"What enemy?" said Troy as he went to bed and slept fitfully.

6
Best Friends

Troy sprang from his bed as his alarm jarred him from a restless sleep. Today was the biggest day of his life. He was graduating as valedictorian, and he could hardly wait for the graduation dance, similar to prom but only for the graduating class, afterward. When his best friend, Renée Peyton, refused to even go to prom, he had taken Kelly Gibbs, the younger sister of his predecessor as starting quarterback. He was going to this dance with Celina Ortiz, the one girl he had tried to get a date with his entire four years in high school. Finally, she had said she would go out with him. Life was perfect—almost. He still had not been able to convince Renée to go to the dance.

Troy grinned as he thought his plan for his best friend through one more time. She would go to the dance tonight if he had to drag her. Troy bounded down the hall to where his mother scrambled eggs to go with the sausage, toast, and cantaloupe.

"Good morning, Mom!" he greeted happily as he poured himself a big glass of orange juice.

"Good morning, sweetheart. This is your big day," Eva replied, full of pride in her only child.

"Yes, ma'am. I just have to get Renée to the dance tonight to have a perfect day."

"I thought you and Ben had worked out that little detail," Eva said uneasily.

"Ben agreed. Now I just have to convince Renée."

Eva sighed, "Renée would do almost anything for you. Maybe if the right man asked her to the dance, she would go. Think about it, Troy."

He nodded. "Renée's my best friend. I'm trying to find her the right man."

With a heavy sigh, Eva said, "Never mind."

Troy gulped down his breakfast, rushed to his room to dress, and darted out the door to the trailer next door. Renée was up and attired reluctantly in a dress because it was required for graduation.

"Wow!" said Troy when his friend let him in. "Guess what I dreamed about last night."

Renée rolled her eyes. "Let me guess—dragons. Troy, when are you gonna realize that was a childhood fantasy, and a ridiculous one at that?"

"Nope. For once that's not what I dreamed about. I dreamed you were dancing at the dance with me."

She laughed bitterly. "You do have absurd fantasies."

"Renée, if you don't go to the dance, I won't go."

"Bull!"

"I mean it. I cannot go to our last high-school experience without my best friend." He plopped onto the brown-and-gold, plaid couch in the living room.

"I still remember what happened the last time I let you bully me into going to a class function." She shook her head. "And you would, too, go. You went to prom. Besides, Troy, who would want to go to the dance with me? You're the only person in our whole class who gives one iota about me, and you have a date."

"Ben."

"Ben Matthews? How much did you pay him?"

"Renée!" He slapped the sofa. "Ben has hung out with us several times. Why must you think the worst?"

She crossed her arms and glared at Troy. He crossed his arms and glared back. "Ben says he will gladly go to the dance with you if you will for once in your life dress like a girl."

"Oh, so there's a condition!"

"Come on, Renée! Please? Please do this for me? Go with Ben and Celina and me."

She laughed hard. "I am soooo sure your date wants me to tag along."

"Jeez!" Troy shouted. "What happened to you? You were the prettiest thing I ever saw and the happiest, most fun person I ever met. What happened? I have been through just as much bullshit as you. I haven't given up on life. What is your problem? For one night—" He held up his index finger—"Just one, can't you, please, be the pixie you once were and sprinkle some fairy dust in my life? I am so tired of your bullshit! Many people, boys included, would like you if you would give them half a chance."

Renée gave Troy an exasperated look. "Even if I wanted to, I can't afford a dress."

"Then, you'll go?"

She put her hands to her face, "Troy!"

He pried her hands from her face and looked at her imploringly.

She screamed, "I give up! You win."

Troy grabbed her by the hand and pulled her out the door and across the trailer park to his home. He dragged her down the hall to his room where he told her to sit on the bed and close her eyes. She did so with some consternation. She heard Troy's closet open and close and felt a box on her lap. "Okay," Troy said, "open your eyes."

Renée opened her eyes and stared at the box. "What's this?"

"Open it."

Inside the box, lay a pink, satin, spaghetti-strap dress and a pair of matching pink pumps. Renée laid the box beside her and ran her hand across her brow. "Troy, why did you spend your money and buy this?"

He squatted in front of her and put his arms on her knees. "So, my best friend would go to the dance. Now, all you need is to let Mom fix your makeup. You can be a fairy princess tonight."

"You don't need to rescue me from myself." She patted his cheek. "I'll do this for you, but you must stop trying to make me into something that I gave up long ago. Troy, I'll be leaving here in August and going to UC Berkeley. I have my scholarship. I'm going to be a corporate lawyer. You'll be going to Florida State and then to medical school. There is no magic that will get us through any of that. It will be our hard work if we become successful. Troy, grow up."

"Have it your way," he sighed in exasperation.

As Renée got up to leave to finish getting ready for graduation, he asked, "Renée, who is Rennin O'Rourke?"

The girl wrinkled her nose. "I think that was the name of the man who wrote the stories Daddy read to me long ago. Why?"

"Have you ever told me his name before?"

"I don't think so. Why?"

"In my dreams, the dragons call me Rennin and compare me to the first Rennin O'Rourke. If there is no magic at all, how could I have known that name?"

"I must've told you and just don't remember. We were only five years old. If you'll stop dwelling on this, I'll see if I can find that old book, and you can read it for yourself. And if you will stop nagging me, I'll go to the damned dance tonight with Ben just to shut you up."

"Will you let Mom do your makeup?"

Renée made cat claws and screamed. "I will even wear makeup and dangling earrings just this once."

She went home for her shoes so that she, too, could graduate with high honors.

Troy grinned. "Let's see how much magic I can make tonight." Then, he picked up the phone and called Ben. "Okay, man. I'll give you the hundred fifty, but if she ever finds out that I paid you, you are a dead man."

7
Dancing in the Dark

Graduation went off without a hitch and at precisely seven o'clock, Ben Matthews knocked at Renée's door. Eugene let the young man in as Renée came down the hall. Her slim five-feet-six-inches had donned the pastel pink dress Troy had bought, and Eva had meticulously applied subtle makeup for the girl. She still wore her platinum-blonde hair in a pixie cut, but tonight she wore pink chandelier earrings. Ben was positive he had come to the wrong address because he felt certain Renée could never have looked so lovely. He stared at her, speechless.

Renée shook her head. "Ben, are we going?"

"Oh. Yeah." He handed her a pink orchid corsage for her wrist.

"Thank you," she acknowledged the gift. "Miss Eva has seen to it that I have a boutonnière for you." She pinned the carnation to Ben's lapel.

Renée kissed her father. "Good night, Daddy."

Eugene said, "Wait! Eva told me to be sure and take some pictures. You do look beautiful, darling."

After several snapshots, the couple left. They met Troy and Celina at the dance. Celina had her soot black hair arranged in an adult fashion and wore a strapless scarlet dress. She commented to Troy, "Renée does clean up well. Are you sure that's not some imposter?"

Transfixed by the sight, Troy murmured, "No, that's my pixie in true form."

Celina scowled and put her arm around Troy's.

The teenagers danced late into the night. Renée was surprised at the number of invitations she had to dance. It seemed everyone had asked her to dance except Troy. Celina held tightly to him for most of the evening. However, while Celina excused herself to go to the ladies' room, Troy finally found his chance to dance with Renée.

She looked at him and said, "I thought you would never ask. How is your dream supposed to come true if you don't make it happen?"

As the slow mellow tune droned and the lights dimmed, the dance between Troy and Renée felt magical. He held her right hand near his heart while her left hand gently caressed the ends of his hair at his neck. She closed her eyes and for a brief moment thought of confetti and glitter and magic fairy dust. Troy rubbed his cheek against the top of her head and without realizing he spoke his thought aloud whispered, "You're the most beautiful thing I've ever seen."

The spell was instantly broken when Celina tapped Renée on the shoulder to cut into the dance as the music stopped. Renée retreated to the restroom, and Troy went to get Celina a glass of punch. At the punch table, Ben sauntered next to Troy and slipped his hand into his friend's hand. Troy felt a wad of paper. "Take it back," said Ben. "You'll never have to pay me to take her anywhere. She's wonderful. How have you kept her to yourself all these years? All that's missing is the money for the corsage." Troy realized Ben had returned almost a hundred fifty dollars, but he didn't realize Celina had partially overheard the exchange.

As Celina touched his arm, Troy hurriedly stuffed the money into his pocket and handed Celina the punch he had come to get. She watched her date's gaze as Renée returned from the restroom. She set down the cup and whispered in Troy's ear, "Let's go somewhere so we can be alone."

He looked down at the Latin beauty as she smiled seductively. "Let me tell Ben and Renée we're leaving."

Celina detained him. "They'll be fine on their own. Now's your chance to be alone with me. There will be no other if you don't take this one."

Parked at the beach, Celina turned on her charms and passed a flask filled with some of her father's best scotch whiskey. She kissed Troy the way he had dreamed of for four years and touched him in places he had never dreamed this girl would touch him. Before he could think logically, he and Celina were in the back seat of his old used Monte Carlo he had restored to near showroom appearance and performance, and Troy was no longer a boy while it was clear to the rational mind Celina had not been a virgin for a long time. However, at that moment in time, Troy was neither logical nor rational. In the heat of passion, he made one fatal error. Without consciously thinking, he breathed the name Renée as he fulfilled a deep lust with a determined Celina who had an agenda all her own.

Ben walked Renée to her door and attempted to kiss her good night. As she pulled back, he said, "Troy's right. You really don't realize how beautiful you are, do you?"

As a slight smirk played around her mouth, Renée asked, "Did Troy say I was beautiful?"

"He said you don't know how beautiful you are. Let me show you how beautiful I think you are." Ben leaned forward to kiss Renée again. This time she allowed him one long-remembered good-night kiss before she slipped inside.

Troy sneaked in as the sun streaked the sky only to find Eva waiting anxiously on the couch. "Troy, what have you done? Do you have any idea what time it is?"

Guiltily, Troy replied, "Everything's fine, Mom. You should've gone to bed. Remember I'll be leaving in two months. You have to let me grow up."

"Is that what you did tonight—grow up with a girl that thinks she's too good to come to your home to meet your mother?"

"Mom, it's not like that. Celina's just..."

"A snob?"

"No, she just..."

"Has money and you don't. I don't trust her, Troy. She's using you for something."

"Mom, can't it be that she likes me?"

"No. If she liked you, she would've liked you years ago."

"You worry too much. Why don't you ask if I had a good time?"

She put a hand on her son's neck. "It's obvious that you had a good time. You have the scars to prove it. Please, tell me that you at least used protection."

"Mom!"

"Troy, I'm not a fool. And you are no longer a little boy. You have too much at stake to take stupid risks. You have a promising future. Don't mess it up. Now, go and get some sleep. You start your job at noon."

Troy stopped to look at himself in the bathroom mirror. Celina had left a huge hickey on his neck, as well as other places that were not visible clothed. His one thought was how to tell Renée what had happened. He gazed at himself in the mirror. *I can't. She would never forgive me.*

Troy slept fitfully. His mystical dragons all whispered to him, "Don't be a fool...She's all wrong for you...She will only destroy your future...Stop it now while you can."

Troy awoke in a cold sweat. He dressed and went to work.

8
Cloudy Future

Renée stopped Troy as he came in from his first day on his summer job. She kissed him softly on the cheek as Celina drove up in her new Mustang.

"What was that for?" he asked.

"For thinking I'm beautiful." Renée rolled her eyes. "Your girlfriend's here."

Celina smiled grudgingly. "Hello, Renée. Did you have fun at the dance? Your date seemed to."

"Yes, I actually did. Good night, Troy."

Celina tried to look innocent. "Did I offend her?"

Troy shrugged and said loudly enough for Renée to hear on her way home, "What are you doing here? I just got off work, and I'm tired."

Celina pouted. "Too tired to see me?"

"Actually, yes. I didn't sleep at all last night, and I've worked for six hours in the heat. I'm just plain exhausted."

"Oh," she said dejectedly. "Maybe I should've called first. I apologize, but I thought after last night you'd want to see me."

Troy sat down on the steps to his trailer and put his fingers to his temple as if his head were splitting. "About last night. I think we should take a step backward. We moved way too fast. I really don't think I'm ready for that kind of relationship with you. I'll be leaving for college in two months. It just is not a wise move on our part to get that serious."

"Well, if that's how you feel!" Celina stomped off to her car.

Troy stared after the Mustang as it sped away. *Wow! Talk about a temper.* However, he felt little compunction to go after the angry girl. Rather, he walked across the way to Renée's trailer and knocked.

Renée opened the door in surprise, sticking her head out and looking both ways. "She left so soon?"

He shrugged and brushed the comment off with his hand. "I really didn't want to be with her tonight. I think she was a big mistake."

"Whoa," Renée teased. "The boy's thinking with his big head for a change."

Troy grimaced at a memory only he knew. "Let's go to the carnival and eat corn dogs and cotton candy," he suggested.

"I thought you were tired."

"Naa. I'm never too tired to get stuck at the top of the Ferris wheel with you." He grinned impishly. "Just let me grab a shower."

The two friends laughed gaily for several hours as they rode dare-devil rides and ate massive quantities of junk food. The beach carnival had added a new attraction, a fortune-telling station. They had a palm reader, a tea-leaf reader, a crystal-ball gazer, and a Tarot-card reader. Troy pulled Renée into the tent. "Come on. Let's see what our futures hold. Which one do we do first?"

"None of them. This is silly."

"Renée, it's just for fun. Let's remember what they say and see what happens in twenty years, or are you chicken?"

She punched him in the arm. Since the tea-leaf reader's line was the shortest, they went to her first. They drank their tea and the wizened old gypsy swirled their cups. First, she interpreted Renée's. In a heavy Baltic accent, she said, "Hmmm. I see a ladder vith some broken rungs. You are upvard bound, my dear, but be careful of de steps you take to get dere. Some are treacherous."

Then, she turned to Troy's cup. "My, my. I have never seen dis before. Dere is a dragon. Dat means you vill do battle, but it is not clear vhat kind of battle."

Troy gesticulated victory. "Yes! I'm gonna play in a super bowl. You'll see, Renée."

The girl had to admit that the encounter was harmless enough, so they moved on to the palm reader who was a pretty, young gypsy. She took Renée's palm. "Your life appears long, but there are barbs all along your lifeline. You will have serious obstacles to overcome. Your love line is chaotic. You will find the one you choose to be false, but there is a constant abiding love who will never forsake you entwined in the line. You are a lucky woman."

Unflinchingly, Troy offered his palm. "Let me see again." The girl reached for Renée's palm. "Yes, the same pattern is there. You two are interwoven although there seem to be breaks in the line that are reformed. Now, your lifeline diverges as if you have two lives. That is an unusual pattern, as if you are two separate identities."

"I didn't like that part about your having multiple personalities," worried Renée as they waited for the crystal ball.

Troy laughed a fake witch's laugh. "Just call me Sybil."

"That's not funny, Troy."

"Lighten up, Renée. You don't take this stuff seriously. But if you do, remember we're *interwoven*." He put his arm around her and pulled her close for a tight, friendly squeeze.

Renée had to laugh despite the disquiet she felt. As they continued to wait, she pointed out, "They must be three generations of the same family." The four women of the ages to indicate three separate generations bore strong resemblances to one another.

"Exactly," said Troy. "It's like a circus act carried on from one generation to the next. They're performers. They tell people what they think will be enticing and interesting. So, chill."

Finally, Troy and Renée reached the table where the middle-aged woman bade Renée to sit. Then, she looked at the couple, "No, sit together. The ball already tells me you will wander in and out of each other's lives forever."

Troy plopped onto Renée's lap. "You're heavy," she chided. "Trade places." He obliged.

The fortune-teller continued. "I do not like dark fortunes. This one is very cloudy. I see turmoil and strife and secrets. I see rays of sunlight trying to shoot through, but the clouds are thick. I see blood. And I see..." The woman jumped up from the table. "No more."

"What did you see?" demanded Troy.

"It cannot be. I saw dragon fire."

"Oh, good grief," Renée barked. "Troy, let's go home. We have to work tomorrow."

"But we haven't done the Tarot cards."

"Forget the damned Tarot cards. I know what we'll get. First, will be the one with its eyes covered indicating it's hard to predict our future. Oh, but there will be a broken heart for unrequited love, and there must be death lurking somewhere." Renée spoke loudly enough to be heard throughout the tent.

Even as she spoke, the young Tarot-card reader crooked her finger at the couple before she took the next person in line. They paused near the table as she spoke distinctly, "Those are exactly the cards I turned over as my mother read the ball for you. Do not scoff, my dear." Troy looked down at the table, and those were the cards that were face up. The woman continued, "Would you like to see the last one?"

"Yes," said Troy.

"No," said Renée simultaneously.

The woman flipped the card. "Lies and deception, both in your pasts and your futures."

Renée dragged Troy from the tent.

Celina did not call Troy for several weeks, and he worked long hard days with the contractor who had hired him for the third summer while Renée worked as a courier for the law firm where

Eva was secretary. Renée surprised Troy by going on several dates with Ben, who lived at the front of the trailer park. Three weeks after she stormed from the mobile-home community, Celina called Troy and told him she needed to talk to him. When she arrived at dusk, Renée and Troy sat on the steps into his trailer. He had just pulled into his parking place and was still grimy and sweaty.

Celina feigned courtesy as she spoke. "Hello, Renée. When do you leave for Berkeley?"

"Four weeks." Renée stood to leave. "I'll talk to you later, Troy." The look that passed between the two women could have indicated murder on both their parts.

Troy graciously invited Celina into his home, but she acted as if she might contract a disease as she entered or if she touched Troy as he was. Nonetheless, enter she did. "What did you want to talk about?" he asked candidly.

"Apparently, you don't believe in small talk."

"No. I'm tired, I'm hot, and I need a shower. I think we both know there's very little we have in common. So, please get to the point of this very awkward visit."

"Very well. You might consider trying to get used to talking to me. I'm pregnant."

Troy fell onto the couch as his stomach lurched. "What did you say?"

"You heard me clearly. I didn't stutter or use euphemisms."

"Are…are you sure?"

"Yes, Troy. Now, what are we gonna do?"

"What *can* we do? What choices do we have? Oh, God! What have I done?" He pushed, sweaty, sticky hair back from his forehead.

"Well, Troy, you know I'm Catholic just as you are. I cannot have an abortion."

"That thought never crossed my mind, but so much for my bright future. I guess I won't be going to medical school or playing in a super bowl. Have you told your parents?"

"Not yet. I thought I should talk to you first. I wanted to see your reaction."

"My mother will be devastated. I'll be such a disappointment to her."

"Troy, what are we gonna do?"

"We have no choice. We'll have to get married."

"But you don't love me. Why would you marry me?"

"It's my duty, my responsibility. It's the right thing to do."

"Well, I have to tell my parents. I would like it if you were with me."

"Of course. When? We still have to tell my mom, too. And..." He waved his hand as if erasing a chalkboard. "Never mind."

"I'll call you. I have to think." Celina left.

Troy made himself a glass of ice water. He took a sip and subsequently threw the glass at the door, shattering it to smithereens. He sat back down, buried his face in the cushions of the couch, and sobbed.

As the Mustang drove away, Renée heard the glass shatter against the door and came in to see her friend in distress. "Troy, what's wrong?"

"Oh, God! Renée, I'm a fool."

"What did she say?"

"She's pregnant."

Renée stared at Troy. "Is it yours?"

"It must be. That's why she came to tell me."

"I don't think so. It's too soon since the dance for her to know she's pregnant with *your* child. But you *are* a fool. Why did you do it, Troy? Why? My God! Why didn't you at least cover the damned thing up? What were you thinking?"

"I don't know why. I wasn't thinking. We were drinking. She made me want to so much. I regretted it even before now."

"Why do you regret it if she was what you wanted?"

"She's not what I wanted. I only thought she was at the time because she had been such a challenge for so long."

"What do you want, Troy? What are you gonna do now?"

"Do you really want to know what I want?" His green eyes locked with her blue ones. "I want *you*! And I want my future back, but I have to take responsibility for my actions." Troy picked the ashtray up from the coffee table and it joined the debris from his water glass.

Renée ignored his tantrum. "I'm telling you, you are *not* the father. Celina has slept with half the senior class and some outside. She lost her virginity before she had boobs. She's using you because she knows you'll do the right thing. I won't let her get away with it. It's my turn to save you from yourself."

Starting out the door, the girl paused. She barely whispered, "You know, Troy, you've *always* had me if you had just taken the time to notice." More loudly she said, "Clean up this mess and stop throwing fits." Renée stomped out the door and slammed it behind her.

Renée's motor scooter came to a stop at the gate to the Ortiz house. She pushed the call button.

"Yes, may I help you?" came the voice over the speaker.

"Renée Peyton to see Celina."

"Does my daughter know you?" asked the woman's voice.

"We were classmates. I need to talk to her about her future plans."

"Very well. Come up to the house. I'll call Celina down."

Renée walked into a house full of ostentatious lavishness. She could hardly believe her eyes as she took in the marble tiled floors and crystal chandelier just in the entry. Through a set of glass French doors, she could see the tile continued, and the few furnishings she glimpsed without moving from the front door were deep rich mahogany. A hand-woven Persian rug lay on the other side of the French doors.

Celina stepped into the foyer to see her. "I suppose Troy told you?"

"Yes, he did, and I'm not gonna let you get away with destroying his future. Both you and I know damned well this is not his baby."

"Shhh." Celina waved her hands frantically and closed the glass doors. "Keep your voice down."

"Why? Don't they know they're having a grandchild?"

"No!"

"Well, if you're so desperate to trap Troy, they should know. I'm sure they'll help you do what's right."

"I'm not trying to trap Troy. I don't want Troy."

"Then, why did you tell him you're having his baby?"

"I have to do *something*. Troy'll do what's right. I saw what he did for you, and you're just a friend. He never had sex with you. He has honor."

"And the sleaze ball that knocked you up doesn't?" Renée clenched and unclenched her fists. "I won't let you do this."

"And how are you gonna stop it?" Celina crossed her arms over her chest. "Are you gonna tell him about this little conversation? Do you think he cares so much for you that he'll listen? Why don't you ask him how much he paid Ben to take you to the dance?" A crooked grin spread across her face. "He thinks you're so pathetic he has to buy you some company."

"Troy told me he didn't pay Ben. Ben told me Troy didn't pay him." Renée's eyes welled with tears, making them resemble tiny lakes.

"And you believed it? I saw them exchange the money at the dance."

"It doesn't matter." She pressed the heels of her hands to her eyes. "Troy doesn't deserve to have you ruin his life. Have the decency to treat him right. Don't you think the real father should know?"

"He does. Troy was *his* idea."

"Jeez! You really are a spoiled little bitch, aren't you? Whatever I have to do, Troy will *not* marry you and ruin his future.

He might be a fool, and I may never speak to him again, but he will not marry you. I'll see to that."

"Good luck. You know he'll stand by me."

"We'll see." With that, Renée left and rode back to Troy, her insides roiling like a volcano about to erupt.

Renée knocked on Troy's door. He let her in, and she immediately said, "I see your mother isn't home yet."

"No. She called to say she'd be late."

"Good." Renée pummeled him across the face repeatedly.

"What the hell?"

She shrieked, "You paid Ben! Admit it! You had to bribe someone to take me to the damned dance! How could you, Troy? How could you?"

He grabbed her wrists. "He gave the money back! He said I never had to pay him to do anything with you because you're wonderful."

"But you felt like you had to buy me company! Am I really that hideous and pathetic?"

"I would've done anything to get you to that dance."

"Except ask me yourself!"

"I didn't think you would go with me. You wouldn't go to prom with me."

"Because I couldn't afford it, you idiot! And you don't ever think! You didn't think twice about fucking some slut who's pregnant and trying to pin it on you. I ought to let you suffer the consequences and spend a lifetime of hell with her, but I happen to care about you!" Renée threw a mini audio cassette player at Troy. "Here! This is your proof, so you won't ruin your future. You are *not* the baby's father. But don't *ever* speak to me again!"

Renée ran from the trailer in tears and called Ben to pick her up. She dragged Ben along the beach to a secluded place where she told him she was leaving for California early, but she wanted to tell him good-bye in a way he would never forget. She slipped from the only sundress she owned to show she wore nothing beneath. Ben stared at her in disbelief. Renée said, "What's wrong, Ben? Don't you want me? Or has Troy not paid you enough to fuck me?"

Ben stammered, "T-t-troy would never have to pay me to be with you. You really are gorgeous."

"Really? Prove it."

Ben took Renée to the ground.

9
A Million Miles Away

Four weeks before she had planned to leave, Renée once again knocked on Troy's door. She hugged Eva good-bye and handed Troy a copy of an old, tattered book entitled *Memoirs of Magic* by Rennin Drake O'Rourke. All she whispered to Troy as she turned to leave was, "I would never lie to you. Ben was my first, thanks to you because all you could do was to sell me to the lowest, most desperate bidder rather than have what should have been yours. You are a fool. Good-bye."

For weeks, Troy could not believe the most special person in his life had simply left for California with no other word. However, Renée still protected him when he played the tape for Celina, and she had to leave without a marriage proposal. He could not imagine why Celina had connived to trick him into a marriage without love. Finally, the day came for Troy to go to Florida State on both a football and an academic scholarship. Eva beamed with pride in the boy she had reared. Troy felt as if everything and everyone he loved were a million miles away as he recalled a dragon's voice warning him not to wait too long to realize Renée was real.

Eugene, though disappointed in Troy's actions, gave the boy Renée's address in California. Troy wrote to her repeatedly asking her to forgive him. After the sixth letter, he received a reply:

Troy

I forgive you. Now leave me alone. I'm well as it appears you are also. I see you're still unmarried. (Thank God.) See to your priorities. Good luck with your future.

Mine is here in California. I won't be coming back to Florida except for brief visits with my father. I've decided to grow up. Now it's your turn.

P. S.

Tell Ben I'm sorry. He really is a nice guy and didn't deserve what I did to him.

Troy did not know what to make of such a message. All he knew for certain was his best friend was on the other side of the country, and he missed her desperately. He continued to drop her letters from time to time because he could not let her go completely. Apparently, Renée could not completely sever their tie either for she would send short replies such as:

Troy,

I'm proud to hear you were red-shirted. That means you'll get playing time. Keep your eyes open for the pro scouts. You have the talent but keep the grades up and prepare for med school. I made the dean's list and I've actually joined a sorority—yes, me, if you can believe it. I figure it'll help me in the future. Sometimes it's not what you know, but whom you know that lands you the job.

Remember that. Make some connections. I'll be in Florida for Christmas. I suppose I'll see you then.

Troy felt relieved that Renée was speaking to him, but he could still feel the strain that his good intentions had caused. He did not know how to make amends and resigned himself to accept the little relationship that was left. He did make connections, but not the kind that Renée had suggested. Although he joined a fraternity, it was just for the social involvement. The connections Troy made during his college years were to his wide receivers and tight ends, professional scouts, and multiple women, with only one relationship lasting more than three dates.

Troy dated a young woman by the name of Melanie Pryor, who was from the small town of Puma Pass, California, which was in the Bay area and near Renée. Her father was a senior partner in a law firm, and being around her, gave Troy a feeling of connection, not only to Renée, but to something he could not finger. However, the relationship ended during the Thanksgiving break when Melanie went home and was tragically killed in a car accident.

The first year of college passed with just the short visit at Christmas with Renée. Troy went home for the summer and worked with the contractor that he had worked with every summer since he was fifteen. Renée stayed in California, clerked for the same law firm Melanie's father headed, and went to summer school. Renée did write Troy a brief note over the summer:

Troy

I thought you might find this tidbit interesting. The town where I'm working was founded in the 1850s by a man named Rennin O'Rourke. Apparently, one of his great-great-grand-somethings is the person who wrote that fairytale after he immigrated to America in the 1600s. I will say this: He could spin a yarn. Have you read it yet? Have a great summer and stay out of trouble. Avoid Latin lovers.

Renée

So distraught had Troy been when Renée left for college, he had not even thought about the old book, but to keep himself occupied in the evenings during that summer, he decided to read it. He found the story fascinating and his dreams returned, but they were not as pleasant as his childhood dreams. Many times, humans in his dreams bickered with the dragons, and those with the last name of O'Rourke had to stand as mediators. He found himself being pulled almost to the breaking point in his dreams. Troy chalked the turmoil in his subconscious up to the strange story and his guilt that remained about Renée.

The young football player happily returned to Florida State where he had many things to occupy his mind. He partied with his fraternity and dated frequently. More importantly, he won the position of second-string quarterback. Troy knew it would have been foolish to expect to be able to be first-string against such a talented senior as Dustin Caples. Nonetheless, Troy got his chance to start after the third game of the year when Dustin broke his leg. He did not disappoint his team, winning six of the seven games he quarterbacked.

Over the next four years, Troy proved himself both on and off the gridiron, and he looked forward to his yearly visit with Renée, despite the number of young women who kept him company in many ways on the campus of Florida State. However, the visits with Renée came to an abrupt halt when Eugene had a massive coronary and died. Renée did not come back to Florida after her father's funeral. She had found a home in Puma Pass where she took the LSAT and entered law school at Stanford after only three years of undergraduate study.

Troy, too, had an exciting future ahead. After winning the national championship with the Seminoles his senior year, he was drafted by the Oakland Raiders, which made Troy more excited than merely playing professional football because Oakland was close to Renée. Even in the wake of the excitement of being able to play professional football, he took the MCAT with outstanding results. He figured that after a few years of football he would go on to medical school. He knew most football careers were short-lived and could be cut even shorter by a major injury.

Eva, though proud of Troy, was distressed that now he would be on the other side of the country. She asked him why he couldn't play football for the Dolphins. Troy shrugged and explained, "Mom, when it comes to football, a new player like me can't just decide where he wants to play. The Dolphins don't need a quarterback as much as the Raiders. I have to go where I'm needed."

"What about medical school, darling?"

Troy hugged his mother. "I won't play football forever, Mom. I might even be able to take some classes in the off season. They have excellent medical schools in California. And…"

Eva stepped back. "And Renée is there?"

"I don't know, Mom. Renée seems a lifetime ago. I'm not sure if there ever really was anything there. Maybe it was all just a childhood fantasy."

She touched her son's cheek. "Well, you know where home is. You are *always* welcome home."

"I know, Mom." Troy went to bed and slept for the last time in a Miami trailer park. That night he dreamed again of dragons who called for him to come to them. When he awoke, he felt home might be a million miles away.

10
Power Struggle

Troy left for training camp with great expectations. The first call he made after settling into his new home was to Renée; however, she cut the call short, telling Troy that she was extremely busy helping to research a case for court in just a few days that involved a law suit against Mercier Memorial Hospital. She congratulated him on his selection and wished him luck.

Feeling greatly rejected, Troy entered training camp and poured his energy into making the team. He did not call Renée again until he made the final cut and was assured a place on the squad. Of course, Troy was a back-up quarterback, as he knew he would be as a draftee. Nonetheless, he craved a celebration with his oldest friend, so he called Renée. She informed him that she had plans for the evening. She was going to dinner with the client whose case the firm had just won and who happened to be on the board of directors at Mercier Memorial Hospital. She commented that her friend might be a good contact for Troy to make for the future and a medical school internship.

The man sighed deeply on the other end of the phone and asked, "Can't you meet me for one glass of champagne? It can be a double celebration—my place on the team and your firm's victory. Bring your client if you like. Hell, you'll help me make a contact."

Troy could hear conversation behind Renée before she agreed to meet him. "Very well. James and I will meet you at Brew Masters at seven. He says he would like to meet you anyway since I've known you most of my life and you're playing for his 'Bad Boys.' He watched you during the preseason and isn't sure you're mean enough to be a Raider." Renée laughed an affected laugh, one Troy had never heard and did not seem genuine.

He pretended to chuckle back. "Rest assured I can be as mean as I need to be on or off the field, or have you forgotten entirely? I'll see you at seven."

Troy arrived early at the bar and grill because he wanted to see just what this James character looked like. While he waited, he drank several Killian's on tap, the only beer he really cared for. He saw Renée enter with a fellow who Troy thought old enough to be her father. The man stood about five feet, eleven inches, had dark hair with gray at the temples and hazel eyes, and dressed as if he had money to spare. Renée looked like a model from a business magazine in a navy-blue, tailored, pin-striped suit.

Troy made his way to the couple and Renée introduced the two men. "James Wilburn, I'd like you to meet Troy Tomerson. Troy, James." James seemed reluctant to shake hands with the younger man, but he did so after a slight hesitation.

"It's nice to meet the new arm of the 'Bad Boys,'" said James. "I'm just surprised Oakland picked up a quarterback."

"I'm not," countered Troy. "Sims is getting pretty old by NFL standards, and Jenkins, if I may be so bold, is not as good as I am. Those are just the facts. So, shall we have that champagne? I understand congratulations are in order for your case, Mr. Wilburn."

"Please call me James."

Troy looked the man over once more. He felt the strangest sensation they had met before, but with a nod he acknowledged, "James it is."

Troy, Renée, and James took a table and ordered a bottle of champagne. They toasted one another's success. Renée put her hand in James's and said, "You know, James, Troy is eventually planning to go to med school. He has already passed the MCAT with remarkable scores. Mercier Memorial could use someone with Troy's ingenuity. He can concoct all kinds of plans. That's why he makes such a good quarterback. Did I ever tell you about the time he paid someone to take me to our graduation dance?"

Troy looked flabbergasted that Renée would mention that incident and defended himself. "Renée, please? We were kids then, and I made a foolish mistake. Can't we put that behind us?"

She waved her hand. "Yes. Yes. It's just an example of what lengths you'll go to in order to accomplish what you want. You see, James doesn't know you or how mean you really can be. I can just imagine what you'll do on the field once you get command."

Troy gave Renée a sarcastic grin. "Whatever it takes to win, but that wasn't the incident I was referring to on the phone. No, I was remembering a freshman kicking the shit out of three seniors because they hurt his best friend."

Unaware that he was witnessing a power struggle, James commented, "Well, maybe you're not such a nice guy after all."

"Maybe not," agreed Troy. "I think I could be a dragon at heart. I go after the treasure I want, and I could probably kill to keep what's mine. The prize I want right now is another Killian's." He signaled the waitress and ordered.

"I think you may have already had a few too many," Renée said, instantly in protective mode. "You smelled like a brewery when we came in."

Troy leveled his gaze at her. "I plan to have several more. You're welcome to join me. James?"

James replied, "I'd love to, Troy, but we have dinner reservations. Perhaps another time."

The rookie quarterback stood to see the couple off and shook hands with James. Troy suddenly blurted, "Corrine."

"What?" said James, dropping Troy's hand.

"Your wife's name."

"Yes, it was. How did you know that?"

Flummoxed, Troy said, "I don't know."

James took a deep breath. "You must've read about us in the papers. Corrine, my wife, was abducted and murdered almost ten years ago. It made the national news."

"That must be why you look familiar," said Troy apologetically. "I'm sorry to have brought up such painful memories."

"No need to apologize," James said. "What's so strange is that you bear an uncanny resemblance to someone I once knew, but he died over twenty years ago."

"It's said we all have a twin," Troy said, trying to relieve the tension.

"True. True," affirmed James. "Well, we must be going. Good night, Troy. It was a pleasure." As he started to turn, James added while pointing at the beer Troy had ordered, "Don't drive home. I would hate for my team to lose such a promising talent so soon."

"Yes, sir," scoffed Troy with a mock salute. Then he took Renée's hand and bent to kiss her on the cheek. He whispered in her ear, "I thought it was unethical to sleep with your clients. Is this one of those times where it's not what you know but who you know? He's old enough to be your father and unscrupulous to boot. Can't you tell, or is your agenda so blurred you're blind to it? Are you really that ambitious? He just might be one of the broken, treacherous rungs on your way up the ladder of success."

Renée sneered back into Troy's ear, "Give it up. You threw me away graduation night. Since you were so willing to pass me to Ben, I gave him just what he wanted for free. Are you willing to cough up enough money to bribe the richest man in the area to let me go? Some things can never be recaptured."

Troy argued, "You once told me to grow up. Now, I'm telling you. Get over it before you hurt yourself irreparably."

They parted company, and there was no winner in the struggle for power. On the contrary, the battle had just begun.

11
Promotion

Sunday after Sunday Troy paced the sideline waiting for his chance to prove himself. Unknown to the anxious football player, Renée and James attended every home game. James, of course, assumed Renée attended the games to please him because he never missed a Raiders' game. The truth, however, was she came to watch Troy, hoping he would get his chance to play. During his first year with the team, Troy got to play three minutes of two games. Nonetheless, he managed to put points on the board in both his appearances.

The one thing Troy did not do during the season was to call Renée. He had come to the conclusion at their last meeting she had become what she had always despised—a social climber. He decided he would not put himself through the stress of constant reminders he had made a drastic mistake as an immature boy. Troy focused on his career and, as had always been the case, did not lack female companionship. However, for him, that is all any relationship amounted to, for no matter how he tried, the one woman all others fell short of in comparison was Renée.

True to Troy's prediction, Sims retired at the end of the playoffs when the Raiders were eliminated after the wild card game. Troy took one class at the University of California at San Francisco Medical School during the off season and trained hard to become the best quarterback for his team.

Meanwhile, Renée finished law school and, thanks to an important connection named James Wilburn, was hired where she had clerked as a junior associate at Pryor and Associates, a prestigious law firm whose main office was located in the town of Puma Pass where Baxter Pryor, the nephew by marriage to one Rennin O'Rourke, had established his office just before the start of the War Between the States. In the beginning, the fact the founder of the law firm and the founder of the town were related escaped Renée's usually sharp mind for details. And the fact Melanie Pryor's father had headed a law firm escaped Troy's.

Renée put forth the effort to let Troy know of her good fortune because somewhere in her heart she could not completely block the boy who had saved her life at the age of six from her mind. Troy congratulated her coolly and snidely told her he would get her to negotiate his new contract when he made starter if James approved.

Renée snarled at Troy, "Oh, can the jealous act. How many women have you slept with in the last nine months?"

"Seven," answered Troy matter-of-factly. "But not a one of them has any bearing on whether I get the starting position. If I get it, I will earn it."

"You jackass!" shouted Renée. "What are you implying?"

"Nothing. I'm sure your sugar daddy didn't pull a single string for you. You made a good connection. That's the long and short of it."

"Troy Tomerson! James is not my sugar daddy."

"No? Since when can a struggling law student from a Miami trailer park afford the diamond Rolex I noticed on your wrist when we last saw each other?"

"Troy, James and I have been dating for over a year. The watch was a gift. As for your starting position, I'm sure your little bimbos can think of all kinds of nice positions for you." The phone clicked in Troy's ear. He threw his cell phone against the wall, shattering it to pieces.

"Damn it," he muttered to himself. "I need a drink." He went to Brew Masters for several rounds of Killian's.

Troy went into training camp in the best condition of his life. He had put on fifteen pounds of pure muscle and was running the forty at his best time ever. The media picked up the scent of a good controversy surrounding the up-and-coming, left-handed, Florida State quarterback that had taken his team to the national championship in his senior year and the veteran, Jenkins, who had started briefly in Atlanta before he was traded to Oakland and played back-up to the successful Sims for several years.

After weeks of practice and preseason games, Coach McClarty walked into the locker room and hollered over the din, "Tomerson, in my office!"

Half-dressed, Troy went into the office with trepidation. Coach McClarty indicated the chair across from his. "Sit down."

Troy's heart was in his throat. With this kind of visit, he half expected the coach to cut him from the team. He sat down on the edge of the seat.

The coach started, "Well, Tomerson, you've got balls. I'll say that. You changed that last play I sent in. It worked this time, but I don't like my calls to be changed. If I screw it up, it's on my head. If you screw up, I'll be on your head. Don't do it again. You have *not* earned the right to change my calls yet. On the other hand, you *have* earned the job. It's yours, so get your damned lawyer or agent on the phone and start negotiating a new contract. Our starter can't make peanuts."

"Yes!" Troy shouted clutching his fist in the air and grabbing the coach's hand. "You won't be sorry. I'll play my heart out for you."

"I knew that last year, son. You just needed some seasoning. You're still fresh meat. If I have to bench you, I'll do it in a heartbeat, especially if I think some broad is taking you out of your game. You come to me with your head on straight. Leave everything else outside when it's game time. Do I make myself clear?"

"Absolutely, sir."

"Now, get out of here. Go have a few rounds of your favorite beer on me."

The first thing Troy did on his way to Brew Masters in his forest green Camaro convertible was to make a call to Miami. Eva answered sleepily for Troy had totally forgotten about the time difference.

"Mom!" Troy gushed. "Buy that house you always wanted. I got the position. I want you out of that miserable trailer park tomorrow."

Eva yawned. "Troy, it's two o'clock in the morning here."

"So? Big deal. Open that bottle of champagne I sent you for this occasion and have a drink over the phone with me right now."

Eva woke up somewhat and popped the cork on the champagne. She poured a glass and said, "To my Troy. Congratulations, baby. I'm so proud of you."

"I love you, Mom. Guess who I'm gonna get to negotiate my contract."

"Let's see. Could it possibly be Renée?"

"You bet."

"Troy, are you doing this to goad her?"

"Yep. But I bet she won't mind taking my money now. She's changed, Mom."

"No, she hasn't, son. She thinks she's a woman of the world, but she's still our little pixie."

"I wish I could believe that."

"Troy, do you love her?"

He laughed mirthlessly. "I always have, Mom. I just wish I had understood that years ago. It's too late now. She's hooked up with some guy old enough to be her father, just so she can move up the corporate ladder."

"Tell her how you feel."

"A lot of good that would do."

"Don't give up on her, baby."

"I didn't give up on her, Mom. She gave up on me."

"I just wish you both were here. I would have a word or two for the both of you."

"I am sure you would, Mom, but tonight the word is *celebrate*. And seriously, go house shopping tomorrow. Get out of that dump."

"I will, honey."

"Good night, Mom. I love you."

"I love you, too. Congratulations, baby. 'Bye."

Renée called, "Come in," to the knock on her office door. A hand holding a yellow rose with a white handkerchief tied to it came through the crack. Renée looked up. She smiled despite herself.

"Only Troy Tomerson would do something like that. Come in, Troy."

He entered the office with a grin on his face. "Forgive me for being a jackass?"

"Yes, but that's not why you came, is it?"

"Not entirely. I told you I wanted you to negotiate my new contract when I got the starting position."

Renée ran from behind her desk and threw her arms around him. "You did it! I'm so proud of you."

He held on to her longer than a client should hold on to his lawyer and breathed the soft fragrance, Taboo, that she wore. Finally, Renée pushed herself free.

"Well, let's get to work. We have a contract to draw up. If I keep bringing in business like you, maybe I'll make partner before I turn thirty."

12
Look Me in the Eye

Renée negotiated a lucrative contract for Troy as starting quarterback for the Oakland Raiders, and the two old friends seemed to be on pleasant terms once again. Troy even bit his tongue and went to dinner with Renée and James. On the other hand, he brought his own date to dinner, a stunning young Hollywood starlet by the name of Paulette Shubert.

Troy and Paulette had started dating just before training camp while she was shooting her first film in which she had the female lead. The young actress was tall and thin, standing five feet and eleven inches and weighing about one hundred twenty pounds. She wore her platinum hair long and straight and had lipid brown eyes that gave her a look of innocence. Paulette Shubert and the two-hundred-twenty-five-pound, six-foot-four-inch-tall, chestnut-haired, jade-eyed Troy Tomerson made an impressive couple. Even Renée had to admit the combination was startling.

That dinner proved to be a pleasant, uncomplicated affair. Neither Troy nor Renée criticized the other's companion. Dinner turned into a frequent occasion during the football season. Troy had a successful run during his first year as starter, getting his team to the AFC Championship and missing the Super Bowl by a field goal.

On Valentine's Day, Renée and James hosted a large dinner party to which Troy was invited. By that time, Paulette was shooting on location in South Africa and had decided she and Troy should see other people, not to Troy's disagreement. He had quickly tired of the vapid beauty. Therefore, he came to the party with Ashleigh Lightsey, a petite, carrot-topped medical intern at Mercier Memorial Hospital whom he had met during his class at UC San Francisco Medical School. Both knew the date was simply a night of companionship, and neither expected nor desired more from the other. It was purely platonic as Troy was taking another class in the off season, and Ashleigh had other interests.

The party proved a raucous event with the open bar being frequented by most of the guests, Troy not in the least. After a dozen tequila shots, he danced with any lady who gave him the honor, which were many. The band struck Revel's Bolero, and a happily intoxicated Troy grabbed his hostess's hand. "You have not danced with me."

Renée shook her head vehemently. "Not the tango, Troy."

His eyes glinted with mischief. "Yes, the tango, just like we did in the dance contest in high school. Do you remember it?"

"Yes."

The crowd cheered Troy on, and Renée let down her inhibitions for a short time. The result was a sexy, steamy, sensationalized rendition of a sensual dance. The onlookers applauded loudly as the last chord sounded. Ever the showman, Troy bowed graciously and indicated his partner, who blushed to the roots of her hair and sashayed off the dance floor to the arm of James Wilburn, who kissed her on the cheek and whispered, "I never knew you to be so daring."

"I'm not," she replied with a slight shudder. "Troy can be very convincing. Maybe he should be the lawyer."

"Well, that little dance makes me want to make our announcement early."

Renée patted James's arm. "Don't be silly. Follow the plan, darling. Troy has always been an exhibitionist."

James squeezed Renée's arm a little too hard. "Very well. I need to talk to a couple of business friends in the library. Excuse me."

Not to relinquish his flow of tequila, Troy came up behind Renée and presented her with a margarita as he whispered, "Was he jealous?"

"Troy!" said Renée in exasperation as she stepped onto the patio leading to the rose garden and into the cool night air.

Troy followed her, took her hand, and led her into the labyrinth of the rose bushes. "Was he jealous, Renée?"

"Don't be ridiculous. Was your date jealous of a little dance?"

"She doesn't care. We're only friends. James is a different story. Was he jealous?"

She made a little snorting sound and pushed Troy slightly away from her. "Why should he be jealous of my dancing with my oldest friend?"

"Because I wanted to take you to the floor right then and there," answered Troy candidly. "Don't deny that you felt the passion."

"It's the nature of the dance. Besides, you've consumed way too much tequila to think straight," Renée argued as she started back into the house.

"I don't think so," he said holding her hand tightly.

"Troy, let me go," she said, agitated.

"You don't want me to let you go."

"Yes, I do," demanded Renée as she jerked her hand free from Troy's.

He set their glasses on a bench located nearby and looked long and deeply into Renée's eyes. Then, he took her face in his hands and kissed her passionately.

She pushed herself free from him after several seconds. "Troy, you're drunk. Don't ever do that again." She raced into the safety of many partygoers.

Troy rubbed his lips, closed his eyes, whispered to himself, "Your words and lips say two different things," and returned to the party just in time to hear James call the crowd to attention.

"Ladies and gentlemen, give me your attention, please. I have an announcement that you, as Renée's and my closest friends, should be the first to hear. This beautiful lady has agreed to be my wife on June first. Raise your glasses: To my fiancée, Renée Peyton."

There was much tinkling of glasses, applause, and chatter. Troy walked back to the bar.

"Another shot, Mr. Tomerson?" asked the bartender.

"No, give me the whole damned bottle," said Troy grouchily.

"Yes, sir."

Troy took the bottle, found Ashleigh, handed her the keys to his Camaro, and said, "Drive me home, Doc. I'm about to be too damned drunk to drive."

Troy awoke the next morning to Ashleigh's setting a tray beside his bed.

"How's the head?" she asked jokingly.

"It hurts like hell. Why did you stay?" Troy responded covering his eyes with his hand.

She shrugged. "I'm a doctor. I figured I'd better not let you die of alcohol poisoning. You guzzled the whole bottle."

The tequila bottle still lay beside Troy on the bed. It was obvious Ashleigh had guided him to the bed and let him pass out fully dressed. He felt the bottle, picked it up, and threw it across the room, shattering it against the wall.

"Temper. Temper," chided Ashleigh. "Now, you have a mess to clean up. I won't do that for you."

Troy groaned, "Can you believe she's going to marry that pompous prig?"

"Maybe she loves him, Troy."

He sat up in bed and grabbed his head. "No way in hell! She wouldn't have kissed me the way she did last night if she was in love with James. She's just too damned stubborn to admit it. I'm not gonna let her marry that bastard."

"Troy, what has the man done to you to make you hate him so?"

"I don't know. I just feel it in my gut."

He fell back on the bed. "Ashleigh, please give me something for this headache."

"Poor baby," laughed Ashleigh as she handed him four Advil and a cup of black coffee, along with a glass of orange juice.

The spring sped into early summer, and Renée refused to see Troy unless it had to do with his contract, which was not up for renegotiation. Nonetheless, Troy received his official invitation to the wedding of Renée Peyton and James Wilburn, as did Eva Tomerson in Miami.

Troy's phone rang just a week before the wedding date. He answered wearily, "Hello."

"Explain it, Troy. Why is Renée marrying this man?"

"Hi, Mom. I don't know. I've tried over and over. She's acting just like she did about Ben. She won't talk to me."

"Well, I'm flying out there. Should I talk to her?"

"No, Mom. She'd only be mad at you, too. Just come out here and get me through this. I have to get back to training very soon. At least that will take my mind off the numbskull. She's making an uncomfortable bed to lie in. I'll introduce you to my friend, Ashleigh. Yes, we've been together, but don't start. She's not my girlfriend. I was an adventure according to her because her significant other is overseas. Her name is Joanne. I heard your jaw drop. Mom, you must remember that I'm living in the San Francisco area, not the Deep South. And it's not like Miami doesn't have its share of same-sex couples."

"Very well, Troy. I'll be there Wednesday. The wedding isn't until Saturday. Something may happen yet."

Eva arrived safely and spent a couple of hours with her son before she went to Renée's office. The younger woman was genuinely happy to see the older woman. "Miss Eva!" she said gleefully as she hugged the lady who had been like a second mother.

"I'm surprised you're still working. When will you take time off?"

"This is my last day in the office until we return from Greece."

"Greece! Whoa!"

"Yeah. Nice honeymoon, huh, Miss Eva?"

"I'd say. Is James a very wealthy man?"

"Yes. He owns a good chunk of everything around here, especially in Puma Pass. He's the last living relative of the founders, the O'Rourkes, of a number of the businesses around here."

"I see," Eva replied distractedly.

"Aren't you going to ask about Troy and me?" Renée asked seriously.

Brought back to reality, Eva replied, "No. Troy told me not to."

"Why can't he let me be happy and just leave me alone?"

"He loves you, honey. That's the only word I'm gonna say. Now, do you need me to help you with anything for the wedding?"

"Only if you might sit in for my mother."

"No, honey, I can't do that. It would be like betraying Troy. I'll come and see you make this commitment, but I cannot do that to Troy."

"Is he coming to the wedding?"

"Do you really want him to? He might just stand up and object. You know he's stubborn enough to do it."

"I can't imagine my wedding without Troy," Renée said with a sigh.

Eva stated bluntly, "I can't imagine your wedding not being *to* Troy. I have to go now. I'll see you Saturday."

Eva left. Renée sat behind her desk and sobbed into her arms.

Troy waited in the moonlight as James Wilburn's Mercedes pulled away from the curb late Friday night. He walked across the street and knocked resoundingly on Renée's door. She opened the door without looking to see who it was. "James, I told you to go home. I'm old-fashioned about that superstition. You can't see me until I walk down the aisle." She paused ever so slightly before she shouted, "Troy! What are you doing here?"

"I need to talk to you."

"There's nothing to say, Troy."

"Then you can listen." He slammed the door behind him.

"Have you been drinking?" she asked, alarmed at her friend's demeanor.

"No. I'm stone cold sober." He took a step toward her, and she backed up.

"Are you afraid of me, Renée? Damn it!" He did a full three-sixty with his hand in his hair. "You know I would never hurt you. Don't you realize I love you? I always have. Please don't marry James. I know you love me. You're just too stubborn to admit it."

She covered her face and exhaled a long, exasperated breath. "Troy, go home. I wish you would support my decision, but if you can't, then, just leave me alone. Please?"

He gently pulled her hands from her face. "Look at me, Renée."

She looked at Troy as tears welled in her eyes.

He took her face in his hands. "I read that book you gave me. Rennin O'Rourke said the most beautiful words I've ever heard to the woman he loved. 'Heart of my heart, life of my life, you are my reason for breathing; and I will love you until the day I die.'" Troy kissed Renée from the depths of his soul, and she melted in his embrace. He lifted her into his arms and carried her to her bed where, although he had been with several women, he made love for the first time. He poured his heart and soul into every kiss, every caress, every breath.

Around two o'clock a vicious thunderclap startled Troy awake. Renée stood at the window watching the jagged lightning split the sky. Troy walked behind her and gathered her in his arms. She turned on him like a wild animal and slapped him across the face as hard as she could. She screamed, "Get out, Troy! Get out!"

Stunned, he stammered, "W-w-what?"

Sadistically, she spat, "Do you really think you mean anything to me? I finally found a way to hurt you as much as you hurt me. Now, get out!"

Angrily, Troy grabbed Renée by the arms and kissed her hard. Imploringly, he said, "You tell me that meant nothing to you. You look me in the eye and tell me that meant nothing, and I will walk out that door and never bother you again."

Coldly and calmly Renée said, "That meant nothing at all to me. I hate you with a passion. Now, get out of my life."

Troy dressed as he walked out the bedroom door. He slammed the front door and disappeared into the storm.

Saturday evening remained heavily cloudy and threatened a deluge. Renée Peyton walked down the aisle alone to wed a man twenty-one years her senior. Her gaze scanned the crowd and took note of one conspicuously missing guest.

Troy Tomerson sat at the bar of Brew Masters and took double shots of a vintage Irish whiskey.

13
Bird in a Gilded Cage

James and Renée Wilburn landed in Athens, Greece, where they toured all the ancient ruins and enjoyed exquisite Greek dining. The sights and sounds were breathtaking and unforgettable. After several days of roaming without any real agenda, the newlyweds began a luxurious cruise of the Greek Isles. Renée videotaped the entire event.

James treated Renée as if she were a princess and bought her whatever she desired until they returned to the mainland for the last week of their extended honeymoon. They wandered aimlessly once again through the streets of Athens and found themselves passing the Greek Orthodox Church where a group of gypsies congregated. Several of the children brushed against James, and he cringed in disgust before one old decrepit gypsy grandmother gently stroked Renée's hair and spoke to her as if she knew her although the old woman spoke only her native tongue, and Renée could not understand a word she said.

James pushed the old woman roughly away from the younger woman saying, "Get away from my wife, you filth."

Renée spoke more gently. "James, don't be so harsh. She's harmless."

A young boy came to the old woman's side and interpreted what she was saying to the bride. "Grandmudder says you know her daughter. She has spoken to you before. She varned you years ago about a treacherous ladder."

Renée gasped as James reiterated, "Oh, get away. You people are disgusting." He pushed past the old woman, causing her to fall to the ground.

The grandmother grasped Renée's hand as James pulled his wife through the throng and muttered again as she removed a trinket from her neck and handed it to the young woman. The boy said, "Grandmodder says you should vear this. It vill protect your heart and mind. She says she knows you believe even dough you try to deny it."

Without looking at the object, Renée thrust it into the pocket of her slacks as James jerked her forward. "Come on, Renée. Leave that vermin behind. She only wants you to give her some money."

Renée waved kindly toward the old woman and the young boy as she noticed a tear course down the old woman's cheek.

Back in their hotel, James grumbled about the old gypsy. "What did that old cow give you, Renée?"

"I don't really know," she replied as she pulled the item from her pocket. She held a delicate crystal dragon with a ruby heart inside and a pixie upon its back. "Oh," Renée breathed. "It's lovely."

"Get rid of the damned thing right now," commanded James as if in panic. "Throw it away."

"No," argued Renée. "It's exquisite."

"I said for you to throw it away," snarled James as he snatched the dragon from her, causing the chain to slice through her fingers.

She screamed, "James!"

He threw the pendant to the floor and stomped it with his foot. Nothing happened to the necklace. It remained intact. A scream akin to the sound of a banshee escaped his throat. "Oh, hell no!" he ranted. He picked up the tiny dragon and flung it into the blazing fire in the fireplace. He grabbed Renée fiercely by the arms and shook her. "You will have nothing to do with that superstitious bullshit, Renée. If you are to be my wife, you will have to grow up. Do you understand me?" James finished as he glared into her face.

James pushed her from him and stormed out the door.

As the furious husband left the room, Renée noticed the dragon as it lay on the hearth in front of the fire, completely undamaged. She picked it up and carefully hid it in her makeup bag. As she placed the precious piece of glass away, Renée could have sworn she heard a voice say, "I am watching over you. You do not need to be afraid."

Sometime later, James returned to the room in a much calmer mood, but Renée had left her arms bare so that he could not help but see the imprints he had left on her arms. All three of her middle fingers on her left hand were wrapped in gauze. From behind his back James retrieved a golden cage with a pair of lovebirds inside. Contritely, he said, "I'm sorry I overreacted this afternoon. I didn't mean to hurt you. That ancient superstition really bothers me. Please accept these little birds in place of an imaginary glass beast. Give them names and cherish them as much as I cherish you."

Renée said softly, "James, I did *not* like the person I met today. Please tell me that's not what I have to look forward to in this relationship."

"I'm sorry," James said again. "Forgive me?"

Renée sighed, "Yes," and took the cage from James's hand. "They're beautiful. I think I'll call them Cam and Tam."

"Why those names?" asked James.

"They remind me of a couple I read about that displayed true love."

"I see," said James in a completely different voice from the one he had used earlier. He said, "You remind me of the song by Guns and Roses." Then he softly sang lines from "Sweet Child o' Mine" and how Renée's eyes reminded him of bluest skies and that he'd never want to cause her pain. He went on to sing about how her hair was his haven, as when he was a child and hid from storms. James mysteriously whispered, "Maybe somehow through you I will be freed and can find salvation."

Renée looked into James's eyes and for the first time saw something soft and warm. It lasted only a moment before it was replaced by the cold, calculating expression she was used to seeing in the shrewd businessman she married. James's whole demeanor changed abruptly as he commanded, "Dress for dinner. This is our last night in Greece, and we're dining with a business associate. I don't want to see any dragons or pixies. I want to see a young, brilliant attorney." He strode into the bathroom to change his clothes.

Renée gingerly stroked her lovebirds as she whispered. "I think I might be as confined as you are. I think I, too, am a bird in a gilded cage." She glanced toward her makeup bag and confided in Cam and Tam, "My dragon's heart faded. I pierced it through. He didn't come and object. What have I gotten myself into?" A sob caught in her throat.

"Oh, Troy, I am so sorry."

14

Reckless

On the Monday morning after Renée's wedding to James, a bleary-eyed Troy stomped into Pryor and Associates and asked to speak to the top partner. Troy demanded a senior partner take his account or he would take his business to another firm because he and Mrs. Wilburn had come to a parting of the ways. Troy remarked offhandedly, "You see, she has a tendency to sleep with her clients. If you want me to stay with your firm, someone else will have to negotiate any further contracts or anything else I might need."

Peter Pryor, the great-great-grandson of the founder of the firm and the father of the young lady Troy had dated briefly before her tragic death, agreed to take Troy on as a client and to speak to Mrs. Wilburn when she returned. Peter felt a strange kinship to the obviously heartbroken young man and was astounded by how much Troy reminded him of his long-dead, but dear, friend and partner, Michael, and Peter was aware that this was the same Troy his daughter had once mentioned. Peter talked to Troy for a while about the person they had in common.

Peter pushed a paperweight around on his desk, "You do realize you dated my daughter, right?"

Troy crinkled his brow. "Wow. You're Melanie's father. I just hadn't realized. She"—He bit his bottom lip to stop it trembling—"She was special. I wish..." His thoughts trailed off.

"She thought you were pretty awesome, too. Please feel free to come to me if you need anything. If things had worked out differently, you might have been my son-in-law."

Troy came away feeling he had made a friend.

Nonetheless, he returned to training camp in a slump. After several days of playing like a high school quarterback, Coach

McClarty once again shouted through the locker room, "Tomerson, in my office!"

"Yes, sir?" queried Troy as he entered the inner sanctum of the head coach.

"You look like hell. You're playing like shit. I told you not to let some bitch get into your head. Now, you get your act together, or you *will* be sitting on the bench." McClarty threw a sealed cup at Troy. "Piss in that for me."

"What? Why?"

"I gotta make sure you're not on drugs."

"I'm not using drugs, Coach," Troy defended as he slammed the cup on the desk.

"No. You're drowning your sorrows in the bottom of a bottle of booze. I know the look. I'll send your ass to rehab in a heartbeat, boy. Is that what you want?"

"No, sir."

"Then, tomorrow morning you will *not* have a hangover. If you wanna play like you're in high school, I'll treat you like you're in high school. Do I make myself clear?"

"Yes, sir."

"Get the hell out of here," growled McClarty.

Troy went back to his quarters, pulled out a bottle of whiskey and poured a shot. He stared at the glass for several minutes, and just as the door opened, he threw the glass and the bottle at the door, sending glass and whiskey all over the floor. His training-camp roommate, an offensive lineman named Jake Muñoz, dodged the glass shards, but not the whiskey bath.

"Well, that's a better place for it, Troy."

Troy started to punch the wall, but Jake grabbed his hand. "Uh-huh. This baby stays intact. Troy, I can protect your ass on the field. That's my job, and I'm damned good at it. If you will let me,

I can be a friend in here. I make a pretty good friend, too. What, or should I say who, has gotten you so torn up? Talk to me, man.

Troy fell onto his bunk. "I wouldn't know where to begin."

"A name."

"Renée."

"Ah. I knew it had to be a woman. Man, I'm twenty-nine, and I've already been married and divorced twice, and I have two children to support. First wife ran off and left me with a baby. Second wife is raising both kids. Trust me, I can understand. So, spill your guts. You'll feel a lot better. You'll play better. Troy, McClarty won't just bench you; he'll trade your ass in a New York minute. If he thinks you're hurting the team, you *will* be gone."

"Maybe I *should* go somewhere far away from her."

"Bullshit, man. You've got it bad. Now, talk."

Troy launched into the lifelong story of Renée Peyton. Jake's response was, "Cold-hearted bitch. Let her go. You have your pick of anybody you want."

"But I want *her*. Jake, I know she loves me. She's just the most stubborn human being I have ever known."

"Then, let her think you've gotten over her. Maybe she'll come crawling back to you. Concentrate on the game and find a hobby. Do some of the shit I do."

"Like what?" asked Troy in a less angry mood.

"Skydiving. Man, that's the time I feel free. After training, go skydiving with me. Just stay out of that bottle." He pointed toward the door. "And bed as many women as you want—safely. Hell, with your looks all you have to do is snap your fingers and some woman will fall at your feet."

Troy sighed. "After making love to Renée, I don't think any will compare."

"Give it time, man."

Troy returned to his true form, thanks to a steady gaze from Coach McClarty, who kept a specimen cup conspicuously at hand, and solid encouragement by his newfound friend. The regular season began with a trouncing of the team across the bay. At half time Troy scanned the spectators to see if James and Renée were there, and sure enough, in their box seats they cheered with the rest of the crowd.

Troy cornered Jake during the brief intermission. "Man, she's here."

"And?"

"Think how I feel."

"Okay. So, you can't date one of our cheerleaders. That doesn't mean you can't date one of the Forty-niners' cheerleaders. Walk across the field and get a date right in front of her. She'll see she lost you."

Troy did just that. Then, on Monday, he went skydiving for his first time with Jake.

The more reckless the activity, the more Troy enjoyed it. He began skydiving, hang-gliding, rock-climbing, and amateur stock-car racing, his favorite for the sheer speed although the feeling he got from hang-gliding reminded him of his dreams of soaring on the backs of dragons. He bought a new Ferrari. For every activity, he acquired a different female who liked the same thing. The tabloids plastered his picture every few weeks with a different woman.

In the line at the grocery store, Renée read the insinuations in each headline. A few had the audacity to couple her marriage to James with Troy's wild behavior. In Miami, Eva read the same headlines and wrote to her son, knowing he would not listen to words on the phone:

Troy,

    Are you trying to prove that you're a true Raider by becoming a really bad boy? What's going on with you? Has the rejection by Renée driven you insane? Are you trying to get yourself killed? You have almost died on me twice. Do not make it a third. I'm too old to take the stress. If one of your new hobbies doesn't kill you, one of the women might. Troy, people die from diseases. Stop being a fool. I taught you better than that. Don't make me sorry I made you my son.

                          Mom

Eva wrote the last line of the letter without thinking about what she said.

Troy read his mother's letter with little attention. He felt he had to fill the emptiness in his life in some way. Nevertheless, he called her.

"Mom, I'm not stupid. I'm careful about all my activities."

"Really? How are you guarding your heart? What about your reputation?"

"So, I'm a bad boy, Mom. Do you think I was such a good kid? I wasn't, Mom. I just never got caught. Think about all the trouble I caused in school, especially art class. I never told you about beating up three seniors during my freshman year or about Celina trying to blame her pregnancy on me, did I? Mom, I've never been the little angel you wanted me to be."

"Yes, you were! I knew about the fight at the beach party and the booze. I saw your knuckles, for heaven's sake! And I told you Celina was up to something. You made the same stupid mistakes other kids make, but you were a great kid. On the contrary, you are not the hellion you want Renée to think you are. Let her go, son. Don't try to get her attention in any way."

"I hear you, Mom. Really. I do. Give me some time to get her out of my system. I really am careful, Mom. I wear my seatbelt or a helmet or safety harness or a condom."

"Oh, Troy. I'm going to church to light a candle for you tonight."

"You do that, Mom. Keep praying for me. I probably need to go to confession, too, but I don't feel compelled to do so. Actually, I think I would like to fly away on a dragon." He laughed. "I still think about Renée's dragons. Am I damned to an eternity with that woman on my mind?"

"I don't know, baby. I will continue to pray for you."

"I know you will, Mom. Thanks. I love you. 'Bye."

"'Bye, baby."

Eva left immediately to light a candle for Troy. While she was there, she also lit one for Renée.

Troy went to sleep and had a conversation with an ash-colored dragon who advised him to take a step backward. "Look at the big picture. Follow your heart, Rennin," advised the creature. Troy awoke feeling better in the face of a broken heart.

Renée acted rashly in her own way by taking on the most challenging cases. She often defied the partners at the risk of losing her job. Luckily for her, she was an excellent barrister and won all but one of the cases the partners would have rejected. Because of her success, and despite her indiscretions, she was offered a junior partnership at the age of twenty-five.

Near the end of the season as the playoffs loomed big, Troy often found himself on the ground due to several injuries in his offensive line. Desperately needing to score a touchdown in the last few seconds of the last regular season game, he broke McClarty's cardinal rule. He changed the play that was sent in to him. With twelve yards to go for a touchdown and seven yards to go for the first down and only eight seconds left on the clock on fourth down and no timeouts, rather than pass, Troy kept the ball and ran it in for a touchdown. The crowd went crazy. Coach McClarty went insane.

15
Benched Bad Boy

Coach McClarty could be seen in the face of his young reckless quarterback. The screaming match ended with Troy being benched for the first playoff game. McClarty put his finger in Troy's chest. "I told you not to change my plays."

"I was gonna end up on my ass again, Coach. I did the right thing. The only lineman I have out there right now worth his salt is Jake. I might be young, but I cannot keep getting hit. Sooner or later I'm gonna fumble the damned ball."

"I don't give a flying leap. You do what *I* say. After you've played five years, maybe, then, you'll have the reasoning to change my plays."

"Coach, can't you admit I did the right thing? I didn't have a time out left to run it by you. I caught them totally by surprise. We won!"

"This time! This is what you're gonna do. You're gonna sit and watch during the first playoff game so you can see how to take orders."

"This is not the damned military! You need me out there."

"I understand Miami might be in the market for a quarterback. How would you like to go home?"

Troy bit his tongue and stormed off the field.

That night Jake and Troy went to Brew Masters. Troy said, "Jake, don't tell me not to drink."

"No. A few brewskies are just what you need tonight. I'll have some with you, but we both have to take taxis home." Jake confiscated Troy's keys and gave both his and Troy's to the bartender for safekeeping.

Troy and Jake made a bet as to which one could drink more Killian's. Jake believed his body weight could handle more than Troy's. Troy argued that somewhere deep down he must have Irish blood. The contest began in earnest. After twelve apiece, neither man could have walked a straight line, but the contest continued. They had drawn an audience. A tall shapely brunette massaged Troy's shoulders as he got ready to down his next beer. Troy finished it with a belch. Then, he took the girl's hand and brought her around to sit on his lap commenting, "Here, beautiful, sit here for luck." The girl complied willingly.

After eight more beers, Jake's face hit the table. The crowd cheered Troy, and he shouted, "Hey, Jim! Send Jake home in a cab."

Troy kissed the girl on his lap. "How would you like to go home with me?"

"Sure, but I can't go without my friend, Paige." She indicated a girl with mousy brown hair who had been standing slightly to the side.

"Hell, I'll take both of you home with me," boasted a drunk Troy.

Leaning heavily on both girls, the trio left the bar. Troy reminded the bartender to take care of Jake and gloated, "You don't have to worry about me. I have a ride."

Outside, he turned his attention to his two escorts. "Who's driving?" asked Troy.

"I will," volunteered the girl called Paige. "Who's car are we taking—yours or ours?"

"We had better take yours. Jake gave my keys to the bartender. Besides, mine only holds two people."

They came to a hot pink Volkswagen Bug where the girls deposited Troy in the back seat.

"Hold on," he argued. "You don't intend to make me sit back here by myself, do you?"

The brunette climbed in the back with him. He kissed her. She responded eagerly. Within minutes Troy had already removed the girl's shirt, and the girl already had his jeans unzipped. When they arrived at Troy's condo, he carried the girl who had her legs and arms wrapped around him inside while Paige followed closely behind. Several hours later, Troy awoke with two naked women in his bed.

Still inebriated, but more cognizant of his behavior, Troy shouted, "What the hell?"

The two girls woke up and scooted closer to him. Realizing that he had picked up two girls at Brew Masters he relaxed and asked the brunette, "What's your name? I don't want to have made love to a nameless beauty." Turning to the other girl he said, "I think I remember you're Paige."

"Casey," the brunette replied.

"Casey? Hey! Did you know that Coach McClarty has a daughter named Casey?"

"Yes, I did."

"How? Do you know McClarty? He's pissed off with me, but I did the right thing, damn it!"

"Yes, you did, and yes, I know him."

"How?"

"That's my dad."

Troy came abruptly to his senses. He stammered, "Y-y-you're Casey McClarty? Shit! You're like only sixteen."

"That didn't seem to matter a few minutes ago."

"A few minutes ago, I didn't know you were only sixteen."

"Oh, come on, Troy. Do you think you're the first guy I've gone home with?"

"I don't care how many guys you've been with. I don't want to be one of them. Does your father know where you are?"

"Are you kidding?" she screeched. "He would skin me alive, but you wanted to be one of my men earlier."

"McClarty would do more than skin me. He would kill me. Worse—he would trade me." He grabbed a handful of his own hair. "What have I done? You have got to get out of here."

"Get a grip, Troy. My dad will never know I've been here. I spent the night with Paige. Calm down. Think of it as your way of getting even with my dad. I do."

Troy turned in alarm, "What about you? Get dressed, both of you."

Paige shrugged, slipped out of bed, and put her clothes on before she commented, "Troy, relax. We do this kind of thing all the time. We have never been caught."

"God!" shouted Troy. "You're sixteen and you get into bars, pick up men, and...and... What the hell *did* we do?"

"Not a damned thing but make out," said Casey derisively. "You were too drunk to perform. I had really hoped for a lot more."

"Thank God I was too drunk," Troy said snidely as he sprang from the bed and dressed. "I don't screw little girls. Now, please, get out of here."

Casey dressed sulkily. "You know, Troy. Maybe if you stopped calling women Renée, it might make you be able to get it up."

"What?" Troy asked in amazement before he commanded, "Oh, please, go home."

Paige was not as cruel. She patted Troy's arm. "Chill. Mr. McClarty will never know we were here, and if you love this Renée person, don't give up on her."

"Great advice from a kid. Besides, she married someone else. And *I'll* know you were here. How do I look Coach McClarty in the eye?"

"Oh, for God's sake, Troy!" hissed Casey. "When we leave, go back to sleep. This was only a dream—it didn't really happen." She waved her fingers in a hypnotic fashion in his face. "You aren't the bad boy that you want everyone to believe you are."

The girls left. Troy bolted his door. He fell back on his bed with a groan. "What do I do now?"

A distant voice said, "Grow up. Then, follow your heart, Rennin."

When Paige drove her Volkswagen into her driveway at three A. M., she and Casey were surprised to see a light in the kitchen. As they sneaked in the front door, Paige's parents, along with Gerald McClarty, came through the kitchen door.

Paige's father asked sternly, "Where have you been?"

The girls froze in their tracks. Paige's father held out his hand. "Keys," he demanded. Paige reluctantly and forlornly handed over her car keys. "Now, where have you been? It's three o'clock in the morning."

"We were just out cruising," answered Paige.

"What poor boy have you hoodwinked this time, Casey?" demanded McClarty. "And to think you would drag Paige along."

"We haven't hoodwinked any boy, Dad. We were just out," answered Casey in a surly tone.

"Yeah," said her father sarcastically as he leaned near his daughter. "Since when do you wear Polo cologne?"

"Oh, all right," said Casey belligerently. "So, we went with some friends to celebrate your victory. What's so wrong with that?"

McClarty held out his hand, "Purse."

"No way," defied Casey.

"Purse, now!" shouted McClarty.

Casey handed over her purse. McClarty opened Casey's wallet and discovered her fake I.D. and two condoms. "Where did you go, Casey? Don't you know the bar owner could have his business shut down for your being there. Granted, you showed him some identification that says you're twenty-one. Where did you go?"

"We went to a party."

"No." McClarty shook his head. "You were at Brew Masters. The bartender almost stroked out when he found out you were underage. He told us you left with a man."

"So, we gave a friend who was too drunk to drive a ride home. Now, that was a good thing to do," Casey rationalized as a way to defend her behavior.

Gerald McClarty scowled and growled at his daughter, "Casey, I am on the verge of having my quarterback arrested for statutory rape. Jake Muñoz was at Brew Masters in a stupor, and Troy's car was there. I know exactly where you went. What I want to know is how much Tomerson knows. Did he have a clue he was leaving with two children?"

"I don't know what you're talking about."

McClarty grabbed Casey by the shoulders and shook her, "Do you want this man to go to jail because of his stupidity and your deceit?"

Casey folded her arms across her chest and refused to speak.

"Fine!" shouted McClarty. "Let's go." He turned back to Paige's parents, "Lee, Dolly, give me a couple of hours before you call the authorities for me unless I call you and tell you not to. As stupid as Paige may have been, she is at least sixteen and can actually consent to sex. Casey, on the other hand, may never live to see sixteen. I might kill her. Or Troy might if he doesn't know how old she is." McClarty glared at Casey. "If the man has a clue you are under the age of consent, he is gone to jail for fifteen years as a sex offender. That will be on his record for life. He will never play football again. When he gets out, he'll be too old to pick up a football, but he'll still be famous. Every one of his neighbors will know that he's a registered sex offender. They will know he screwed a little girl and worry he might touch their daughters. Is that really what you want?"

Lee and Dolly Knight agreed, and Gerald McClarty forced his daughter into his car and drove straight to Troy's condominium.

Troy awoke to the pounding on his door. "I'm coming!" he yelled irritably.

Troy opened the door to see his coach and Casey standing there. McClarty did not wait but snarled at Troy, "You have two options: talk or jail."

"Whoa!" said Troy, holding up his hands in surrender. "Nothing happened, Coach. Honestly, I was too drunk to do anything. And I had no idea who she even was when the girls brought me home. I sure as hell had no idea they were only sixteen."

"I thought as much. Casey won't be sixteen for two more weeks. Casey, talk. Or do you really want me to send Troy to jail? Remember what I already told you—registered sex offender for life."

"Dad, nothing happened. Troy was too drunk to even stand up. We put him to bed. When he found out who I was, he unceremoniously threw us out. Troy did not have sex with either of us. There is no reason to arrest him at all. And don't you dare trade him to another team. That's what he was so damned worried about when he found out who I was. Trading him would be just plain stupid. You need him. And he made the right decision in the game. You need to get over your need to control everything all the time."

"Obviously I can't control you!" McClarty roared. "But you're going to an all-girls' boarding-school in Switzerland as soon as I can make the arrangements."

"That's a good idea," said Troy, "but don't send Paige to the same school. They feed off each other."

"Mind your own damned business," snapped McClarty. "It's almost five o'clock. I expect to see you in one hour on the practice field."

"Excuse me?" countered Troy.

"You heard me. Unless you want to be on the next plane to New York, Miami would be too cushy, you'll be there."

McClarty dragged Casey from the room. She was in Switzerland on Friday.

Troy trudged to the practice field before the sun rose. Coach McClarty waited. No other players were required to show up on Monday. McClarty snapped, "Twenty laps. Move it."

"You can't be serious," Troy said.

McClarty started singing an off-key rendition of "New York, New York."

Troy finished twenty laps and threw up at McClarty's feet. The coach jerked his player up by the scruff of his neck. "Now give me fifty wind sprints."

"You're crazy," Troy whined.

McClarty began a rendition of "Nights on Broadway."

Troy managed to eke out the wind sprints and collapsed with searing pain in his side. He coughed and heaved, but there was nothing in his stomach to come out. McClarty rolled Troy over with his foot. "One hundred sit ups and then one hundred pushups."

Troy glared at his coach but did not make a single comment. He groaned through every sit up and started the pushups. After thirty, he fell flat on his face and gasped, "I can't, Coach. Not now."

McClarty took out his cell phone and dialed a number. "Stephanie. Hi. It's Gerald McClarty. Sorry to wake you so early, but Troy Tomerson needs to sell his condo. When can you show it, and how much can you get for it?"

"No, I don't!" yelled Troy.

"Hold on a minute, Stephanie. I think he might have changed his mind."

Troy started the pushups. "Thirty-one."

McClarty pushed Troy down with his foot. "Start at the beginning."

Troy finished the pushups while McClarty chatted with the person on the other end of the phone. "What now, Coach?"

McClarty ended the phone conversation. "Go home. Get some sleep. Be here at six in the morning. And if you as much as drink Nyquil before the Super Bowl, you *will* be in New York. Do I make myself clear?"

"Yes, sir."

"You're not a child, Troy. Stop acting like one. And you had better be very glad you didn't sleep with my daughter because I wouldn't've hesitated to put your ass in jail."

"I'm sorry," Troy said contritely as he lay prone on the ground.

McClarty offered Troy his hand and helped him up. "Sit down a minute, Troy."

The younger man complied, and Gerald McClarty talked to him like a father. "I know I'm hard on you, but you have more natural talent and intelligence than anyone I've ever coached. Even with that on your side, you might get ten good years in this league if you stay healthy. What I want to know is why you're so self-destructive. You drink yourself to unconsciousness. You sleep with anything female. You participate in the most dangerous hobbies. You have too much to offer to care so little for yourself. What is it, Troy? What has you so torn up?"

Troy leaned his head back on the bench and closed his eyes. Tears flowed unchecked down his cheeks. He unburdened his soul. He told Gerald McClarty all about Renée from the day she moved into the trailer park. He spoke about the disquieting dreams he had and finished by saying, "Half the time I don't know who or what I'm supposed to be."

McClarty put a hand on the man-boy's shoulder. "First of all, Troy, who do you want to be? You have to decide what's best for you. Second, let the woman go. If she was ever meant to be yours, eventually she'll come back to you. Last, Troy, do you have faith? Do you ever ask God for guidance? You might try it sometimes. I'm a cantankerous old coot. That's where I find my strength."

Troy sighed, "You sound like my mom."

"You have a wise mother. Now, go home and rest. I'll see you at six in the morning."

Unknown to either man, the paparazzi that had been following Troy since the game, snapped many shots of their morning together to go along with the ones they had taken of Troy and two young girls the night before, and the next issue of the tabloids plastered them on the front page with captions such as, "Tomerson in Tryst with Coach's Daughter" and "Benched Bad Boy."

Troy worked harder than he had to make the team. The Raiders' first playoff game was in Miami. The only joy Troy took from the visit home was being able to see his mother briefly. He gave her tickets to the game, the first she would be able to see him play in person.

Eva did not say a word about the tabloids. She simply laid a copy of every one of them in front of Troy as he had coffee with her.

He whispered, "You can stop worrying, Mom. I'm not drinking at all, and I'm not seeing any woman at all. I *am* still racing, climbing, parachuting, and hang-gliding. I *have* to have some release, Mom, but I've decided to grow up for real. I promise."

Eva nodded and kissed her son's head as she stood to refill their coffee mugs.

Troy hugged his mother and laid his cheek against her chest as she soothingly stroked his hair and kissed him on top of the head again. He said softly, "I love you, Mom."

Eva rubbed his back as she had when he was little and said, "I love you, too, Troy."

In the locker room, McClarty gave the start to Jenkins. Troy sank onto the bench and looked imploringly at the man who had heard his confession. "You can't be serious. Haven't I redeemed

myself? I swear to God that I *will not* change your plays. My mom
is actually here. Jesus." He crossed himself.

"Was that a prayer?" asked McClarty.

"Would it make any difference?" asked Troy.

McClarty shrugged. "Could be."

The quarters dragged by. The Raiders were down by fourteen
at half time.

Troy beseeched the coach before they left the locker room,
"Coach, give me my team."

"Your team?" McClarty said, wide-eyed.

"Yes. Please, Coach? I know you want to do what's best for
the team. Jenkins isn't a bad quarterback, but I'm better. You know
it."

"Let's go," McClarty commanded the team, unmoved by
Troy's pleas.

Back on the field, Troy shadowed McClarty's every step, and
made suggestions for plays. Some of them McClarty used with
success; however, with three minutes left, the Raiders were still
down by ten points. McClarty bellowed, "Tomerson!" and turned
around right into Troy. "Get in there and send that moron to me."

Troy scampered onto the field. Seven plays later, the Raiders
were down by three. They went for an onside kick and recovered
it. Miami's defense pounded Troy, two sacks in a row. Jake trotted
in from the sideline. Troy asked, "Well, what does he want me to
do?"

Jake replied, "He said to do whatever it takes to win this."

"He didn't send in a play?"

"No."

"Jake, cover my ass. I can't get the ball down the field if I'm
on the ground."

Troy took over, making plays reminiscent of his childhood
hero, Dan Marino—perfect passes to the sidelines.

With eleven seconds left, Troy was faced with going for the
win or overtime. He quickly spiked the ball to save his last time
out and sprinted to the sideline. "Coach, what do we do?"

McClarty said, "You make the call."

"Overtime means they could get the ball before us."

"And going for the win means we could go home in a few seconds."

"Coach?"

"Follow your heart, Troy."

A gargantuan glistening gray dragon loomed into Troy's consciousness. He jogged onto the field. "It's now or never," he said in the huddle and made his call. The pass landed perfectly in the tight end's chest in the end zone.

Gerald McClarty was the first to engulf Troy in a bear hug as he whispered in Troy's ear. "You've earned the right to call what you see on the field."

Four weeks later Troy paced the floor in his hotel room in Pontiac, Michigan, as he awaited his first Super Bowl appearance against an almost perfect Dallas Cowboys team who had lost only one regular season game. He sat on the bed and spoke aloud to the darkness. "God, I haven't prayed since I was a little boy. I don't remember the last time I went to confession. Half the time I don't know what's real and what's in my head. Please help me, not just tomorrow, but all the time. Forgive me for being a fool." A sob caught in his throat. "And, God, please watch over Renée."

Troy did not know James and Renée Wilburn were two floors above him at that very moment, but he fell asleep with a sense of relief and dreamed of soaring on the back of Smoke, the misty gray dragon while the pearly one named Draco called affectionately from a pristine beach, "He's just like the first Rennin, isn't he?"

"No," Smoke replied. "He's worse, or is it better? I never thought I'd meet anyone with more gumption and spunk. This kid is the one we must have. He must come home, but how do we get him here?"

"We'll figure it out in time," assured Draco.

Troy awoke refreshed and reassured. Twelve hours later, Troy kissed the Vince Lombardi Trophy.

The party that night in celebration of the Super Bowl victory lasted into the wee hours of the morning. During the celebration Troy asked McClarty, "Is it alright for me to drink tonight, Coach?"

McClarty laughed raucously. "Yes, Troy. Tonight, I'll drink with you."

Troy's revelry was short-lived as James and Renée walked into the party. James shook Coach McClarty's hand and introduced his young bride. McClarty dragged James toward Troy saying, "Let me introduce you to the real hero of the evening."

Troy took a deep breath as McClarty began an unnecessary introduction. Troy extended his hand. "Hello, James. How are you? Marriage seems to agree with you."

James shook Troy's hand vigorously. "Well-played game, Troy. Congratulations."

"So, you two already know each other," surmised McClarty.

"Yes, yes," James replied. "Renée and Troy have been friends for years."

McClarty turned a pallid face toward his quarterback and then put a protective, fatherly arm around the young man's shoulders. "Well, how nice," said McClarty. "Now, James, if you'll excuse us, there are a few other guests I'd like Troy to meet."

"Of course," said James as Renée came to his side.

Troy took Renée's proffered hand and kissed her socially on the cheek. "It's good to see you, Mrs. Wilburn. You look well."

"As do you," Renée replied cordially. "Congratulations, Troy. I'm proud of you."

"Thank you. Now, excuse us. Coach has someone he'd like me to meet."

McClarty steered Troy onto the terrace of the hotel convention suite. "Your Renée is Renée Wilburn? Do you really have a death wish?"

"What do you mean?"

"Troy, you do *not* want to cross that man. He has underworld ties. No matter how popular you are, you could be sleeping with the fishes."

"Is Renée in danger?"

"Troy, are you listening to me? Don't trifle with James Wilburn. Many think his first wife's disappearance was his doing. They can't prove it, but…"

"I have to protect Renée."

"No, you don't. Does she have anything James could possibly want?"

"Not that I know of. She grew up as poor as I did. She's a brilliant young attorney, but that's all."

"Then, maybe she's safe as James's trophy wife. You are not safe. That nice Ferrari's brakes could fail very easily. Are you getting the picture? Stay away from that woman. She will get you killed."

"I hear you, Coach. Do you think I could slip out of here unnoticed? It's really hard to be around her. Can you understand that?"

"Yes, son. You did a good job covering your feelings just now. I'll make your excuses. You're exhausted. How much have you had to drink?"

"Not enough."

"Troy?"

"I'm going to my room."

"Very well. Go on."

Troy stopped at the bar and picked up a bottle of good Irish whiskey. On his way out the door, Troy collided with Renée returning from the restroom. She scowled as he hit her shoulder.

"Sorry," he said curtly, but he noticed the grimace. "Are you all right?"

"I'm fine. I fell off my horse a couple of days ago and my shoulder's still tender."

"I recall the horses on the carousel being safer," Troy replied as he longed to touch this woman.

"So was the beast master," she said mysteriously as she remembered James's spooking her horse.

"What does that mean?"

"Nothing. Are you leaving so early? And with a bottle?"

"What do you care? You hate me with a passion, remember?"

"Troy…"

"Don't, Renée. I can't do it anymore. You've already ripped my heart from my chest. This should be the happiest day of my life, and it was until you walked through the door. I just cannot play your game anymore. It hurts too much."

"Troy, please don't hate me."

Troy laughed derisively. "I don't hate you, Renée. It's much, much worse than that."

A small sob caught in her throat.

"I love you, Renée." He turned toward the elevator.

Renée detained him, "Troy, wait."

"No," he said. "I have to get out of here. I cannot watch you with him."

"Troy, please? I-I-I lied. I don't hate you. I-I-I love you." Her voice faded to a whisper.

He smiled sadly. "What happened to the fact that you would never lie to me? Don't you think it's a little late for that declaration? You have a husband. You benched me." He kissed her softly on the lips. "Good-bye, Renée. I do want you to be happy. Truly." Troy took the elevator to the first floor, walked out the door, and hailed a cab.

"Take me to the racetrack." He handed the cabbie a fifty and told him to keep the change. Troy had almost finished the bottle of whiskey by the time the fifteen-minute trip was up.

"Would you like me to wait, sir?" asked the cabbie.

"Yeah," Troy replied, holding up the bottle. "You had better." He handed the man another fifty.

Troy went into the garage to check on the race car he had decided to purchase while he was in Michigan. It was a red suped-up Celica on which Troy had had painted a white dragon on one side and a gray dragon on the other. He climbed behind the wheel. To his amazement, the key was in the ignition. "What the hell? Why not? The track is empty," he said aloud to himself.

The cabbie got out of his vehicle and watched momentarily while Troy flew around the track. The older man had read many of the stories about Troy in the tabloids. He had the presence of mind to call the hotel and have Gerald McClarty paged.

"Hello," said McClarty irritably.

"Mr. McClarty, my name is Vince Smith. I'm a cab driver. I just brought Mr. Tomerson to the racetrack and he's driving a racecar around the track like a bat out of hell. He has also just about finished off a fifth of whiskey. I think you should get down here, sir. Your quarterback's trying to kill himself."

Gerald McClarty did not even say good-bye. He hailed a taxi and took off to the track. He got out of his cab just in time to see the Celica hit the wall and flip three times.

McClarty reached the wrecked car within seconds. Troy sat there laughing and crying at the same time. McClarty jerked the door open. Troy looked at his ashen-faced coach. "Even when I actually try, it doesn't work, Coach. I'm still alive."

"Troy, have you lost your mind? Did you see that woman again?"

"There she was in the doorway as I was headed back to my room. Do you know what she said? She loves me. Here she is married to some underworld figure, and she says she loves me. Can you believe that bullshit, Coach?" At that point, Troy was crying like a baby.

"Hush, Tomerson," chided McClarty. "Stop being a baby. Let me get you out of there. Whose car have you destroyed?"

"Mine." McClarty let Troy lean on him, and Troy grunted in pain.

"Well, hell!" said McClarty as he felt Troy's collarbone. "It's broken." He looked Troy over before he surveyed the totaled car. "How do you walk away from that with only a broken collarbone?"

McClarty dismissed his cab driver and spoke to Troy's. "Smith, take us to the hospital. The fool broke his collarbone. I might break his neck for him."

In the emergency room, Troy got a brace for his collarbone, but the doctor wanted to keep him due to his intoxicated state. "No," said McClarty. "I'm taking him with me. I am not going to let the little shit out of my sight."

Not quite true to his word, McClarty stopped back by the party after he deposited Troy in bed and saw that James still mingled with the revelers but heard that Mrs. Wilburn had gone to bed. McClarty knocked insistently on the door to the Wilburns' suite. A weary-looking Renée opened the door. "Coach, McClarty? James is still at the party."

"I didn't come to see James. I came to see you."

"Please come in."

"No need. I can say what I need to say from the doorway. I'll get straight to the point. Stay the hell away from my quarterback. Don't tell him you hate him. Don't tell him you love him. Don't say a damned thing to him. That boy almost died tonight because of you—from what I hear that's the second time. Stop playing with his head. You made your bed, now lie in it. I really *do not* think you want your husband to know you have feelings for another man. In my experience, James is not the forgiving sort. *Leave Troy alone!* Let him get over you. Lady, you are benched from his life as of this second. Good night."

Renée stared, aghast, as the imposing figure of a coach who loved his player like a son stormed from her presence.

Part Two

Blessed Be the Tie That Binds

16
Old Photographs

A year later Troy had not heard a word from Renée, but he had finished his third class in medical school, which would either have to be put on hold for a while since the classes would be requiring clinical time or football would have to be put on hold. Troy chose the former, and returned to the Super Bowl, leaving without a victory in the wake of an overwhelming Chicago Bears' defense. As a matter of fact, the new second-string quarterback, Raymond Fitzgerald had to finish the game after Troy played through bruised ribs but could not pass after he dislocated his thumb against the helmet of an oncoming defensive linesman's rush.

During the off season, Troy paid a visit to his mother in Miami. While there, he ran into Celina Ortiz, who looked as if she had aged twenty years rather than ten. She talked pleasantly to Troy and apologized for her despicable behavior years before. She confessed the father of the baby had been the softball coach, and she had given the baby up for adoption. She told Troy that seemed like another lifetime to her and gave him a picture that she still had from the dance. She also told him that although being with him had been a part of her deception, she had actually enjoyed him very much and wished it had been under different circumstances.

He laughed. "You know, you were my first."

Celina replied, "I would never have known if you hadn't called me Renée. That's when I knew in my heart that you had subconsciously saved yourself for her. I hated her. She was lucky."

The man sighed deeply. "Sometimes I think back to those days and wish you'd had my baby. Maybe then I wouldn't be in so much pain." He raised his hand in the cast.

Celina touched Troy's chest. "I think your pain is here. I'm really surprised you never married Renée. She fought for you like a mother tigress."

Troy smiled weakly and kissed Celina on the forehead. "She weaned the little cub and put him out on his own."

He also spent a great deal of time with Eva. His mother did not bring up the subject of Renée for she could see in her son's eyes his heart could not stand the pain. Eva had never known about Troy's wreck after his first Super Bowl. He refused to burden her with his "stupidity." McClarty had paid good money to keep the story out of the press.

Eva and Troy spent time on the beach and touring sites which residents never sought, but tourists always looked for. Troy laughed about pretending to be a tourist in his own home.

The professional football player took a day and spoke at his alma mater. He was inundated with autograph requests and signed every one of them awkwardly with his broken hand.

In the evenings, mother and son relaxed and watched television or looked at old photographs. Eva showed Troy pictures of a naked baby with sandy hair.

"Who's that?" asked Troy.

"My baby," answered Eva quietly.

"That's me?" said Troy in disbelief. "My hair was almost blond. And my eyes look more blue than green."

Recovering from her silence, Eva replied, "They changed as you got older."

When he got ready to leave, Troy asked if he could have one of his baby pictures to show his friends in Oakland. Eva gave him the whole scrapbook.

When Troy returned to his condominium in Puma Pass, where he had taken residence, Jake and a few other teammates visited to play with a new computer program Troy had in which they scanned their baby pictures to see if the computer made them look like themselves with an aging program. Jake was not as heavy in his computer-generated picture, but he was recognizable. The other guys were unmistakable. However, Troy looked nothing like himself at all. The fellows teased him mercilessly that he belonged to the mailman or that the hospital mixed him up.

"Very funny," Troy snapped. Although he knew his teammates teased him, he felt a strange uneasiness once again, as if he belonged somewhere else. He also recalled the gypsy fortuneteller talking about his two lives. He could not shake his disconcerted feeling.

Meanwhile, Renée moved in high social circles and made significant contacts to advance her law practice, albeit some of the contacts proved to be less savory than she had expected. One associate of James's that gave her a huge account and someone she had never expected to encounter again was Glen Thomas. He commented to James, "How did you end up with this smashing lady without Troy Tomerson breaking every bone in your body? I tried many years ago when I was young and stupid, although the wrong way, which I truly regret. I ended up with a broken jaw, two broken ribs, and a partial plate." To prove his point, he popped out three of his front teeth. "I missed my senior year of football and a scholarship to the University of Miami. As I recall, I deserved something, but I sure would like my teeth back." He shook Renée's hand and the past was forgiven; but from reviewing his case, Renée saw that Glen still preyed on those weaker than himself. Although she took his retainer, she felt a sense of conscience, and she could hear Troy's taunting voice, "He's unscrupulous...unethical...really that ambitious."

Many nights Renée spent alone reading or watching television. The nights stretched into days at a time when James left town on business. On those occasions she found herself rambling through the huge estate and finding things that had heretofore gone unnoticed. She wandered into the attic and found exquisite furniture containing etched dragons and a grandfather clock with a mother-of-pearl dragon on the pendulum. She wondered why such priceless pieces were stowed in the attic and remembered a passage from the old book of fairytales, "I want these pieces to always go to someone with the last name of O'Rourke. May a devastating curse fall on the man who takes control of them if he is not a true O'Rourke."

Renée thought it strange that a Wilburn should own such pieces. She thought maybe that was why they were hidden in the attic—James was not an O'Rourke. Perhaps he had read those stories and knew of the founder of Puma Pass and the man's namesake and believed in curses.

Renée continued to plunder through the attic. In an antique trunk she found a myriad of old photograph albums, some of which dated from the 1850s. She thumbed carefully through the sensitive pages. On the first page of the oldest book was a faded daguerreotype with the caption below it: *Rennin and Rebekah O'Rourke—New Orleans Honeymoon*. Renée stared at the picture for ages before she realized she had said aloud, "My God. That could be Troy." She stayed in the attic for hours looking at the old photographs until the pictures became more and more modern. The recurring theme in the photos was the name O'Rourke. Finally, she found an old yearbook from Puma Pass Academy in with the photo albums. She thumbed through it, instinctively looking for the name O'Rourke. She found two, apparently a set of twins because they were in the same grade. After reading the names and staring at the pictures in stunned silence, a lightning bolt shattered Renée's brain and she dropped the book with a thud—Corrine Elizabeth O'Rourke and Michael Aidan O'Rourke. *James's first wife was an O'Rourke. The dragon pieces are the original ones from the book I read as a child.* She stared hard again at Michael O'Rourke's high-school senior portrait. It was the spitting image of Troy Tomerson at eighteen, and Troy had asked all those years ago who Rennin O'Rourke had been. Renée snatched the last book from the trunk with her mind racing. It proved to be a baby book filled with photos of a small dark-haired, green-eyed boy named Rennin Duncan O'Rourke. She gently traced the outline of the photograph that looked exactly as Troy, minus the dirt, had looked the first time she ever laid eyes on him when he was five years old.

Renée jumped in terror as she heard the front door open and the twittering of Cam and Tam, the lovebirds. James was home early. He was not due back until tomorrow. She hastily laid the books back in the box and rushed down the stairs, feeling as if she had stumbled onto some dark and sinister secret.

17
Old Documents

Renée ran into James's arms to his surprise. "What's this greeting?" he asked.

"I missed you," she answered.

"Enough to go to bed with your aged husband?"

"What a silly question," she said, locking her arm through James's and walking him to their bedroom where she gave herself reservedly to a man who did not take time to be a lover.

The next morning at breakfast, Renée was pensive. James kissed her on the cheek as he came into the breakfast nook. "A penny for your thoughts."

"Make it a partnership," she muttered without considering her response.

"Oh, ho! The little vixen's agenda becomes clear."

"That's not what I meant, James."

"No? Then tell me what has you so preoccupied this morning."

"I was wondering about your first wife. You've never told me much about her."

"What would you like to know?" His countenance darkened. "When she died, we were contemplating a divorce. That's why many authorities questioned my involvement in her murder. I don't like to talk about her."

"Before that, when things were good between you. What was her maiden name?"

"O'Rourke. Her great-great-great-great-grandfather was Rennin O'Rourke who founded Puma Pass after he struck gold. This is the very house he built for his wife, Rebekah."

"I see. Well, where is the rest of her family?"

"Her parents died while she was still young, and the household servants reared her and her twin brother, Michael. Michael, his wife, and son were killed twenty-six years ago in an Ameri-Rail derailment."

"An Ameri-Rail wreck?" asked Renée in astonishment.

"Yes, why?"

"It's just such a coincidence. Troy's father was killed twenty-six years ago in an Ameri-Rail wreck."

"Really? I knew his mother brought him up alone and he grew up poor, but I had no idea why. That *is* strange."

Renée shivered. James noticed. "Are you cold, dear?"

"No. It's all this morbid talk. Let's change the subject. It's Saturday. You don't have to go into the office, do you? I thought we could do something fun together. I would like to add some of my own touches to the house. What do you say?"

"What would you like to do?"

"To be honest, I discovered some gorgeous antiques in the attic. I would like to move them downstairs."

"No." replied James decisively.

"Why not?"

"It doesn't matter why. Those things stay in the attic. Don't bother them. You may go shopping for anything you want to add to the house, new or antique, but those things remain undisturbed."

"Why don't you sell them if you don't want them in your house?"

"I really should do that. They remind me too much of Corrine, but I don't know anyone who would want those eerie things around."

"I can think of someone."

"Who?"

"Does that matter? If I can get rid of them for you, will you let me do it?"

James thought for a minute. "Give them to the Salvation Army if you like, but I do *not* want them in my house."

A little over two years from the last time Troy spoke to Renée, his phone rang to her voice on the other end of the connection. "Troy, it's Renée."

"What's wrong?"

"Nothing. I have some things that I would like to give you. I think you'll find them fascinating. Will you come to my house this afternoon?"

"Renée, I don't think that would be a good idea."

"Why? James won't be here. He's in London."

"An even worse idea for me to come over there."

"Bring Jake or Coach McClarty with you if you're afraid of me, but I promise not to bite you. Oh, and bring a truck or U-Haul. You're gonna want these things."

Troy and Jake arrived at the Wilburn home about four o'clock. Renée was taken aback to see Troy really had brought a bodyguard with him, but, then, she reasoned that if Troy took the furniture, he would need help moving it.

She greeted both men cordially and served them whiskey on the rocks. When she offered Troy a second glass, he refused, to her second surprise of the day. Troy laughed lightly. "I'm not an alcoholic, Renée. I've learned when to stop. What was it you so earnestly wanted to give me?"

The woman could see that this was going to be strictly business, so she showed Troy and Jake to the attic and the furniture etched in dragons. Troy dropped to his knees and caressed the old clock as if making love to a woman. He breathed almost inaudibly, "These should be mine."

"They are if you want them and don't believe in curses," said Renée.

"What do you mean, 'curses'?" asked Troy.

"Well, do you remember that old book of fairytales I gave you?"

"*Memoirs of Magic?*"

"Yes. These are the actual pieces of furniture that Rennin Drake O'Rourke purchased in Boston for his wife Morgan. Do you remember how he said anyone who was not an O'Rourke would be cursed if he had possession of them? There are no direct descendants from him left. Corrine, James's first wife, and her brother, Michael, were O'Rourkes, and they're both dead without any heirs. So, are you willing to tempt fate and the dragon's curse?"

Troy laughed. "I've had the dragon's curse since I first met you. Yes, I'll take these pieces."

He wandered around the attic for a few minutes before he happened upon an old wardrobe in a simple cherry veneer. Staring at the clothes cabinet, Troy suddenly clutched his chest and started to hyperventilate. "Jake, get me out of here. I can't breathe."

Jake shook Troy. "What is it, man?"

Troy pointed at the wardrobe. "He locked me in there once."

"What are you babbling about, Troy?" asked Jake in alarm.

Troy realized how foolish he must sound. "Nothing. Yes, Renée, I'll take the pieces. May I send a mover for them on Monday?"

"That'll be fine," she said, dumbfounded.

The two men left. Troy asked Jake to drive and was quiet for the entire ride home.

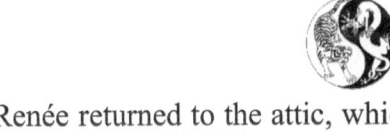

Renée returned to the attic, which had become her sanctuary. She opened the wardrobe that had sent Troy into a panic attack. The only time she could remember him behaving so strangely was in the third grade when Billy White had pushed him into the coat closet and leaned against it, trapping Troy inside. Troy had kicked the door so hard that he had broken the doorknob and had then punched Billy, blackening his eye, and both boys had received three days in detention and a paddling by the principal. Inside the wardrobe were stacks of old documents: deeds, birth records, marriage records, and death records. There were old newspaper clippings, as well as an old family Bible, and an elaborately embroidered tapestry with a dragon background.

Being the consummate corporate attorney, Renée was fascinated by the documents. She spent hours poring over each one in detail. It was obvious from the papers that as the only living relative of the O'Rourke family line, James did, indeed, own most of the town of Puma Pass.

Renée read the documents and the old Bible pages that established the bloodline of the O'Rourke family, finally coming to a birth certificate for Rennin Duncan O'Rourke, who was born March 12, 1980. Directly behind the birth certificate lay the death certificate for the same child, dated August 7, 1982. Paper-clipped to the two legal documents were numerous newspaper clippings regarding the Ameri-Rail tragedy that had claimed the child's life. Officials had apparently ruled the wreck a result of foul play. Parts of a bomb had been found in the compartment that belonged to a couple from Miami, the Tomerson family. When the explosion which caused the derailment occurred, it appeared that the only member of the family in the compartment had been the father who was killed instantly. Mrs. Tomerson and her son, a child of two named Troy, had escaped with only minor injuries. The couple in the compartment next door had not fared so well. Michael O'Rourke, age twenty-five, Denise O'Rourke, age twenty-four, and their two-year-old son, Rennin, had been killed in the blast. Although badly burned, the adults had been identified by wedding rings and a diamond engagement ring that miraculously survived the heat of the fire, but the child was charred beyond recognition. The only identifiable item for the child was his medical alert bracelet stating his severe allergy to penicillin.

Renée dropped the article as her mind raced. *Troy is deathly allergic to penicillin. He constantly wears a medical alert bracelet after he was run over by the school bus. The only time he takes it off is during a football game, but even then, he leaves it with his coach in case something happens to him during the game.* His family had been in the compartment next to the O'Rourke family. The rest of her thoughts were unfathomable. *What if? No, it's too bizarre...*

Renée laid the papers aside and examined the tapestry. Apparently, whoever made it believed in a magical, mystical world. Renée read the lineage embroidered into the dragon tapestry, drawing comfort from the strength it radiated:

The O'Rourke Family Line
Family Tree for Rennin Duncan O'Rourke

Generation 1

Alexander O'Rourke:

Born, c. 1530, Willow Hollow, Ireland

(Wizard, Island of Draconis.)

Married, Genevieve Brady

- Elizabeth Gilhooley (Mother–Quazel Rodriguez Morales)

- Duncan Sean O'Rourke*

Generation 2

Duncan Sean O'Rourke:

Born c. 1550, Stonebridge, Ireland

(Also known as King Satin, Ruler of Draconis.)

Married, Priscilla Cecelia Callahan

- Anna O'Rourke (Died in infancy.)

- Aidan Duncan O'Rourke*

Generation 3

Aidan Duncan O'Rourke

> Born 1576, Stonebridge, Ireland
>
> (Liberator of Draconis.)
>
> Married, Caitlin Leanne Fitzpatrick
>
> - Kieran Sean O'Rourke
> - Rennin Drake O'Rourke*
> - Genevieve Marie O'Rourke
> - Shannon Michael O'Rourke

Generation 4

Rennin Drake O'Rourke

> Born 1596, Draconian Waters
>
> Married, Morgan Celeste Fitzpatrick
>
> - Donovan Alexander O'Rourke
> - Cameron David O'Rourke*
> - Duncan Paul O'Rourke
> - Colin Aidan O'Rourke
> - Rachel Leanne O'Rourke

Generation 5

Cameron David O'Rourke

> Born, 1615, Draconis
>
> Married, Holly Montague (Also known as Kolehah of the Iroquois Tribe) 1632 (Died, 1633 in childbirth.)
>
> Married, Tammy Patrice Martin, 1643

- Rowan Patrick O'Rourke* (Mother--Holly)
- Holly Morgan O'Rourke
- Docia Ruth O'Rourke
- Kieran Duncan O'Rourke

Generation 6

Rowan Patrick O'Rourke

Born, 1633, Ohio Territory

Married, Ellen Brent, 1653

- Cameron Rennin O'Rourke*
- Patrick Oliver O'Rourke
- Geoffrey Ian O'Rourke

Generation 7

Cameron Rennin O'Rourke

Born, 1654, Boston, Massachusetts

Married, Nancy Shay Montague

- Ian Sean O'Rourke
- Devlin Daniel O'Rourke*
- Sylvia Suzanne O'Rourke
- Colleen Diane O'Rourke

Generation 8

Devlin Daniel O'Rourke

Born, 1675, Boston, Massachusetts

Married, Melissa Beecham (*Last surviving member
of the Beecham family of Salem, Massachusetts.
Parents tried and hanged as witches, 1690.*)

- Barbara Anne O'Rourke
- Melanie Louise O'Rourke
- Josephine Christine O'Rourke
- Rennin Patrick O'Rourke*

Generation 9

Rennin Patrick O'Rourke

Born, 1695, Lexington, Massachusetts

Married, Catherine Churchill, 1712 (*Died, 1713 in childbirth*)

- Aidan Cameron O'Rourke*

Generation 10

Aidan Cameron O'Rourke

Born, 1713, Concord, Massachusetts

Married, Frances Haughton, 1730

- Gayle Ann O'Rourke
- Janice Leigh O'Rourke
- Duncan Shane O'Rourke
- Donovan Michael O'Rourke
- Jeannie Ruth O'Rourke
- Colin Sean O'Rourke*
- Seamus Ian O'Rourke
- Timothy Daniel O'Rourke

Generation 11

Colin Sean O'Rourke

Born, 1732, Boston, Massachusetts (Died, 1777,
Battle of Saratoga.)
Married, Patricia Simmons, 1752
- Rowan John O'Rourke*
- Roland Thomas O'Rourke

Generation 12

Rowan John O'Rourke
Born, 1753, Boston, Massachusetts (Died, 1781,
Fort Griswold.)
Married, Liza Danaher, 1770
- Rennin Duncan O'Rourke*

Generation 13

Rennin Duncan O'Rourke
Born, 1771, Boston, Massachusetts
Married, Michelle Riley, 1790
- Rowan David O'Rourke*
- Leslie Renée O'Rourke

Generation 14

Rowan David O'Rourke
Born, 1791, Pittsburgh, Pennsylvania
Married, Abigail Johnson, 1810 (Died, 1828)
- Caitlin Danielle O'Rourke
- Catherine Mary O'Rourke
- Candace Elizabeth O'Rourke
- Cassandra Leanne O'Rourke

- Constance Celeste O'Rourke
- Camille Patrice O'Rourke
- Rennin Aidan O'Rourke* (Mother—Caitlin O'Rourke)

Generation 15

Rennin Aidan O'Rourke

Born 1828, Minnesota Territory

(Also known as Friend of Dragons; Colonel Union Army, wounded, Pennsylvania; California State Representative, Founder Puma Pass, California, Puma Pass Academy, Mercier Memorial Hospital, and O'Rourke Enterprises)

Married, Rebekah Suzanne Sinclair (Also known as Eyes of a Dove of the Pawnee Tribe.)

- Firelight O'Rourke (Daughter of Rebekah and Black Cloud, honored brave of the Pawnee Tribe, stillborn)
- Gabriel Braden O'Rourke*
- Michael Rowan O'Rourke
- Stanley Knox O'Rourke (Adopted)
- Jedediah Bartholomew Franklin (Guardian)
- Stephen Shane Mercier (Guardian)
- Christopher Aidan Mercier (Guardian)
- Keturah Suzanne Mercier (Guardian)

Generation 16

Gabriel Braden O'Rourke
Born 1850, Puma Pass, California
Married, Deborah Fischer, 1871
- Michael Shane O'Rourke*
- Ryan Donovan O'Rourke
- Caitlin Rebekah O'Rourke
- Patrick Aidan O'Rourke

Generation 17

Michael Shane O'Rourke
Born 1873, Puma Pass, California
Married, Anita Anne MacMillan, 1894
- Mary Catherine O'Rourke
- Genevieve Patrice O'Rourke
- Rennin Jacob O'Rourke*
- Daniel David O'Rourke
- Caleb Colin O'Rourke

Generation 18

Rennin Jacob O'Rourke
Born 1896, Puma Pass, California (Died, Ypres, 1915)
Married, Melanie Sarah Pryor, 1914
- Samuel Aidan O'Rourke*

Generation 19

Samuel Aidan O'Rourke

Born 1914, Puma Pass, California (Died, June 6, 1944, Normandy, France)

Married, Sheila Marie Davies, 1933

- Matthew Rennin O'Rourke*
- Katie Danielle O'Rourke
- Carolyn Celeste O'Rourke

Generation 20

Matthew Rennin O'Rourke

Born 1936, Puma Pass, California

(Colonel, United States Marine Corps, MIA, Vietnam, 1970)

Married Tristan Alexis Monroe, 1956; (Died, 1960)

- Michael Aidan O'Rourke*
- Corrine Elizabeth O'Rourke

Generation 21

Michael Aidan O'Rourke

Born 1957, Puma Pass, California

Married Denise O'Hara, 1978

- Rennin Duncan O'Rourke*

As she heard the soft cooing of her set of lovebirds, Renée strained her eyes for the stitching, apparently done by Denise to pass on to her son and future generations, had abruptly ceased, but there appeared to be shadowy writing to continue the tapestry. She held the cloth up to the light, and shooting from the dragon's mouth in silhouetted flames were the words:

Generation 22

Rennin Duncan O'Rourke

Born 1980, Puma Pass, California

Married Renée Samantha Peyton

and no date.

Renée Samantha Peyton Wilburn dropped the tapestry and fled the attic in a cold sweat.

18
Love on the Rocks

For weeks Renée did not enter the attic. When the movers Troy sent for the dragon furniture pieces arrived on the Monday after Renée was scared out of her wits, she directed them up the stairs to the attic with directions that they could not miss the pieces. Ironically, the unsuspecting movers chose to throw the old tapestry over some of the furniture to protect it during transport. Renée was glad to see it leave.

On the other hand, when the tapestry arrived with the furniture, Troy thought it belonged with the other things. He, too, read each name in succession until he came to the last one. "You're the same age as me," he whispered to an unseen entity. He felt such a connection to the tapestry that he had it mounted on his wall over the fireplace mantel.

Three years after their Super Bowl win, the Raiders had a dismal year, only breaking even. With a long face, McClarty called a team meeting at the end of the season.

"Okay, men. Some of us are about to have new homes."

Troy's heart lurched. McClarty recognized the deer-in-the-headlights look on Troy's face. "Don't worry, Tomerson. You're safe, at least as long as I'm here. The problem is that I'm not certain how much longer that will be. You know Al likes to start chopping at the top. I'm the head. Troy, you're the neck. He has no love for one man, but his team. So, since his love for us is on the rocks, we have to pull something together, or we will be elsewhere. There will be some trading in the next few weeks, and I need a good draft. There are very few of you that I can promise anything. Not even you, Jake."

"I understand, Coach," replied Jake Muñoz, Troy's right arm. "Just give me the heads up if you think something is coming down so I can make it look like it was my decision, and I can find Troy a new babysitter."

The team laughed uneasily. Although Jake's words were said in jest, each player felt the same. Theirs was an uncertain future.

The draft came and went, as did training camp. At least for one more year, McClarty, Jake, and Troy had a home, but it was the last year on Troy's contract. Either he or the team could make a change the next year without consequences. Troy realized it was time to pay Pryor and Associates a visit. He placed a call to Peter Pryor. "Peter, how are you?...I'm fine. It's just that it's almost time for a new contract. You know the boss gets jumpy when the team flounders, so I need to start planning now. I need to ask you something. Will you give me back to Renée?...I grew up Peter. I'm not a jealous little boy anymore. She's the best. We both know that." It was agreed that Renée Wilburn would handle negotiations for Troy when the time came. Troy also made another decision. If he did not play in the Bay area, then, it was time for medical school.

James Wilburn was out of the country more than half the time. Renée felt the loneliness she had felt as a teenager. Finally, after recovering from the fright of the tapestry, she ventured back into the attic. She looked through the pictures again and reread many of the papers in the wardrobe. Her sharp mind noticed that conspicuously missing from all the documents was anything dealing with Corrine's disappearance and murder.

Unable to shake the feeling that something was amiss, Renée began to research her predecessor thoroughly. In the hall of records, she was surprised to find a prenuptial agreement that left James high and dry should the couple divorce. It disturbed Renée that James had said he and Corrine had been thinking about a divorce before she was killed.

Renée's continued research uncovered several complaints with the local police of domestic violence in the Wilburn home after the death of Michael O'Rourke. Bits of conversations floated through Renée's mind. Troy's words when he first met James haunted her, "He's unscrupulous…are you too blind to see?" James's own words came to mind, "Questioned my involvement in her death…" She even remembered some of the words of the fortunetellers at the carnival when she was seventeen… "The one you choose to be false."

Every time James left for his extended business trips, Renée's uneasiness grew. She returned to the attic, feeling certain she would find something to help her. She discovered a small locked trunk. Determined to see what was in the trunk, she pried it open. Inside she found a perfect diamond in a rose-cut setting, two loops of golden chain, and a jade dragon pendant. Once again, she recognized the items from the book, *Memoirs of Magic*. Before she went a step further, she boxed the trinkets and mailed them to Troy with a note that said simply:

Troy

I found some more items I think you should keep safe.

Renée

She returned to her attic refuge and opened what appeared to be the original copy of *Memoirs of Magic* that Rennin had read to Rebekah. She caressed the cover and remembered confetti-and-glitter fairy dust. She found a large Ziploc bag into which she gently placed the precious old book.

Then, Renée pulled out a leather-bound journal, handwritten by Rennin Aidan O'Rourke, along with a copy of the same journal that had been put into print. She took the time to read the narrative. This, too, she placed in another Ziploc bag, thinking that the historical preservation society of Puma Pass would greatly appreciate the original writing. The next day, Renée knocked on Troy's door. He was cordial, but did not invite her in.

"Thank you for the jewelry pieces. They must be priceless. Why didn't you keep them and wear them?"

"I don't think James would have liked seeing them. I just came by to bring you something else. I couldn't trust this to the mail." Renée handed Troy the copy of *Memoirs of Magic*. "It's the one Rennin, who founded Puma Pass, read to Rebekah, his wife, and this is a copy of his journal, which tells all about their life together before he and she went in search of Draconis."

Troy stepped back from the door with the books in his hands. "Come in, Renée."

"Are you sure you want me in your house?"

"Yes. Come in."

The first thing She saw was the tapestry over the fireplace. She caught her breath. "Troy, did you read that tapestry carefully?"

"Yes, I read every word. Isn't it gorgeous?"

"Did you read the fire coming from the dragon's mouth?"

"What fire?"

"Go and look."

Troy examined the tapestry. "Renée, I don't see anything."

"Put more light on the dragon's mouth. I know what I read. I did not hallucinate."

Troy shined a flashlight directly onto the dragon's mouth and saw the silhouetted fire in which these words appeared:

Generation 22

Rennin Duncan O'Rourke
Born 1980, Puma Pass, California
(Also known as Troy Lane Tomerson.)

"What the hell?" Troy dropped the flashlight.

Neither could see what the other saw, and when they searched again, nothing unusual appeared. The two old friends discussed what they had seen and felt the connection they had felt at five.

"Do you believe in ghosts, Troy?" Renée asked seriously.

"No, Renée. Maybe we're both looking for some part of the happiness we once felt. Honestly, I don't believe in anything much these days."

As Renée started to leave, she turned and said, "What if..."

Troy put his finger to her lips. "Shhh. It's too late for what-ifs."

Silent tears fell from Renée's eyes, but she only nodded and went home.

Behind the closed door, Troy shed his own tears. "Oh, God, I love her so much. How do I go on?"

For the first time in fifteen years, Troy went to church and really prayed. He came home and slept after a long conversation with the old minister of the small Episcopal Church around the corner as dragons whispered, "Follow your heart, Rennin."

Renée went home and tried to sleep. She awoke in the middle of the night thinking she had to read the last book in the chest before James got home the next day. She made her way to the attic where she sat on the floor and opened another diary. This one was penned in a woman's hand. The name on the cover read: Corrine O'Rourke Wilburn.

The early passages read like a schoolgirl in love. Corrine resented the fact that her brother, Michael, did not approve of her beau, James Wilburn. Michael married Denise. Corrine adored her sister-in-law. At Denise's urging Corrine had James sign the prenuptial agreement. Corrine had a nephew. She loved and doted on Rennin and wanted to have a baby with James. She went to the doctor to find out why she was having trouble getting pregnant but was told she was perfectly healthy. Corrine came in while James was supposed to be watching Rennin until Michael and Denise returned. She found the two-year-old locked in the cherry wardrobe in the guest room. Renée paused. What had Troy said the day he saw the wardrobe? "He locked me in there once." Renée wondered if some sort of spirit was trying to gain justice from the grave.

She continued to read. Corrine was devastated by the loss of her brother and his family. She spent a year in a psychiatric facility. She took massive doses of antidepressants. Corrine had questions about James's business practices. She felt some of the men he did business with were criminals. She confronted James. James slapped her, and she called the police. James pushed her into the wall and strangled her. She called the police. Corrine threw James out of their bedroom. She had a private investigator follow him. He met with some shady businessmen. Funds were missing from some of the O'Rourke companies. Corrine found evidence linking James to the bomb on the Ameri-Rail train. Corrine confronted him. The last entry was the day before Corrine was abducted.

Renée's head spun. *Have I married a murderer?* She was genuinely terrified. She went to her office before dawn where she photocopied the entire diary and placed the original in her office safe.

When James returned from New York that evening, Renée met him at the door. She handed him the photocopied pages as Cam and Tam began to flutter wildly as if in terror.

"What is this?" asked James.

"Did you kill her, James? Did you kill Corrine? Did you kill Michael and Denise and a *baby*, for God's sake?"

James thumbed silently through the pages before he exploded. The next thing Renée knew, James had her pinned against the wall with his hands around her throat. "You stupid bitch!" he roared. "You nosy, stupid bitch. You couldn't leave it alone, could you? I have no desire to hurt you. You fit perfectly into my plans. I fit into yours. I can get you what you want, a partnership before you turn thirty, which is just over a year. All you had to do was to be a beautiful, dutiful wife. You, a little guttersnipe from a Miami trailer park, live in the lap of luxury. Do you really want to throw all that away?"

Renée dug her nails into James's hands. He yelped in pain and loosened his grip but did not let her go. "Let go of me you son-of-a-bitch!" demanded Renée.

"Not until we come to an agreement."

"You can't be serious."

"Oh, but I am, and if you don't agree, you *will* be dead."

"I'm getting out of here," declared Renée as she managed to push James away from her.

James caught her by her arm. "You're not going anywhere." He pulled her back to him and punched her hard in the stomach. Renée doubled over. James jerked her up by her hair and threw her onto the couch where he proceeded to force himself on her as she screamed and tried to free herself from his grasp.

When James was done, he stood over Renée. "You will not report any of this to anyone. If you aren't afraid for your own life, then think about those you care for."

Renée laughed hysterically. "I don't have anybody, you fool."

"Really? What about Troy Tomerson?"

"You wouldn't!" snapped Renée.

"In a heartbeat, baby. You know how much he likes to drink. Drunk driving in that Ferrari. Or his parachute conveniently doesn't open on one of his skydiving adventures. Or the rope breaks while he's rock climbing. Or, God forbid, his neck snaps under the weight of a three-hundred-pound lineman. Do you get the picture?'

"What has Troy ever done to you?"

"Nothing, but he's the closest thing you have to family. So, if you aren't afraid to die, consider his wellbeing. Now, I have to go to the Caymans in the morning. You will be here just as always when I return, or the Raiders will be prematurely looking for another quarterback."

Renée was terrified. James grinned triumphantly. He knew he had played the right trump card.

19
Shattered Dreams, Wounded Hearts, Broken Toys

While Renée scoured the attic to settle her uneasiness before James returned, Troy sat quietly on the back pew of a small Episcopal church near his condominium. He stared in a bewildered and hypnotic state at the flickering candles near the altar. Feeling as if the roof might cave in or lightning strike at any minute, he fidgeted and murmured under his breath, "God, I know I came here to talk to You, but I don't have the foggiest notion what to say."

At the front of the church, an old man in shades of gray entered the sanctuary from a side door. He started as he realized he was not alone and became aware of the young man's presence. The gray gentleman spoke in a clear resonant voice, "Did you say something, young man? May I be of service to you? I'm Reverend Ogden, pastor of this congregation."

Troy replied still dazed, "I-I-I don't know. I came to talk to God, but I don't know what to say."

"Hmmm," grunted the minister. "I understand." He made his way to where Troy sat and took the pew in front, placing his back against the side, swinging his legs onto the cushion, crossing them at the ankles, and pivoting on the seat to face Troy, his elbow resting on the wooden back. He continued, "I've had numerous experiences where the words just wouldn't come or came out jumbled. Scripture says that's when the Holy Spirit intercedes for us. However, I think there's more. Perhaps, there's just too much on your heart, Mr. Tomerson. Maybe a good old-fashioned confession would help."

Troy guiltily looked at the floor. "You recognize me. I thought, perhaps, I could hide in here for a time."

"Well, at least the paparazzi don't have the nerve to come into a place of worship yet, but you can't hide from God. He knows you at all times. Don't worry that I recognize you. Even men of the cloth like football. I set my VCR every Sunday. May I call you Troy?"

The younger man nodded.

"Troy, anything you say to me will be held in the strictest confidence. What you say to your minister is as sacred as what you say to your doctor or attorney, maybe more. I would love to be your minister if you want."

"I don't know where to start." Troy sighed and dropped his face into his hands. "I'm a hellion. Can God really forgive me for all I've done? All the stories you've heard are true. I was raised Catholic, but I just can't bring myself to believe a priest who is as sinful as I am can grant me absolution. My coach says all I need is to confess to God and ask His forgiveness. What's the truth?"

"I was locking up for the night. Walk to the rectory with me. Have you had dinner? We can talk over a BLT and a brandy. I think you need more than the general rhetoric. What do you say?"

"Okay. Thanks. I need some good advice."

The older man locked the church, and the two exited through a back gate onto a sloping yard that lead to the house the congregation furnished for its minister. Inside the house, Rev. Ogden handed Troy a bottle of brandy and told him to pour two glasses while he fried some bacon and prepared BLT sandwiches. Sitting in a private, relaxed atmosphere Rev. Ogden came directly to the point. "Troy, Coach McClarty is right. Tell God all about it, ask His forgiveness, and trust in the work of Christ who lived the perfect life for us because we are unable to do so, was crucified as a blood sacrifice and atonement for our sins, and was raised again. However, confessing and talking to someone who understands can relieve the guilt and burden you bear. I've often heard it said that sometimes we need God with skin. That's what I offer my congregation as a servant of God. Why not tell me what's on your heart? Then, we can pray together. Sometimes it's easier with a little guidance. Troy, I wasn't always a kindly old man who serves God. I was a hellion in my younger days, too. Talk to me. You'll feel better."

Troy stared into his brandy snifter. After a few moments of contemplation, he unburdened his soul. He finished by saying, "Reverend, I know it's wrong, but I love Renée with all that I am. What do I do?"

Rev. Ogden patted Troy's shoulder. "First, confess your sins, and, yes, it is *sin*, not mistakes. Admit it to yourself and to God. Ask His forgiveness and have faith. I don't have all the answers. My wife of thirty-five years died last year." The old minister refilled their glasses. "Beth was not my first wife, and I was not her first husband. I married a German girl when I was in the Army and stationed overseas. We had a daughter, Karina. Greta, my first wife, left me less than a year after Karina was born. I had a really bad temper in those days, and she was afraid of me. Beth was married to an abusive alcoholic. She left him. They also had a daughter. Karina came to live with me when she was five. Beth's daughter, Susan, was the same age. Beth and I were married shortly after that. We had two boys together. All the kids are grown and doing well. They live all over the country. It may well be that one day, somehow, you and Renée will be together. On the other hand, it might also be time to move on. Time will tell. There's a song that might help you. Some of the lyrics say, "'Give them all...'" He closed his eyes and dipped his head in rhythm. "'...Shattered dreams, wounded hearts, broken toys...'" The old man sang in a melodious voice. "'... and He will turn your sorrow into joy.' Give them all to Jesus, Troy."

Troy nodded penitently. "I want to have faith, but I'm a strong-willed person. I can't change that."

"God doesn't expect you to change everything overnight. As a matter of fact, most of your personality traits don't need to change at all. You just need to focus your energies in a new direction. From the visit we've had tonight, I can tell that you're not the hellion you want everyone to believe you are. Actually, part of you is still a scared little boy. You're a good man, Troy Tomerson. Just let the Lord guide you."

Troy agreed, "I want to."

"Then, put it in God's hands and wait. I think Renée is your shattered dream, wounded heart, and broken toy all rolled into one."

"What about the dragons? Do you think I'm crazy?"

"No. A long time ago I had a dream in which a florescent green dragon visited me. She told me to minister to the needs of the people. It was weird because many Christians see dragons as evil beings, but I listened. I was never happier than when I did what I was told to do. No, Troy, listen to your dragon's advice. Perhaps, you're 'entertaining angels unawares.'"

Troy laughed softly. "I never thought of it like that. Will you pray with me now? I think I need to get some sleep."

The old man of God prayed for the young man with a child's faith, and Troy went home. He began attending services at the little church where he had found his faith as often as possible with his schedule. That night, although sure of himself, Troy still had an uneasy feeling in his spirit regarding Renée. After lying awake for quite a while, Troy whispered aloud, "Okay, God. I give her to You. Whatever happens, I will wait upon You. I love her, Lord, but You know best. Please, send Your angels to watch over her. Help me keep faith. Amen."

Finally, Troy slept.

20
An Affair to Remember

When James came down the stairs before sunrise next morning to leave for the airport, Renée had not moved from the couch. He commented menacingly, "Good girl. I'll be back in about a week. Remember what I said: One word to the authorities and Troy Tomerson is history."

Renée's hand shook as she dialed Troy's number as soon as she heard James's car leave. Troy yawned into the phone, "Hello."

Momentarily there was silence at the other end of the line until Troy's instinct roused him. "Renée? What's wrong?"

Her voice quivered. "Troy, I need you."

The dragon's heart inside the man sprang awake even in the predawn hours. "Renée, what's wrong? Where are you?"

"My house."

"Is James there?"

"No."

Troy's red Ferrari pulled into Renée's driveway twenty minutes later. He did not even knock on the door but burst through it to see Renée in a heap upon the sofa. She met the man in three steps, flung her arms around his neck, and wept uncontrollably.

It took Troy about two seconds to see the finger imprints on her neck. He held her back from him and asked fiercely, "Where is he?"

"On his way to the Caymans."

He started out the door, and Renée grabbed his arm and screamed piercingly, "No, Troy! Please, don't go after him. He'll kill you."

"What are you talking about? I'm gonna kill *him*."

Shaking her head, Renée pleaded, "No. Please, just hold me."

Troy pulled her into his arms. "Shhh. Don't cry. Tell me what happened."

She shook her head against his chest. "I can't. I can't tell anybody. He will kill you if I do."

Troy put Renée slightly from him and smoothed her hair from her face. "Baby, what can he do to me? He was bluffing you."

She argued, "No, he's not. He has already deliberately killed four people and many others who just happened to be in the way, including your father. I can't let him hurt you. I love you too much."

He breathed deeply and held her close again. "Renée, what happened to the tigress who took on Celina Ortiz?"

"Troy, that was a joke compared to James. He's a ruthless killer."

"Renée, you might as well tell me the whole story. You've started now."

"No," she said, still in terror of what her husband might do. "I just need to be with you. I need to keep you safe."

She ran her fingers into Troy's hair and pulled his face to hers, kissing him desperately.

"Renée," Troy hesitated. "We can't."

"Yes, we can. James won't be back for a week. I need you, Troy. Make love to me."

He could not fight his heart another minute. He carried Renée to her bed and gently undressed her until he saw the bruises across her abdomen. "No," he muttered. "I swear, Renée, I will kill him."

"Don't think about James. Lose yourself in me."

Troy did, and for the next several hours no one existed except him and Renée, and the only sound that interrupted their heartbeats was the soft cooing of two lovebirds.

It was December with only two regular season games left and the Raiders were once again in play-off contention. Troy hated to tear himself away from Renée, but he had obligations. She told him to go. "I'll be fine. So long as I keep quiet, we're both safe.

Now, go. You're already late, and McClarty will have you running laps."

"I could jump hurdles today," he breathed into her hair as he held her one more time. "I love you, Renée. God, how I love you."

He kissed her again and opened the door. He turned with one more word, "There's a key in the begonia basket. Will you be at my place when I get in, or was this a one-time thing?"

"I'll be waiting for you." There were no games in Renée's agenda. She only had to figure a way to be free.

Troy was half an hour late for practice. McClarty glowered at him. "I had an emergency, Coach." With that said, he took off around the field, imposing his own laps upon himself. Twenty laps later he jogged to McClarty.

McClarty spat on the ground. "Do you want to talk about it?"

"Nope."

"Is it Renée?"

Troy did not answer. McClarty continued, "Remember what I told you about that bastard she's married to?"

"I remember. Do you think he's seriously capable of murder?"

"I do."

"Would he kill Renée or me?"

"Troy, are you sleeping with her? I thought you had gotten past her."

"I thought so too until I saw the bruises on her neck, Coach."

"He actually left bruises where they could be seen?"

"Oh, yeah." The younger man leaned on the bench.

"Troy, he's not being as careful as he used to be. There were never any visible bruises on his first wife."

"What do I do, Coach? How do I get her out of there?"

"That's a step she'll have to take for herself. In the meantime, I suggest that you not get caught. Do you really love her that much?"

"I have loved her since I was five years old. She brought magic into my life. She's my reason for breathing, and I will love her until the day I die."

"Oh, boy," sighed McClarty. "James Wilburn could see to that sooner than later. Troy, I've never said this to any other player on any team I've coached. I love you. Please, be careful."

"I will, Coach. Well, let's get to work."

Troy slipped quietly into his own house. He did not see Renée. He said to himself, *I knew it was too good to be true.*

He went into his bedroom to change into something comfortable and lazy. Lying on his bed in a black lace teddy was Renée. She rose to her knees and held on to one of the posts on Troy's four poster bed. "Surprise," she said seductively.

Troy took several deep breaths as he watched Renée wrap a leg around the post. Then, he boldly strode to her and tightly entangled his fingers in her still short blonde hair and commandingly laid her back on the bed. In the fading twilight, Troy and Renée made hot, passionate love before the sun sank completely on the horizon.

Nestled in an embrace under the sheets, he finally broke the spell that captivated him. "I'm starving."

"Me, too," agreed Renée.

He slipped into a pair of silk boxers and looked at the blonde pixie on his bed. "I know you didn't wear that teddy over here."

"Actually, I did. I just wore a blouse and a skirt over it."

Troy laughed and tossed a Raiders t-shirt to Renée who slipped it on.

"That makes a nice dress for you." He smiled.

She pulled the neck to her nose and breathed deeply. "It smells like you. That's all I need."

"Well, I need food," said Troy. He held out his hand. "Come on."

In the kitchen, Troy whisked some eggs and handed Renée a chunk of sharp cheddar and the cheese grater. "Grate some cheese."

She grated cheese while he gently stirred the eggs in the skillet. Then, she looked in the refrigerator and asked, "Do want some ham, too?"

"Only if you chop it. I'm too lazy."

Renée sliced a thick chunk of ham from the spiral ham she found in the refrigerator and chopped it into cubes. Troy sprinkled the ham and cheese over the eggs and Renée popped some sourdough rolls into the toaster oven and found strawberry jam in the refrigerator. She chuckled holding up the jar. "Some things never change."

Troy shook his head. "Nope. I have always loved strawberry jam."

He scooped a perfect omelet onto a plate while Renée buttered the rolls. Troy poured a glass of wine for each of them, and they sat at the table in the kitchen to eat together as they had so many years ago, only this time he held her hand while they ate. Between bites of omelet and rolls coated in butter and jam, he kissed her hand.

"Troy," giggled Renée, "you're gonna get my fingers sticky."

He promptly sucked her fingertips in retaliation. She started to withdraw her hand, but he held onto it gently, yet firmly. "What's the matter?" he asked tenderly.

Once again tears welled in her eyes. "Why didn't you come to the wedding and stand up and object? Miss Eva said you were stubborn enough to do it."

Troy's heart failed him at the sadness in Renée's voice. "Is that what you wanted me to do? You had just told me you *hated* me. At that moment in time, I believed you."

She started to cry earnestly. "I'm so sorry, Troy. How can you still love me after everything I've done to you?"

"I have never stopped loving you since the day you threw fairy dust on me and put me under your spell. Please, don't cry. If we can only have each other during stolen moments, let's make the most of them without regrets or tears." He knelt in front of her and softly brushed her tears away with his thumbs. "Someday you will be all mine one way or another. When that day comes, I will say before the world the same words Aidan spoke to Caitlin and Rennin spoke to Morgan. 'Heart of my heart, life of my life, you are my reason for breathing; and I will love you until the day I die.'" Troy reached up and touched the bruises on Renée's neck, and she flinched because the pain had set in. "And I mean it, Renée. If that bastard ever lays another hand on you, I will kill him. As God is my witness, I will kill him."

Troy led Renée back to his bed where they made love again softly and tenderly. She slept in his arms all night and they planned another stolen moment before he left for practice.

The Raiders made the play-offs again and Renée gladly went to all the games with James so that she could be sure nothing happened to Troy on the field. When the team was eliminated before the AFC championship, Renée secretly rejoiced because it meant Troy would have free time, and since she had begun negotiations for a new contract, she had a legitimate reason for seeing him.

When Troy came to her office to review the two-year renewal, James was there. It was everything Troy could do not to throw him out the sixth-floor window. James sat down as if to stay for the meeting.

Troy objected. "Excuse me, James, but this meeting is a client-lawyer thing. The details of my new contract will be public soon enough. Watch the tabloids. I'm sure they'll have the information before any reputable newspaper."

Put out, James left Renée's office. She trembled. She put a finger to her lips and shook her head. Then, she sat down and went over the terms of Troy's contract.

On a notepad she scribbled, "*I think the office might be bugged, and I don't think we should meet at either house from now on.*"

Troy nodded in understanding and signed the contract. When he left the office, James waited in the outer office. He stopped and shook hands with James, commenting, "Well, now since that is taken care of, I think I might spend a couple of weeks in Miami—visit my mom. I think I might drive down though and take in some sights along the way. I need a serious vacation."

"I understand. I wish I could talk my wife into going on a vacation with me, but she really wants to be partner. All she ever does is work."

"She has always been like that," said Troy. "She used to keep her nose in the books while I played and goofed off. I'm surprised she wasn't valedictorian. It would've been fairer."

"Well, I'm leaving day after tomorrow for Caracas. You know they have a booming oil business in Venezuela. I'll be down there at least six weeks, maybe more."

"Negotiate some good contracts so we won't be so dependent on Middle Eastern oil. Good-bye."

Troy wanted to make sure James's plane crashed, but instead he hired a private detective to follow James. "Get anything you can on him and let me know immediately if he doesn't go where he says or if he comes home. It could be a matter of life and death."

The next day, Renée received a plane ticket to Aspen in the mail along with the confirmation of a lodge reservation and a note that read: **Don't pack anything. QB.** James asked if there was anything of interest in the mail. "Not particularly," Renée answered. "I left it on the coffee table." She slipped her mail into her handbag.

The night before he left, James once again felt amorous, and forced Renée into submission. He knew she loathed his touch, but he reveled in humiliating her. However, he was surprised she gave in without a serious struggle. He did not understand Renée was even at that moment protecting Troy for she knew Troy could not see another bruise on her without acting rashly.

James left for South America at ten, and an unobtrusive, bald man boarded the plane behind him. Renée's flight left at three. In the meantime, she made one more trip to the attic. Some unexplained nagging told her she had missed something. She searched the old trunk and discovered a lock of baby Rennin's hair sealed in an airtight container. She took it, along with the mesmerizing photograph of the child taken only weeks before his death.

Still unsatisfied, Renée searched the wardrobe again without consolation. Last, she looked in the small trunk and wedged in a corner in the bottom she found a perfectly shaped teardrop emerald attached to a heavy chain. How she could have missed it, she did not know.

Feeling compelled the items she had with her on the way to the airport needed to be better safeguarded, Renée stopped at her office and deposited the lock of hair and the pendant in the safe in her office where she forwarded all her office calls to her cell phone as she had done the house phone before she left. The photograph, along with her lovebirds, she took to her friend in the private criminology lab located in the basement.

Skyelar Jacobson, an effeminate, open homosexual greeted Renée affectionately. She thrust the photograph into Skyelar's hand. "Skye, can you use that aging program on your computer to see what this baby might look like at thirty?" Then she set Cam and Tam on his desk.

Skyelar replied, "Well, of course, I can. How long can you give me?"

"I'm on my way to the airport. I'll be gone several weeks. Just have it ready when I get back or call my cell if it's really shocking." She pointed at the birds. "And take care of my babies."

"All right, girl. Where are you going? That miserable husband of yours finally taking you on one of his trips?"

"No!" snapped Renée venomously. "I'm going to Aspen with…a friend."

Skyelar pawed at the air. "Oh, you go girl! You've found yourself a man. And about time, too. Now, get out of here. I'll call you if it's something you might want to know immediately. Otherwise, I'll have it when you get back."

Kissing her friend's cheek, she said, "Thanks, Skye." Renée paused as she thought about the lock of hair in her safe. "And when I get back, I might ask another favor."

"Anytime, girlfriend. You go on and be a lovebird, and I'll take care of these two."

Renée boarded the plane to Aspen expecting Troy to be in the seat beside her. When he wasn't there, she became fearful James had played some kind of trick on her but flew on to her destination. She shivered as she left the plane since Aspen was covered in a sparkling blanket of white, and she wore only a lightweight cream-colored sweater and a pair of black slacks. To her great relief she saw Troy in the airport lobby. He engulfed her with a cozy down parka before he kissed her soundly.

"Thank you," Renée whispered. "I was freezing."

"I told you not to pack. I have everything you need."

She put both hands on his chest and teased him. "Anything to wear besides a parka?"

He winked and took her hand as he led her from the airport to his waiting Ferrari.

"You didn't fly?" asked Renée.

Troy cocked an eyebrow. "Technically, no. But this baby flies." He opened her door. "Shall I show you?"

"No," chastised Renée. "You will drive safely."

"Party pooper." He pretended to pout as he drove reasonably to the cabin at the lodge he had rented for a long weekend.

Inside, a fire already roared in the fireplace, and Troy prepared two cups of hot chocolate the moment they stepped in from the cold. The next three days they spent skiing, having snowball fights, building snowmen, and making love by the fire.

Bright and early on Monday morning, Renée was jarred from a peaceful sleep as Troy announced, "Wake up, Sleeping Beauty. We have to hit the road."

"What?" she asked groggily.

"This is only the first stop. We have places to go. Now, move it." Troy popped Renée's behind affectionately.

She sluggishly rolled from the bed and asked, "Troy, where are my clothes? I can't go anywhere naked."

"Oh, yeah." He pulled another suitcase from the closet and handed a leather, fleece-lined jacket to Renée. "You won't need the heavy parka, and the clothes in here are appropriate for the next leg of our journey. I already sent the other things to my place. Jake will hold them for you."

"Does Jake know about us, Troy?"

"Don't worry. Jake knew about us before we knew about us. He's surprised it took so long."

"Are you sure you can trust him?"

"With my life."

"Okay. If you trust him, I will. Now, where are we going?"

"It's a secret."

"Troy?" Renée coaxed.

As she wheedled Troy, her cell phone rang. It was James. Renée answered sleepily. "Good morning, darling," said James mockingly. "I thought I had better check on you."

"Do you know what time it is, James?"

"Barely dawn, but what better time to catch my wife at home?"

"Well, I want to go back to sleep for a while. Do you have a problem with that?"

"No, no. You need your beauty sleep. Thirty is fast creeping up on you." James hung up.

Renée looked alarmed. "He's checking up on me, Troy. I'm scared."

"Could you tell where he was?"

"I heard a lot of Spanish in the background. I hope he's in South America."

"I haven't heard anything differently."

"What do you mean?"

"Never mind. Don't worry about it. He's just trying to intimidate you. Fuck him."

"Troy!"

"I mean it, Renée. That bastard will not ruin your life any longer. You once saved me from a fate worse than death. Now, let me take care of this. Let me be your knight."

"I want you *alive*."

The man hugged the frightened woman. "I'm not afraid of James Wilburn. Trust me. His world is about to crumble around his ears. He is neither omnipotent nor omniscient. Do you remember when I told him I might be a dragon at heart?"

She nodded.

"Then, relax, my love. Let the fiery beast do its job."

Renée held tightly to Troy and buried her face in his chest. "Oh, Troy, I can't lose you. I love you."

"And I love you. Now get dressed so we can continue our little adventure."

She complied, and the couple drove east, stopping at a motel in the Oklahoma panhandle for the night. The next day, they drove into a lavish hotel in Hot Springs, Arkansas, where they spent three days relaxing in the natural hot springs and thinking about no one but themselves.

On Friday, Troy once again told Renée they were headed out, but he would not tell her where they were going. At dusk, they drove into New Orleans and the swankiest hotel in the French Quarter. While Troy swept her into his arms as the bellboy opened the door to their room, Renée took in the sight in an instant. "Oh, my God. This is the same room where Rennin and Rebekah O'Rourke spent their honeymoon."

"Yes, it is," said Troy triumphantly. "I researched it in detail after I read Rennin's journal. And do you realize what next Tuesday is?"

Renée shook her head. Troy grinned. "Mardi Gras." He lowered her to the floor and tipped the bellboy.

"Troy!" squealed Renée. "You really did plan this trip in detail, didn't you?"

He bowed. "Guilty as charged, counselor."

She slipped into his arms. "I love you, Troy Tomerson."

Once again, he lifted her into his arms as he carried her to bed.

During their long weekend in New Orleans, Troy and Renée dined on the finest Cajun and Creole cuisine at both Antoine's and Emeril's. They toured the most popular attractions. They went to the zoo and the aquarium and the D-Day Museum, and they had their caricatures drawn by a street artist in Jackson Square. They took in a haunted ghost tour and had goosebumps on their skin when a member of their tour group asked the guide about Marie LaVeau and voodoo, and as if on cue, haunting strains from a saxophone from a street musician wafted on the cool night breeze. They watched the Mardi Gras festivities from the balcony of their room just as Rennin and Rebekah had done a hundred fifty years earlier. There were no gunshots, but there were fireworks when Troy and Renée made love as Ash Wednesday approached.

As they lay in bed in the early hours of Wednesday morning, Renée asked, "What are you giving up for Lent?"

"Not a damned thing," laughed Troy. "No, wait. Asparagus."

Renée laughed loudly. "You hate asparagus."

"Exactly." Then, Troy sobered a bit. "I don't think God wants us to do things like that. I think He looks at the condition of the heart. He definitely knows what I do on Monday, so why confess it on Saturday? He already knows. Why should I ask some man to grant me absolution from some perceived sin when God knows my heart? Isn't it logical to assume God is the only One who can grant absolution? That's what both Coach McClarty and Reverend Ogden think, and it makes perfect sense to me."

Renée said, "Troy, I've never heard you discuss religion before."

"That's not religion. That's simple faith. God doesn't expect us to be perfect. He was perfect for us. All we need to do is believe. And, yes, I believe. Since I am no longer a good Catholic, I think I'll skip Ash Wednesday. It's time for us to go to our next destination."

"Where is that?"

"Home."

"Draconis?"

"What?"

"What did I say?"

"Never mind. We're going to Miami to visit my mother."

"Troy, what will she think of me?" She pushed back from her lover.

He smirked. "You have finally come to your senses."

"Troy, maybe you've decided not to be a good little Catholic boy, but Miss Eva is a devout Catholic."

Troy kissed Renée's fingertips. "She will understand we are completely and totally in love. You know she loves you, too." He kissed her and whispered, "Make love to me one more time in this magical room where past, present, and future seem to be one." Troy and Renée melded as one in an affair to remember.

21
DNA

Just as the sun topped the palm trees that lined the street, Troy's red Ferrari with tinted windows roared into the driveway of the modest, but pleasant, home in a Miami suburb Eva Tomerson had chosen. Anything fancier would not have been her style, but she was no longer in the dingy trailer park where Troy had grown up. He had not informed his mother he was coming. She hurried from the door of her home in great excitement at the surprise visit, hugging her son and surveying him critically.

"My, you look wonderful. You look happy for a change. What's up with you?"

He held up a finger as he walked around the car and opened the passenger's door. Renée stepped out anxiously. Eva clapped her hands over her mouth in awe. "My girl," she said with as much love as she had for Troy. Eva embraced Renée as tears streamed down her cheeks. Then, she eyed the two of them. "Explain," she commanded gently.

"What's to explain, Mom? Isn't it obvious?" asked Troy secretively.

Bluntly Eva asked, "Did James die?"

"Not yet," replied Troy, "but I'm working on it." He put a protective arm around Renée.

Eva looked from Troy to Renée and back. "Adultery? Under my roof?"

"Take us or leave us, Mom," Troy answered.

"I'll take you," replied Eva as a rapturous smile spread across her face. She ushered her two children into her home and knew in her heart Troy and Renée were no more sinful than she.

In the light of the house, Troy surveyed his mother and observed, "Mom, I might look great, but you don't. What's wrong?"

She patted his hand. "I've just been a little under the weather. Nothing for you to worry about."

He was sure that Eva was not telling him everything, but he let her play the mother hen and make breakfast. Eva questioned the couple about how they had finally come together and received cryptic and incomplete answers. After breakfast, Troy excused himself to unload the car and shower. While Eva and Renée talked over another cup of coffee, Eva said, "Renée, what happened? Tell me everything. Leave nothing out."

Renée poured out the whole story. Eva sat in stunned silence. She whispered, "Secrets and lies always come back to haunt you." As she stood to put her coffee cup in the sink, the room spun wildly, and Eva lost consciousness.

Renée dashed down the hall and threw open the shower curtain. Troy grinned but saw the look of horror on her face. She gasped, "Troy, your mother fainted. Something is really wrong."

He hastily wrapped a towel around him and hurried to the kitchen. Eva sat precariously on the chair at the table with her head on her hands. Troy knelt beside her. "Mom, what's wrong?"

Eva confessed, "I'm sick, Troy. I need to go to the hospital now. My doctor's number is on the refrigerator. Will you, please, call him to meet us there?"

Renée found the number and called Dr. Goldberg, and Troy drove his mother's car to the hospital. Eva dozed in the back seat as they drove. Renée ventured, "Troy, Dr. Goldberg is an oncologist."

He looked at the woman he loved with real fear in his eyes. "Under the weather? She has cancer and didn't tell me?"

Renée took Troy's hand. "It'll be all right. I'm with you."

They arrived at the emergency room where Dr. Levi Goldberg waited for them. He checked Eva into the oncology wing and met with Troy and Renée.

"How bad is it?" asked Troy. "She hasn't told me a thing."

"She didn't want you to worry," replied the doctor. "I told her to tell you. Mr. Tomerson, she needs a bone marrow transplant. At this advanced stage of her leukemia, it's the only option. You're the only living relative she has. As such, you're her best chance for a match for the transplant. She didn't want you to take time out from your position as quarterback to do the transplant. It's a very painful procedure, and you'll be unable to practice or play football for several weeks."

"To hell with football! What do I need to do?"

"I thought you'd feel that way, but she's a stubborn woman. I've been scanning for potential donors on a daily basis. First, we need to see if you're a match. Even as her son, there is no guarantee you'll be a perfect match, but you're her best chance."

"Let's do it," said Troy authoritatively.

"Me, too," volunteered Renée. "Just in case. Even if I don't match her, I might be able to help someone else. I don't have to die to donate bone marrow."

"Very true," responded the doctor. "I wish more people felt that way. Follow me." He showed Troy and Renée to the oncology lab and began the necessary tests to find Eva a marrow donor.

As Troy and Renée awaited the test results, Renée's phone rang. To her great relief, it was Skyelar. "Hey, girlfriend. I know it took me a while, but we had a real case come up that needed my attention. Nonetheless, when I got these results, I had to call you. You won't believe who this baby looks like."

"Troy Tomerson," said Renée.

"Right you are, darling. Is this some sort of paternity case for you? Has your old friend fathered a child?"

"Something like that. I can't say anything more. I have to go now. I'll call you later."

Dr. Goldberg came toward Troy and Renée with a long face. He earnestly asked, "Mr. Tomerson, were you adopted?"

Taken aback, Troy responded, "No, why?"

The doctor took a deep breath. "Honestly, Mr. Tomerson, you are not even close to a match. You are more distant than Mrs. Wilburn, who doesn't match either, but she actually has more of the same DNA markers as your mother. You have a few, but are you certain you weren't adopted?"

Troy did not know how to respond. He was both confounded and dumbfounded. Renée sat on the sofa in the waiting area and thought aloud, "Can this be real?"

Suddenly, Dr. Goldberg was paged to Eva Tomerson's room.

Troy clasped Renée's hand. "Renée, now I really need you. Help me understand what's going on."

"I will, darling. I think I know, but I need a little more undeniable proof."

Dr. Goldberg returned and spoke compassionately. "She wants the two of you. Be gentle. She won't be with us much longer."

As Troy and Renée entered Eva's room, Eva held a weak hand out to Troy. He grasped her hand with tears on his cheeks. Eva comforted him. "Don't cry, baby. You have been my one happiness for almost twenty-eight years."

"I'm almost thirty, Mom," Troy said without thinking.

"Don't hate me, Troy. I love you more than anything in this world."

"I love you, too, Mom."

Eva looked at Renée, "You know, don't you, my darling girl?"

Renée nodded.
"Help him understand. Love him."
Renée nodded again. She could not speak.
Eva's hand slipped from Troy's, and she was gone.

22
Family Plot

Back in Eva's home, Troy made funeral arrangements, and Renée made a phone call to Skyelar. "Skye, can you do DNA testing on hair?"

"You know I can if the follicle is intact."

"Listen to me carefully and don't let a word of this slip out. In the safe in my office is some hair in an airtight container. Do a profile on that. I will get you the other DNA sample somehow." She gave Skyelar the combination to her safe.

Almost simultaneously as she hung up from her conversation with Skyelar, her phone rang. James's voice bellowed on the other end, "Where the hell are you?"

Renée's backbone had grown over the last several weeks and she answered confidently, "I'm in Miami with Troy. His mother just died unexpectedly, and he needs me here to help him make arrangements."

James grunted, "I'll be there tomorrow."

She told Troy James was on his way to Miami.

"What the hell for?" he hollered as he realized the detective he had hired had not called, or had he? Troy checked his voicemail and had four messages from the detective. He realized the incident with his mother had overshadowed his protection of Renée.

He cried on her shoulder, "I'm sorry, baby. I let you down."

"Hush, Troy. You just stay cool when he gets here. I'm your best friend, and I'm here to help you through this difficult time."

"God!" Troy groaned. "This was supposed to be the culmination of our trip before we had to go back to reality."

She took his face in her hands and spoke assertively. "This is reality right now. I love you. You love me. It's just you and me, baby, just the way it has *always* been. We will do what we have to do. Do you understand me?"

Troy nodded and drew strength from the fire his pixie had found once again. Renée led him to the bedroom they had planned to share while visiting where she made love to him and made him forget his sadness for a time.

James arrived as Troy and Renée dressed for Eva's funeral. Renée had purchased a simple black business suit and a suit for Troy.

Renée glared at James. "Troy is still in shock. Don't make a scene. It really was not necessary for you to come."

"Be glad I'm acting the part of a concerned friend. I even brought some of his cohorts with me. Jake Muñoz and Gerald McClarty flew down with me. By the way, I bought a jet, so I never have to deal with the public airways again."

Renée peeked into the living room to see Troy was in good hands. She said honestly, "Thank you for that."

The funeral was a simple affair as Eva would have wanted it, and Troy buried her next to her dead husband in the small family plot that belonged to the Tomersons. There was room for two more. Troy supposed it was meant for him and whomever he might marry.

At the house, Eva's friends gathered to pay their respects and comfort Troy. The old attorney for which Eva had been a secretary most of her life, spoke to Troy and told him he needed to stay a few days to decide how to dispose of Eva's property. Troy acknowledged the request and asked Renée if she would help him.

James replied for her. "I wish she could stay, Troy, but she really must come home with me today, or there could be some disposal I will need to do."

Both Troy and Renée perceived the underlying threat. Jake and McClarty asserted they would stay with Troy. Consequently, Renée flew to Puma Pass just a few hours after Eva was laid to rest.

Arriving around four o'clock in Puma Pass, Renée insisted she had to go to the office. "James, you know I dropped everything in such a hurry. I really have to check in. I'll be back before dark."

Renée went immediately to Skyelar who questioned, "Girl, what are you doing back?"

"I'll tell you later," she responded urgently. "Did you get that profile done?"

"Oh, yeah. Do you have the other sample you want me to compare?"

Renée reached into her purse and handed Skyelar a hair sample she had taken from Troy's brush. "Skye, this is Troy's hair."

"Troy? Are you having an affair with him, honey? Are you trying to find out if he has a kid?"

"Something like that. I need this fast. How long will it take, Skye?"

"I'll rush it, honey. Give me seventy-two hours."

"I owe you big time." She kissed her friend on the cheek and scurried home. "I'll get Cam and Tam now," she said, snagging the birdcage as she left.

Back in her house, Renée showered and changed into a pair of jeans and a Raiders t-shirt that was too big but smelled like Troy. She walked down the street at dusk and visited the O'Rourke family plot in the cemetery. Kneeling beside the headstone that read, "Rennin Duncan O'Rourke, May 12, 1980-August 7, 1982," she cried real tears for the loss of a woman she had loved dearly and wondered what "Troy" would have been like. *Would he have been as wonderful as the man I know and love as Troy Tomerson? Would he believe in a world of magic?* She shook her head. *No. That would have to be Rennin. It's in his blood. But how can I help*

him deal with the fact his whole life has been a lie? She remembered the Tarot cards at the carnival and the palm reader. *Lies. Two lives.*

A surly voice snarled behind her, "What is this? Are you deciding where you would like to be laid to rest?"

Renée wheeled on James. "I want a divorce. I don't want anything from you, and your secret is safe with me. I just want to be free of you." She pushed past him.

He grabbed her arm roughly. "The only way you will be free of me is to be in the family plot." Then, James threw Renée to the ground and forced himself upon her, caring not if bruises were visible.

23
A Question of Paternity

Renée could hardly get out of bed the next morning, and when she gazed into the mirror, she was happy Troy was still in Miami because she looked as if she had gone ten rounds with a champion boxer. She limped back to the sofa and sank in despair.

As James came down the stairs, he commented, "Aren't you going to the office, darling?"

Renée got off the couch and glared at him. "Are you kidding? How would you like me to explain this?" She ran a hand down her side.

He looked at her with loathing. "Let's see. Last night at dusk you went for a walk to the cemetery. I'd say you were mugged. Some vagabond sleeping among the gravestones saw a pretty, rich lady and took all her money."

"In Puma Pass where the crime rate is zero and the worst thing the police have to worry about is underage drinking and tobacco use? That's a very plausible story," she retaliated. "Not to mention I didn't call the authorities."

"Maybe you were attacked by a puma that wandered in from the mountains. I really don't care what you tell them, Renée. This evening I'm flying to Buenos Aries. I don't plan to come back, so in seven years when you're too old to care if a man looks at you, you can have me declared legally dead. Then, you'll be free, but by then Troy will have moved on to some bimbo just like he always has."

"Troy is free to be with whomever he pleases."

James laughed viciously. "The problem is Troy Tomerson likes fucking my wife."

"What are you talking about?" Renée said with her mind in frenzy.

James opened a large manila envelope and threw photos at her. There were pictures of her and Troy in Aspen, Hot Springs, and New Orleans. "What? No denial, Renée? Just because I was in South America doesn't mean I couldn't have you followed. Actually, I had *Troy* followed from the moment he left your office. What did you tell your lover, Renée?"

"Nothing."

"Yes, I actually believe that. With his hot-headed temper, he would've confronted me. And you're so scared of what I might do to him. So, tell me, darling, how long have the two of you been sleeping together?" James continued as he pushed Renée down onto the couch and sat beside her.

Refusing to be dominated, she shot, "Since the night before our wedding."

"Well, now, that *does* surprise me. Maybe he *is* willing to stick around. I guess I'll have to postpone my trip. I want to see what *he* does when I show *him* these pictures. So, tonight you and I are going to Hawaii. Yes, that's a good plan."

"I'm not going anywhere with you.

"Yes, you are because you don't want to see Troy in a pine box. I have to run out and get my new jet ready to go. You pack while I'm gone. Don't pull any stunts. I have already disconnected the phone. Give me your cell phone."

When Renée did not reply or respond, James repeated, "Give me your cell phone."

"What?"

"Give me your cell phone. I don't believe your hearing is damaged. Oh, and your car keys."

"I will not."

James backhanded her. "You will and now."

He followed Renée's gaze to where her purse lay and snatched it before she could move to it. "I'll be back in a couple of hours, dear." He pinched her face between his thumb and fingers and kissed her on the mouth.

Renée would not be bullied. She knocked on the door of three neighbors before someone answered. The elderly lady who opened the door saw the bruised face of the young woman and let her in instantly. Renée asked to use the phone. The first call she made was to Troy who did not answer. In desperation, she left a message on his voicemail. "I need you home now, Troy. James knows about us, and he's trying to make me go to Hawaii. Please, hurry."

Then she called Skyelar. "Skye, please tell me you were able to get that profile faster than seventy-two hours. I'm desperate."

"Yes, I did, honey, but you won't believe the results. I was just about to call you."

"Skye, I don't have time for games. Just tell me. Troy and the baby are the *same* person, aren't they?"

"Yes."

"Skye, get to my house as fast as you can and bring Mr. Pryor with you. It's an emergency. Oh, and look in my safe. I have an extra set of car keys there. James took mine."

Saying to herself, "Troy is with Jake and Coach McClarty. They'll keep him safe," she called the police.

When James drove past his house he kept driving because there were four squad cars in the driveway. He thought to himself, *she's got more balls than a man. She'll be so sorry.*

Meanwhile in Miami, Troy and his two dear friends waited for Eva's attorney to read her will, which basically left everything she had to Troy to dispose of as he saw fit. Troy told the lawyer to sell the house and give the proceeds to his mother's church and to give the clothes and other items that were of no use to him to charity. The old white-haired man handed Troy an envelope. "Eva told me to give this to you in the event of her death. I have no idea what it contains."

Troy opened the envelope to find several pages in his mother's handwriting:

My Darling Troy,

Now that I have gone on and will never know if you can hate me or forgive me, the time has come for you to know the truth. No matter how much this information shocks and hurts you, please remember I did all for the love of my child.

Many years ago, you asked me a question I could not believe you could have remembered at such a tender age. You asked me, "Mom, who is Rennin O'Rourke?" The answer to that question, darling, is you. You were born Rennin Duncan O'Rourke in Puma Pass, California, May 12, 1980.

Troy's hand flew to his mouth. The mysterious writing on the tapestry flooded his mind. The fortunetellers' words about lies and two lives bombarded his memory. His stomach roiled, but he continued to read.

When I first took you as my own, I didn't know who you were. To me you were a lost little boy who needed a mother. I became that mother. Let me explain the story to you.

You already know of the Ameri-Rail derailment that killed my husband. What you don't know is my son, Troy, also died in the wreck. There was carnage all around. I must have been in shock—I honestly don't remember. I remember looking at the body of my dead husband and my baby who was charred beyond recognition. When the explosion occurred, I was not in the compartment we had reserved. I had gone to the dining car to bring dinner back to us because Troy was so tired, he couldn't have endured eating in the dining car. That's why I didn't die at the same time.

Well, I must have dragged my family out of the wreckage. As I've said, I do not clearly remember. Nonetheless, there they lay. Nearby, lay another couple severely burned and dead. I think I pulled them out too. Sitting by the couple was a precious little boy with dark-brown curly hair and vivid green eyes. He was crying his heart out. All I could think of was to stop the child's pain. When I reached out to him, he came to me willingly and hushed his tears. At that moment, I believed God had given my Troy back to me, just in a different form.

The precious little boy wore a medical alert bracelet, which I didn't read, but I took it off and put it on my own child's wrist. That's why years later I didn't know you were allergic to penicillin, and you almost died on me again after the accident with Renée and the school bus.

I brought you home with me; and you became Troy Lane Tomerson; and you were the greatest joy in my life. Well, at some point, I came to my senses and realized what I had done. I watched the news reports and heard how the accident was actually an act of violence and how the bomb had gone off in the compartment my family had. The strange thing is the train line had confused the O'Rourkes' compartment and ours. My husband and Mr. O'Rourke spoke, and since the compartments were identical, it really didn't matter where we slept; so, both parties stayed where they were for the sakes of two very tired little boys. The irony is the O'Rourke family took the train as a lark because they had never traveled by rail. However, it was obvious to me that someone had tried to kill the O'Rourke family, regardless of how many others were injured or killed. It was then that I knew you were safe with me. Whoever tried to kill you had failed. I felt compelled, even called by God, to care for you. You had to remain Troy Tomerson, and, I will confess, I was terrified of going to jail for kidnapping, although that was never my intent.

Hearing Mr. O'Rourke's first name shocked me, too. Michael O'Rourke. I did a bit of genealogy research on myself. My great-grandfather was named Michael O'Rourke. He fought with Roosevelt in the Spanish-American War. He died in Cuba where he met his wife, who, along with four daughters survived him. My digging proved that Michael O'Rourke had a twin, Gabriel, who lived and died in Puma Pass, California. It seems the Depression hit Michael's family hard, and the daughters lost most of the money he left to them. Still, I knew God had brought you to me for safekeeping, for we were distant relatives.

You cannot imagine my surprise when Renée moved next door with a book written by Rennin O'Rourke, but you did not know that at the age of five. (Actually, you were six.) When you asked me who he was, my life almost ended on the spot. However, I knew that there was a reason Renée was sent to us, and I also knew that someday I would have to tell you the truth. I think somewhere in your heart you have always known there was more to you than a trailer park in Miami—and it was not just a football field.

Silent tears streamed down the young man's face, dripping onto the ink and causing a few smudges.

Troy, or I guess it's time to call you Rennin, you never went hungry or needed anything as you grew up although you had to work hard for niceties and luxuries, which probably taught you to be self-sufficient and independent. I will not apologize for instilling those values in you; but, darling, you are one of the richest men in America. You should own all the things James Wilburn owns. They are yours by right.

My heart tells me that man is dangerous, especially after I met him. He may have even been the one who tried to kill you all those years ago. That I do not know. I do know that you and Renée belong together. Do whatever it takes to get her away from that man. Although she never became my daughter, I love her almost as much as I love you.

I know what you have just read must boggle your mind. I'm so sorry for any pain I've caused you. You have been the light of my life since you were two. No matter what you may think of me now, I have loved you with an everlasting love and a mother's heart. I can only pray you will always consider me Mom. I love you.

Eva Tomerson

Troy handed the letter to his coach, and McClarty and Jake read it together in disbelief. The three men returned to Eva's house to make plans to get back to Oakland. Troy checked his voicemail and announced they had to leave immediately.

Gerald McClarty flew back with Troy while Jake volunteered to drive Troy's Ferrari back for him. Troy went immediately from the airport to Renée's house where he found her safe and under police protection. Skyelar Jacobson had not left Renée's side until Troy returned.

Troy held her tightly in his arms and joked that he wasn't sure Skyelar would have been any help if James had returned. Renée hit him playfully, "Troy Tomerson, that is just plain mean."

He just raised an eyebrow and simultaneously he and Renée said, "We have to talk."

They sat on the couch. "Ladies first," said Troy. Renée pulled out the photograph of baby Rennin and the aged computer generation along with the DNA profiles Skyelar had done. Troy said, "Well, if it's a matter of reading something…" He handed her the letter from Eva. They exchanged documents.

The two looked at each other for a long time before Troy said, "Well, do you love Troy or Rennin? I'll be the one you want me to be."

Renée burst into laughter. "Do you want to be rich or poor?"

Confused, Troy said, "I don't think I'll be poor either way."

"Well," said Renée, "it seems James has either squandered or embezzled most of the O'Rourke family fortune. You still own this house and part of Mercier Memorial Hospital and Puma Pass Academy. Other than that, Rennin O'Rourke is strapped."

Troy interrupted with a chuckle. "Ian Montague said in that book the O'Rourkes would one day lose their fortune for being too nice. He never met me."

Renée rolled her eyes. "On the other hand, Troy Tomerson is a successful football player who has made wise investments and has a lucrative income from endorsements."

Troy sighed. "First of all, James will get what's coming to him, and I'll get my family fortune back for the dragons. Second, I'll still have everything Troy has made. So, I have no idea what to do. You're the lawyer. What should I do?"

"Call a press conference," she said confidently, "and make public what we know. Issue a challenge to James. He won't be able to help himself. He'll come gunning for you. Ask the public what you should do. And do you really believe there are dragons somewhere waiting for Rennin O'Rourke?"

He shrugged. "They are at the very least in my dreams. You once believed they were real."

"Sometimes I still do." Renée smiled and told Troy about the dragon necklace the old gypsy had given her in Greece. She retrieved it and put it on.

Troy held the trinket gently in his fingers. "Well, maybe they'll whisper to me what to do."

The next morning, Troy called a press conference and revealed the past secrets to the public. He publicized both the letter and the DNA evidence and made a clear declaration that both he and the authorities were seeking James Wilburn in conjunction with the

Ameri-Rail tragedy in 1982, the murder of Corrine O'Rourke Wilburn, the physical assault of Renée Peyton Wilburn, and the misappropriation of funds in a number of businesses that were a part of O'Rourke Enterprises. He asked his fans as well as the public in general for their support and prayers as he made decisions regarding his future. He ended his proclamation by saying, "Ladies and gentlemen, this morning I don't even know what to call myself. Am I Rennin O'Rourke or Troy Tomerson?"

On a sofa in a plush villa in Argentina, James Wilburn threw his glass of scotch at the television screen and a strange screeching voice wailed, "Damn those O'Rourkes! Won't they ever die?"

He picked up the phone and made a call to America.

Gerald McClarty pounded on Renée's front door. She opened the door to a distraught man asking, "Is Troy here?"

"Yes," Troy answered for himself as he descended the stairs.

McClarty collapsed in a chair. "Oh, God. It was Jake."

"What are you talking about, Coach?"

"Your Ferrari was outside Brew Masters. When it cranked, it exploded. Jake was still on his way to deliver it to you."

Troy sank to his knees and sobbed as Renée gathered him in her arms. "I think James has raised the stakes, Renée."

Jake Muñoz's funeral was a solemn occasion with a sea of black suits and silver ties. Troy had to stop several times in the delivery of his best friend's eulogy, but his spirit to fight and his killer instinct rose to the surface. He surveyed the audience before he spoke his final words. He looked compassionately at Jake's two children, Sergio and Nidia. He knew they had different mothers, but it was hard to believe they were siblings with such contrasting skin tones. His heart broke for them because he understood growing up without a father. "Jake Muñoz knew the meaning of friendship. He was like a brother to me. Jake was murdered in an attempt meant for me. I *dare* the coward who took from us a father, a son, a lover, and a cherished friend to face me eye-to-eye like a man. If you want me, come for me. Don't plant a bomb in a car or a train. Don't send a hitman with a sniper rifle. Don't try to get a linebacker to break my neck. Do it yourself. I *dare* you."

McClarty clamped Troy on the shoulder as they left the cemetery. "Balls, Tomerson, O'Rourke, or whoever the hell you are. You have balls."

The next few weeks were uneventful except for the fact McClarty drafted a quarterback in the NFL draft, to Troy's consternation. McClarty explained, "In case James Wilburn meets your challenge at Jake's funeral."

Troy officially moved into Renée's house with her and brought all the dragon pieces with him, proudly displaying them in the appropriate rooms. He also hung his tapestry over the fireplace and caressed the dragon's mouth as he whispered, "Tell me what to call myself." In an act of compassion for Eva Tomerson, for Troy dearly loved the woman who had been his only remembrance of a mother, he had her real son's body moved to rest beside her in Miami.

Renée returned to her office, but always with a bodyguard. Troy refused to leave her unprotected. She bought a house in remote Alaska, claimed residency, and filed for divorce on the grounds of abuse and desertion. Peter Pryor called Renée into his office and asked her to be seated. She felt nervous as a fox trapped by hounds. With all the publicity surrounding her, she felt certain Pryor and Associates' conservative reputation had been tarnished.

Peter shoved a document across his desk toward her. "Read it and tell me what you think."

Renée looked up from the pages and asked, "Are you serious?"

"Absolutely. I've been waiting for an O'Rourke to come aboard as my partner since Michael died. He was as brilliant as you. You know it was Pryor, O'Rourke, and Associates. Michael's grandfather and my grandfather were partners. Michael's father was not the lawyer type but joined the military and went missing in Vietnam. Michael had just graduated law school and inherited the position. He decided to go off on one more excursion with his family before he settled down to practice law with me when he was murdered. You will be an O'Rourke when you marry my godson. Yes, Rennin is my godson. You are aware that as Troy Tomerson he dated my daughter at Florida State before she died in a car accident, aren't you? You are going to marry him, aren't you?"

"Yes, I knew he dated Melanie. I think she might have been the one person who could have captured his heart and made him forget me, but he hasn't asked me to marry him, even now."

"He will."

"He also hasn't decided to change his name."

"He will. The dragons will insist. He won't be able to resist their pull. So, what do you say? Until such time as your name officially changes, it will be Pryor, Peyton, and Associates. Renée, this offer doesn't have a damned thing to do with James Wilburn. The man is scum and should be shot at sunrise. I have never represented him. I represented Mercier Memorial Hospital. You're a young, vibrant, brilliant attorney. I want you as my partner. The fact that once you marry Rennin you will be family is merely icing on the cake. I would have offered you this partnership quite soon anyway. Now, give me an answer, or do you want to discuss it with my godson first?"

"I say, 'yes.' It's what I've wanted forever. Peter, do you believe in dragons?"

"Yes. They sent you to me. So, welcome, partner."

Renée stood to shake Peter's hand, and the room went black.

A few minutes later she came to as he bathed her face in cool water. He commented, "I think Rennin had better marry you as soon as possible."

"Why?"

"I only know one reason why strong, healthy women faint like that. You're pregnant, dear."

She muttered, "No. No, I can't be."

Eva had been dead six weeks. Renée recalled with both joy and sadness her last night in Miami. In the same thought, she recalled with disgust and terror the very next night in Puma Pass. She drove straight from her office to her doctor. She was in too much shock to even call ahead, but Dr. O'Neil saw her without hesitation and confirmed Peter's prediction. Her security detail followed her discretely.

Rather than the joy he expected from his patient, Renée burst into tears. "Oh, God! What do I do? I don't know if James or Troy is the father."

"Oh, I see," said Dr. O'Neil sympathetically. "I think I know who the father is."

"How?"

"If I recall correctly, many years ago I had a patient by the name of Corrine Wilburn. She came to me to find out if there was something wrong with her because she had tried for years to get pregnant. There was not a thing wrong with her. I never examined James, but the odds are he had the problem. Now, if she never conceived with him, and you never conceived in all the years you were married to him, what should you think?"

"Dr. O'Neil, I so want to believe that. But how can I know for sure?"

He patted her hand. "Have faith, dear. Go home and tell our newfound Mr. O'Rourke that he's going to be a father. And in a few months when you are about twenty weeks, if you desperately need to know for certain before the baby comes, we can do an amniocentesis for a DNA profile."

"But if I wait that long, what options do I have if it proves to belong to James?"

"You would still have options, but I won't do it."

Renée cried some more. "I wouldn't do it anyway. I think it's wrong. You're right. I was married to James quite a while, and never got pregnant without the use of birth control. How dangerous is the amnio?"

"There are risks, but I've never lost a patient or a baby yet."

"Then, I just have to have faith. This baby belongs to Troy. Nothing would make me happier except to be married to the baby's father."

"When will your divorce be final?"

"Thirty days from the date I became an Alaska resident.

Dr. O'Neil quirked an eyebrow.

Renée shrugged. "I'm circumventing the law a little, but I refuse to wait six more months to be officially free. And knowing James, he'd contest the divorce from whatever rock he's crawled under. Believe me when I tell you Troy paid the struggling attorney up there a hefty sum to get me away from that jerk. We didn't file in Florida even though I could probably have still claimed residency because James might have expected that."

"Then, there's plenty of time."

All the way home Renée rehearsed how to tell Troy she was pregnant until she had talked herself into a fit of happiness. She bounced in the door and passed the post where a policeman had been stationed for six weeks. "Troy! Troy, where are you? I have something wonderful to tell you."

24
A Vanishing Act

Renée bounded up the stairs. Troy was not in the bedroom. Neither was he in the kitchen. She could not shake an unsettled feeling as it dawned on her there was no policeman outside her house. Her private security left as usual when she got home, thinking she would be under police protection. She called Gerald McClarty. He had not seen Troy all day but told Renée he was on his way to her house to find out why his quarterback had missed practice and had not answered his phone all day.

McClarty arrived in as much a state of panic as Renée. He called the police. After a quick search of the property, the authorities found the body of the policeman who had been on duty outside the woman's home. Renée was near hysterics. She called Peter Pryor who came over immediately. Then, she called Skyelar and asked him to bring the emerald pendant from her safe and said she didn't know why she wanted it, but felt it held some key to finding Troy.

Skyelar arrived at the same time as a courier. Skyelar handed Renée the pendant, and a voice whispered for her to put it on. The courier handed her a package, which the police confiscated. Bomb professionals opened the package. Inside was a video cassette. The policeman in charge put the video into the VCR and pressed play.

As the tape began, all the spectators in the room saw a candlelit room and heard James Wilburn say, "Hello, Renée." She screamed in sheer terror and backed as far from the television set as she could for what she saw on the screen was a hideous creature bearing little resemblance to a human. Those around her thought she was afraid of the man on the screen. The voice droned on. "I have something to show you." The camera panned to a coffin. "The pine box for your beloved at nine this morning." The picture blipped and came back on. The creature waved a hand. "The pine box at noon." Troy's lifeless-looking body lay in the casket. The picture blipped again, and the creature waved a hand again. "The pine box at three o'clock." More hideous figures lowered the coffin into a grave. "He's not dead just yet, Renée. I want him to know who did this to him and why. I might have left you in peace with your little quarterback if he had not turned out to be"—The figure leaned in toward the camera and screamed like a banshee—"an O'Rourke! I have tried for almost five hundred years to get rid of them. What is it about them that they will *not* die? Well, this is the last one unless by some magical miracle you can find him before his air supply runs out." The tape ended.

Lt. Bass, the commander, ordered helicopters and questions of every cemetery within a hundred miles for freshly turned graves. Renée placed a protective hand over her womb. Nobody besides Dr. O'Neil and Peter knew she was pregnant. That thing would come after her baby. Nobody could know. But nobody else had seen what she saw. Unknown to her, neither had anyone else heard the part about five hundred years. They had only heard the word years.

Renée clasped her hand over the emerald as she remembered the story of Draconis and the witch Quazel. Nobody in the room would believe her. Maybe McClarty because he loved Troy if she made him wear the pendant and watch the tape again would believe her.

She approached Gerald McClarty and tapped him on the shoulder. "Will you do something for me?"

"Sure, honey. What do you want?"

"You'll think I'm crazy."

"Just ask."

She took off the pendant. "Will you wear this and watch that tape again? Tell me I have not gone insane."

McClarty slipped the pendant over his head and said, "Turn it on."

What he saw sent him scurrying over the back of the couch. He jerked the necklace off. "Renée!"

185

"You saw it, too."

He nodded. She continued. "Troy won't be in a cemetery. We're going to have to find him—you and I. They won't be able to." She grasped the man's hand, and they left unnoticed through the front door.

As Troy Tomerson, sporting only a pair of black silk boxers, stepped onto his front porch for the morning paper in the heavy, oppressive, frigid fog that rolled in from the bay at night, he felt something akin to a wasp sting in the side of his neck. In an instant, he could not move or speak, but he saw a blurred streak of black behind the police officer, who had turned to wave his usual morning greeting, on the sidewalk plunge what appeared to be an ice pick into the officer's neck. Troy felt his full two hundred twenty-five pounds crumple.

Two men dressed as police officers carried him to the cruiser in front of his house and deposited him in the back seat. Troy was sure they drove across the bay from the sound the tires made. Still, he could not move.

The car pulled onto a side road in a secluded, wooded area, and moments later, Troy was hauled from the car, carried into a building, and dropped resoundingly into what he thought had to be a coffin. It smelled like pine. Sometime later, James Wilburn's face peered over the edge of the box and sneered.

"Hello, Rennin O'Rourke. You said you wanted me to look you in the eye. I'm doing so."

Troy tried frantically to move some part of his body, but even his eyes were fixed straight ahead.

"Relax," taunted James. "You might as well not struggle in your mind. You won't be able to move for at least another hour, maybe longer. You've been shot with a poisoned dart dipped in curare. It paralyzes you, so you appear dead to all except your own mind. Many South American tribes use it to paralyze their prey, and it is often used by voodoo priests in the making of zombie powder. It's how the hoodoo religion has created the myth that they can bring people back from the dead and that zombies exist. Of course, if they're buried, they actually do die—thus enhancing the lore of vampires when the bodies are exhumed, and the dead have turned over in their graves. On the other hand, the priests are placed in a crypt or catacombs—thus, zombies as they walk out alive eventually. But normal humans just do not return from the grave.

"Why won't you O'Rourkes die?" He ran perfectly manicured fingers through his dark graying hair. "Why must you make my existence so miserable? When I first met you, I felt a strange stirring within." He tapped his chest over where his heart should be. "Yet, you died when you were two, or so I thought. I should have known who you were though because you look so damned much like Michael. You know your great-times-seventeen-grandfather survived a dose of this poison. His grandfather just had to let Aidan lie in state for the mourners' benefit. Alexander left Aidan out long enough for the damned poison to wear off. I don't think you'll be so lucky."

James picked up a tube and ran it along the padding inside the casket. "This is air for you. Oh, no. You won't die immediately. I want you to think about what's happening to you. I've adjusted the air flow so that at precisely six A.M. on the sixth of June, the air stops. You should be dead about three minutes after that, maybe a little longer. That gives that delicious slut of yours about forty-two hours to find you. By the way, there are a couple of bottles of water for you. I wouldn't want you to dehydrate before your appointed hour." James laughed wickedly. "And, oh, the humiliation of when your bodily functions take over. Damn! Why didn't I think about installing a camera so I could watch? Ah, well, I suppose hindsight is twenty/twenty, as they say.

"You, know, Rennin, if you had just stayed Troy Tomerson, I was prepared to walk away from that tasty little morsel and let you have her. I think it's sweet you appreciate leftovers. I suppose that comes from your humble upbringing. By the way, have you ever had anyone fresh—a virgin?" He licked his lips. "It's amazing. I really wish you could at least speak, but, alas. I would like to compare notes on Renée. Was she as good for you as she was for me?

"By the way, I'm truly regretful about Jake." He wiped a non-existent tear from his cheek. "The moron I sent after you didn't pay attention to the driver, only the car. And you were correct. If you want something done right, do it yourself. Therefore, I'm doing this myself. I have to close the lid now. I do remember your being a bit afraid of tight, dark spaces, like the cherry wardrobe. However, I'm not a liar. I told Renée I would put you in a pine box." James ran his hand over the lid of the coffin. "This is lovely, fragrant pine." James slammed the lid, engulfing Troy in utter darkness.

Troy felt the coffin being carried down some sort of slope and lowered into the ground. He heard shovel after shovel of dirt being tossed upon him. The plods of dirt became muffled until all was silence and darkness.

After an eternity of stillness, Troy felt his leg twitch. He had lost all concept of time. After several more minutes, he was able to move with ease. He slid his hands along the lid of the coffin. He thought, *I will not die in here.* He pushed against the top of his tomb with all his might, to no avail. Troy pushed, punched, and kicked until his muscles ached. He screamed into nothingness, "I will not die in here!"

Troy tried to breathe calmly. *Renée,* he thought. Closing his eyes in concentration, he focused every thought on Renée the way Clifton Spell, his karate instructor, had taught him to do before a fight. *Feel me, Renée. Feel me.*

Troy must have slept for dragons came to him again and whispered encouragement, "You must fight, Rennin. We need you. You must win this battle."

Troy spoke words to the majestic beasts. "Help me. I can't do this alone. Help me." He awoke to the sound of his own voice calling, "Smoke, help me. I need you. Please, help me."

In a land that time forgot, a glistening gray dragon raised his head as he heard his name called in desperation. He walked to the mouth of his cave and spoke to the night air. "I cannot come to you yet. I have not been freed to leave this world. Listen to my voice. Draw from my strength. You are Rennin O'Rourke. You must fight. You are smart. Think. You will find a solution." The magnificent creature took flight to the very edge of his domain. There he waited, willing the frail human to fight.

Renée pulled her BMW to the side of the road and looked at the gray-haired man with her. "I hear him, Coach. He's calling to me."

Still clutching an emerald pendant in his hand, Gerald McClarty replied, "I believe you, darling. Concentrate."

Renée laid her head on the steering wheel and opened her heart and mind to the man she loved. How long she focused her energies, she did not know. She saw a gossamer winged shadow pouring his strength into a gulf. She roused herself as she spoke one word, "Rennin."

Renée peered into the eyes of Gerald McClarty and asked, "Where do we find dragons here?"

"Chinatown?"

Renée drove to San Francisco and Chinatown. Once there, she turned to McClarty again. "Where to now?"

"I have no idea. Every souvenir and gift shop will have some kind of dragon."

Renée parked, and they walked. She felt certain she would know where to go if she saw the right place. For hours they stopped in shop after shop until Renée saw a sketch of a dragon on crinkled, yellowed parchment within a dusty old frame. Renée went in and addressed the shop owner, "That sketch of the dragon—how much?"

The small jaundiced man walked to the window and took the frame from its resting place. "It is very old. It came from the old country."

"How much?" asked Renée impatiently.

"There are legends associated with this picture."

"How much?" demanded Renée loudly.

"Five thousand."

To the shop owner's amazement, Renée took out her checkbook and wrote a check for the amount the man asked without dickering once. She practically ran back to her car with McClarty keeping stride.

In the car, Renée said excitedly, "Look at the signature."

In the lower left hand of the old picture in bold penmanship was the name *R. O'Rourke*.

Renée babbled on. "The book never said Rennin signed the picture. It must have been a habit, so he didn't think it was important."

"What book?" questioned McClarty.

"I can't explain now." Renée rubbed her hands over her face. "I'm so tired."

"No wonder," said McClarty. "Renée, it's sunrise. You need some sleep."

"I can't sleep," she protested. "That thing buried Rennin alive. I have to find him."

"Rennin?" said McClarty uncertainly.

"Yes, Rennin. That thing didn't want to hurt Troy Tomerson. It was after Rennin O'Rourke. Troy Tomerson may have gone into that box, but, Coach, Rennin O'Rourke will be coming out."

McClarty was totally befuddled, but his love for the young man who was missing was not contingent upon a name.

Troy lay in the utter stillness and whispered, "Smoke, don't leave me. Talk to me." A calm rage rose in the man's chest and he struck the lid of the coffin with a palm heel punch. His hand broke through the satin lining and he felt wood, but not smooth wood. He felt wooden crossbars. *James was too cheap to buy a well-made coffin with smooth planed wood. I wonder if he buried me six feet. Probably not.*

He managed to turn himself over, and he began to rip the satin from the bottom of the casket. Finding the wooden crossbars on the bottom of the coffin, he pried one loose. With his makeshift lever in hand, Troy rolled onto his back and ripped the rest of the satin from the lid of the coffin. Then, feeling in the dark, he used the rigged lever to pry the three crossbars he felt loose from the top.

Troy scratched across the top of the coffin until he found the grooves where the pieces of lumber were fitted together. Using a crossbar, he hammered at a groove until dirt showered him in the face. With renewed vigor, he pounded at the spot where the dirt had fallen through. With every blow, he said aloud, "I am Rennin O'Rourke. I will not die in here. I am a descendent of Alexander, Duncan, Aidan, and Rennin. *I will not die in here.* I am meant to soar on the backs of dragons. *I will not die in here*! I have magic waiting for me. *I WILL NOT DIE IN HERE.* I am Rennin O'Rourke. *I! WILL! NOT! DIE! IN! HERE!*"

Too exhausted to drive any further, Renée agreed to find a place to rest for a few hours. Driving down a side street, she slammed on the brakes in front of an apparently deserted old mansion guarded by two massive, hideous gargoyles that were supposed to resemble dragons. "What is this place?" Renée asked Gerald McClarty.

"I don't know. It looks as if it has been deserted for a long time. It's secluded from the rest of the area and appears to have been left to rot."

"We're going in there."

"Renée?"

"Please, Coach?"

McClarty got out of the car and examined the lock on the gate. He motioned for his companion to roll down the window and stuck in his head.

"The lock is new, but the chains are old. Someone has been here recently."

"How can we get in?"

"Let's go to a hardware store and come back."

Renée drove until she found an Ace Hardware just opening for the day. McClarty went in and came out with bolt cutters.

Returning to the gate of the haunted-looking hall, McClarty cut the chain with the bolt cutters and swung the creaking gate open for Renée to drive through.

Back in the car, they started up the bramble-covered driveway. "Stop a second," said McClarty.

He got out and examined the driveway. "Something has driven over this recently. Let's find a place to park where the briars aren't so thick and walk around the property."

Renée drove slowly up the driveway toward the dilapidated manor until she came to an area of tall overgrown weeds without the wild blackberry vines and other briars. The two searchers got out of the car. Renée shivered at the caw of a raven.

"This place gives me the creeps too, Renée, but we'll be fine. I would never let anything hurt you. Give me your hand."

They walked around the house but saw nothing out of the ordinary. McClarty whispered, "Exactly what are we looking for?"

"Freshly turned earth."

In his premature grave, every blow brought dirt into Troy's face, and with every strike he muttered, "I am Rennin O'Rourke. I will not die in here." Nonetheless, in the realization that continued hammering would only fill the coffin with dirt, he lay back to think. He was through the wood. He had created a hole about three inches in diameter. "Think," he ordered himself, feeling the dizziness from his exertion, the low amount of air, and his claustrophobia.

Still clutching the crossbar, Troy felt for pieces of satin. He used his teeth to tear the material into strips. Fumbling in the dark, he used his hands and his teeth to securely tie crossbars together two at a time. On the first crossbar, he attached a large splotch of satin. He pushed hard, forcing the crossbar into the hole in the lid of the coffin and plunged it into the dirt. He connected another crossbar to the bottom of the first and pushed again. He repeated the steps until his push felt no resistance. Then, he pushed a little more to be sure his flagpole was clear. Troy had used the four crossbars he had loosened. Each was about two feet long. He was, indeed, six feet underground. The knowledge of this weighed heavily on his chest and he began to have difficulty breathing.

"Breathe, damn it!" he chided himself. Then he muttered, "I am Rennin O'Rourke. I will not die in here." His declaration he followed with three pleas. "Smoke, don't leave me. Lord, let Renée hear me. Feel me, Renée."

At the thought of Renée, silent, unwanted tears escaped his eyes. From sheer exhaustion, the man slept.

The estate on which the old mansion sat was extensive. In the twenty-four hours since Troy had been discovered missing, Renée and Gerald McClarty had bonded. The rings beneath the young woman's eyes prompted him to assert his fatherly nature, and he insisted she sleep.

"Where?" she groaned.

"Right here," said McClarty as he sat and leaned against a tree. "Renée, if you make yourself sick, you will be of no help to Troy. Sit down. Put your head on my lap. Take a short nap. And call your house to let them know we're not missing, too."

Reluctantly, Renée complied with all Gerald's requests. As she drifted off to an uneasy sleep she said, "I can feel him, Gerald. He's here somewhere. I know it."

As the sun gilded the sky, Renée awoke with a start and jarred Gerald McClarty from a fitful sleep. "How long did we sleep?" Renée questioned as she jumped to her feet and instantly hit the ground in a dead faint.

McClarty gently tapped Renée's cheeks to rouse her and asked softly, "Renée, is there someone else we need to be concerned about besides you and Troy? That is exactly what my wife did when she was pregnant with Casey."

Wide-eyed Renée begged, "Please don't tell anyone. That thing."

"Shhh. Everything will be all right, but you need some food and something to drink."

"Not yet," pleaded Renée. "We have to keep looking."

"Renée, we have looked all over the grounds. There's nowhere left to look."

"Yes, there is."

She shot toward the old rundown house. All the doors were locked. At the look of determination on Renée's face, McClarty said, "Oh, hell," as he took off his undershirt to wrap around his hand before he broke the glass in the door and turned the bolt.

Inside the floorboards squeaked beneath their feet, but they began searching for the entrance to the basement. McClarty called, "Renée, here," as he swung open a door in the kitchen with steps leading down. "There's no electricity and it's extremely dark."

Feeling no remorse for rifling through the drawers in the kitchen, Renée found candles in one of them. McClarty pulled a lighter from his pocket and shrugged. "Cigars. We all have a vice." They lit a couple of candles and made their way cautiously down the stairs.

The misty dragon took flight at the first sign of morning on the second day. "Wait, Smoke. Don't leave me," called a haunting voice after him.

The dragon replied, "All is well, Rennin. All is well."

Troy's eyes popped open as he heard a soft beeping and realized the pump on the air canister had stopped. He nudged the makeshift flagpole up another couple of inches and cried loudly, "I am Rennin O'Rourke. I will not die in here."

To his disbelieving ears he heard scrapping and the lid of the coffin sprang open. The man breathed into the air, "I am Rennin O'Rourke. I will not die in here."

25
A Rose by Any Other Name

"**I** am Rennin O'Rourke. I will not die in here," were the words that greeted a weary and heartsick Renée as the authorities, who had been called, hoisted a filthy disheveled man from his would-be grave. The paramedic who pulled him up said, "We need to take you to the hospital, Mr. Tomerson."

Flashing green angry eyes looked the paramedic full in the face and the man spoke. "I am Rennin Duncan O'Rourke, and the only place I'm going is Buenos Aries."

Renée grabbed her lover's arm. "You're going with me."

The look in the man's eyes did not change. "Then, you're going to Buenos Aries."

The police lieutenant who had been searching for the missing man spoke sympathetically, yet commandingly, "Mr. Tomerson, Argentina is a non-extradition country. Even if Mr. Wilburn is there, we can't bring him back."

The emerald eyes leveled a malevolent gaze on the policeman. "Perhaps you did not hear me. I am Rennin Duncan O'Rourke. I am going to Buenos Aries. I have no intention of bringing James Wilburn back to this country. I have every intention of leaving his carcass to rot in some remote area of Argentina. You may try to stop me if you like, but eventually I will go after him. And since Argentina is a non-extradition country, you can't bring me back either."

McClarty could stand no more. He grabbed the young man by his shoulders and shook him soundly. "Stop it!" he commanded. "I don't give a flying leap what name you choose to use. You still have responsibilities here. You have a team to guide, and a woman to marry."

The newfound man tried to pull away from McClarty's grasp. McClarty tightened his grip. "No. You will listen to me. You have a team to guide, and a woman to marry if you are not so pigheaded that you do not get my drift. And, Troy, Rennin, whoever you want to be, you have no idea exactly what you're up against. Trust me. Have I ever steered you wrong? When the time is right, both Renée and I will go to Buenos Aries with you. The time is not right. You need medical attention, and you need to know *everything*. Besides, that thing might not even be in Buenos Aries anymore. You cannot let that Irish temper send you running off half-cocked."

All the tension seemed to release the young man. "I do have a temper, don't I, Coach?"

"Yes, you do. Jake and I cleaned up enough glass from your little tantrums over the years to go into the recycling business."

The green eyes peered sorrowfully at the older man. "Coach, Troy Tomerson is dead."

McClarty loosened his grip on the man and patted his shoulder. "I know. Renée said he would be."

"Rennin can't be your quarterback. I can't be your quarterback. It's no longer my calling."

"I know that, too. I drafted a great kid in the spring, remember? But we have to think about what we're going to do about you."

Nobody had left the basement, and all were anxious to know what steps to take next. McClarty seemed to be in control of the situation, so all eyes turned to him to coach the next plays.

McClarty laid out a plan that formulated as he spoke. "Lt. Bass, you seem to be a man of integrity. You didn't see on the tape what Renée and I saw. When we go back to the house, I want you to watch it again. Rennin." The devoted coached choked out the name. "You need to watch it, too.

"Gentleman, Troy Tomerson cannot leave this basement alive to the public. James Wilburn must think he accomplished what he set out to do. Hear my proposal.

"There's already a massive congregation of media above us. For their benefit, and in order to keep Rennin alive, we carry the body of Troy Tomerson out of here straight to the morgue of Mercier Memorial Hospital, where Renée's friend, Skyelar, will be waiting to drive the living Rennin O'Rourke to my cabin in the Sierra Madres. Skyelar is perfectly capable of tending the minor injuries Rennin has sustained." He rubbed his chin.

"Lt. Bass, you will hold a press conference declaring that although we miraculously found where Troy's assassin buried him, we were too late to save him. Renée, it's time for you to be an actress. I hear you can be pretty convincing. You must be grief-stricken. The man you loved is dead.

"We will have a funeral and bury a coffin in the O'Rourke family plot. The day after that, I, myself, will drive Renée to my cabin because she really needs to get away in the face of all she's endured. By that time, I will most likely be jobless as well. Without Troy and Jake, I'm useless. Al is ready to get rid of a broken-down old man anyway and infuse his team with some new younger blood. I think I'll announce my retirement and preclude being fired. With the murders of two of my Pro Bowl players, I can't continue.

"Rennin, get your detective friend to find where that sack of shit is hiding. At that time, we'll worry about phase two of our plan. None of this can leave the basement of this place. Lt. Bass, are you in agreement?"

Lt. Bass agreed and swore all present to secrecy. The paramedics carried the shrouded body of Troy Tomerson to the morgue to await the coming of Skyelar Jacobson, who arrived with clothes, nourishment, and supplies to clean and bandage Rennin's splinter-riddled hands. Other than those minor injuries, the man was unharmed. After Rennin showered and changed clothes, he and Skyelar, left through the mortuary entrance, and drove to McClarty's cabin.

"Well," said Skyelar impatiently as he drove, "are you going to tell me what happened? I'm doing just what Renée asked me to do, but I'm completely in the dark. That just isn't fair."

Rennin put his head back on the seat. "I'll tell you later. Skyelar, don't be offended, but I just can't be buddies with you the way Renée is. I do appreciate all that you've done. You're Renée's best friend. Jake was mine. I cannot risk losing anyone else right now. Suffice it to say that I have decided to be the man I was born to be, Rennin O'Rourke, and because of that James Wilburn really wants me dead. I have agreed to hide temporarily like a little pansy so that I can formulate a rational plan. Now, I think I just want to sleep for a while. You have the directions to the cabin. If you need me, wake me up."

Renée's performance over the next few days was worthy of an Academy Award. She began her charade by collapsing over the sheet draped body as the paramedics carried Rennin away and wailing hysterically, professing her undying love and blaming herself for the apparent outcome of their affair. Gerald McClarty lifted her off the body and she continued to sob into his chest as Lt. Bass gave his contrived press conference. The deep circles under Renée's eyes at Troy's funeral were real for during the days between the press conference and the funeral, morning sickness hit her with a vengeance. She lost weight and could hardly hold her head up. As Gerald McClarty held her hand before he pronounced Troy's eulogy, he whispered, "Damn, you're good. You look like hell."

Renée whispered back, "Give that credit to another actor in the troupe," and patted her tummy.

McClarty smiled softly and kissed Renée on the cheek as he whispered, "Good boy."

"Girl," argued Renée.

McClarty delivered Troy's eulogy through real tears for he felt a loss of one he dearly loved. After the interment, McClarty also announced to the press that had assembled he was retiring from coaching altogether and the next day he and Ms. Peyton would be leaving town for a much-needed rest.

One of the reporters actually asked, "Coach McClarty, what are your intentions toward Ms. Peyton? After all, you are a widower, and she has shown a penchant for older men." Unable to control his Scottish temper, McClarty belted the man in the mouth.

Renée had to pull McClarty off the rude man and spoke for herself. "Gerald McClarty is a man of honor and integrity unlike many in our midst." Her insinuation did not go unnoticed. "He has been like a father to me through all of this. The only affinity I have for an older man is for the vermin to which I was once married to be brought to justice. He thinks he has escaped prosecution for a number of crimes, but if you would like to report it, you may let him know one day I will find him. The authorities may not be able to extradite him from Buenos Aries, but I am a private citizen with a great deal of wealth and power at my disposal. He is *not* safe from the vengeance of a woman scorned. He has taken the most important thing in the world from me. I will not rest until he pays for his crimes."

"Where did that come from?" asked McClarty in the back of the limousine on the way home.

"I hope it scares him enough to betray his whereabouts to Detective Zane."

The next morning, Lt. Bass came to the house to watch the video once again. He thought he might find a clue, but he left the house in a deep dread after he watched the video wearing the emerald pendant, for he was dealing with forces beyond his comprehension.

Gerald and Renée left shortly after the lieutenant's departure and had to lose several paparazzi that followed them. "Damn those people," declared McClarty. "Can't they leave anyone alone to grieve?"

Renée laughed. "They're hoping to get a picture of you and me in each other's arms. It's their nature. They have to find a scandal somewhere even if they invent it."

Once McClarty shook the reporters from his tail, the rest of the drive proved uneventful. When they arrived, Skyelar was packed to leave and declared, "How can you survive like this—no television, no telephone? I'm surprised you have electricity and running water. This is too primitive for me." He kissed Renée on the cheek and waved good-bye to the two men. "Good luck!"

"Hallelujah!" shouted Rennin as he gathered Renée in his arms. "Renée, I know he's your friend, but I was ready to strangle the whiny bitch."

Renée rolled her eyes in exasperation. "You're still the same— just a different name."

As Rennin and Renée went into the cabin, McClarty unloaded the car, including a small TV-VCR combination. He walked into the cabin. "Where do we start?"

Rennin and Renée were locked in a deep passionate kiss. McClarty cleared his throat. "Ahem. I guess we start with a kiss."

Rennin and Renée separated, and the man appraised the woman he had held in his arms. "I think you took this acting a little too seriously. You look terrible."

McClarty said, "Start with that." He pointed at Renée as she began to protest. "I mean it, Renée. You tell him right now, or I will."

She crossed her arms. McClarty crossed his arms. Rennin said, "Renée, the only person I know who is more stubborn than you, is Gerald McClarty. What is he going to tell me?"

Renée protested, "I kind of wanted to do it a little differently."

"No time," insisted McClarty. "You can do the next one differently."

Rennin shouted, "Will someone please tell me what the hell you two are talking about?"

McClarty said, "I prefer he hear it from you."

She sighed in resignation. "Rennin, we're having a baby. Was that simple enough for you, Gerald?"

"Straight and to the point. It works for me. Now, the video."

Rennin waved his hand excitedly at McClarty. "Hold on, Coach." Then he turned to Renée. "Would you repeat that, please?"

She grinned and slid into his arms. "We are having a baby."

"Are you sure?"

"Yes, Dr. O'Neil confirmed it the day you went missing. I came home to tell you immediately."

"When?"

"Dr. O'Neil says January tenth."

Rennin stifled his next serious question. He would not give way to even the thought of the possibility. It was obvious Renée would not. He just held the woman he loved and stammered, "I don't believe it. Me? A father? Is it a boy or a girl?"

"I don't know," laughed Renée. "It's too soon to tell. We can have an ultrasound later to find out. And, even though you won't say what's on your mind, we can have a test done to determine for certain James is *not* the father." She pushed back from his arms. "Admit it. You had the same thought I had when I first found out."

Rennin shook his head, "I won't let that man be the father of anything. This baby is mine. I know it."

"And what if the DNA profile says otherwise?"

Determinedly Rennin vowed, "I swear before God—this baby is mine. I don't care who may have sired the child. This baby is mine. Don't you dare consider anything foolish, Renée Samantha Peyton. Moreover, three weeks from today when your divorce is decreed, we are going to Las Vegas, and we are going to get married. Coach, will you be my best man? Skyelar can be Renée's maid of honor."

Renée hit Rennin in the arm. "Rennin O'Rourke! Lord! I have to get used to saying that. That was just plain mean, but, yes, I will marry you, and I was never considering anything foolish."

"Well," said McClarty, "since we have settled that issue, shall we move on? First, I'm not your coach anymore. And I have to get used to calling you Rennin, too, so call me Gerald from now on. Yes, I'll be your best man and surrogate grandfather to this little bundle of joy. Now, get your ass over here and watch this damned video."

Renée slipped the emerald pendant over Rennin's head, and he asked, "What's this for?"

"Hold on," she said, and she took the pendant off. "Watch the video."

Rennin watched his abductor's taunting video. "And what's so special about that?" he asked.

Renée slipped the pendant back over his neck. "Watch it again."

"Holy shit!" Rennin jumped to his feet and shouted. "What the devil was that?" He jabbed a nervous finger toward the screen.

Renée explained, "Do you remember in *Memoirs of Magic* the pendant Rennin left with Cameron? This is it. Do you remember that Rennin said the pendant showed Quazel for what she really was? Obviously, James is demonic. He's not human, or at least, not anymore. When we go after him, we won't be going after a man."

"What do you mean by 'we'?" demanded Rennin. "You can't go. Not now."

"Like hell!" argued Renée. "Try and stop me. If you thought Caitlin Fitzpatrick O'Rourke was stubborn, you haven't seen anything. You cannot do this without me. Gerald, set him straight."

McClarty hesitated. "I don't want to be a part of this argument, but this time the lady's right. You need both of us. The only other person who has seen James's true identity is Lt. Bass. You need someone who knows the truth to help you. You O'Rourkes might be hard to kill, but not impossible."

Rennin crossed his arms and glared at his assassin squad. Then he threw his hands up in surrender. "Very well. I know when I've lost a battle. You are the two most stubborn people on the face of the earth. How did I get stuck with both of you? I will let it lie." However, in his mind he said, *Neither of you will go after James or whatever he is. I think maybe you're taking some of this way*

*too literally, and neither of you has a clue how to fight. I know
whom I need, but the time is not quite right.*

Renée slipped her arm around Rennin's. "Iron sharpens iron.
Neither of us is half as stubborn as you."

Renée went to sleep early for she was truly exhausted. The
week had taken a toll on her. McClarty walked onto the porch of
the cabin where Rennin leaned on the porch rail and stared at the
stars. Lighting a cigar, he disturbed the young man's reverie. "Do
you want to talk about it?"

"I don't know what to say. I actually miss myself. I mean, I
miss Troy. Sometimes I wish I were back in a Miami trailer park
watching a little blonde-haired pixie descend from a U-Haul, but
she played with Barbie dolls and not dragons. I know what I have
to do and who I have to be, but it's so hard to leave who I was
behind. Troy Tomerson was a good man, a little on the wild side,
but a good man. Who is Rennin O'Rourke?"

McClarty patted Rennin's shoulder. "You're still you. The
person inside you hasn't changed. You're simply having to walk a
different path now. You have chosen to fight a harder battle than
the ones you faced on the football field. You know, Renée made
me read that blasted book this past week. If that's real, and after
seeing that thing on the video, I believe it is, you have no choice
but to become Rennin O'Rourke; nevertheless, the man that was
Troy Tomerson still stands before me."

Rennin heaved a heavy sigh. "You know, Gerald, when I was
seventeen, no, I guess I was eighteen, Renée and I went to a
carnival where we had our fortunes told. The tealeaf reader said I
would do battle—I thought she meant a Super Bowl. The palm
reader said that Renée and I were interwoven, but she also said my
lifeline showed I had two identities. The crystal ball was cloudy,
but there were dragons; and the Tarot card reader told me there
were lies and deceptions in both my past and my future. Wow!

They were right. I just wonder who I actually have to kill for the blood to be on my hands and how many more lies are lurking. Troy was uncomplicated—Rennin is enigmatic."

Gerald McClarty put a protective, fatherly arm around Rennin's shoulders. "I told you once that I love you. You are like a son to me. I don't care what name you use. Neither does Renée. You are a fine man, honed to a precision fighting instrument by the things Troy Tomerson learned. But your heritage, yea, your birthright calls you to something more. Nonetheless you are still you—a man with a dragon's heart. Wasn't it Shakespeare that said, 'A rose by any other name would smell as sweet?' You are merely a rose with a new name, but you smell just as sweet."

Part Three

Transition

26
Mom's Trading Post, Pennsylvania

Renée puttered around the cabin the next morning, perplexed. "Gerald," she said a bit irritably, "is there really *not* a telephone jack anywhere in this cabin?"

"Don't need one," answered McClarty. "When I come up, it's to get away from civilization."

"How am I supposed to use my laptop?"

"You're not."

"But I want to show Rennin something on the Internet. It's a thought I had. We can't stay here forever. Neither can Rennin return to Puma Pass. At least, not while James is still out there."

"Sorry. Nothing I can do about it, dear girl. Just tell him. Use words. You're a lawyer. You're good with words."

Rennin came into the main room from the bedroom with a yawn. "What do you want to tell me? You had to have been talking about me because no one else is here."

Renée whined, "Skyelar was right. This place is primitive." She waved a dismissive hand. "Oh, no matter. I wanted to show you something on the Internet, but there's no phone outlet for my laptop."

"So, tell me. Like Gerald said, use words."

"You won't believe the town I found in Pennsylvania. I thought we might live there at least temporarily."

"Where?"

"Mom's Trading Post. It still exists. It's a small town almost on the Ohio-Pennsylvania border a little over fifty miles north of Pittsburgh. I researched it before we came up here. There's a bed and breakfast there, family owned by the Rileys. Rennin, they have to be distant relatives. They must have descended from Ryan and Rachel, or maybe Ranson and Angela, but I'd bet Ryan and Rachel."

"Your mind works overtime, doesn't it, Renée? How would it look if you just up and disappeared from Puma Pass? Didn't you tell me that Peter just offered you a full partnership? What about your doctor?"

"Rennin, this can work. Gerald, talk to him."

"What have I become, a mediator for the two of you?" asked McClarty.

"What *do* you think, Gerald?" asked Rennin. "I could use some fatherly advice."

"Well, Renée's arguments have merit, but so do yours."

"That's helpful," Renée and Rennin said together.

"Actually, Pittsburgh's in the market for a consulting coach to man the booth. If I got that job, I would be close enough to make sure you stay out of trouble. You could go ahead and find a place to live. If I don't get the job, I'll just have to bunk at your place, so get a place with a spare room besides one to turn into a nursery. Renée will have to tell Peter the truth. The man is your godfather, for heaven's sake. Maybe it's time for Pryor, Peyton, and Associates to have an office in the East, and there are good doctors in Pennsylvania."

"I thought you were retiring from coaching."

"And do what?"

"Be my bodyguard. Or with your education degree, coach high school and take some of the stress off."

"That's an idea. I could mold some more like you: stubborn, willful, prideful, ill-tempered."

"But you love me, and it sounds as if you agree with Renée. Am I wrong?"

"No, I actually think she has a good plan."

"Well, what will *I* do?" Rennin asked pouring himself a cup of coffee.

"What was your college major?"

"Biology and chemistry. I planned to go to med school in another lifetime. Rennin O'Rourke doesn't have a degree. He comes from old money, which has been stolen."

"That can be worked out. I know a couple of college presidents I trust."

"Sounds as if you might have a shady past, Gerald."

"We won't go there. Suffice it to say not all pro ball is on the up-and-up. There are deals made every day that nobody ever knows about."

"Ahem." Renée cleared her throat. "Darling, you could start your own business."

"Doing what, Renée?"

"Construction. You did it for eight years. Or carpentry. You have talented hands."

"And what would I call this business venture?"

"Dragon Construction or Dragon Carpentry. You could have your slogan read: 'Make your home legendary.'" She moved her hand through the air as if pegging the words. "And your logo, of course, could be the sketch by Rennin."

"May I at least have a cup of coffee before my whole life is planned for me?" he asked in agitation. He took his coffee outside and walked alone in the woods.

Sometime later, Renée found the conflicted man dangling his feet in the nearby stream. She slipped her shoes off and joined him in his idleness. "I'm sorry," she said. "It was too much too soon."

He took her hand. "No. It's just that nothing seems to be coming from me anymore. Something or someone is making all my decisions for me. I can't stand that."

"What do you want?"

"Honestly?"

"Always."

"I want to be the kind of man that Aidan O'Rourke was. He wasn't perfect, but he was strong, and he fought for what was right and just. I want to love you the way the first Rennin O'Rourke loved Morgan and the Rennin who founded Puma Pass loved

211

Rebekah. I want to be the kind of father they were. I want to be five years old in a Miami trailer park meeting a true pixie for the first time. I want to throw a football forty yards for a winning touchdown and hear the crowd roar. I want to soar wild and free on the back of a devoted gray dragon named Smoke. And then, sometimes, I just want to disappear into the woodwork and never be bothered again." He shrugged. "I don't know what I want. The only thing I'm absolutely certain about is whatever I must do, I want you. I can't survive without you. We are two sides of the same coin. So, if you want me to go to Podunk, Pennsylvania, to freeze my ass off and make furniture, I will. I don't think either of us is meant to stay there forever. I love you, Renée. I would do anything you asked of me."

He pulled her into his arms. "Don't ever leave me again. When do we go to Mom's Trading Post?"

"Well, when you decide, you expect everything to happen immediately."

"I hate inaction."

"Well, then, Gerald and I need to go back to Puma Pass, so he can do what he must, and I need to talk in-person to Peter. Then, you and Gerald will need to go on to Mom's Trading Post while I make arrangements to get there. I'll join you as soon as I can. Will you be all right here all alone for a few days?"

"Without my babysitter, Skyelar? What *will* I do?" He placed his hand over his heart and rolled his eyes.

"Well, then, we'll leave day after tomorrow. Let's take tomorrow and fade into the woodwork."

Renée and Gerald went back to Puma Pass to start the ball rolling on the plans that had been made. Gerald put his house on the market and Renée told Peter the whole truth and discussed plans to open an office in Pittsburgh.

Rennin fished and pulled out pen and ink and once again put flights of fancy onto paper. He smiled and thought. *I can do this now. That old bat, Mrs. Spencer, needs to know who I am so she can feel very foolish. Why am I thinking about that, Smoke? I need to let it go. That was another lifetime. Troy Tomerson, royal pain in the ass for everyone, is dead. I am Rennin Duncan O'Rourke. I am alive, and I know in my heart you're real.* Feeling truly free, he strummed his guitar and slept and dreamed of flying on dragons.

27
McClarty's Home

Stephanie Pitts, the realtor McClarty had once used as leverage over Troy Tomerson, regretfully placed Gerald's house on the market. They had become good friends over the years with all the real estate he had helped her move between the comings and goings among numerous football players. The house, situated in a quiet, upper-middle-class neighborhood, drew instant takers. In addition, Troy's condo and Renée's house went on the market.

Renée graciously visited Gerald with the intention of helping him pack for moving. He suggested she pack the delicate things because women were better at making sure things didn't get broken. She agreed and began wrapping and boxing glass, dishes, and trinkets while Gerald boxed books from the bookshelf.

Renée picked up a picture from the fireplace mantle, and instantly let it slip through her fingers, shattering the glass. She knelt to pick up the picture as Gerald came to see if she was harmed. "I'm sorry," she said pensively. "So much for women being better with delicate things. Gerald, who is this woman?"

"That's Agnes, my wife. She died in a car accident when Casey was about six months old."

"Tell me about her. How did you meet?"

"Aggie," McClarty said lovingly as he sat down on the raised hearth. "I was still coaching at the University of Miami. She was a waitress at the diner where I usually ate lunch. She was so quiet, but so beautiful. Her eyes were as blue as yours. Somehow, I got her to talk to me, and we started seeing each other. We were discreet about our relationship because Aggie told me she was married to a man who would kill her if he found out she was unfaithful."

Renée snorted bitterly. "I'm sorry. Go on."

"Well, it was then, that I got my first job in the pros. I couldn't bear to leave Aggie. She filed for a divorce and left with me. We had Casey about a year later. Our time together was short, but I have never loved anyone else."

Renée asked, "Gerald, what was Agnes's last name?"

McClarty answered as something dawned in his brain, "Peyton."

She turned her tear-stained face to a man she didn't know whether to love for the man she knew or to hate as the person who had deprived her of her mother. "Gerald, Agnes was my mother. She didn't just leave a husband, who would never have harmed a hair on her head because he adored her, but one who couldn't support her because he lost his job. She left a ten-year-old little girl, who became angry and bitter and cynical."

Gerald stammered, "Sh-sh-she never told me she had a child."

"Gerald, right this minute I want to hate you." Another thought hit Renée in the face. "Oh, my God. I have a sister."

McClarty sighed, "I wish I had known Casey had a sister."

"Where is Casey?"

"She's in school at Columbia. She refuses to come home because I sent her to boarding-school in Switzerland after she..."

"What did she do?"

"Casey was rather wild. I had an impossible time controlling her behavior."

"Okay, but there must have been some serious catalyst that made you send her out of the country."

"She and her friend, Paige, procured fake I.D.s and went to bars and picked up older men. Both girls looked a lot older than sixteen. One night they went home with one of my players. I almost had him arrested, but he had no idea the girls were so young. And both girls swore nothing happened because the man was too drunk. So, for Casey's sake and my sanity, I sent her to an all-girls' boarding-school. She has never forgiven me. She hasn't been home since. Neither have I gone to Switzerland. I haven't seen her since she was fifteen."

"One of your players?" She licked her teeth. "Which one?"

"It doesn't matter."

"Gerald, you can't fool me. It was Troy. There's no other player you would have protected to the point of running the risk of losing your own daughter."

She stood. "Gerald, I think I had better let you pack your own things. This day of revelations has been a bit much for me. You do realize now that we truly are family. You are, albeit unknowingly, my stepfather."

He walked her to the door. "Renée, I swear, I never knew about you. I would never have taken a mother from her child."

"I believe you, but right now it's a lot to absorb. I have wanted to drive a stake through the monster's heart that took my mother away from me twenty years ago, but you're not a monster. I need some time to reconcile what I feel for Gerald McClarty and what I feel for the unknown man who ran off with my mother. I hope you understand."

"I do. But if it means anything to you, I have come to love you as much as I love our Rennin. I'm honored to be your stepfather. I really don't think I can handle both my daughters hating me."

"Call Casey. Work it out. Maybe she's grown up enough to understand. She's almost twenty now."

Renée had left her cell phone with Rennin and purchased another. In the car, she called the one person whose love she had never doubted, even in the times of turmoil.

The man's voice answered ecstatically, "Hey, baby. I miss you."

Renée burst into tears at the sound of his voice. "I need you."

"What's wrong? Calm down and talk to me. Is something wrong with the baby? Has James come back?"

"No." She told him the whole story, finishing with, "What do I do, Rennin?"

"Can you forgive me for what happened with Casey?"

"What? Yes. What does that have to do with anything?"

"I was a grown man, and I acted a fool. Casey told Gerald nothing happened that night. Honestly, I want to believe her, but I was too drunk to remember much at all. That is the one time I had a real alcohol blackout and the last time I ever had more than two or three drinks, with the exception of the victory party where I also acted a fool. I have very little recollection of that night with two teenaged girls. What if something really did happen, and Casey lied? Listen to me, Renée. What if, God forbid, but what if I had sex with your sister, who just happened to have been a child? Can you forgive me for that?"

"Why are you asking me that? I want to know what to do about Gerald."

An exasperated sigh rang in the woman's ear. "Renée, if you can forgive me for being an absolute fool, you can forgive Gerald. Every woman I slept with from the time you married James until we finally got together, I did in an attempt to hurt you. I wanted you to know about every single one of them. I wanted you to know I felt my actions were your fault. They weren't. I was an idiot, but after Casey, I came to my senses. I did a total one-eighty and became completely celibate. I finally had sense enough to wait for you. Nonetheless, because of my rash stupidity, my desire to get back at you, I could be sitting in prison right now and be branded as a sex offender for life. Casey said she was sixteen, but that was a lie, too. The brat was only fifteen. Renée, that is statutory rape. It's possible I *should* be in jail. I probably deserve it. On the other hand, yes, maybe Gerald was a chump for falling in love with a married woman, but he never meant to hurt you. If you want to place blame, place it where it belongs—on your mother. She chose to leave you. After knowing that and after knowing Casey, however briefly, I think it's genetic on your mother's part. I'm glad you took after Eugene."

"Did I? Look what I did with James and even Ben." Renée sighed.

"You were as big a dodo as I was. I'm not gonna sugar-coat what I say to you. You made some poor decisions. But you came to your senses, too. You and I are finally where we belong—together." An uneasy chuckle came across the line. "You know, I always worried my mother, Eva, would marry your dad, and then you would have been my stepsister. Now, how messed up would that have been? Even if there was no blood kin, it might have looked awkward to a lot of people. I imagine right now, Gerald is being torn apart. Look what he forgave me. He's as devastated as you are. He would never intentionally hurt you. Maybe this is some mysterious way God has given you a family. Don't look a gift horse in the mouth. Embrace what you have. That's what I'm trying to do. Hell, the man says he loves me like a son. Well, now he can be my father-in-law. Gerald McClarty is a good man. He made a mistake. Is he any more fallible than I am? Is he any more fallible than you?"

Renée was silent for a long time before she said, "When I told you to always be honest with me, I didn't expect this."

"Yes, you did. I've always told you what I think, whether or not you like it. Did you expect anything different this time?"

"No, I guess not. I expected you to help me think rationally."

"Have I?"

"You have definitely helped me put things into perspective. Thank you."

"Any time. You know I love you."

"I love you, too. 'Bye for now."

Inside, Gerald played with his cell phone for several minutes before he dialed Casey's number.

Casey answered in a surly tone, "Hello, Dad. I'm not in any trouble. I have good grades. I promise."

McClarty said honestly, "I didn't call to check up on you. I just wanted to talk to you."

"Really?" said Casey skeptically.

"Really."

"What do you want to talk about?"

"First, I want to say that…"

"Yes, Dad?"

"Casey, I love you."

"Dad, are you dying or something?"

"No."

"Then repeat what you said because I'm sure I misunderstood you."

"Casey Diane McClarty, I love you. I always have, and I always will. I'm sorry I haven't said it enough over the years. Will you forgive me, and let's start over?"

"Dad, are you sure everything is all right?"

"It will be if you answer yes to the question I asked you."

"Dad, what are you not saying to me?"

"Damn it, Casey! I'm really trying here. I'm taking the advice of someone you're going to have to meet very soon."

"Is it a woman, Dad? Are you getting married and that's what this is all about?"

"Yes, it's a woman, but no I'm not getting married. It's your sister."

"My what?" Casey's voice shrieked through the line.

28
House on the Banks of Beaver Creek

Rennin called McClarty before Gerald left Puma Pass and asked if he would sell his new black Ferrari. After Jake's death, red did not suit him. "Gerald, I think it would be too flashy for a small town in Pennsylvania. Besides, it only holds two people. Trade it in and get me something more reasonable. Then, get Renée's maid of honor to drive it out while you tow yours with the moving van. I have to get to Mom's Trading Post and find a place to live quickly. Make sure Renée sends my dragon pieces. I want those if I leave everything else. And, *please* buy Skyelar a plane ticket home. I'll drop him off in Salt Lake City to fly back to San Francisco."

McClarty hooted with laughter. "I won't tell Renée what you said about Skyelar."

"Thanks. Oh, Skyelar isn't bad in small doses. It has zilch to do with his sexual orientation, but he whines too much. He just begins to annoy me after long periods of time. So, is Renée talking to you?"

"Yes, but she's guarded about everything. Casey's the one who is completely refusing to speak to me now. She won't even accept my phone calls."

"I'm sorry, Gerald. They'll both eventually come around."

"Maybe I should have told Casey I only had six months to live." McClarty laughed sardonically. "She seemed to want to talk to me when she thought I might be dying."

"Maybe I should give her a piece of my mind."

"Whoa, now. She thinks you're dead. How do you suppose she'd react to that little tidbit?"

"Maybe she would think I had come back to haunt her, and it would scare the hell out of her. Damn! I hate all the lies and secrets. Casey will have to know sooner or later."

"Better later with her."

"If you say so. Just get me a reasonable car, one that can hold a baby seat. Hey, Gerald, I'm gonna be a father."

Skyelar drove into the rugged drive of McClarty's cabin three days later in a new white Lexus LS 430 with light brown leather interior and loaded to the hilt. He got out singing the praises of the new car.

"You are going to love this one, Troy, oh, I mean, Rennin. It's like riding on a cloud."

Rennin walked around the car critiquing every angle before he sighed, "No, Skyelar, I *loved* my Ferrari. But this one is respectable. It looks more like something a daddy should drive."

"A what?"

"Renée hasn't told you? We're having a baby."

"Oh, that girl is in trouble when I get home."

"Don't kill her. She's just being cautious because of James. She's worried he might come after a baby O'Rourke. Just be ready to fly to Vegas in a few more days to stand up for Renée when we get married."

"Me?" He put a hand on his chest. "Stand up for Renée?"

"Why not? You're her best friend, aren't you?"

"Well, yes, but I'm not a woman."

Rennin bit his tongue to not make a smart aleck comment and replied, "It's Vegas. Nobody will care."

So, on the drive to Salt Lake City, Skyelar prattled on about what kind of dress to help Renée buy and what he should wear for the occasion. Rennin was just happy Skyelar wasn't whining about the accommodations, but the car really was smooth and elegant. Rennin dropped Skyelar at the airport and bade him farewell. Since it was getting late, he stopped at a motel for the night and went into the bar across the street.

"What'll it be?" asked the bartender.

"Killian's."

"What?"

"I get it. No Killian's. Give me a shot of good Irish whiskey."

The bartender poured a shot, and Rennin downed it with a grimace. "What the hell is that?"

"Whiskey."

"Not a good Irish whiskey. More like firewater."

"You want another?"

Rennin surveyed the bottle and considered the back taste in his throat. "No. I think I'll have a Coke in my room. Good night." He paid for his drink and left. On his way back to his room he asked, "Was that your way of telling me not to drink, God?"

He seemed to hear a voice answer, *"At least not on this trip."*

Rennin followed the map Renée had sent him and drove into a small town of about 7,000. The bed and breakfast Renée had mentioned and a Holiday Inn on the outskirts were the only two places to stay in town. Rennin chose the bed and breakfast.

The proprietor, a man in his mid-forties, stood about six feet and had sandy-red hair and periwinkle eyes. He was a few pounds heavy, but jocund, and greeted Rennin warmly. When he was set for the night, Rennin asked, "I'm thinking about starting a business in this area, and I need to find a place to live. My wife will be joining me as soon as she can take care of some business matters. Are there any places around here for sale and any places that might work for a furniture making business?"

The man rubbed his chin. "People don't move in and out of here a lot although some of the young folks take off to the big city. There's a house about five miles up on the banks of Beaver Creek. Nobody has lived in it for nigh on twenty years. It's a big old Victorian thing. It needs some fixing up, but I bet you could pick it up for a song." The man noted the old-fashioned, sign-in guest register. "Rennin O'Rourke? Is that seriously your name?"

"Yes, it is. I understand my great-times-sixteen grandfather started the first settlement here. I guess, I've sort of come home."

"Yes, well, I guess that makes you family. Rennin O'Rourke was my great times, I guess sixteen or maybe fifteen, grandfather. Well, now, ain't that something?"

"My wife said she'd bet you were descended from Rachel and Ryan Riley. Cameron was Rennin's child that finally got down to me."

"Yeah. All the actual O'Rourkes have either died off or moved off from here, but there are still some Rileys and Montagues. It'll be nice to have all the names together again. As a matter of fact, Travis Montague is the one you want to see about that old house. I'll get him to come over tomorrow morning after breakfast, if you'd like."

"Yes, thank you. I have one more question. Does anybody in town have Killian's on tap?"

Padraig Riley laughed good-naturedly. "This town was founded by an Irishman. Killian's, Guinness, and Jameson if want whiskey. Mickey's Pub is your place. My nephew owns it."

True to his word, Padraig Riley introduced Travis Montague to Rennin during breakfast, and the two men drove to an old Victorian house situated beneath elms and maples with one ancient oak on a knoll on the banks of Beaver Creek. The backside of the house sported a neglected, but once elegant, rose garden around a gazebo. Travis said, "I should tell you the last person to live here was Shane O'Rourke. He died mysteriously in his sleep. I haven't been able to find anyone who wants to live here because folks swear the place is haunted."

"Maybe Shane was murdered by some evil force and wants the truth to be known. I'm not afraid of the ghost of one of my relatives. Renée will love this place," Rennin concluded when he saw that the carving on the door knocker was a dragon and the name O'Rourke already existed on the name plate. "How much?"

"Actually, since you are apparently the only living relative of Shane's, no matter how distant, I suppose it already belongs to you. Shane had no heirs to inherit it. It sits on ten acres, including the stream in front, not that Shane ever kept the kids from swimming or fishing there. It's built on the site where Duncan O'Rourke built his house for Cynthia. I'm just the executor of the estate. I guess to compensate me for not really doing anything but hoping someone would come along and buy the place—a hundred and fifty thousand, and probably back taxes."

"That's all?"

"You will probably put that much into fixing it up."

"I'll take it. How would some of the kids in town feel about making some extra cash helping me work?"

"I can think of five or six I can send you tomorrow."

"That sounds great. I'd like to have it livable by the time Renée gets out here. We're having a baby. I hope she gets all her business settled quickly. I'd like the baby to be born here, not Puma Pass."

"Puma Pass? Good Lord! I knew you looked familiar. You're Troy Tomerson. You're supposed to be dead."

Rennin handed Travis five hundred dollars in cash. "What's this for?" asked Travis.

"It's a retainer. I just hired you as my attorney. You can't say a word about who I once was, or I *will be* dead. If you recognize me, then you should know all about me. I've chosen to become Rennin O'Rourke, as I was born. The maniac who tried to kill me needs to continue to believe he succeeded."

"You don't have to pay me to keep your secret."

"Maybe not, but I don't have a lawyer until Renée gets here, so you're hired. In addition to the house, I need a place to start a furniture building business or a construction company or both. I think I'll call it Dragon Builders."

"Yep," said Travis thoughtfully. "You're related to Shane. He had a thing for dragons, too."

Rennin hit the ground running the next day as six adolescent boys showed up before seven at the old house. Two he set to manicuring the grounds at ten dollars an hour to be paid at the end of the week. Three he put to work on scraping and painting the house at the same rate. Travis had sent the delivery of tools and paint Rennin had requested with the boys. He took note of a brawny young man as he placed a ladder for himself to go onto the roof. Rennin asked, "Are you afraid of heights?"

The boy replied, "No, sir. I'm not afraid of much of anything."

"Then come up here and help me with the roof but be careful. I don't want your parents to kill me the first day I'm here."

The boy laughed sarcastically. "Don't worry. They won't."

By the time Gerald arrived, Rennin had discovered the boys thought that their small high school had a football team that "sucked." The coach was a joke, and the schoolboard was willing to pay for a coach to just coach and not teach if necessary. He asked, "How would you guys like for a former professional football coach and player to take over the team?" The boys could not believe they could have that much luck and wanted to know if the men had been with the Steelers. "No, a rival," he answered, "but they're really good."

The one who had helped with the roof, stayed until after dark. His name was Bobby Willis. Since it was already night, Rennin gave the boy a ride home. During the short drive to the other side of town, Bobby asked candidly, "Mr. O'Rourke, are you one of the men who might coach us?"

Rennin asked, "Why would you ask that?"

Bobby shrugged. "Well, you said the men had been with a rival. I do know my football. You're Troy Tomerson. I thought you died."

A little worried, Rennin asked, "Do the other boys know who I am? I need to keep it a secret because the man who tried to kill me thinks he succeeded."

"Nah," said Bobby with a shake of his head. "If you aren't a Steelers' fan around here, you don't know anything about football. They wouldn't know it was you if you introduced yourself as Troy Tomerson. Most of them are too dimwitted."

Rennin laughed. "Well, Bobby, I think I would like very much to coach football. It's my passion. The only thing I love more is Renée."

"Mrs. O'Rourke?"

"Well, almost. We'll be getting married as soon as her divorce is final."

Rennin stopped in Bobby's driveway. The house was dark. He asked, "Isn't anyone home? What will you have for dinner?"

Bobby shook his head. "My folks are in Cancun. They go somewhere for a month or so every summer. I'll grab a sandwich. Thanks for the ride."

"Hold up," said Rennin. "How about grabbing a burger or something with me? You can tell me more about your team."

"That would be nice. I would like to have somebody to talk to for a while. Let me run in and get some cash."

"No need. It's my treat." Bobby got back in and the two found a Waffle House and pigged out. They talked and ate for a couple of hours, but Bobby avoided talking about his family. He preferred to discuss football and the possibility of having a coach who knew something about the sport. Rennin liked the boy. He thought Bobby had the intelligence to be a quarterback, but his build and brawn suited him for defense. Bobby's position had been guard, but Rennin really thought he should be the nose tackle. Rennin dropped the boy off around ten and looked forward to seeing him the next day.

All the way home, Rennin whistled and thought about the possibility of coaching high school football. He found he relished the idea. He felt a spark of life in his chest and waited for Renée to get to the house on the banks of Beaver Creek.

29
What It Means to Be Family

Gerald McClarty arrived in Mom's Trading Post at the end of the week with a van load of furniture and the information Renée was staying at Peter Pryor's house until they could iron out the logistics of opening an office in Pittsburgh. Rennin eagerly shared the news about the high school wanting coaches. Gerald seemed thrilled at the prospect of coaching kids again. The following Monday he spoke with the school officials who were delighted to bring him aboard as a coach and physical education teacher. He insisted Rennin assist him with quarterbacks and, finding it necessary to explain the whole situation to the school board, secured Rennin a position teaching both advanced chemistry and advanced biology using Troy Tomerson's credentials. It seemed almost everyone in Mom's Trading Post could claim kin to Rennin O'Rourke and informed both McClarty and Rennin that Rennin would be well protected among his family. The only dissent came from the local law enforcement voicing concern over potential threats to the community.

McClarty told Rennin, "I don't like Dubois. He gives me the heebie-jeebies."

Rennin called Renée and asked, "Can you be happy married to a teacher and coach? I promise to still build antique replicas in the basement, but that will be my hobby. You know football's my passion."

"If you're happy, I'll be happy. You'll be happier when you hear what I'm opening as we speak. The address is from my Alaskan attorney." Renée ripped open an envelope over the phone. "Yes! I'm a free woman. No six-month wait for me! Rennin O'Rourke, will you marry me?"

"Yes, ma'am. I'll meet you at six o'clock Friday evening at the Dragon's Lair Restaurant. Make sure you have your maid of honor there."

"Why did you tell Skyelar to stand up for me? You know you can't stand being around him."

"It's the last time I have to see him until our fiftieth wedding anniversary. He's your best friend. I can put up with him for short periods of time, but he cannot know where I'm taking you on our honeymoon. Yes! We're having a honeymoon, and if you argue, we'll be getting divorced on Saturday. Really, Renée, Skyelar is a good person. I can be around him in small doses. I'm very grateful to him for everything he's done. Tell him I said so."

"Where are we going on our honeymoon?" Renée asked eagerly.

"It's a secret. Just have your passport with you. Once again, don't pack anything."

Renée wore a baby-blue, scalloped-necked, fitted satin bodice adjoined to a sleek slightly darker blue, A-line, street-length velvet skirt as she waited for Rennin at the entrance of the Dragon's Lair Restaurant. Skyelar stood beside her in a navy-blue suit, crisply starched white shirt, and a tie that matched Renée's bodice. He commented, "Shouldn't the groom be waiting for you?"

"Hush," scolded Renée nervously. "Don't you think I've made him wait long enough?"

"Well, you do have a point," Skyelar admitted as Rennin and Gerald pulled up in a limousine.

Rennin got out while Gerald waited. "I'm sorry I ran a little late. I stopped at a flower shop." From behind his back he presented Renée with a bouquet of thirteen long-stem white roses. "I also stopped at a jewelry store. I had no idea what you would be wearing, but I think I guessed well. I see you already have on your something blue, so this can be your something new." Rennin presented Renée with a sapphire choker to wear with her dress. He fastened it around her neck. "Last," he said, "this is your something old." Rennin reached into his pocket and pulled out the diamond that had been worn by a bride of an O'Rourke man in every generation in his family line since the first Rennin gave it to Rowan to give to Ellen.

"I have to wear it on my right hand. You better have the wedding rings."

"I do," said Rennin.

Skyelar was the one near tears. "Oh, girl, I wish I had a man like that."

Rennin chortled. "There's not another one like me."

Skyelar continued, "Let's go. I already loaned her a sixpence from my coin collection this morning. It is in her shoe."

"Wait," said Rennin. "I have another small token. It's exactly like Gerald's." Rennin pinned a single white rosebud boutonnière on Skyelar's lapel. He helped Renée into the limo after Skyelar climbed in and they drove to a simple little chapel. The minister proved to be a retired Episcopalian minister.

Before the minister began the exchange of traditional wedding vows, Rennin said, "There is something I wish to say to Renée before we begin. Is that all right?"

"It's your wedding," replied the minister.

Rennin nodded. "Renée, the first time I saw you, I knew you would bring magic to my life. You were my pixie who sprinkled me with fairy dust. Just like in every fairytale, we've endured obstacles to get to our happy ending, although for us this will be the beginning of a wonderful journey together. However, I made a promise to you, and I keep my promises. I don't know if this has been a family tradition for generations, but I hope to make it one today. I do know the first Rennin O'Rourke said these words on his wedding day, and he said them because he had heard his father say them repeatedly to his mother. 'Heart of my heart, life of my life, you are my reason for breathing; and I will love you until the day I die.'"

The minister turned to Renée and asked, "Renée, do you have anything you would like to say to Rennin?"

Never at a loss for words, Renée spoke from her heart, "I had not thought to have prepared any special vows. You think that I brought magic into your life, but it was you who saved me— literally when I was six and figuratively on several occasions. You have always been there to catch me when I fall. You have been my knight. Even when I pushed you away, you never stopped loving me. For those reasons and a myriad more, I will never leave nor forsake you. I will follow you to the ends of the world, yea, to worlds unknown, even unto eternity."

"Well," said the minister, "having heard the words spoken from your hearts, I don't find it necessary to read trite and worn out expressions. Therefore, Rennin Duncan O'Rourke, having vowed to love Renée until the day you die, will you have her to be your wife in both the sight of God and man?"

"I will," Rennin vowed confidently.

"Renée Samantha Peyton, having vowed to follow Rennin to the ends of the world, will you have him to be your husband in both the sight of God and man?"

"I will," affirmed Renée.

"Do you have rings to exchange?"

"Yes," confirmed Gerald and Skyelar together as they handed the chain loops to Rennin and Renée.

Rennin explained the unusual rings to the minister. "These wedding loops were crafted sixteen generations ago from a father's heart, and they have been worn by O'Rourke couples ever since."

The minister nodded. "Then, Rennin, place the symbol of unconditional love on Renée's finger and repeat after me, 'With this ring I pledge myself to you in heart, mind, body, and soul.'"

Rennin placed the ring on Renée's finger and repeated the words with assurance.

The minister turned to Renée. "Renée place the symbol of unconditional love on Rennin's finger and repeat after me. 'With this ring I pledge myself to you in heart, mind, body, and soul.'"

Renée repeated the words confidently as she placed the ring upon Rennin's finger.

The minister became misty-eyed, which was unusual for him, and said, "Having spoken the words God gave you and having vowed before God and these witnesses to receive each other as husband and wife, I hereby declare by the power vested in me by God and the state of Nevada you are husband and wife. Rennin, kiss your bride."

As Renée pulled Rennin to her, the minister stated, "In this case, perhaps, I should have said, 'Renée, kiss your groom.'"

Rennin and Renée released each other and Skyelar applauded and giggled. Gerald shook Rennin's hand and embraced him in a bear hug. Then, he turned to Renée and kissed her cheek softly. She put her arms around Gerald and said, "I love you. The past is behind us. This"—She looked around the little group—"is what it means to be family."

The minister's assistant snapped a few pictures.

Renée hugged Skyelar and handed him twelve of the white roses, pulling one out for herself to keep. Rennin even hugged Skyelar affectionately for once. The entire entourage left for the airport to await their respective flights. Skyelar's shuttle flight left just after nine. Gerald flew back to Pittsburgh at 10:02, leaving the newlyweds to wait alone.

Renée asked, "Are you going to tell me where we're going now?"

"Nope. Suffice it to say I already checked your luggage."

At 10:45, the flight to Chicago was called. "That's us," said Rennin.

"You said I needed my passport," said Renée.

"You do. Chicago, then New York, and then my lips are sealed, but we are not stopping in either city long enough to have a honeymoon."

30
Heritage

As Renée slept on Rennin's shoulder in New York, the intercom announced the departing flight for London. "Wake up," he nudged her. "We're leaving."

"We're going to London?" Renée asked sleepily.

He shook his head. "Be patient."

Aboard their flight, she wheedled, "Don't keep me in suspense. Where are we going?"

Rennin shook his head again. "You know how stubborn I am. You said you would follow me to the ends of the world. Give it up. I'm going to sleep."

Both of them slept until the flight attendant woke them for lunch. An hour and a half later, their plane landed at Heathrow. Forty-five minutes after that, they boarded a shuttle flight to Dublin.

"Ireland," twittered Renée excitedly. "We're going to Ireland."

"Yes, but not *just* Ireland. Just wait."

At the airport in Dublin, Rennin claimed their baggage, exchanged currency, and picked up the rental car he had reserved. About two hours south of Dublin on the Celtic Sea, Renée read a sign: Stonebridge, 2 kilometers.

"Oh my God!" she exclaimed sitting straight up in her seat.

Rennin grinned mischievously. "Are you surprised?"

"Yes!"

They drove over an old stone bridge and into a quaint picturesque Irish village that looked as if it were still in the 1500s except there were electrical wires strung. Rennin stopped the car. On a hill, gleamed a whitewashed stone mansion. Rennin turned to Renée. "That was Elizabeth Gilhooley's house. Would you like to see it up close?"

"You know I would."

He drove the car up the long drive to the mansion. The sign at the gate read: Cypress Creek Inn.

Rennin and Renée went inside. A bell over the door dinged. The house seemed to have remained undisturbed from its original state except for the electricity, running water, and a counter to the side. When Rennin went to the counter, a short, round, bespectacled man came in from a room behind it. Renée looked around the parlor while Rennin spoke to the man. "Rennin and Renée O'Rourke."

"Welcome ta Stonebridge," said the innkeeper in a hearty Irish brogue. "Yer room is ready. Did ya have a pleasant floight?"

"Our room?" said Renée as she had overheard the conversation.

"That's right," said Rennin.

The innkeeper summoned a youth to bring in the guests' bags and to park the car as he led them upstairs. He talked as they walked. "Yes, Mrs. O'Rourke, ya aire in the Master Suite. It is the suite used by the original owner of the house. Legend says she was a witch who married her childhood sweetheart, and they disappeared not long after that. If the story froightens ya, we can change yer room."

"Frighten me? I could never be frightened of Elizabeth and Diggory."

"So, ya aire familiar with the legends of our area?"

"Some of them," Rennin said. "Such as the one about Duncan O'Rourke who went in search of a mythical island. I'm his descendent."

"Well, welcome home, then. So, is this a trip to explore yer heritage?"

"Yes and no," Rennin said as the man opened the door and handed him the key. Rennin scooped Renée into his arms. "We're on our honeymoon."

"Congratulations," the man said as the youth with the help of another boy brought their bags up the stairs.

Rennin stepped over the threshold before he set Renée down. He tipped the men all around and asked, "Would you please send up two house specials and a bottle of sparkling cider? Then, we would like to be undisturbed."

"Very good," replied the innkeeper as he turned to leave.

"Sparkling cider?" asked Renée.

"You can't have champagne right now."

"I would have thought you would have wanted a nice Irish whiskey."

"There's time for me to try authentic Irish whiskey and beer. Tonight, I plan to keep a clear head and focus on the most gorgeous woman in the world."

As Rennin kissed his new bride, one of the young boys knocked with dinner and the cider. Rennin answered and generously tipped the boy again. He set the tray on the table and jokingly asked, "Well, which would you rather have first: dinner or me?"

Renée grinned. "Would you mind very much if we eat? I'm starving. Then, I would kill for a shower. I'm afraid you take third place."

"No, I don't mind if we eat. My child needs nourishment."

"Oh, I see," she teased.

Rennin pulled a chair out for his bride and gestured for her to sit down, which she did. He uncovered two piping hot plates of roast beef, baked and mashed potatoes slathered with brown gravy, cabbage, green peas, fresh baked soda bread, and rhubarb crumble. He opened the cider and poured two glasses. He raised his glass. "To my pixie, may she always be the magic that steers my heart."

Renée raised her glass. "No. To my knight, may his arms always be able to bear the weight of a pixie."

They drank their toasts, and Renée tore into her dinner. Rennin laughed. "I've never seen you eat so ravenously."

She pointed her fork at her new husband. "I have a good reason to eat. Leave me alone."

After dinner, Renée disappeared to the shower. She had to read how to operate it as it was quite different from the States. Hearing the water finally start, Rennin thought for about one minute and said aloud to himself, "Nope. I will not let her get away with this one."

The next moment, she felt his arms around her as she let the steamy water beat on her face. "You told me to be patient," she chided.

Rennin shook his head. "True, patience is a virtue; however, it's one I do *not* possess." He maneuvered her against the shower wall. "Do you want me to leave?" He pressed his swollen manhood against her thigh.

"No," she replied, hooking her knees over his hips as steam billowed through the bathroom.

During their two weeks in Ireland, Rennin and Renée visited many attractions, but their favorite outings were to walk the streets of Stonebridge and trace the possible steps of Duncan and Aidan O'Rourke. Diggory's house had burned a hundred years earlier, but they visited the ruins. The postmaster now lived in the house Duncan O'Rourke had owned, and he graciously allowed the couple to walk through. Rennin rented a sailboat and they sailed to Porpoise Point for a picnic.

Several nights, they visited Malone's Pub where Rennin experienced true Irish drinking. Men and women alike goaded and encouraged as they chanted "Go, go, go," as Rennin bested many a native Irishman in chugging contests. They tried to get Renée to participate, but she refused gleefully announcing to the entire village that she was expecting a child.

"It'll put hair on his chest," prodded one inebriated Irishman.

Renée countered, "What if it's a girl?"

The man roared, "No, we don't want hair on *her* chest!"

All too quickly, the honeymoon ended, and Rennin and Renée O'Rourke were forced to return to reality, but they relished and cherished the adventure into a true heritage.

As their plane landed in Pittsburgh, for Renée would be staying a week in Mom's Trading Post and taking the Pennsylvania bar exam, she said, "If Draconis proves to be a myth, then let's retire in Stonebridge."

"If?" said Rennin a bit shocked. "Are you telling me the pixie believes again?"

She patted his hand. "Maybe she never really stopped. Now, show me my house. You have to carry me across this threshold, too."

As Rennin crossed into the revitalized living room of the old Victorian manor, the surprise that greeted them was nothing compared to the utter terror that greeted the unexpected interloper who had just entered their scheme in secrecy.

31
Sibling Rivalry

In a shrill, horrified voice, Casey McClarty shrieked, "You're dead!" There upon, she fainted at the sight of an apparent ghost.

Casey came to as her father bathed her face in cool water. She heard muffled voices as Gerald explained, "Casey only arrived about an hour ago, and she brought someone with her. This is getting to be more than my old heart can take."

Casey opened her eyes fully and sat bolt upright. "Your heart! Troy's dead. What's he doing here?"

Gerald sat down in a wing-back chair and groaned, "There are a lot of explanations in order here."

"Start with the walking dead," demanded Casey, still frightened

"All right," said Rennin as he turned a ladder-back chair around from the card table in the cozy family parlor and straddled it, resting his forearms on the back. "Troy Tomerson is dead, at least the name. The public believes James Wilburn murdered him. I've chosen to use the name with which I was christened, Rennin O'Rourke. I've moved here to this small town which was started by my ancestors to begin a new life, coaching and teaching. My dear friend, and"—Rennin took Renée's hand—"technically now stepfather-in-law has joined me. My lovely wife will be joining me on a permanent basis in another couple of months when she has established a branch of her law firm in Pittsburgh. That's the story in a nutshell."

Casey leveled a cold malevolent glower at Renée. "You're my"—She turned the same stare at her father—"She's my sister? And she's married to him?"

Rennin stood and felt the need to put a protective arm around Renée. "Gerald, it's your turn. I'm off the hot seat."

Gerald hesitated, but took a deep breath and delved in. "Years ago, I met a woman named Agnes Peyton. I fell in love with her, but she was married. Then, I got my first pro coaching position in Dallas. She left her husband and came with me. We had you, and your mother was killed shortly afterward. I only recently found out Agnes also left a child in Miami. Renée is that child."

Casey scowled at Renée. "Do you have something to explain?"

"Not really," said Renée. "I think they covered it well."

"Well, I think you do," spat Casey. "I cannot believe Troy has forgiven you for what you did to him. You were a bitch to him. He almost drank himself to death. And you forgave her and married her!" Casey finished shrilly, glaring at Rennin.

Rennin held Renée closer. "That's what love does, Casey. It forgives. It does not keep a record of wrongs. I was no angel, now, was I?" he asked pointedly.

At that moment, a small girl of about four bounded down the stairs holding a soft bodied doll. "Mommy, what's wrong? I heard you screaming upstairs in Grandpa's room."

"God, help me!" Rennin said, sinking back onto the chair he had vacated as he beheld a female version of himself. "I think it's your turn to explain some things, Casey." He looked at Gerald. "At least to me."

Casey squatted in front of the little girl. "It's okay. Mommy was just startled because she thought she saw a ghost. Go back and play in Grandpa's room for now."

The child obeyed promptly. All eyes were upon Casey.

She waved a hand toward the stairs. "D'Aubigné Marie McClarty. As you have surmised, I lied to all of you some years ago. Yes, is it Rennin now? She's yours."

"That's obvious," snapped Rennin. "Casey, was I such an asshole you thought I wouldn't take care of my child? You *swore* nothing happened."

"Actually," Casey said coolly, "I thought very little of you after that night. But I guess that's a good place to start my explanation. Back then, I had the biggest crush on you. I knew

Dad would never have allowed me to see you even if you had wanted to. And, at that time, I would have done anything to piss off my dad. I was so angry with him. I felt that he loved his football players more than he did me." Casey glowered at her father. "I still think you love him more than you love me. How could you keep this kind of secret from me?"

McClarty pointed upward, "How could you keep that kind of secret from me? From her father?"

"I never wanted to speak to you again for sending me away. As for her father, I'm sorry. That was wrong, but it kept you out of jail. If you want me to explain, don't interrupt." She narrowed her eyes to slits. "When I realized I was pregnant, Madame Bijou started to call Dad. I threatened her. I told her if she called Dad, I would run away and have an abortion. Madame Bijou is a really good Catholic. She didn't want that on her conscience. Rather, she let me move into her house, have the baby, and continue to attend classes. She told Dad I refused to come home, which was true, and I could stay with her.

"Taking care of d'Aubigné wasn't hard when I was with Madame Bijou. This year at Columbia has been difficult. It's killing me to go to school, work, and take care of a little girl. So, after Dad's phone call a few weeks ago, I started thinking it was time to mend our fences. I came here to introduce him to his granddaughter and ask him to help me. I actually thought I might ask if d'Aubigné could stay with him. I never expected to find anything else."

Casey sat on the sofa. "Rennin, I don't want your money or anything like that. I just want to be able to go to school without working myself sick."

He leveled a menacing gaze at Casey. "Casey, I don't give a damn what you want. You're a lying, manipulative, selfish bitch. However, you're not a little girl anymore. Because of that, I won't mince words with you. That's my daughter upstairs. Now that I know she exists, I have every intention of getting to know her and taking care of her. You're her mother, so I don't want to fight with you; but if you get in my way, I *will* fight. I'll win. I can be a mean son-of-a-bitch if I have to be.

"I think you *should* continue your education at Columbia. I'll even help pay for it. I will formally adopt my child. I want my daughter's name legally changed, and I want her to live with me while you're in school. You'll be free to see her anytime you like. This house is huge. We will decorate a room for d'Aubigné, and you can have the one right next door when you come. When you graduate, then, we'll discuss change of custody and visitation."

The man took a deep breath. "In January, d'Aubigné will have a little brother or sister. I want her to know her siblings. You and Renée have been cheated out of that. It's time for you to grow up. You should get to know your family and realize there are people who care about you. Now, I would like to meet my daughter."

Casey laughed nervously. "I expected you to throw a fit, to maybe break something."

"Casey, I grew up. I'm trying to stay calm. Yes, I'm angry with you, but it's time to mend those fences you mentioned; that includes ours. Let's do it for that little girl upstairs." He pointed upward. "I know we can be friends if we try. I love Renée. I always have. She's my past, my present, and my future. You can have a future too, despite your past mistakes. Let's make sure d'Aubigné has a bright, secure future."

Rennin could feel Renée's nails digging into his shoulder. He glanced up at her, "It's all gonna be fine."

While Casey went upstairs to get d'Aubigné, Renée only said, "You didn't ask me what I want."

Agitated, Rennin snapped, "What do you want, Renée? Do you want me not to want my child?"

"No. That was unfair."

Rubbing his temples, "I'm sorry," he said in a softer tone. "Did I do the right thing? What *do* you think?"

She put her hands on his arms. "I think you're about to explode and break something. Yes, you should have your daughter in your life. I would never begrudge you or your child that, but build

Casey a guest house. I don't want her sleeping under my roof." Renée turned toward Gerald. "I'm sorry, Gerald. That's how I feel. I don't trust her. And demand a paternity test."

"You're probably right," Gerald said apologetically.

Rennin agreed to Renée's request. "I'll get to work on a guest house, but if she comes before it's ready…"

Renée finished, "She can sleep next door to her daughter."

"About that test? The child looks just like me."

"Then, *I* demand it."

Casey washed d'Aubigné's face and brushed her hair. The child complained, "I already met Grandpa."

"I know you did, darling, but now I want you to meet someone even more special."

"Who?"

"You have to come downstairs to find out."

Casey steered d'Aubigné toward Rennin when they descended the stairs. He dropped to one knee in front of the little girl. Casey said, "D'Aubigné, this is your father, Rennin O'Rourke."

The child looked confused. "You said my daddy's name was Troy and he was dead. Did you lie to me?"

"Out of the mouths of babes," muttered Rennin. Then he turned to the child. "No, your mommy didn't lie. She thought I was dead. You see, a very bad man tried to kill me. So, we've played a big joke on him, and we want him to think I'm dead. I changed my name, so he couldn't find me. Can you understand that?"

D'Aubigné nodded her assent. "I think so. So, then, are you my daddy?"

"Yes, darling, I am."

"What do you want me to call you?"

"What do you want to call me?"

"Is it all right if I call you 'Daddy'? I don't want to call any of Mommy's boyfriends 'Daddy.' I don't like them. Oops." The child put her hand over her mouth.

"It's all right not to like them," said Rennin looking knowingly at Casey. "But there's someone I want you to meet I think you *will* like. She's not my girlfriend. She's my wife and your stepmother." Renée knelt beside Rennin. "D'Aubigné, this is Renée."

"Hello," said d'Aubigné. "You have a French name, too."

"Yes, I do," said Renée, "but yours is much prettier. I've never heard your name before."

"Well, do I call you 'Stepmommy'? Yuck."

"No, you may call me Aunt Renée." Renée smirked and looked at Casey. "After all, she *is* my niece."

Casey's eyes bored holes through Renée who never dropped her gaze. Casey knew that without saying a word, Renée had drawn a solid boundary which indicated Renée would gladly accept Casey as her sister, but if Casey so much as looked toward her husband, there would be a war. The nuances of the relationships gave new meaning to the term sibling rivalry.

By the end of the week, Travis Montague had drawn up the documents asserting Rennin's parenthood and custody change. Renée was fuming Rennin had not had the paternity test as she readied to fly back to Puma Pass. At the airport Rennin handed her two labeled Ziploc bags containing hair samples. One read, "Rennin" and the other, "D'Aubigné."

He shrugged. "Does Casey have to know? Can't that genius, Skyelar, do it? He already has my profile. Tell him I asked nicely and will send him a rose—a variegated unusual color, indicative of him, because there's only one Skyelar."

Renée took the two bags and commented, "Maybe you're right that Casey shouldn't know. I don't trust her. When does she have to be back at Columbia?"

"She's leaving next Saturday."

"Not soon enough. Lock your door at night."

"Renée, are you jealous of her?"

She set her lips in a firm line. "She has already had your baby. I don't trust her."

"She's your sister," reminded Rennin.

"And you're my husband. That little vixen still wants you."

He chuckled, "Honey, I love you."

"But soon I'll look like a beached whale. You might be tempted."

"Not with her," Rennin replied scornfully. "Not with anybody," he added quickly as he read the next thought about to escape Renée's lips.

Her final boarding was called, and she had to leave. Rennin called, "Let me know when the sonogram is."

He sent half a dozen roses to Skyelar two days later.

Saturday loomed like a mirage to Rennin as Casey, in Renée's absence, played the real coquette. At last, Saturday arrived, but to Rennin's vexation, Gerald had to leave a good two hours before Casey was scheduled to start her drive back to Columbia. A few minutes after Gerald left, Casey called Rennin to help her load her luggage. His heart leapt for joy because he thought she had decided to leave early. He skipped up the stairs.

The man's demeanor changed abruptly when he went into Casey's room. She stood there wearing a white, spaghetti-strap, clingy satin blouse with no bra beneath, a skin-tight, black leather mini skirt, black fish-net stockings, and five-inch black stiletto pumps, all accessorized with six-inch silver loop earrings and a French manicure. Casey beamed at Rennin as she asked, "What do you think?"

He asked, "Do you really want me to answer that question?"

She sallied near him and rubbed one finger up and down his bustling bicep. In her sultriest voice she said, "I'm sorry I lied to you. I thought you might want to know that you performed extremely well."

Rennin physically lifted Casey by her elbows and put her at arms' length from him. "I haven't answered your question. You look as if you are trying to earn twenty-five bucks a trick on some sleazy street corner. Casey, you're my sister-in-law. I love Renée very much. If you ever flaunt yourself at me again, you will *not* be welcome in my home. Am I making myself clear to you? Casey, don't you have *any* self-respect? You're a beautiful, intelligent young woman. There's a man out there that will love you as much as I love Renée." He took a deep breath and spoke slowly, "I...am...not...the...man...for...you."

He opened Casey's largest suitcase and pulled out a light sweater and a pair of jeans, her Reeboks, and a bra. Then he gathered her bags and carried them to her car.

Following Rennin down the stairs, Casey demanded, "What are you doing?"

He spat back, "You've decided to get a jump start on the traffic. You're leaving, but not until you change clothes. No matter how pathetically immature and annoying your little stunt has been, I don't want you to stop for gas and have some lunatic leave your body in a ditch because you were dressed like a two-bit whore. I don't want to explain to my daughter her mother was a fool, and I don't want to tell your father I did nothing to protect his younger child."

Casey mumbled, "You've just plain gotten old." Nonetheless, she changed her clothes, kissed d'Aubigné good-bye, and departed for Columbia, leaving behind her questionable frock.

Rennin looked down at the little girl and saw two tears on her cheeks. He squatted down in front of her and wiped the tears away as he kissed her on the forehead. He asked, "D'Aubigné, have you ever been fishing?"

"No, sir," the child replied shaking her head.

He stood. "Well, then, I guess we need to go into town and pick out the perfect fishing rod for a little girl to go fishing with her daddy. We'll catch some big fish and have a fish fry with Grandpa for supper." Rennin held out his hand, and d'Aubigné took it as they walked to the garage. He strapped the child into the back seat of his Lexus, and they went shopping for a fishing rod.

Back from town, Rennin packed a picnic lunch, and father and daughter spent a successful afternoon fishing and did, indeed, have a fish fry with Gerald that evening. Gerald taught d'Aubigné how to batter the fish, and she had more mixture on her than on the fish, but they managed to coat the fish. As Rennin made hushpuppies, the phone rang.

Rennin pushed the speaker button. "Hello."

"What's all the noise?" asked Renée's cheerful voice.

"D'Aubigné, Grandpa, and I are having a fish fry. She caught most of them today on her first fishing excursion."

"He's lying, Aunt Renée," called d'Aubigné. "I only caught two, but they were big."

Renée laughed, "That's more than I usually catch. Wish you could send me some. I'm getting ready to go to a business dinner with one of the steel magnets from Pittsburgh. Peter says if we can land this account, we'll be able to open an office there by November. Wish me luck."

Everyone chorused, "Good luck."

Renée continued, "Rennin, Skyelar finished those tests."

"Hold on just a second." He washed his hands, took the phone off the speaker, and walked to the other room with the handset.

"And?"

"For once, she told the truth. I don't get to give you your first child."

"Renée, don't sound like that. This is not a sibling rivalry. I love you, and I love that baby growing inside of you. But I still have enough love left over to love d'Aubigné, too. I hope you can love her as well. She needs a woman in her life that's not a complete screw-up. Renée, if I don't see some change in Casey by the time she finishes college, I'm not giving custody of d'Aubigné back to her. Let me tell you what she did today before I literally threw her out." He told her all about the incident that morning.

"I told you I didn't trust her," said Renée smugly.

"Well, I think I got the point across to her."

"I hope so because she doesn't want *me* to get the point across to her. I won't be as nice as you were. I'll strangle her with my bare hands. It only makes it worse because she *is* my sister."

D'Aubigné tugged at Rennin's jean pocket. "What is it, sweetie?" he asked.

"Grandpa says the fish and fries are almost ready and you need to finish the hushdogs."

Rennin chortled into the phone, "Did you hear that?"

"Yes, I did," said Renée, laughing. "Rennin, tomorrow go and buy her a baby book so you can write all these things down. When you're old and gray and someone is calling you 'Grandpa,' you can show them where their momma called hushpuppies 'hushdogs.'"

"I'll do that."

"Oh, the sonogram is set for August 28th, at nine. Don't even think about trying to come out here. It's too risky. They have a VCR, so we can record the whole procedure. I'll send it to you."

"I hear you. I love you. 'Bye."

"I mean it. 'Bye."

Renée thought that her bladder would burst as she waited for her name to be called. Finally, she heard that long awaited sound. "Ms. Peyton."

She was escorted to a different area where the technician handed her a gown and told her to change after she had been weighed, had her blood pressure taken, and her finger pricked. "Dr. O'Neil will be with you soon."

"I hope so," said Renée. "I have to pee so badly."

She waited only about five minutes before Dr. O'Neil came in. "How are we feeling today?" he asked jovially.

"I feel fine, except I'm about to pee on myself."

"We'll take care of that in just a few minutes. Let's see, you've gained three pounds since your last visit."

"Is that bad?"

"No, just an observation, but that must mean your appetite has returned. However, your iron is a little low." Dr. O'Neil handed her a bottle of pills. "I want you to take one of these along with your prenatal vitamins. You *are* taking your vitamins?"

"Every night."

"Good. Just add one of these. It's just a little extra iron. Well, then are you ready?"

"Yes."

The technician knocked on the door. "Ah, perfect timing, Marilyn. I was just about to call you to run this infernal machine."

"Dr. O'Neil, there's a gentleman out here insisting that he's Ms. Peyton's husband and demanding to be allowed in here. He's getting rather loud."

"He wouldn't have," said Renée as she rose onto her elbows from the prone position she had assumed.

"Renée," said Dr. O'Neil, "should I be privy to something that I'm not? James has disappeared. Troy died. Talk to me."

Renée suddenly became frightened. "What does he look like?" she asked the technician.

"I can't really tell. He's wearing a hooded sweatshirt which covers most of his face."

"What color are his eyes?" asked Renée.

"They are gorgeous. They are a vivid green."

"How dare he!" Renée stormed as she got off the examination table and went up front in her hospital gown.

Renée knew instantly Rennin had risked his life to be with her for this procedure. She would have known it was he just from the way he stood and carried himself. She marched straight to the man, grabbed the drawstring on the hood of the shirt, and snarled through clenched teeth, "Come with me."

She did not speak again until she had dragged Rennin to the sonogram room where Dr. O'Neil and Marilyn waited with breathless anticipation. She closed the door firmly behind her before she bellowed, "Rennin O'Rourke, I told you not to come! It was too risky!"

Rennin lowered his hood. Dr. O'Neil cried, "Holy Mother of God!" and crossed himself. Marilyn stood with her mouth agape.

"Hello, everyone." Rennin grinned sheepishly. "No, I'm not a ghost. Renée, you might as well tell them the whole story. This is your doctor. He can't repeat a word of it. You should've thought about that. And I'm not leaving."

Renée stammered, "I-I-I don't want you to leave. I wanted you to be here, but I didn't want you to take that risk. You're right." Renée told the story succinctly without details, but assured the listeners that Rennin was not a ghost and he was, indeed, her husband.

Dr. O'Neil wagged his head. "I just hope this elaborate hoax doesn't backfire on you. Now, shall we continue?"

"Yes," agreed Renée.

"Renée, back on the table. Rennin," Dr. O'Neil said carefully, "if you come on this side, you'll be able to see the screen easily."

Dr. O'Neil squirted the conduction solution on Renée's abdomen and said, "Let's see if we can hear a heartbeat first. We should be able to hear it distinctly." The sound they heard resembled the sound of several pairs of wings fluttering at once. "Hm," interjected Dr. O'Neil. "I think we *need* the sonogram. I need to confirm a theory."

Marilyn started the procedure and the VCR. During her maneuvering of the imaging device, Dr. O'Neil voiced, "Uh-hum, uh-hum, aha! Stop! There. Can you two see what I see?"

Rennin squinted toward the screen. "It looks like three feet."

"That's right," said Dr. O'Neil. "And we know humans don't have three feet. Go on, Marilyn."

Marilyn moved the device around some more. "Ha!" exclaimed Dr. O'Neil. "There it is. Do you see it—the fourth foot?"

"Fourth foot? Fourth foot?" Renée stammered. "There are two of them?"

"Yes, ma'am. You have a set of twins. Do you want to know the sex?"

"No," said Rennin. "I want to be surprised."

"But that way we'll know how to decorate the nursery," argued Renée.

"Decorate with something neutral. Would you really want me plastering footballs all over the wall if they are boys?"

"Oh, all right."

Marilyn took some measurements and they finished about ten minutes later. Renée zipped to the bathroom. As he and Dr. O'Neil waited for her to get back, Rennin picked up a large syringe on the table and asked, "What is this for?"

"The amnio," replied the good doctor.

"You stick this big thing into her uterus and draw out fluid?"

"Yep."

"No," said Rennin firmly. "I will not allow it. It's risky, especially now that we know there are twins, isn't it?"

"The risk factor has increased."

Renée walked in to hear the last statement. Rennin held up the syringe and shook his head. "Renée, no. I've already told you it doesn't matter. I feel it in my heart. I'm the father. Please, don't do this. If you absolutely must do the DNA testing, let Skyelar do it after they're born."

Renée looked at her doctor and asked, "What do you think?"

Dr. O'Neil answered honestly. "I agree with your husband. I only do amniocentesis if there's a potential problem the parents need to prepare for such as a high risk of Down's Syndrome. You have already said you're going to have these babies, so why risk a miscarriage?"

Renée sat down on the end of the examination table. "I just had the weirdest thought. What if one belongs to each? Is that possible?"

"It's possible, but not very *probable*," affirmed Dr. O'Neil. "If these are monozygotic twins, they have the same father and are identical. They were once one. When the fertilized egg divided the first time, it did not rejoin to continue growing but started another. Monozygotic twins are a fluke of nature.

Rennin interjected, "Just like the Rennin who started all of this."

Renée argued, "If I recall correctly, Morgan had a twin brother."

Dr. O'Neil continued, "If they're dizygotic twins, they're not identical and may even be opposite genders. If that proves to be the case, that means you produced two eggs during ovulation, and both were fertilized. Since you were with both men within a twenty-four-hour period, it's in the realm—the outer realm—of possibility they could be polar-body twins, and that they could have different fathers. However, I've already told you what I think about James. Renée, obviously Rennin is willing to love these little ones because they're a part of you. Keep them safe. If you must know their parentage, wait until they're born. You already have a DNA profile on Rennin. All you will need to do to the babies is to swab the insides of their mouths."

Renée looked at the faces of both men. "Very well, then. Dr. O'Neil, will you find me the best doctor possible near Mom's Trading Post, Pennsylvania? I love you, but I plan to be with my husband by the time these little surprises arrive. And, now, speaking of Mom's Trading Post, when do you go back?"

Rennin said, "Tonight. So, let's hide somewhere for the afternoon."

Rennin tiptoed into the house, but he was met by a wide-awake four-year-old bombarding him with questions. "I couldn't sleep until you came home, Daddy. Do I have a brother or a sister?"

He scooped d'Aubigné high into the air and then held her close to his heart before he set her on his hip. "I don't know whether they are boys or girls, but there are two of them. You have two siblings." Rennin held up the video cassette. "And I have them on tape, so you can see them."

"Oh, boy! Let's tell Grandpa."

"Isn't Grandpa asleep?"

"Yes, but he's on the couch with the T.V. on. He won't mind. We can watch the video."

Rennin set the child down. He could hear her waking Gerald. "Grandpa, I have two siblings, but we don't know if they're boys or girls although Daddy has them on video. We're gonna watch it right now."

Rennin came into the room and spoke commandingly. "No, we are not. It's far too late for you to be up. We'll watch the tape first thing tomorrow."

"Daddy!" argued the precocious four-year-old.

Rennin pointed toward the stairs. "D'Aubigné, bed, now."

D'Aubigné narrowed her eyes as if she wanted to battle. Rennin spoke quietly, but firmly. "I will not argue with you. You're the child. I'm the father. You will obey. I haven't had to punish you yet. Don't start now. Go to bed. We'll watch the video tomorrow, and tomorrow night I'll begin reading you a terrific story. You know the rule here is bed at eight except on Friday. Now, go."

D'Aubigné dragged toward the stairs before she turned back and asked, "Do siblings always make life harder? Do I still get a daddy hug?"

Somehow feeling he had lost the battle although d'Aubigné was headed to bed, Rennin walked to the stairs and took the little girl's hand. "No, siblings are great. Yes, you still get a daddy hug and a daddy kiss. Come on. You can even sleep in Daddy's bed. I want to go to sleep."

32
Competition

The high-school football season started with an unusual occurrence for Scott Montague High School, named for the first man to bring formal education to Mom's Trading Post. They won, a feat that had not taken place in twenty years. The fact they were on the road made the victory even sweeter. Practically the whole town turned out to welcome the team home. Gerald's statement to the media was simple:

> "I can't promise a victory like this every week, but if these boys play the way they did tonight, they stand a dammed good chance. I want to recognize two young men for outstanding play tonight. Chip Riley, our quarterback, showed great leadership and poise under stress. Well done, Chip. And Bobby Willis for that aggressive quarterback sack that sealed the victory. No laps for you on Monday even if you talk back to me. I won't promise that for Tuesday. I will promise this to all you parents and fans and opponents: We Dragons have some competition for you. Bring it on!"

The crowd roared with cheers and applause as Gerald told his team to go home and rest. He and Rennin drove home, chatting excitedly all the way there. Gerald asked, "Does Chip remind you of anyone?"

Rennin replied good-humoredly, "Who? Me? Are you insinuating that I'm corrupting the boy?"

Gerald chortled. "I would like to know what you've been doing with him and the offensive line, who has really shaped up, too, during those private practices."

"You'd fire me if you knew."

"I doubt it. You've brought out the tenacity in that boy. The first time I watched him at practice, my heart sank. Yeah, he had a good arm and he was fast, but he was a pansy about being hit. Now he'll even block a linebacker going for his running back. How did you accomplish that?"

"I hit him."

"What?"

"Seriously. I lined up in a defensive position along with a couple of the offensive linesman pretending to be defense, and we made a point of taking his ass down. If he whined, he ran ten laps. If he did nothing to try to escape the attack, I added five laps for laziness. If the offensive line completely folded and let us through, they gave me ten laps. Then, I told them that if I saw sloppy play on the field, I would pull 'em and make 'em run laps in front of the crowd, and Monday they would be doing wind sprints until they puked."

"I think you got your bluff in."

"I wasn't bluffing. You taught me well. I remember a time when you had me doing laps, wind sprints, pushups, and sit-ups, all with a major hangover. When I puked my guts out, you just got meaner. At least the kids weren't working in the face of hangovers, but it might be a good thing we're not having Saturday practice."

McClarty grunted, "If I find out they're drinking after the games, we will have sunrise Saturday practices."

"See," said Rennin teasingly, "I told you I learned from the best."

Rennin and Gerald came quietly into the house because they did not want to wake d'Aubigné. Jennifer Polson, the teenager Rennin paid to babysit, was transfixed to the television screen and the horror flick she was watching. Rennin put his finger to his lips, tiptoed up behind the girl, and tapped her shoulder. Jennifer let out a blood-curdling scream. Rennin cackled. He knew the girl's shriek must have been heard across the creek.

"Coach O'Rourke, that was mean!" panted the babysitter.

The next sound they all heard was little feet on the stairs followed by, "Daddy! Daddy!"

Rennin picked up his daughter and scolded her gently. "You're supposed to be asleep."

"I was asleep, but then Jennifer screamed. What happened?"

"I apologize. I didn't mean to wake you up. I just couldn't help myself. I scared Jennifer."

"That's okay. Now you get to tuck me in and give me a kiss. I missed my good-night kiss and the story."

"That sounds like a good idea." Rennin put d'Aubigné down. "Run back to bed, and I'll tuck you in just a second." The child complied, and Rennin paid Jennifer. McClarty drove her home while Rennin tucked his daughter back into bed and kissed her goodnight before he went to his own room and called Renée.

"Hello," she answered sleepily.

"Did I wake you? It's not that late in California."

"No, I've just been reading for my newest case. Caldwell Steel is in a struggle. I'll be out there really soon. Another company is trying to take them over in a hostile buyout. I was researching and got sleepy. So, how was the first game?"

"We won!"

"Congratulations. Now, I just hope I win this case. Dade Enterprises is a huge conglomerate, and the firm that represents them is stiff competition."

"I have faith in my pixie. Just sprinkle them with fairy dust. They'll be putty in your hands."

"I wish it were that simple. Who knows? Maybe I'll try it. I can sprinkle a little glitter and confetti across their logo and say an incantation. What if I really do have magical powers?"

"Oh, but you do. You have totally bewitched me."

"Good. I plan to keep you under my spell forever. My competition for your affection hasn't been around lately, has she?"

"Do you mean Casey? The only other female that has my affection is four years old. But, no, Casey hasn't been back. She called to say she would be here for Thanksgiving. You had better be here to keep me from using the carving knife on her rather than the turkey."

"I'll be there permanently by then. Before, if I get this brief done and out there. Let me get back to work."

"Don't tire yourself out. I miss you, and I love you. Sweet dreams."

"Love you, too. 'Bye, darling."

Rennin crept into d'Aubigné's room in the hope that she would have gone back to sleep. On the contrary, she sat there with *Memoirs of Magic* on her lap. Rennin was forced to read to her before she would go back to sleep, but he considered it a joy to read to his daughter.

He went to bed and thought momentarily how ironic it was that he had always dreamed of soaring on the backs of dragons and the football team he was coaching happened to be called Dragons. As he drifted off to sleep, he thought, *We need to update their mascot. It looks more like a green Barney with wings than Smoke. Their colors are green and white. I think we should put Draco on their helmets.*

The next morning while he made waffles and bacon for breakfast, Rennin was on the phone to every school board member with the same proposal: "If you want to spark the football team to be extremely competitive, give them new uniforms. Update the logo and mascot. If you all will agree to the change, I'll pay for the whole thing. It won't cost the school a penny. I'll even outfit the band, the cheerleaders, and other sports teams."

The legendary greed of dragons bloomed quickly among the school officials, and they readily accepted Rennin's proposal. Three weeks into the season, a monstrous white marble dragon found a home on the roof of the school. Coach O'Rourke came to cheerleader practice with a surprise for the squad, new uniforms bearing the new logo and a new mascot suit that resembled the dragon that now topped the school. Rennin joked with the girl who wore the mascot suit, "Now you won't look like an alligator with wings." He, then, paid a surprise visit to the band and presented them with new uniforms.

Rennin was late for football practice, but he grinned at Gerald as he walked up. "I refuse to run laps for you this time. I'm the bearer of good tidings. Call 'em in."

McClarty blew his whistle and the team gathered around him. Rennin spoke to the team. "I apologize for missing practice today, but I have an excellent excuse. I want everybody inside to check his locker."

The players raved about the new uniforms and put them to good use over the next several weeks. By homecoming, they were 8-0. Even if they lost their last two games, they were assured a winning season, something they had not had in fifteen years.

After homecoming, Rennin and Gerald came home to an unwelcome surprise. Casey sat in the living room with a young, light-skinned Haitian man, who wore dreadlocks and dressed like a reject from the 1960s, and d'Aubigné. Apparently, Casey had sent Jennifer home. Casey sprang to her feet. "Hello, Dad. I thought I'd surprise you. Don't worry; we're only here for the weekend, Rennin. I wanted to see my daughter and introduce all of you to my fiancé."

"Your what?" spat Gerald as he sprayed Rennin with the scotch he had made himself the second he saw Casey.

Undaunted, she continued, "Jacques, this is my father, Gerald McClarty and my brother-in-law Rennin O'Rourke. Dad, Rennin, this is Jacques Picard."

Jacques spoke politely in halting, heavily accented English as he extended his hand. "Eet ees a pleasure to meet bof of zhou. I have heard a great deal about zhou. But, um, where ees Renée?"

"California," Rennin answered cryptically. He shook Jacques's hand. "Jacques. We've heard nothing about you. Please, sit down." Rennin turned to his mentor and friend and whispered, "Breathe."

Then, he turned to d'Aubigné. "Why are you still up?

"Mommy wanted me to visit with her and him."

"Well, the visit is over for tonight. Casey, d'Aubigné's bedtime here is eight o'clock on every night except Friday. That's her late night. She's allowed to stay up until ten. It's almost midnight. I'm late getting here because it was homecoming. Who took Jennifer home?"

"Oh, she called some boy to pick her up and said she was going to the game to watch some kid named Bobby play. Don't worry. I paid her for the whole night. She only hesitated to go to homecoming because she said she needed the money."

"Casey, Jennifer's fourteen. When she babysits for me, I'm responsible for her safety. You will never allow her to leave with anyone again. Now, I'm putting d'Aubigné to bed. Come on, darling."

"You're right, Rennin," Casey said defiantly. "Jennifer's fourteen. So, why should she not get to be a kid just because she needed the money? She obviously really wanted to see this boy play. She's a freshman in high school, and she was missing her first homecoming. Couldn't you see past your rules on one special night? You could have even taken d'Aubigné to the game with you, just for homecoming."

Rennin's stubbornness did not want to admit Casey's argument had some merit. He just grunted, "No matter. It's time for d'Aubigné to go to bed."

The four-year-old raised her arms for Rennin to pick her up, which he did, and he disappeared upstairs, leaving Gerald to meet his future son-in-law, but he paused on the stairs and spoke over his shoulder. "Casey, I'm in the process of building you a small guest cottage for when you visit, but it's not ready yet. You may still sleep in the room you used last time you were here. Jacques, you may not use that room. I'm not a prude, but I have an impressionable four-year-old here. Please, take the one across the hall from Casey. I'm sure since you're only here for two nights, you'll be comfortable without Casey for that short time." He did not wait for a reply but continued up the stairs.

As he started into d'Aubigné's room she whimpered, "No, Daddy. Can I, please, sleep with you tonight? That Jacques scares me. He talks funny. He looks funny. And he smells funny."

Rennin pushed her brown waves from her face. "Yes, you may sleep with me, but we still have to get your pajamas. Have you even had your bath?"

"No, sir."

Rennin opened d'Aubigné's door and asked, "Which PJs do you want tonight?"

"The lavender ones with the butterfly on the shirt. Those are my favorite ones."

Rennin gathered the pajamas, underpants, and bubble bath for the little girl. Then he took her hand and said, "You can take a big-time bubble bath in Daddy's Jacuzzi tonight. D'Aubigné, would you have liked to have gone to the football game tonight?"

She answered honestly, "Yes, sir, I would have, but you were busy coaching. I guess I could've sat with Jennifer though. She could've been my babysitter at the game, and I could've watched Draco play on the teams' helmets."

"What did you say?" asked Rennin. "Who is Draco?"

"A white dragon. You put him on the helmets of your team. You've read to me about him, and sometimes he visits me when I sleep."

"Does he?"

D'Aubigné nodded. Rennin asked, "Aren't you afraid of a dragon?"

"Oh, no," said d'Aubigné with vehement head shaking and wide eyes. "Draco would *never* hurt me. He loves me. He says I remind him of Duncan, but I don't know who that is."

"Yes, you do. Don't you remember King Satin?"

"Does Draco mean *that* Duncan? Wow! If I remind him of a king, then I must be a princess."

Rennin laughed. "Yes, you must be. You're Daddy's little princess at the very least." And although it was well past her bedtime, Rennin read to her before she snuggled into the crook of his arm and fell asleep.

In Puma Pass, Renée packed her bags to surprise her husband. As she closed her briefcase with all the materials she needed for the next week in Pittsburgh, she found herself dropping glitter-and-confetti fairy dust inside the satchel and saying quietly, "*Vici meus hostis*." (Conquer my enemy.)

As she drove to the airport, she thought about what she had done and laughed aloud. "Wait until I tell Rennin what I did. He'll torture me forever with it." She checked her bags and made the shipping arrangements for her car. An hour and half later, she bade farewell to Puma Pass.

Renée's cell rang, but it was off during her flight. Rennin grumbled, "Where is she?"

33
Trick or Treat

Since Saturday was Halloween, Rennin went into town to get treats for the kids. On the way, he tried to call Renée again. Still he received the message that the number was out of range.

Jennifer had agreed to walk around with d'Aubigné. The sight that Rennin beheld when he walked back into his family parlor caused him to use words that he instantly wished he could take back. "What the fuck is this?"

Unaffected by Rennin's outburst, Casey answered, "Costumes for Halloween. I figured since you said I looked like a streetwalker when I wore this before, it would make a great costume." Casey wore the outfit she had worn when Rennin had thrown her out to go back to Columbia.

Rennin looked at Jacques and bluntly asked, "And what are you supposed to be?"

Wearing a purple rayon suit, Jacques looked confused. "Casey said zat black men een Amereeca often call zeir girlfriends zeir hos, and since she ees dressed like a ho, and I am Haitian, zen I am her peemp."

Rennin roared with laughter. "No, Jacques. *Decent* black men do *not* refer to their girlfriends as hos. A ho is a prostitute, and her pimp is the man who sells her. But if that's what you and Casey want to do, it's your prerogative. However, you will not be a pimp and ho in front of my daughter."

Rennin then turned to Jennifer. "What are you?"

"Oh, I'm just a Goth."

He shook his head. "So long as you don't show up in my biology class looking like that." He squatted in front of d'Aubigné and asked, "And what are you all dressed in flowing white robes? An angel?"

"I'm a virgin sacrifice."

"You're what?" Rennin said, his ire rising rapidly. "Who told you that?"

D'Aubigné started to cry because Rennin had never spoken to her in anger. "I don't know. I just heard someone say it."

Still angry, Rennin took the child by the shoulders and said crisply, "You are *not* a virgin sacrifice." He rounded on the others present. "Which one of you told her that? It's not funny, not even as a joke. Casey, did you say something like that?"

"No!" shouted Casey defensively.

"Jennifer?"

Jennifer shook her head. "No, Coach. I promise."

Before Rennin could even ask, Jacques declared, "No way, mon. Wif zee hoodoo releegion een my country? I am not zat fooleesh. And I am not a peemp." Jacques swung Casey around. "And zhou are not ho. Shange clothes. Go and put on zhour bellbottom jeans and a headband. You can be a heeppy. I weell be a reggae seenger wif a bongo. Zat ees strange enough for zis communeety."

The child was crying in earnest at that point. "Daddy, are you mad at me? Mommy only yells at me when she's mad at me."

Rennin realized he had been bellowing. He softened his voice. "I'm sorry, baby. No, I'm not mad at you. I just do not like the idea that someone told you that you were a sacrifice. D'Aubigné, there are some crazy people in this world who believe that, and they might want to hurt little girls. Let's see if we can change you into an angel right quick. Jennifer, will you, *please*, find me three coat hangers and a piece of white string and bring them into the kitchen? I think there's some kite string in the garage."

Rennin took his daughter into the kitchen and placed her on the counter. Jennifer came in with the coat hangers and kite string. Rennin straightened one hanger and made a loop in one end. He handed aluminum foil to Jennifer. "Wrap this around the hanger for a halo. Leave about two inches at the bottom uncovered." Then, he twisted the other two hangers together by the hooks. He covered the two triangles formed by the hangers in foil. Jennifer handed him the halo, which Rennin attached to the hooks and finished covering with foil. He made two slits at the apex of the triangles where they joined and ran the white kite string that Jennifer had found through them. Then, he turned to d'Aubigné who watched attentively and lifted her off the countertop. "Stand up for me, baby." Rennin tied the string around her waist. The halo floated over her head, and she had two silver wings. He rubbed her chubby little cheek with the back of his hand. "There. That's much better. Now, you're Daddy's little angel. Go look in the mirror in the bathroom. And guess what."

"What, Daddy?"

"I've decided to walk around with you to show you off. Grandpa will have to pass out the treats all by himself."

D'Aubigné went to see her new costume in the full-length mirror and came downstairs with Casey and Jacques who were new creatures as well. Rennin nodded. "Okay. That I can have walking around with my daughter. Much better. Thank you, Jacques." Rennin took d'Aubigné's hand.

"Are you going, too?" asked Casey.

"Oh, yeah," he answered curtly.

"Renneen, may I speak to zhou een private one moment before we leave?" Jacques asked.

"Jennifer and d'Aubigné, wait on the porch for me," Rennin commanded gently. "Casey, you go, too."

He spoke to Jacques. "I apologize if I offended you."

"No," said Jacques, lifting his hand like a shield. "Zat ees not what I weesh to speak about. Zank zhou for makeeng zeengs clearer. My Engleesh ees steel not very good. I do not always understand slang. I deed not understand zat 'ho' ees slang for whore, and peemp ees not a word zat I was fameeleear wif. I want to speak about zee voice d'Aubigné heard. Renneen, I feel an eveel force here. I am very fameeleear wif voodoo and hoodoo reetuals een my country. Most are just mumbo jumbo and harmless. However, some of zee deepest eveel practeeces of Santeria eenvolve sacreeficeeng virgeens, usually young cheeldren, especially een my country because girls lose zeir virgeeneety early een life. Perhaps I was sent here to warn zhou. I do not know, but guard d'Aubigné closely. I sense zat zhou disapprove of my relationsheep wif Casey, also. Ees eet because of zee deefference een race, or do zhou have some feeleeng for her as well?"

"The feeling I have for Casey is wanting to wring her neck. She's my wife's sister. Did she tell you about d'Aubigné?"

"Yes, she told me zee circumstances surroundeeng her conception and birth and zat she lied to zhou and her fazer. Casey steel has much groweeng and learneeng to do. Steel, I zink zhou feel a need to protect her from me. I care very much for Casey. I would not eententionally hurt her. Yet, zhour and Mr. McClarty's reservations are reasonable. Contrary to Casey's concept of zee future, I have not offeecially proposed to her. We have deescussed zee posseebeeleety. Much depends on government eessues een my country. Right now, I am not safe een my country. I hope for asylum een Amereeca. An outside force has moved een and my life would be een danger eef I returned home because I know of zis man's supernatural eenvolvement, and he ees a reech, powerful Amereecan. I must say I am surprised zat zhou have not scoffed at my belief een zee supernatural."

"I don't know what to think about you anymore, Jacques." Rennin released a long huff. "At first, I thought you were, perhaps, using Casey to get a green card. I'll be honest. I would never scoff at supernatural occurrences. I have experienced some myself. And, if you knew the history of my family, you might ask yourself if the evil you feel is standing before you. Thank you for your candor. I'll watch d'Aubigné closely. But, believe me, Casey is all yours if she's truly what you want."

Rennin took his daughter trick-or-treating.

D'Aubigné found the treasure trove in candy and other Halloween treats. Rennin allowed her to pick out four things to eat before bed. Casey said, "Oh, come on, Rennin. Let her stay up and have some fun."

He cut Casey a look of reproach even as d'Aubigné climbed onto his lap. "Help me choose, Daddy. I know I want a Reese's."

"That's one," he said.

"May I have two chocolate things?"

"You may have any four items you choose because it's a special night, except gum. Save the gum for tomorrow."

D'Aubigné chose a package of M and M's, a Hershey bar, and a Milky Way. Her saucer-like eyes looked at Rennin. "Daddy, may I pick one out for you, too?"

"For me? Do you want me to share your candy?"

"Yes, sir."

"All right. Which one do you think I'll like?"

The child shook her head the same way Rennin did. "Daddy, you must think I don't pay attention to you. Every time you buy me a Reese's at the gas station, you get a Snickers." She promptly handed her father a Snickers bar.

Rennin popped the bite-size candy into his mouth and mumbled around it, "You are very bright and observant. Thank you."

D'Aubigné put her hands on her hips. "Daddy, don't talk with food in your mouth."

"Yes, ma'am," he replied after he swallowed. "Now, eat your treats and off to the bath." He turned to Jennifer. "Do you want to help her and wash some of that off you at the same time?"

"Not this time, Coach. I'm going to a party at the old gristmill. Bobby Willis is supposed to pick me up at 8:30." Jennifer looked at her watch just as a car honked. She started out the door.

Rennin walked with her. "Nope. If he can't walk to the door to get you, you can't go with him. Are you sure your parents know you're going?"

"Yes, Coach. My mom is the one who suggested Bobby and I go to this thing. You can call them if you like." Bobby honked the horn again.

Rennin hollered from his porch, "Willis, if you want to go on a date with this girl, you have to walk up here and get her. Behave like a gentleman or you get fifty wind sprints Monday."

Bobby Willis, who was a sophomore nose tackle, thanks to Rennin's suggestion, jogged to the porch steps. He had on a skullcap with what appeared to be a hatchet buried in his head.

Rennin laughed, "Which one of Jason's victims are you?"

"Probably his thousandth."

"Is there booze at this party?"

"Not for me, Coach O'Rourke. I heard what Coach McClarty said he would do to us if he caught us drinking. We have two more regular season games. I plan to be on the team when we go to the playoffs."

"Good answer," said Rennin, "but, Bobby, if anyone is drinking or if there's any trouble, call me, and I'll get you home. I'll take care of you." He lowered his voice. "And I won't tell Coach McClarty. I know what he does when he's pissed."

"Thanks, Coach."

"Have a good time but stay out of trouble."

Rennin closed the door as d'Aubigné, ready for bed, descended the stairs. Behind her, came Casey in a golden negligee.

"Casey," began Rennin.

"I'm going to bed, Rennin."

He knelt to his daughter's level and squeezed her tightly. "Umm. You smell good."

"Mommy put some of her bath oil in my water. Mommy's going to tuck me in tonight. Is that okay, Daddy? I still want my kiss though. I guess I have to miss the story tonight."

"Yes, it's fine for Casey to tuck you in. Did you brush your teeth?"

"Yes, sir. I brushed extra-long because of all the chocolate."

"That's my girl." Then, he kissed her forehead and both cheeks and pecked her on the lips before they rubbed noses, the bedtime routine they had developed. Rennin hugged d'Aubigné one more time and whispered in her ear, "I love you. Sweet dreams."

The little girl called over her shoulder as she went up the stairs, "I love you, too, Daddy. Good night."

It dawned on Rennin that was the first time he had said aloud to his daughter he loved her.

Rennin poured himself a shot of expensive imported Irish whiskey and tossed it back. He poured another, which he had in his hand as he flipped off the porch light. Casey descended the stairs, still wearing the golden negligee. "What now?" he asked irritably.

"I have something I want to say to you."

"It will keep 'til morning when you have on clothes." He tossed back his second shot.

"But I want to say it now. Are you drinking again?"

"I wasn't before you came. But I think I am now." He poured another drink and went to lock the door.

A car door closed unnoticed outside. Renée, wearing a frilly, pink maternity top and matching slacks, a play tiara, and carrying a toy magic wand in one hand and her briefcase in the other came onto the porch.

Casey dogged Rennin's steps. "What?" He demanded before he could turn the dead bolt.

"I have a question for you. What was that stunt this afternoon about the pimp and ho?" Casey ran her hand up Rennin's arm. "You can't handle a little competition?"

Rennin clutched both of Casey's wrists, spilling the whiskey all down the front of her negligee. Simultaneously, the front door opened, and Renée said, "Trick or treat."

Renée froze in mid-thought as she saw what could have been interpreted as an intimate moment. Meanwhile Jacques clutched the banister at the top of the stairs as he watched the scene below him. Five seconds elapsed, but it could have been an eternity, before Renée exploded like unstable nitroglycerin. "You bitch!"

she screeched in fury. Casey took a step back from Rennin. Before she thought about what she was doing, Renée hit Casey full in the face with her briefcase, knocking her to the floor and breaking her nose. Renée straddled Casey and pounded her head against the wood flooring.

Casey screamed, "Get off of me." Her face was covered in blood, but she threw punches back at Renée, striking her across the cheek and eye.

Rennin wrangled Renée off Casey and held her firmly. "Let go of me! I'm going to kill her!" Renée screamed. The next thing Rennin knew, Renée gave him a back fist to his nose and was on top of Casey again.

Rennin saw Jacques at the top of the stairs. "Don't just stand there. Help me."

Jacques replied, "But I want zee the blonde lady to keeck Casey's ass."

"Jacques, please," coaxed Rennin. "Can't you see that she's pregnant? Think about the babies."

Rennin pulled Renée off Casey again, but he pinned her arms to her sides this time. Meanwhile Jacques jerked Casey to her feet.

Casey bawled, "You broke my nose, you bitch."

"That's not all I'm gonna break," Renée yelled back as she continued to struggle against Rennin's restraint, trying to stomp his feet, which caused the two of them to jump up and down like Mexican jumping beans as Rennin kept his feet clear of his angry wife's attempts.

"Renée, settle down," he commanded.

Casey continued to whimper about her nose. Rennin shot at her, "Shut up, Casey, before I turn Renée loose on you. Both of you be quiet before you wake up d'Aubigné and Gerald," he finished through clenched teeth.

Renée stopped struggling and stood with her arms folded across her chest, breathing heavily.

Casey tried to step behind Jacques. "Do not get behind me," Jacques said angrily. "I saw what zhou deed to Renneen. Why, eef zhou are een love wif heem, deed zhou breeng me here to meet zhour fazer and eentroduce me as zhour fiancé? Casey, he ees married to zhour seester. How could zhou do somezeeng like zat to zhour seester?"

Jacques started up the stairs as Casey called out, "Jacques, wait."

"Do not profess zhour love to me, l'enfant. Eet ees a lie. Zis weekend has shown me one zeeng. Zhou love only zhourself, eef zat. Perhaps my purpose here zis weekend lies een zee conversation I had wif Renneen earlier. Now, come. I weell attend zhour wounds, but we are no more. Zat zhou brought upon zhourself."

Rennin and Renée were left standing in the foyer. Renée finally dropped her arms and started crying. "Rennin O'Rourke, what is she doing here?"

"I tried to call you last night *and* this morning."

"I must have been in the air. I wanted to surprise you. I even dressed as close to a pixie as I can right now."

He gathered her in his arms. "You were a lot more than a pixie. I recall Tinkerbelle tried to kill Wendy for the love of Peter. And you definitely surprised me. Come to the kitchen."

She followed her husband to the kitchen. Rennin made an ice pack. "Put this on your cheek. You're gonna have a black eye."

"No, I can't," cried Renée. "I have court on Monday."

"I'm sorry," he said. "I'm sure you'll find a way to use it to your advantage. I have never seen you in a rage, not even with Celina Ortiz or when you found out about Ben—not like just now. Remind me not to set you off. So, what did you do, fly in for the weekend and court?"

"No," said Renée. "I'm here to stay."

"Yes!" he said, triumphantly raising a fist in the air. "For that treat, we have to go to church tomorrow. There's a neat little nondenominational church here where I take d'Aubigné to Sunday school."

"Well, do you mind if we go to bed? Will you, please, bring in my luggage?"

"You go on up. I'll bring your things."

Rennin stopped in the foyer as they started to their destinations. "Renée, do you want your briefcase? It's open, and the contents are all over the floor."

She walked in and started picking up the contents of her briefcase.

"What's that?" asked Rennin.

"Fairy dust. And I put a spell on it, too."

Renée walked up the stairs without further ado.

Renée slept peacefully, but Rennin tossed and turned until he finally sat up in bed at almost midnight. He heard a voice call his name and started to turn on the lamp.

"Don't turn on the light. It would only disturb Renée. You can see me just as well without it." A shadowy figure of a benevolent-looking, gray-haired man appeared at the foot of the bed.

"Stay calm," said the voice. "It was you who said you were not afraid of a ghost of your relative. I mean you no harm. I am Shane O'Rourke, at least I was. I'm proud to see you escaped James Wilburn. I was not so lucky. Yes, I would like to see him pay for his crimes, but I think you already know he's not what he appears. Neither is he what you have thought. There are others like him even among those we think we know. Be discerning. Protect those you love, even Casey, for you do love her in a strange way. Even tonight, you will be called upon to battle a touch of evil. The battles will become increasingly difficult. Draw strength from the ancient beings. You have sensed them all your life, just as I did. There will come a time for you to decide to be a man of this world or of something unknown. Just as I decided to be a part of the unknown, my life was stolen, even as yours almost was. Last, do not be surprised of what blood flows in your true love's veins. She is of Celtic origin. She has not admitted to herself the deep magic that flows within. Finally, form a hedge of protection around your girls, all three of them." The ghost paused as he saw Rennin's mouth open.

The apparition lifted a finger to its wavering lips. "Oh, you didn't know. Remember what d'Aubigné said she was for Halloween. Do not take that omen lightly. It has been over four hundred years since the spirit sought one of Quazel's bloodline. No matter how diluted, d'Aubigné is of that bloodline, and so are any other daughters you might have, but your firstborn is special. You will be amazed when you find out how special. Know this too; Jacques has been sent to *you*, not Casey. She was only the instrument to bring him here. D'Aubigné's discomfort near him was a spiritual awakening she is not quite ready for. Now, I can rest in peace for I have delivered to you, the last of an exceptional breed, what you need to know. I had feared I was the last, but that is *your* destiny. Go with the Lord's blessings."

As the specter disappeared, Rennin's phone rang.

34
A Touch of Evil

Before he finished saying hello, a frantic voice begged, "Coach O'Rourke, it's Bobby." Rennin slipped from the bed and took his phone into the hallway, not wanting to disturb Renée. The boy continued, "My folks went to Pittsburgh for the game tomorrow, and I don't know Jennifer's home number. You said you would help if we needed you. Coach, something crazy is happening up here. I'm really scared. Jennifer's hurt or something. I've locked us in my truck, but these people are insane." Rennin heard a loud banging sound before Bobby burst his eardrum, "Oh, God! Coach, please, hurry!"

Rennin did not take time to answer but dressed as quickly as possible without thought of not disturbing his wife. "Rennin, what's wrong?" Renée asked.

"I don't know," he replied as he tied his sneakers. "Bobby Willis just called in absolute panic and terror."

She started to get dressed. "No, and don't argue," he said. "If there is some kind of danger, you three do not need to be there." He kissed Renée on the forehead.

"At least take Gerald with you."

Rennin nodded agreement and marched down the hall to bang on Gerald's door. Without waiting for an answer, Rennin went in. "Gerald, get up. Bobby Willis just called for help. He sounds as if this is real trouble."

The older man was dressed in a matter of minutes, and the two coaches took off, but before they got out the door, Jacques appeared in the hallway. "May I be of help, Renneen?"

Rennin flung over his shoulder, "Yes, take care of my family while I'm gone."

When Rennin and Gerald arrived at the old gristmill, it seemed to be deserted although several bonfires still burned. The only sign of life was Bobby's old pickup. Rennin wondered why the boy had not driven away, but then he saw all four tires were slashed and every window looked like spider webs. Rennin seized the door handle, but the door was locked. He tapped gently on the fragile glass. "Bobby, it's Coach O'Rourke. Open the door."

Bobby responded, "Are those maniacs gone? Who else is out there?"

"I don't see anyone here. Coach McClarty's with me."

Bobby tentatively opened the door, and Rennin jerked it wide open. Except for being ghostly pale, Bobby appeared unharmed. On the other hand, Jennifer sat on the seat beside Bobby and stared into space as if she were in shock. Then, Rennin looked at the boy's shirt and hands, which appeared to be covered in blood.

Taking the boy's hands, Rennin inquired, "Bobby, are you hurt?"

Bobby shook his head. "It's not my blood. I think it's Jen's."

"Come on, Bobby. Get out of the truck. Gerald, take him to the car."

Rennin climbed into the truck and gently shook Jennifer. "Jennifer, it's Coach O'Rourke. Look at me."

The girl did not respond. Rennin took her face in his hands. "Jennifer, look at me." At that instant, she commenced screaming and slapping at Rennin.

"Get off of me! No! No! Get off of me!"

He tried to calm the girl to no avail. Finally, in sheer desperation, he slapped her hard. She stopped screaming and resumed her soulless stare. Rennin examined her as best he could in the dark. Indeed, the blood covering the front of Jennifer's costume appeared to belong to her. He tried again to communicate with the girl. "Jennifer."

She turned toward the sound of her name. "Coach O'Rourke?"

"That's right. We need to get out of the truck now. Coach McClarty has called the authorities." Even as he spoke, the constable and a rescue unit arrived. Rennin got Jennifer out of the truck and left her with the paramedics. The constable was shaking Bobby.

"Whoa!" shouted Rennin. "He's a victim of something here. Stop treating him as if he were a criminal. He'll tell us what happened." Rennin turned to Bobby. "What *did* happen?"

"It was crazy, Coach."

"Relax," soothed Rennin. "Look at me. Forget anyone else is here. Tell me what happened."

The paramedics interrupted, "We need to transport the girl to the hospital. How do we contact her parents?"

Rennin said, "I must be going crazy." He dialed Jennifer's home and spoke with her father, who seemed more upset about being woken up than what he heard on the phone. His wife was not home. Gerald rode to the hospital with Jennifer while Rennin stayed with Bobby.

After the rescue unit drove off with siren blasting, Rennin said to Bobby once more, "Okay, now. Tell me what happened."

"Well, you know the flyers have been up for weeks about the haunted gristmill party, and Jen's mom practically insisted we come. She seemed to think we would have a blast. At first, we were all having a lot of fun. We were roasting wieners and marshmallows. We were dancing to the music. Almost everyone wore a costume, so I don't know who all was here. It was more than just those of us from Mom's Trading Post though. There were probably about two hundred people here.

"Then, this group of about a dozen people wearing red robes showed up. We thought it had something to do with the entertainment. They went inside the mill. Strange noises started coming from inside, so we all sort of moved in to see what was going on." The boy shivered from head to foot.

"Jeez, Coach! These robed people were dancing around a pentagram on the floor. It was actually thirteen people, one man. There were candles everywhere. There was a goat's head. The women started taking off their clothes. Then, they cut the heads off of chickens and started coating themselves in the blood. That's when I told Jen it was time to leave. That's when the man in the robe pulled Jen through the crowd up there with them

"I kept trying to get through, but it seemed everyone just wanted to watch what was going on. There was this weird yellow haze, like powder in the air. I kept pushing my way through the crowd. They kept pushing me back. Then, Jen started screaming. Coach, I think I punched a couple of the people in the crowd. I finally got to the front. I don't know what that guy did to Jen." Bobby balled his fists in anger.

"Yes, I do. I'm gonna kill him, Coach. I lunged for him, but he side-stepped me. He had also carved that damned pentagram on Jen's stomach. Jen was just screaming. We had to get out of there. I grabbed Jen's hand, and we ran for it. I don't know if he was going to kill her or what.

"It was like the crowd was hypnotized. They didn't do anything to stop those people from hurting Jen. When we got to the truck, the tires were slashed. I locked us in and called you. I guess I should have dialed 9-1-1, but you said to call you if we got into any trouble, so I did."

Rennin said in disbelief, "I was worried that you might get drunk at the worst."

"Well," Bobby continued, "the crowd followed us, and you see what they did to my windows. Then, they all left. It was totally silent. Jen wouldn't speak. I was terrified, Coach." Tears formed in the young man's eyes.

The constable asked, "Did you get a look at their faces?"

"No, they wore these hideous looking masks. I can probably identify their boobs though. One thing, they were *not* teenagers. They were adults, you know, the ones that are supposed to protect us from things like that. The man was about six feet and had dark hair with some gray. I saw that when his hood slid back, but I didn't see anybody's face."

"Okay, Bobby, I know how to call you, but I don't think you should go home alone," said the constable.

"I'll take him home with me," Rennin volunteered

Bobby said seriously, "Coach, my folks won't answer their phone before that game is over tomorrow. They went to see the Steelers play. Nothing else will matter until after that game is over."

"You can stay at my house as long as you need to. Now, I think you want to go to the hospital and get checked out."

"I'm not hurt, Coach," protested Bobby.

"I want to be sure," Rennin gave Bobby his shut-up stare. He drove Bobby to the hospital. On the way Rennin explained, "I thought you might want to check on Jennifer. I take it she's your girlfriend, or was this your first date?"

"We've been going out since last May, before I got a driver's license. I'm sorry I didn't tell you about her before. Coach, who do you think those people were?"

"Evil people, Bobby. Very evil people."

Rennin, Gerald, and Bobby left the hospital with heavy hearts. Jennifer had been raped, and her parents were angry, but their anger seemed to be about the fact they were inconvenienced. Bobby whispered to Rennin, "Coach, would you think I was crazy if I told you I think one of the women there tonight was Jen's mom?"

"You must be mistaken. I cannot believe a mother would let that happen to her daughter, let alone participate in it."

The trio entered the O'Rourke home near dawn to find Renée, Jacques, and Casey anxiously awaiting news. Rennin sent Bobby off to bed and told his family what had occurred.

By the light of day, Rennin, Renée, and Jacques revisited the gristmill. Rennin and Renée stood aghast at the grisly sight they beheld. However, Jacques seemed unperturbed. Rennin said to him, "This doesn't shock you?"

"No," replied Jacques. "I have seen zis many times een my country. I am amazed to see eet here."

Constable Dubois rushed to the three people who had entered the gristmill waving his arms madly. "You can't be in here. This is a crime scene."

Rennin waved his hand at the man in a gesture of ignoring him and said, "I need to be here right now."

A bit dismayed the constable stammered, "Yes, yes. Mr. O'Rourke and his companions need to be here right now."

Jacques's expression caught Rennin's eye. "What?" asked Rennin.

"Zhou have zee geeft."

"What gift?"

"To sway zee mind."

Rennin shook his head and spoke to Constable Dubois. "I want to look around. Don't bother me."

The constable ordered, "Mr. O'Rourke needs to look around. Stay out of his way."

Jacques gave Rennin a look that said, "I told you so."

The three would-be sleuths began their inquiry into the site. In the center of the room and splattered with blood was the pentagram just as Bobby had said. Decapitated chickens littered the area, and the stench was already becoming pungent, even in the chilly air on November 1st. Suspended from the ceiling was the baphomet. An altar of sorts was situated against the wall. An upside down cross adorned the altar and a stone table sat in front of it. On the table lay a dagger and grail.

Jacques broke the silence. "Zese zeengs were not put here for one Halloween party. I would say zhou have a very sereeous coven een zhour meedst. Zis ees more zan a touch of eveel. Zis ees a serious perversion of even zee darkest practeeces of Santeria."

Turning to leave, Rennin looked down. Inside the grail lay an onyx cuff link. Rennin carefully picked it up. Monogrammed into the onyx were the initials J.W.

Rennin said, "I know this evil well. Renée, he knows I'm alive. This travesty was meant to let me know. My God! When Gerald warned me James had underworld ties, I thought he meant the Mafia. It's much worse. We are talking about *The* Underworld, Hell itself."

That evening before Jacques and Casey left, Rennin and Jacques had another private conversation. Jacques told Rennin, "I zink zat God sent me to zhou zis weekend. I fear zat Jenneefer was only to be a replacement for d'Aubigné. I know een my heart zat zee voice d'Aubigné heard and zee eenceedent wif Jenneefer are leenked. Jenneefer ees only alive because of zee zhoung man seeting een zhour leeving room. He might someday be zhour daughter's salvation as well. He needs zhou een hees life, Renneen. I do not zink he has zee guidance he needs. Zhou were sent to heem even as I was sent to zhou. Renneen, zhou and I are not feeneeshed wif our assoceeation. I do not know how we weell be connected, but from zis weekend forward we are bonded. I tell zhou zis: Zhou have true magic een zhour soul, deeper zan zhou can eemageene. Zhou have been touched by ancient beings full of mysteecal power. I know. I have spoken wif zem, too. I shall pray for zhou, and I am certain we shall meet again."

For one of the few times in his life, Rennin was speechless. His otherworldly message came back to him. He took Jacques's offered hand but felt compelled to embrace the younger man. He whispered in Jacques's ear, "Jacques, I would kill anyone who tried to harm my daughter. I truly would, without regret or hesitation. I think I really might need you around. If I can help with your case for asylum, let me know. Renée is an excellent lawyer. You are always welcome here." He laughed softly. "Even with Casey."

Casey had said very little since the fight with her sister. She drove away without a good-bye to anyone except d'Aubigné.

With the knowledge that James Wilburn apparently knew their whereabouts, Rennin insisted Renée carry a gun on her commutes to and from Pittsburgh for evil lurks in the hearts of many. Perhaps, one such evil is greed.

Renée entered the courtroom shakily after the weekend's events, but confident in the merit of her case. William Caldwell drummed his fingers nervously on the table. Renée covered his hand with hers. "It'll be fine," she encouraged her client.

Anxiously, Caldwell whispered, "Ms. Peyton, you have a black eye."

"And I plan to use that to our advantage. And from now on, I'm Mrs. O'Rourke."

It came time for Renée to present her opening statement. She stood and greeted the jury that would be settling the case. "Good morning, ladies and gentlemen. I'm sure you have all noticed my black eye. I have this shiner because I fight for what I believe in and for what is mine. You should see the other person." She laughed lightly. "You see, another woman came into my house to try and take what was mine although she has her own. That is greedy, and greed is one of the seven deadly sins.

"Let me tell you a story:

'There were two men in a certain city, one very rich owning many flocks of sheep and herds of goats; and the other very poor, owning nothing but a little lamb he had managed to buy. It was his children's pet, and he fed it from his own plate and let it drink from his own cup. He cuddled it in his arms like a baby daughter. A guest arrived at the home of the rich man. But instead of killing a lamb from his own flocks for food for the traveler, he took the poor man's lamb and roasted it and served it.'"

Many of the jurors stretched their eyes wide in horror while a few nodded at the recognition of the story.

"This is the story the Prophet Nathan told King David after David had taken another man's wife. Listen to the reaction of the king:

> 'David was furious. "I swear by the living God," he vowed, "any man who would do a thing like that should be put to death; he shall pay four lambs to the poor man for the one he stole and for having no pity."'

"Ladies and gentlemen, William Caldwell is that poor man. He owns a small company by conglomerate standards, a company that his great-grandfather started. On the other hand, Dade Enterprises owns some business in every state in the Union and some overseas. And now they have tried to take the poor man's little lamb. That is greed, ladies and gentlemen."

She walked to the bar separating the jury from the courtroom and softly laid her hand on it, palm down. "Heed King David's righteous indignation. No, we are *not* asking anyone with Dade Enterprises be put to death. We *are* asking you to prevent the rich, greedy man from taking the little lamb. And, perhaps, King David made your job easier. We are asking you to put a stop to this takeover and to compensate Mr. Caldwell. King David suggested four times what the greedy man had taken. And since he was the father of King Solomon, the wisest man the world has ever known, that sounds like a good number to me."

Renée walked back to her table and picked up a document. "Mr. Caldwell's company's estimated value, though to many of us sounds enormous, was 8.7 million dollars at the last accounting. Dade Enterprises has a net worth of 700.3 million dollars. Greed, ladies and gentlemen. You must see a touch of evil here.

"Mr. Caldwell, like me, might leave here with a black eye for staying in the fight for what is his. But, ladies and gentlemen, it is up to you whether he leaves with his lamb."

Renée presented solid evidence of unethical business practices by Dade Enterprises that had caused Caldwell Steel to lose profits. She presented witnesses to under-the-table deals that had almost driven Caldwell Steel into bankruptcy. At the close of court on Thursday, the judge instructed the jury to make a wise decision and to think about the case overnight. The parties involved returned to court Friday morning to wait. The wait was short. The jury returned a ruling to halt take-over proceedings by Dade Enterprises and a compensatory judgment in the amount of thirty-five million dollars, a rounded four times the value of Caldwell Steel.

As Renée packed to leave the courtroom, the CEO of Dade Enterprises approached her. "Mrs. O'Rourke."

"Yes?"

"Would you have found a way to win my case?"

"Mr. Abbott, I have nothing against big business. I'm partner in a very prestigious law firm. My husband's family holdings once tripled yours and will again. If I had been arguing your case, I could have won because I know how to find loopholes. However, in this instance, you were just plain wrong."

"I agree. That's why I would like to ask two things of you. First, will you provide me, not my lawyer, with the documents you have so I can ferret out *who* in my company is so unscrupulous? Mrs. O'Rourke, I swear I had no idea these shady dealings were going on. Second, since I just fired Giles and Giles because I think they were involved, will you come on board for Dade? I know, you're thinking conflict of interests. I'm sure you can find a loophole there, too. I mean, when you pulled out the story of David, I asked Giles to settle right there. They refused to settle. Mrs. O'Rourke, I'm a Christian. My company would never have engaged in the practices you presented with my knowledge. I admit that I've taken a back seat and let others do the work when I should have been keeping a closer eye on my vineyard, to use another Biblical analogy. I need you because my company is about to become much smaller. I will not have disreputable men or women working for me. Mrs. O'Rourke, to use your sheep metaphor, I'm a shepherd and my flock is scattered. I'm about to gather them in and do some shearing, maybe some slaughtering. When I do, I'm sure to be slapped with multiple lawsuits. Think about it. Talk it over with your partners. You have my number."

Rod Abbott shook Renée's hand and left, passing the court reporter in the doorway. The reporter approached Renée. "Mrs. O'Rourke, a courier just asked me to give you this."

Renée took the small envelop and opened it. She unfolded the note and read:

"Renée, is it mine? James."

35
The Hand That Rocks the Cradle

For the first time since Rennin insisted she carry a firearm, Renée laid the .38 revolver on her seat as she drove home. She called Rennin as she drove.

He answered in the middle of football practice, "What's wrong?"

"Nothing," she lied. "I just wanted to talk to you."

"Liar. Did you lose the case? Are you upset?"

"No, I won. Then, Rod Abbott asked me to represent Dade."

"Then, what's bothering you? You don't like to talk on the phone while you drive, so 'fess up."

"Rennin, just be home when I get there. I have something to show you."

Rennin picked up d'Aubigné at preschool and drove up just minutes before Renée. "Now, what's up?" he demanded before she got out of the car.

She handed him the note. Rennin said bitterly, "His spies are better than mine. I still have not heard a word about where he's hiding, except he never returned to Buenos Aries."

"I'm worried now, Rennin. What if he comes after the children? We already know he's not above murdering innocent children. He was already here, I think, for d'Aubigné."

He placed a protective arm around his wife. "Don't worry. Tomorrow I'll have a security system installed. The preschool already knows that only four people are allowed to pick up d'Aubigné. When the other two get here, I think I'll hire a live-in nanny. And I still have Zane looking for that thing. Renée, when I find it, I *am* going to kill it."

After the note, James seemed to hide once again. Life was good in Mom's Trading Post. For the first time in history, Scott Montague High had a perfect record and won the class A championship. Chip Riley, the quarterback and Chuck Stevens, the starting wide receiver, were selected as first-string all-stars and were talking to several college scouts.

Even on the family front, life seemed less stressful as Casey came in for the Thanksgiving holiday. She came alone and spent most of her time with her daughter. She did not dress provocatively or come on to Rennin once, and she and Renée did not fight. She informed Gerald that she would not be there for Christmas because she was flying to Haiti with Jacques.

Jennifer came to the house for a visit. She asked Rennin and Renée if she could babysit for d'Aubigné and the twins when they arrived. Rennin was pleased to see Jennifer coming to grips with what had happened on Halloween and was attempting a normal life again.

Even with all the good things in his life, Rennin still felt this was just the calm before the storm. He was in daily contact with Detective Zane, and once again, he heard dragons whisper to him in his sleep. They told him to do what must be done without hesitation or regret and then pled for his help.

Rennin played Santa Claus for the first time in his life and was delighted to see the excitement in d'Aubigné's eyes when she found her first bike and her hand-crafted doll house on Christmas morning. Rennin had also spent his spare time after the high-school playoffs crafting matching cradles of mahogany with dragons in flight carved on the ends. The family attended a special Christmas pageant at the small community church and returned to a feast mostly prepared by the men in the house because Renée's cooking left a lot to be desired, although she made a mean eggnog that gave a very merry Christmas buzz.

After the meal and several glasses of eggnog, Rennin and Gerald settled in front of the television for an afternoon of football. D'Aubigné crawled onto Rennin's lap. He whispered to her, "You need to take a nap."

She whispered back, "I can take a nap right here just like Grandpa."

Rennin noticed that, indeed, Gerald dozed in the recliner. Renée joined the group as she sat down on the couch and propped her swollen feet on the coffee table.

"She's right," said Renée. "We can take a nap right here, just like Grandpa. Don't bother me for at least an hour."

Rennin sighed, "I'm outnumbered. Let's all take a nap right here."

D'Aubigné nestled down into the crook of Rennin's arm and laid her head on his chest. A couple of hours later the group awoke to the sound of carolers. They opened the door to the football team and the cheerleaders, along with several others, caroling on their front lawn as a light snow began to fall.

Renée gasped, "Look, Rennin! Snow! How long has it been since I last had a white Christmas?"

"I've never had one," said Rennin.

Renée set about making hot chocolate for the lot. The teenagers milled about for a while and chatted among themselves. Rennin noticed Jennifer had drifted to the cradles and gently rocked one back and forth.

"Merry Christmas, Jennifer," Rennin said softly.

"Merry Christmas, Coach. Did you make these yourself? They're beautiful."

"Yes, I did. Thank you."

"Oh, and thank you and Mrs. O'Rourke for the bath salts. I plan to soak when I get home. It was the nicest gift I got."

"You're very welcome. Are you sure you're up to babysitting soon?"

"Yes, sir."

"Well, I plan to take my wife out for New Year's Eve. Can you be here at eight? And if you want to bring Bobby, it's fine."

"We broke up."

"Why?"

"I can't even look him in the eyes these days. I feel so dirty, Coach."

"Jennifer, are you going to the counseling sessions?"

"Yes, but I still have a hard time being around Bobby. My counselor says I should bring him with me, that he needs to express his feelings, too. Do you think I should?"

"I think that is very good advice."

"Then, maybe I will. It looks like we're leaving. I'll see you New Year's Eve."

By the time all the carolers left, a light blanket of snow covered the ground, and it was time for a late supper and bed. As Rennin tucked d'Aubigné in she said, "Daddy, I'm supposed to tell you what Smoke said."

"What did you say?" asked Rennin.

"I am supposed to give you a message from Smoke."

"Who is Smoke, darling?"

"A gray dragon. He talks to me sometimes when I sleep, but Draco usually talks to me. I *told* you that once. Smoke said he talks to you, too, and I shouldn't be afraid of him just like I'm not afraid of Draco."

"Yes, he does. What did Smoke tell you?"

"He said, 'Beware the hand that rocks the cradle.'"

"What does that mean?" Rennin said musingly.

"I don't know, but that's what he said."

"Well, you did a good job. Is there anything else?"

"Yes, I want you to paint Smoke on the side of my doll house, so he can protect my babies. I would put Draco on there, but he's white and wouldn't show up. Besides, Draco is the overseer, but Smoke is the defender."

"Can you explain that, d'Aubigné?

"It's simple, Daddy. Draco watches over all of us, but Smoke will fight for us. So, will you put him on my house? I want him to keep the monsters away."

"I'll do it first thing in the morning. Good night. I love you."

"I love you, Daddy."

Rennin fell asleep contemplating his daughter's analysis of the roles of dragons. Her relationship with these creatures seemed deep, not a childhood fantasy. He whispered to himself, "They *are* real. I *know* they are."

Rennin copied the sketch of Smoke onto the side of d'Aubigné's doll house as he had promised and began to think he should do the same to the real house. The rest of the week passed without event until the snow started about noon on New Year's Eve.

Rennin had not told Renée of his plans for their first New Year's Eve as husband and wife because he wanted to surprise her, and she had insisted she had to go into the office for a while. She said she had several loose ends to tie up before the twins came, and she was due any day.

The snow started at noon and began to swirl thickly by two. Rennin called Renée at her office, but she had gone to lunch. He tried her cell, but apparently the snowstorm interfered with the satellite reception. He reassured himself Renée was fine, and she was a safe driver.

Renée returned to her office, and her secretary had already left. Looking at the weather, Renée decided she should head home just as her phone rang. Thinking it was probably Rennin she answered, "Pryor and O'Rourke."

The female voice on the other end of the phone asked, "May I speak with Mrs. O'Rourke, please?"

Renée replied, "This is she. How may I help you?"

"Renée, this is Casey."

Renée was surprised to hear Casey's voice because first she was supposed to be in Haiti and second Renée would never have expected Casey to call her. She asked, "Casey, where are you?"

"I'm in Pittsburgh at the airport. I wouldn't have bothered you, but I can't get through to the house and it's a blizzard out here. I'm surprised to catch you in the office, but I took that chance. Is there any way you could give me a ride to your house?"

"Is Jacques with you?" asked Renée.

"No, that's why I'm here. Renée, Jacques is missing. His mother made me leave." A sob caught in Casey's throat. "Renée, I'm scared. You might not know, but Jacques was seeking political asylum here. He only went home to try and bring his mother here, too. Renée, what if they caught him? He could be dead. Please, take me to Dad."

Renée hesitated a moment. The thought of being alone in the car with Casey for an hour infuriated her. Casey's voice brought her out of her thoughts.

"Renée, please? I know you hate me, and you have every right to. I've been despicable. I'm not very good at saying I'm sorry, but I am. I really need you to...to be my sister."

The pathetic tone in Casey's voice cut Renée to the quick. She said softly, "Casey, do you love him?"

"Yes, I love Jacques, but I'm not *in love* with him. He's my very best friend. That's why I went to Haiti with him. I wanted to help him get his mother out of the country. Do you really think I would have missed Christmas with d'Aubigné unless it was very important?"

"No, I don't think you would have. It'll take me about twenty minutes to get there. Casey, I don't hate you."

On the way to the airport, Renée had a cramp in her side, but she shrugged it off. The snow was almost blinding. It took nearly an hour for her to make the drive to the airport. As Casey got into the car, Renée had another cramp. She thought aloud, "No, it can't be."

"Can't be what?" asked Casey.

"Nothing," said Renée, trying to convince herself. "Everything's fine. We need to get going before the storm gets worse."

Thirty minutes into the countryside, Renée stomped the brakes as a severe cramp hit her. Casey gasped, "Renée, what's wrong?"

Renée breathed hard for several minutes. "Oh my God," said Casey, attuned to what was happening. "Renée, are you in labor?"

"I don't know. That's the third cramp I've had since you called. What do you think? You've done this before?"

"Yeah, and I ended up having a C-section. Besides that, d'Aubigné was almost two months early."

"You did? She was?"

"Maybe it's just Braxton-Hicks. Don't worry about what happened with me. I was only sixteen. That probably played a huge factor in my complications. Do you want to go home or back to the hospital?"

"I want Rennin," said Renée like a child.

"Then let's go home. Do you want me to drive?"

"I think I'm fine now. Let's see what happens."

Renée and Casey drove slowly through the ever-thickening snow and falling darkness. Renée hit the brakes again and slammed the car into park as she bellowed very unladylike, "Fuck!"

"Renée? Talk to me," said Casey, genuinely concerned.

"I'm in labor, Casey. My water just broke. I think it's time to turn back to the hospital. You'll have to drive."

The two women changed places. Casey slowly turned around in the middle of the road and headed back to Pittsburgh. Renée let out another expletive. Casey tried to remain calm. "Renée, look at your watch right now. Count the minutes until the next contraction. When it hits, count the seconds it lasts."

"Okay," said Renée, suddenly glad her sister had called her to come and get her at the airport. Ten minutes passed before another contraction of thirty seconds hit.

Casey felt as if the car had not gone a mile because she was driving so slowly, but visibility had become nil. Suddenly, on the country road they had exited onto to go home, a tractor trailer roared out of nowhere, side swiping the BMW. The car spun wildly before it slid down the embankment and into a tree. Both Renée and Casey sat motionless, stunned at the suddenness of the accident and the fact Renée's airbags had not deployed.

Casey was close to tears as she murmured, "I'm sorry, Renée."

"It wasn't your fault," grunted Renée as another contraction hit with a vengeance. She pounded the car door with her fist and moaned as the contraction subsided, "Casey, now I really need you to be *my* sister. What do we do? We're in the middle of nowhere in a blizzard. A blasted maniac just ran us off the road and didn't bother to stop, and I'm having twins. Neither of us can walk anywhere. My cell isn't working. Is yours?"

Casey tried her phone. She shook her head. "No, the storm's too bad."

Renée screamed. "Casey, are contractions supposed to be this bad so soon?"

"They weren't for me," answered Casey. "I was in labor for hours."

Casey rubbed her hands across her forehead. "Renée, do you have emergency flares?"

"In the trunk, I think."

Casey got out of the car. "What are you doing?" Renée asked in alarm.

"I'll be right back," assured Casey. "I'm going up the embankment and set the flares off. I'm not going to leave you, Renée."

Casey struggled up the embankment in the blinding snow and managed to set the flares. She slipped and slid back down to the car. Her short time in the elements had chilled her to the bone. It was almost dark as Casey got back into the car, shivering all over.

Renée snarled, "There is no doubt these kids belong to Rennin. He's notorious for doing things the hard way. They're just like their daddy."

Despite the circumstances, Casey could not stifle a chuckle. "Renée, we need to get organized here. I think you need to get in the back seat, so you have room. You have a first-aid kit and an emergency blanket in the trunk. I'm gonna get that. Then, we're gonna alternate running the car and turning it off. We can warm up, then deal with the cold for a little while and warm up again. We might be here all night."

"I'll kill him!" snapped Renée.

"Who?"

"Rennin. He did this to me."

"I think you both had something to do with it," said Casey matter-of-factly.

Casey got the first-aid kit and the blanket. Then she settled down to do what she could for the sister she had finally found.

By nightfall Rennin was frantic. He could not get through to Renée's office or her cell. Then his house phone went out along with the electricity. D'Aubigné was so scared that she would not leave her father's side. Gerald tried to convince Rennin that Renée was smart. "Rennin, she wouldn't have driven in this weather. She's smarter than that. She's spending the night in her office. Her phones are out, too. That's the long and short of the matter. Relax. Let's stoke the fire and wait to bring in the New Year with this gorgeous little lady." He ambled to the door. "D'Aubigné, help Grandpa for a minute. You bring that small log, and I'll get the big one." The child reluctantly let go of Rennin's arm to help her grandfather. Gerald whispered to Rennin, "You are *not* helping d'Aubigné right now. You have to have more confidence in Renée."

Rennin tried to show outward calmness after that, but his insides churned. Nonetheless, with the howling wind and the swirling snow outside, and the blazing fire in the fireplace, Gerald, d'Aubigné, and Rennin all fell asleep in the parlor and missed the midnight hour.

Inside the BMW, Renée had almost ripped a hole in the leather. She had resigned herself to the fact that she was going to deliver two new babies in the backseat of her car. Using what she had at her disposal, Casey washed Renée's face with melted snow.

After a contraction that seemed interminable, Renée barked, "What time is it, Casey?"

"Almost midnight."

"You had better mark what time these O'Rourkes are born. I might get the first baby of the new year," Renée gloated, trying to find some bright spot to her predicament.

"Could be," said Casey as Renée contorted again. Casey set the alarm on her watch to sound at midnight.

Just as the alarm beeped, Renée let out a blood curdling scream. Working only in the light from the overhead and a flashlight, Casey said to Renée, "I think you can push now. I see a head."

Renée shrieked, "Just get it out!"

Again, Casey calmly said, "Push, Renée."

Renée heard faint crying. "It's a girl," announced Casey. "12:03." Casey snipped the cord with the small scissors in the first aid kit, tied the navel section off with dental floss she found in the kit, and wrapped the baby in one end of the blanket while Renée screamed through another contraction. Casey tore the bow off her sweater and tied a little bow on the baby's foot. She tried to sound encouraging, "In case they're identical, we'll know which was first later."

"Thanks," moaned Renée. "Casey, is the other one ready. I'm dying here."

"Not quite."

Three more contractions and Casey announced, "It's another girl at 12:07, and they look alike to me."

A few minutes later after she delivered the afterbirth, Renée relaxed. She said, "I want to see them."

Casey maneuvered the twins into their mother's arms as best she could. Renée asked, "Do they look all right to you?"

"They look great. You did a good job. Have you picked out names yet?"

"First names, yes. The first one is Caitlin. What's your middle name, Casey?"

"Diane, why?"

"Caitlin Diane O'Rourke."

"Are you serious?"

"Yep, she's gonna be named for Aunt Casey. The other one is Morgan. Morgan Denise, for Rennin's biological mother. Casey, I'm so tired."

"Go to sleep. I'll take care of you and my nieces until someone comes in the morning."

At the first sign of light, Rennin took Gerald's four-by-four toward Pittsburgh. He knew the route Renée always traveled. Although the snow had stopped, the roads were still hazardous, and progress was slow. Rennin's eye caught a flash of blue about twelve feet down the embankment headed toward Pittsburgh. He stopped to see if someone needed help. Out of the truck, Rennin instantly recognized Renée's BMW.

Throat constricted, heart pounding, he raced down the incline and wrenched the door open. He could hardly believe what he saw.

Casey started awake with the blast of cold air and quipped, "Well, good morning, Daddy. It's about time you found us."

Renée slowly opened her eyes and smiled weakly as she saw Rennin's face. "They couldn't wait." Indicating with a nod of her head, she continued, "Meet Caitlin Diane and Morgan Denise."

Stunned to silence, Rennin finally managed, "What happened?"

Casey unfolded herself from the car. "Get us all to the hospital so we can get checked out and we'll tell you all about our little adventure."

Casey took the babies and looked at the steep bank. "Daddy, we might need some help."

Rennin managed to help Casey and the babies to the truck where Casey crawled into the small rumble seat and laid one baby on each side of her. She looked at Rennin. "Can you get Renée by yourself? I don't want to leave them unattended, but she doesn't need to try and struggle up the hill."

"Casey?" Rennin started.

She preempted the questions. "It's a long story. Just get my sister up here so we can take care of business."

Rennin got Renée into the truck and started for the hospital. On the way, Casey and Renée took turns telling the story from the fact that Jacques was missing in Haiti to New Year's babies.

Once at the hospital, all parties checked out fine and Renée's doctor pronounced them fit to go home, although Rennin had to buy two new baby car seats. Upon the arrival of both his daughters, Renée and Casey had to tell the story all over again to Gerald, who sent them both packing off to bed along with his two new granddaughters.

After Renée nursed her children for the first time, Rennin tucked them snuggly into their cradles. D'Aubigné tiptoed into the room and asked to see her sisters. Rennin let her peek at the babies. She asked, "Daddy, how do we tell them apart? They look just alike."

Rennin picked d'Aubigné up and said, "Do you see that little pink ribbon your mother took off her sweater?" D'Aubigné nodded. "Well, until they get a little older and we can tell the difference, Caitlin gets to wear that ribbon on her ankle."

D'Aubigné got a little wrinkle in her brow, prompting Rennin to ask, "What's wrong?'

She turned her jade saucer eyes on her father. "Daddy, now that you have two more little girls, do you still want me?"

He gently pushed his daughter's hair from her face and kissed her chubby little cheek. "D'Aubigné, Daddy will *always* want you. I love you very much. But you know what?"

She shook her head. He continued, "Daddies can love a lot of children. I love you. I love Caitlin. I love Morgan. Someday Aunt Renée and I might have another baby, and I will love him or her, too. But even if I have a hundred children, I will always love you. You're my first child. That makes you really special." He got a creased brow, identical to his daughter's as he remembered what he had read in *Memoirs of Magic* and Elizabeth saying that in olden times children born through Caesarian Section were thought to be more than human because they were not "born of woman." Then he remembered what Shane's ghost had said about d'Aubigné. He had just learned that day that she had been delivered via C-section. *Can she really have some extraordinary ability?* Her words brought him back to the present.

"Even if you don't love my mommy?"

Rennin heaved a great sigh. "D'Aubigné, can you keep a secret?"

The little girl nodded. He whispered, "I do love your mommy, just not the same way I love Aunt Renée. She has a special place in my heart because she gave you to me. But I am not in love with her. I think Jacques is in love with your mommy. That might be a good thing because your mommy needs to know we all love her in our own special way."

Rennin turned around to take d'Aubigné down the stairs and saw Casey in the doorway. She mouthed the words, "Thank you," and went off to get some much-needed rest.

He came back to where Renée and the babies slept and before he did anything else, he kept his promise to Renée. He swabbed the babies' mouths to send the samples Federal Express to Skyelar. Then, he sat in the bentwood rocker he had found time to make. Assured his family was safe, he drifted off to sleep. Somewhere in his subconscious he heard Smoke's voice again guiding him along a murky path. "Rennin, I told you to beware the hand that rocks the cradle."

Rennin jumped in his sleep and opened his eyes. Kneeling between the cradles, Jennifer gently rocked them to and fro as she hummed a lullaby.

36
Casey's Sacrifice

Rennin leapt to his feet and stammered, "Jennifer, w-w-what are you doing here?"

She put her finger to her lips. "You'll wake 'em up. Everybody in town knows the twins have come. I just wanted to see my little charges."

He led Jennifer into the hall. "Who let you in? You scared me to death when I woke, and you were here."

"The door was open. I guess everyone must be asleep. It was a long night. I didn't mean to scare you."

"I know you didn't. It's all right. How did you get up here?"

"I walked. I do that a lot these days. I walk and think and listen to the voices."

"What voices, Jennifer?"

"The ones in my head."

"What do the voices say to you?"

"Different things. Sometimes they argue. That's when I get scared. Do you think I'm crazy, Coach O'Rourke?"

"Jennifer, when did the voices start talking to you?"

"Halloween."

"No, I don't think you're crazy. I think you're trying to work out what happened to you, and sometimes it's hard. Have you told your counselor about the voices?"

"She thinks I need pills." Jennifer pulled out a prescription bottle. "Wellbutrin. Every morning. She says I'm depressed and suicidal. I wasn't suicidal until I started taking the pills. I haven't taken them since Christmas. They scare me. Sometimes I think I could be homicidal if I saw those people again. Sometimes I hear your voice, at least it sounds like you. I feel protected then. Sometimes it's my mom's voice and their voices that I hear. Then, I just wanna scream."

Rennin was concerned for his student. He wanted to hug her and tell her he understood but thought it would be inappropriate. Therefore, he tried a different kind of solace. "Jennifer, don't listen to those voices. Those people were evil—pure evil. If you hear the voices, call me. I understand. Sometimes I hear voices, too, but they're wise and encouraging voices. Last year, a very wicked man tried to kill me for the third time. He buried me alive. My voices kept me sane and strong until Renée found me. My voices belong to dragons."

Jennifer's sullen expression changed, and she laughed nervously. "Thanks, Coach. Now, I know someone is crazier than I am. I'm sorry I scared you earlier. Did one of your dragons tell you I was here?"

"Actually, yes."

"Okay, Coach. If the voices scare me again, I'll call you." She stepped into the biting cold.

"Don't you want me to drive you home?" asked Rennin.

"No, I'll walk. I'll be fine, Coach." She reached into her pocket. "I have my cell phone." The slender, shapely, almond-haired girl walked down the path.

The next day, life took on a new routine with feedings and diaper changes. Rennin still could not shake his uneasiness. He took d'Aubigné to town with him, but this time he drove into Pittsburgh where he sent the swabs to Skyelar and took his daughter shopping. They bought a horn and a basket for her new bike. She found some bath oil that smelled like Casey's. As they passed the accessories store, d'Aubigné said, "Daddy, may I get my ears pierced?"

"Aren't you a little young for that?" he surmised.

"No, sir. Lots of kids in my class have earrings. Please, Daddy?"

"Your mommy might get mad if we don't ask her."

"Mommy won't care. She wears her whole ear full of earrings, and she has a belly-button ring and a tongue ring and a tattoo on her back. I just want one hole in each ear. She won't mind."

"You're probably right. She'll think it's cool. But she might get mad that we did it without her. Maybe we should at least call her and ask. What do you think?"

The child shrugged. "If it will make you feel better, call her."

"Okay. I'll call, but you ask her."

Casey's cell was off, so they called the house number. A female voice answered. D'Aubigné knitted her eyebrows together just like Gerald did, and for the first time Rennin had to admit that he saw a lot of Casey in this little girl, her strong-willed independence for one. She was as free a spirit as her mother. He had no desire to quell her spirit but to channel it in a constructive rather than destructive path. He listened to the one-sided conversation.

"This is d'Aubigné. May I speak to my mommy, please?" A moment's silence passed before the child said, "Mommy, when I get through talking to you, Daddy needs to talk to you. Daddy says I can get my ears pierced while we are at the mall if it's okay with you. He won't do it without your permission. Will you tell him it's all right with you?"

D'Aubigné handed the phone to Rennin. He heard a ruckus in the background. "Casey, what's going on there?"

"Your house has been invaded by a giggling gaggle of teenage girls and their mothers. They've thrown a surprise baby shower."

"Who answered the phone?"

"Jennifer. I think the whole thing was her idea, but it was a sweet thought. All your students are here with their moms, except Jennifer. She's by herself."

Rennin lowered his voice. "Casey, keep an eye on Jennifer. She's been acting weird since Halloween."

"How would you act, Rennin, if you'd experienced what she did?"

"I understand that, but, Casey, I can't betray her confidence. Just watch her. I almost wish you weren't going back to Columbia. Can you believe I just said that?"

"No," Casey laughed. "I *have* to go back now that I finally know what direction I want to take. Renée inspired me. I'm considering obstetrics nursing. But while I'm here, I'll be vigilant. Now, I want to enjoy this shower, too. It's fine for d'Aubigné to get her ears pierced, but I really appreciate your thoughtfulness."

D'Aubigné picked out a pair of ruby, her birthstone, posts and walked out of the accessory store before she reached her arms up for Rennin to hold her. He picked her up, and she buried her face against his shoulder. He felt the warmth of silent tears. "What's the matter?" he asked.

"It hurt, but I didn't want strangers to see me cry. And that one fat lady made fun of my ears. She whispered to the other one that I have 'Spock' ears, whatever that means."

"Well, I have points on my ears too, and it's over now, and the next time we come to the mall, we can pick out some fancy earrings. Now, I'm starving. May I take the prettiest girl in the mall to lunch?"

D'Aubigné dried her own tears. "I'm okay now, Daddy. I just needed to cry. What are we gonna have for lunch?"

"Whatever you'd like."

Giving a child the choice of what to have for lunch means only one thing—Happy Meal. After lunch at McDonald's, Rennin told d'Aubigné he needed to go to the hardware store and get some paint.

"What are you painting, Daddy?" she asked.

Without even considering what he was saying, he replied, "I'm painting Smoke on the side of our house, so he can protect my babies."

"That's a good idea," agreed the gifted four-year-old.

On the drive home, a small streak of charcoal darted in front of Rennin's car. Instinctively, he swerved to miss the animal. Not knowing whether his attempt to dodge the creature was successful, he pulled over to see so he could either get the body off the road or put a wounded animal out of its misery. D'Aubigné followed her father. He scolded her. "You should've stayed in the car. It's dangerous to walk on the road." In actuality, he did not want her to see if he had to euthanize the animal.

She replied undauntedly, "I'm safe. I'm with you."

Rennin took her hand and they came to the spot where the creature should have been if it made the crossing safely. Cowering and shivering beneath the roadside holly, they discovered an inky-black kitten about six weeks old. D'Aubigné reached out for the animal as her father warned, "Be careful. He might scratch you." She cautiously reached for the kitten, which ironically rubbed its head on her hand. She gently picked it up and cradled it in her arms.

When the two saucer eyes looked up at Rennin, he knew what was coming. "Daddy, look. It's a baby Satin. May we keep him?"

"So, you've already named him, huh? What makes you think I want a cat?"

"Because you're a daddy and you have enough love for furry babies too."

Rennin knew he was beaten from the get-go. "Bring him on. Just don't start a menagerie, and make sure he doesn't eat Cam and Tam."

"What's a menagerie?"

"I'll tell you later."

Casey went back to school but started the habit of calling d'Aubigné every night to say good night. She also started driving back to Mom's Trading Post every other weekend where she stayed in her guest cottage at night and visited with her family during the day. The month of January proved uneventful. Casey had no word about Jacques's whereabouts. Neither did Rennin receive any new information regarding James Wilburn.

The weekend before Valentine's Day, Casey showed up with Valentine gifts for everyone. She brought d'Aubigné a teddy bear that was as big as she was and a box of chocolates. She bestowed the twins with small bears. Gerald received chocolates and a mushy card that said what she could not verbalize. To Renée she gave a specialized card for her sister, a chocolate rose, and a floating-heart necklace. She handed Rennin a card that simply read, "For a toad, you are some prince," along with a green stuffed frog wearing a crown. Rennin smirked at the joke.

Casey shrugged. "I started to get a pair of silk boxers that had 'hot stuff' on them, but I thought that might be misconstrued."

"Hey," said Renée, "that's what I got for him. And it's about time for him to show me hot stuff again."

Rennin turned beet-red as Renée and Casey gave each other a high five at his expense. He could not believe the changed relationship between the two women. They had truly found sisterhood. Gerald could not believe the person Casey had become. He was sincerely proud of her.

As they all bustled around the kitchen preparing an Italian feast, Casey's cell phone rang. She had no idea who would be calling her as she answered, "Hello."

"Casey?" replied the voice on the other end through great static.

"Jacques?" Casey squealed. "Where are you? Are you all right?"

"Casey, leesten." The static interfered with the reception. "Casey, no time…love…zhou…tell Renneen…Weelburn." She heard the rat-a-tat-tat of machinegun fire. The connection was lost.

Casey hollered into the phone, to no reply. For the first time since she was five years old, she fell into Gerald's arms, sobbing. He steered her to a chair and tried to soothe her fears. "Sit down, Casey. At least you know he's alive."

She choked, "He was when the call started. I don't know now. I heard machineguns."

Rennin handed her a glass of water. "Drink this, Casey, and if you want a whiskey, I'll give you that, too. What did he say?"

She took a swallow of water just to gain control of her voice. "I think he tried to tell me he loves me. Then, he told me to tell you something. All I heard was Wilburn."

Rennin pounded the table. "A rich, powerful American interfering with his government. That's what he said to me. James is in *Haiti*. It's a non-extradition country and swathed with black magic. It makes perfect sense he would go there."

Rennin called Harvey Zane who booked the next flight to Haiti. He had orders to find both James and Jacques. Rennin took Casey's hand. "Casey, now that we have a clue, I'll do whatever I can to find Jacques. Zane's a good man. He'll find him."

Casey tried to draw strength and comfort from her family. Driving back to New York was the hardest thing she had ever done. She wanted to stay with the people who loved her, and she could not come back until spring break because she was working on a research paper. Casey's cell phone bill skyrocketed. Rennin paid it.

Casey left a day early to come home for spring break. She did not care that she missed three classes. She felt pulled to get back to Moms' Trading Post. She arrived about one o'clock and decided to pick up d'Aubigné at preschool. The late March air still bore a chill as she hurried inside.

The new receptionist at the entrance to the preschool told Casey d'Aubigné had already been checked out. "Who checked her out?" asked Casey.

The woman looked at the checkout log. "A Miss Polson."

Casey went livid. "Did you refer to the checkout authorization? Miss Polson is not authorized to check my daughter out of school."

Casey called Rennin immediately, but his phone was off in the classroom. She called the office at the high school and demanded to speak to Coach O'Rourke. The secretary tried to tell Casey Rennin was teaching. Casey raged into the phone, "Lady, you get Rennin O'Rourke on the phone right now, or I will be barging through your front door. This is an emergency."

The secretary paged Rennin to the office. "What's wrong, Myrtle," he asked as he walked in.

"There's a woman on the phone demanding to talk to you. Her name is Casey."

A look of alarm spread over his face as he snatched the receiver. "Casey, what's wrong?"

"Jennifer checked d'Aubigné out of school, Rennin. I'm at your house now."

Casey did not knock on the door but rushed straight in calling, "D'Aubigné! Renée!"

There was no one downstairs. Casey raced up the stairs. First, she went to her daughter's room and then to Renée's. Renée lay in a crumpled heap on the floor with a handful of light-brown hair in her fingers. Casey exclaimed, "Oh God! Rennin, get home! Caitlin and Morgan are gone, too! Renée is out cold! Hurry!"

Rennin dropped the receiver and bellowed at Myrtle, "Send the authorities to my house immediately."

Rennin charged through the door and ran up the stairs three at a time. Renée was coming around when he came through the door as Casey washed her face with cool water. Renée screamed, "Jennifer!"

It took a few seconds for Renée to get oriented to her surroundings. She finally realized Casey and Rennin were there.

"What happened?" Rennin demanded abruptly while trying to remain calm.

Renée gasped, "Jennifer took the girls. She hit me with something. I tried to stop her."

In addition to his children missing, Rennin fretted that Renée probably had a concussion, but she would not go to the hospital.

The constable arrived, and a massive search began, but as darkness fell, the children had not been found. Both Renée and Casey were frantic. Casey could not sit still. The constable began to talk about waiting until morning to continue to look. "Like Hell!" Casey shouted at the man. "Now you get some search lights and some hounds. A fifteen-year-old could not have gotten far with two infants and a little girl. I frankly don't think you're trying very hard. Have you even bothered to call her boyfriend? He might be helping her."

"Bobby wouldn't do that," mumbled Rennin, but he placed a call to the boy anyway as the constable stammered some lame excuse and Renée lashed out at him.

"You heard my sister. Get the bloodhounds. You must not want to keep your job."

The solidarity of the two sisters strengthened Rennin's resolve. He kept having visions of James holding his daughters. When he hung up from talking to Bobby Willis, Rennin suddenly announced, "I'm going out to look for myself. Now, Bobby's panicking. He's afraid someone will hurt Jennifer, but he has no clue where they are. Ladies, are you coming?"

Renée had wandered to the kitchen wall. She tapped her fingers on the calendar. Thinking aloud she said, "Today is the spring equinox. A virgin sacrifice. Rennin!"

In unison the three chorused, "The gristmill."

Casey shouted, "Take the four-by-four. You can cut cross country with it."

It did not take long to note Renée had deduced correctly. An eerie light sneaked through the cracks of the old mill, and bawling could be heard distinctly. Casey leapt from the moving four-by-four and was to the door before Rennin and Renée got out of the vehicle. The babies, wearing only a diaper and wailing as if they understood their predicament, lay on the stone altar. Beside them, d'Aubigné was bound and gagged wearing a white robe and fiercely struggling to free herself. The noises that she uttered around her gag were pure rage.

Lighted candles lined the walls and in the center of the pentagram was what appeared to be a cauldron with some sort of bubbling liquid in it. Jennifer stood by the altar wearing a black robe and holding the dagger that should have been in the evidence room at the police station. She appeared to be having an argument with herself. She was crying. "I don't want to hurt them. Please, don't make me do this." Every time she argued, she appeared to contort in a painful seizure.

As Rennin headed across the room to the altar, Renée called, "Rennin, stop. You can't walk across the pentagram."

"Watch me," he retorted.

"You *can't*," insisted Renée. "Only a priest or priestess of Druidic descent can walk across it. If you go that way, the oil in the cauldron will catch fire and you'll be consumed. Rennin, you talk to Jennifer. Whatever is making her behave strangely, she's resisting it. She'll listen to you. Circle around and talk to her. I'll get the children. Casey, don't move. You can't enter the pentagram either."

"What are you going to do, Renée?" asked Casey.

"I'm going to get the children," Renée said as she stepped into the circle around the five-point star. Nothing happened. She assessed the colors of the candles. "Someone has perverted all of it, but the sequence has to be the same." Renée stepped carefully from candle to candle as Rennin coaxed Jennifer to listen to only his voice.

"Today is Ostara—The Spring Equinox marks the first day of spring. It's the time when the god grows to maturity. The night and day are equal; therefore, it's a time of balance when our lives can be brought into harmony. It's a time of beginnings of action."

She carefully placed her toe beside another candle. "Next will be Beltane—Beltane is the emergence of the god into manhood.

He falls in love with the goddess, and their union results in the goddess being with child. Beltane is a celebration of their coupling and the fertility of the Earth goddess and all living things. Beltane marks the return of vitality and passion. Then, oh, what is next?"

She bit her lip in thought, and she moved forward. "Summer. Litha—Midsummer falls on the longest day of the year. On this day the god begins his journey towards death as the days begin to get shorter."

She leapt to the next candle. "Followed by Lammas—Lammas is the celebration of the successful growing season. The grain is ripe but is just beginning to be harvested. The god loses strength as the days grow shorter. It's a time to address and overcome fears and anxiety.

"Then, it should be Mabon—Mabon is the celebration of a successful harvest." She swiped sweat from her brow. "Once again, night and day are equal, the fall equinox. It's a time to address the balance in our lives and to be thankful for our success. The god continues to fade with the sun, while the goddess mourns his loss but rejoices in her pregnancy." Stomach roiling, she released a nauseous breath.

"Then, the actual beginning, Samhain. This is why they wanted the virgin sacrifice on Halloween. Jennifer didn't succeed in what she was to do. Now, she's also being punished.

"Samhain—Samhain is the first day of the Celtic New Year. At this time, the god passes into the otherworld to be reborn to the goddess at Yule. The division between the worlds is thin, and it's a time to remember one's ancestors and to reflect on the past year, and sometimes spirits return to claim a new body."

She stood stock-still and rubbed her neck as the tension began to make her muscles clench.

"God! It's been so long since I read about this and thought about this and traced my own family line. Let me think." She massaged her temple. "And my head really hurts. Yule! Now it's Yule—Yule is a time of rebirth and renewal. At Yule, the goddess gives birth to her son, the god who is symbolized by the sun. His birth brings hope and the promise of the coming summer.

"Last, we will go to Imbolc—Imbolc marks the growth of the god into a strong boy, as the days grow longer, and the sun gets stronger. It also marks the recovery of the goddess from giving birth to the god. It's a time of initiation, a beginning, as the seeds begin to wake from their winter sleep. We have made the circle of life."

Renée stepped out of the pentagram beside the altar.

She knelt by d'Aubigné who still wriggled and struggled against her bonds. It was obvious the little girl was a fighter from her battle scars. Renée soothed, "D'Aubigné, sh. Aunt Renée is here." She took the gag from the child's mouth. D'Aubigné's shrill cries pierced the air. Renée rubbed her cheeks gently. "D'Aubigné, please, be quiet. I know you're scared, but you have to listen to me." Renée untied the child's hands and feet. The child clung to her aunt. Renée took her face into her hands and looked directly into the eyes of the terrified little girl. "D'Aubigné, what you need to do now is to run around the outside of the circle to your mommy. *Do not* step inside the circle. Can you do that for Aunt Renée?"

D'Aubigné nodded. "Go!" commanded Renée. "Casey, she's coming to you. Get her out of here."

Meanwhile, Rennin still pled urgently with Jennifer, and she was within his reach. She grabbed her head and screeched, "Stop it! Leave me alone. I won't do it. I love them." She fell unconscious into Rennin's outstretched arms.

"Get her out of here, Rennin," commanded Renée. "I have the girls."

As Casey pushed the door open, she came face to face with the constable and his drawn weapon. She put d'Aubigné behind her and took a step back.

The constable wagged his head. "You really do have nine lives, don't you, O'Rourke? James was right about you. You have really messed up the balance of things around here. We were free here to practice our religion until you came. Just like your ancestors, you just had to meddle. But we also saw a definite advantage to having you here when your little bastard showed up. The one thing we had needed to consecrate our temple. And then! You gave us two more opportunities if we didn't succeed with the first one."

"How can you be sure of that?" snapped Rennin. "They could belong to James and are mine in name only."

"No, no. We grilled the little faggot and he squealed like a stuck pig. I give him credit though; he put up a good fight first for a little pansy-assed fairy."

"What did you do to Skyelar?" asked Rennin, truly remorseful.

"The last I saw him, he was lying in his laboratory with his guts all over the floor. That was last night."

During all the posturing, Renée had managed to slip to the back-emergency exit of the mill with the twins. She somehow managed to catch d'Aubigné's eye and motioned for her to come to her at the same time she pointed at the circle. D'Aubigné let go of her mother's hand. Casey was too terrified to tear her eyes from Rennin and the constable to see why. Rennin's quarterback eye caught the movement as d'Aubigné dropped to her knees and crawled toward the back of the mill. He continued to goad the pompous, corrupt law enforcer in order to keep the man's attention away from the children. "Gerald was right about you. He sensed something was off the second he met you."

Jennifer stirred as Rennin took a step toward the pentagram. "Well, Constable, what do you plan to do now? It seems your little sacrifice has failed once again. As I recall, James Wilburn is not the forgiving type. You've failed him twice."

"That's true, but I can finally kill you for him." The constable jerked Jennifer by her wrist and shoved her through the door. "Your mother was so wrong about you. Get out of here, you useless piece of shit." Then he slid his nine-millimeter into firing mode.

"No!" railed Casey as she threw her small weight against the obese villain, but it was enough to throw him off balance, and Rennin wrestled the gun from him; but in one fluid motion, the rotund constable slung Casey forcefully across the room into the pentagram.

Just as Renée had said, the cauldron tipped, and the candles ignited the oil therein. Flames engulfed Casey. As if in a dream, Rennin emptied twelve rounds point-blank into the fat, greasy man who had served as law enforcement in Mom's Trading Post before he dropped the gun, and with no thought for himself, he plunged into the flames for Casey.

Outside, Renée locked the girls in the truck and flew back to the blazing building as Rennin stumbled out, carrying Casey gingerly in his blistered arms.

37
Zane's Report

The wait at Mercy Hospital seemed interminable. Jennifer had been admitted to the pediatric psychiatric unit. Her doctors suggested that she displayed early signs of paranoid schizophrenia. Rennin disagreed, saying that she was possessed, and he vowed to get her alone with a qualified priest in the near future. Jennifer's parents looked annoyed that Jennifer had once again disrupted their lives and horrified at the suggestion that a priest should go anywhere near her. Rennin felt uneasy about the whole situation.

The three children were physically unscathed except for a few bruises and scrapes on d'Aubigné where she had struggled.

Renée proved to have a mild concussion, but she refused to be admitted and stood vigil for his sister.

Also refusing to be admitted for treatment, Rennin only allowed the emergency physicians to treat and bandage his burns, which encompassed his chest, arms, and hands. He insisted on waiting in the ICU with Gerald, Renée, and the children. He still could not fathom the reckless, yet selfless, act that had brought Casey to this serious juncture in life. In addition, visions of a disemboweled Skyelar plagued his mind. He could not bring himself to inform Renée what the constable had told him while Casey barely clung to life in a cubicle down the hall.

Several hours after Casey had been brought into the emergency room, Dr. Craig Jamison, a burn specialist and cosmetic surgeon who had been called in, emerged with a dour expression. Gerald, as Casey's father, was the one the doctor approached. Seeing the look on the doctor's face, Gerald said simply, "Don't hold back anything. What are her chances?"

Gravely, Dr. Jamison replied, "Casey has third degree burns over eighty percent of her body. The lining of her lungs is scorched. She refuses to let us put her on a ventilator to help her breathe before she talks to all of you. She's the most stubborn woman I've ever met. And so beautiful. In the short time I've known her, I admire her strength and dignity. If she makes it through the first twenty-four hours, she has the tenacity to live, but most people with this much damage don't survive. If she *does* survive, she'll need to undergo years of reconstructive surgery, but she will have some scarring no matter what. I will perform every operation for her. I'm sorry to present such a bleak prognosis, but Casey wanted complete honesty." Dr. Jamison gawked at Rennin and demanded, "Why are you not in a bed upstairs?"

Rennin replied absent-mindedly, "I can't leave Casey. She's here because of me. I won't leave her."

"Is it a family trait?" asked Dr. Jamison.

"What?" asked Rennin bringing his eyes from the floor.

"Stubbornness. Are you Rennin?"

"Yes."

"Casey wants to talk to you alone."

Rennin stood and realized d'Aubigné had been sitting on the floor leaning against his leg when she locked her arms around his leg and cried desperately, "Daddy, don't leave me."

Gerald pried d'Aubigné's fingers loose from her father and held her tightly in his arms. Rennin rubbed a bandaged hand across her cheek. "Daddy's not leaving you. I'm going to talk to Mommy. I'll be back in a few minutes."

Even with Rennin's assurance and her grandfather's strong loving arms around her, d'Aubigné cried after her father. The sound of her sobs broke Rennin's heart, and he prayed that Casey could not hear her daughter's crying as he entered the cubicle where the woman lay.

The first words Casey uttered were, "What's wrong with d'Aubigné?"

"She's crying because she's afraid I left her."

Casey's voice was a raspy wisp. "I don't want her to see me like this."

"She already saw you at the gristmill."

"So, you think I should talk to her?"

"Yes, I do."

"Then, bring her in here with you for a minute."

Rennin went back for his daughter, who cleaved to his leg in horror. Tears dripped down Casey's cheeks. She could hardly find any voice at all as she squeaked, "D'Aubigné, Mommy is so sorry. Now, you listen to me. Mommy's going to have to go away."

"No," cried the child frantically.

Casey continued, "D'Aubigné, listen to Mommy. I won't be able to come back. Remember no matter where I am, I will always love you. You're the one good thing I ever did. You listen to your daddy and your aunt Renée and Grandpa. They will take good care of you. Now, I want you to go sit with Grandpa while I talk to Daddy."

D'Aubigné reached out and touched Casey's singed hair. "Mommy, I love you. I don't want you to leave me."

"Mommy doesn't want to leave, baby. I don't have a choice. You be a good girl for your daddy. And I will always be in your heart. Now, go to Grandpa." Casey choked out her last words. D'Aubigné obeyed.

Rennin argued with Casey. "You *do* have a choice. You fight to stay with us—all of us."

Through extremely labored breathing, Casey continued to speak, "Rennin, stop right now. Don't blame yourself for this. It's not your fault. I know you will take care of our daughter, but I want you to make me a promise."

"What? Name it."

"When you find James Wilburn, make him suffer. Don't kill him quickly like you did Dubois. Let him know what it feels like to suffer."

"Casey, you stick around and help me. I need someone like you in my corner. Casey, you're the only one who knows I shot that bastard. Why don't I feel any remorse for killing a man?"

"Not much of a man." She tried to laugh. "He deserved it. You did the world a favor. Don't dwell on it, Rennin, or it'll drive you mad. You had no choice. You did what you had to do. Do it without regret." Her breath rattled. "So, now, you finally see that I could have been good for you? You need me around."

"Casey," Rennin kissed her gently on the forehead. "You have a good man that loves you. You might think about hanging around for him."

"I wish I could. Rennin, you find Jacques, too, if he's alive. Tell him I love him and I'm sorry. None of you seem to understand though. Yes, I love Jacques for his ideals and his dedication and loyalty. I am *not* in love with him. He's my best friend, not my lover. Halloween showed both of us that was not our path. He's not my soul mate. Maybe I don't have one, so it's all right for me to leave. Now, I want to talk to Dad."

Rennin kissed Casey's forehead again. "You know, if I had met the lady you've become, I could've fallen in love with you."

"No, Renée is your soul mate. I know that now. Yet, it feels good to know you care about me. Show it by loving d'Aubigné."

"I promise." Rennin left Casey and sent Gerald to her.

Gerald could not find words to speak to his daughter. Casey simply said, "Dad, I love you. I'm sorry for all the grief I gave you. Now that I have d'Aubigné, I know you only did what you thought was best for me. Thank you."

"I am so proud of you, Casey." Gerald choked on his words. "You're all I have. I love you so much."

She shook her head. "I'm not all you have. You have Renée and Rennin and three grandchildren. Please help Rennin care for d'Aubigné."

Gerald managed a bittersweet smile. "She's so much like you."

"I know," said Casey with a shuddering breath. "That's why Rennin will need your help. Don't let her make the kinds of mistakes I did. Promise me."

"I promise."

"Dad, I want to talk to Renée. Please ask her to come in."

The person that entered Casey's ICU cubicle was not what Casey had expected. The sapphire lakes that were Renée's eyes instantly became cascading waterfalls as she openly and honestly wept from the depth of her soul. "Casey, I can't lose you. I just found you. Don't you dare leave me."

With all the strength she could muster Casey commanded, "Renée, stop crying. I need you to be strong for me right now. I have to ask something of you because you're the only one I trust to do it."

Renée sniffled as she stifled her tears. "What can I do for you, Casey? How can I ever repay you for what you did tonight? I still have the love of my life because of you."

"First," said Casey, "you can be d'Aubigné's mother."

"Stop it, Casey. Don't talk like that."

"Come on, Renée." She wheezed. "Both you and I know that my chances of living through the night are slim. And if I do live, what will I be—a roasted marshmallow and pin cushion for several years? I'll never be completely whole again. I need you to be my lawyer right now, not my sister, though I love you dearly. Please, Renée?"

Renée took several deep breaths to calm her nerves. "What do you want me to do—a will?"

"I leave everything I have to d'Aubigné. That's my bequest. I want you and Rennin, of course, to be her parents. Renée, adopt her. Be her mother. The next thing is the hardest. I want to see it in writing. Renée, if I die, don't let them bring me back. I want you to draw up a DNR."

"No!"

"Renée, please? Be logical and rational. I cannot live like this. Neither Dad nor Rennin could do this for me. You're the only one who can possibly understand. If God sees fit to have me survive, then I'll endure whatever I must, but if He sees fit to take me out of this, do not usurp His authority. Renée, I'm in agony." Casey rolled her eyes toward the I.V., which had been necessary to connect to a vein in her neck because her arms were too badly burned. "I would almost ask you to increase the dose of morphine and let me slip into peace, but even you, the strongest person I've ever known, couldn't grant me that. But, please, Renée, if you love me, let me go."

Renée nodded as she whispered, "I'll take care of it. You have my word. Casey, I do love you. I just wish I had found you sooner."

"Me, too. Maybe a big sister could've kept me out of trouble."

"Or caused more with you."

Dr. Jamison came into the cubicle. "I think she needs to rest. Casey, the ventilator will help you breathe. Even with the massive dose of morphine I gave you, you must be in excruciating pain. Let me help."

Casey tried to reach out a hand. "Renée."

Renée puffed out her cheeks. "I'm sure Dr. Jamison has the appropriate forms." She looked the doctor in the eye. "She wants a DNR."

Dr. Jamison stared at Casey. "Are you certain of that? Casey, you're so young. Think about your little girl."

"I am. I didn't say not to do everything possible to keep me from dying, but if I do, please let me go. And, yes, I am in pain. Can you give me some…more?"

Dr. Jamison hesitated. "A little, but the ventilator will ease your breathing difficulty. You won't be able to talk, but it'll give you some relief."

Casey nodded as she locked eyes with her sister. Dr. Jamison saw the exchange. "Renée, you may come back in an hour to visit. I think there are two little girls who need you out there right now. They are giving their father and grandfather fits."

Renée kissed Casey's forehead and whispered, "Don't leave me. Be strong. I love you."

For Casey's family, the waiting proved the hardest. Every hour on the hour, an adult sat with her for five minutes. In the wee hours of the morning, Dr. Jamison told them that Casey's condition had worsened. She had slipped into a coma and was not responding to stimuli. Still, they waited.

Near dawn, the family had an unexpected visitor as Harvey Zane, balding man weighing about a hundred sixty pounds and not quite six feet tall entered the waiting area. His hazel eyes showed depth of character and his words of compassion were genuine. He handed Rennin a large manila envelope, which Renée had to open.

The detailed report contained pictures of a heavily guarded compound where James Wilburn had holed up. There were other disturbing photos of people being carried in and out of the compound. Most who entered did so unwillingly. Some were brought out and unceremoniously dumped outside the gate, battered and tortured, but alive so they could report to their people or obey some command. Others were never seen after they entered, and some were obviously dead when they were thrown onto a flatbed truck and carried away. Zane had managed to capture one truly disturbing photo of a young Haitian man being tortured, resisting James's interrogation. Rennin stared hard at the photo before he asked, "Zane, do you have any closer up?"

"I used the telephoto lens on him because I think he's the one you're looking for." Zane thumbed through the photos. "Here."

There was no doubt as Rennin and Renée exchanged looks. Rennin asked, "Is he still alive?"

"He was when I left. Obviously, Wilburn wants something from him, and he isn't giving it up."

"I can bet what it has to do with," said Rennin bitterly.

As they talked, loud beeps blared from Casey's room. "No!" cried Renée. "Not now."

Medical personnel poured into Casey's room. The family raced to the doorway as they heard Dr. Jamison speak authoritatively, "Leave her alone. She's a DNR."

"What are you talking about?" Rennin shouted over the hubbub.

Renée put a steadying hand on her husband's shoulder. "Rennin, it was what she asked for."

"No, damn it!" he bellowed as he pushed through the medical staff to see the flat line on the monitor. Rennin knelt beside the bed and talked coercively to Casey. "Casey McClarty, don't leave us. We all need you to stay with us. I need your help. I found Jacques. He needs you. Don't make me have to tell him you gave up the fight. James Wilburn has been torturing him for months. *He* has not given up the fight. You said you love him. You stay here and fight." Rennin shook Casey, causing his own wounds to bleed and ooze. "Listen to me. I know you can hear me. I already have to tell Renée that Wilburn used Dubois to kill Skyelar. Don't let Wilburn win. Don't let him take another person I care about. He'll come after d'Aubigné again. I need your help."

Renée had walked behind her husband and had heard all he said. Though heartbroken over the loss of her friend, she laid her hand on Rennin's head as he released Casey and sobbed uncontrollably. She whispered as tears streamed down her own face, "Let her go. Her suffering is over."

Casey felt herself floating. She felt no weight, no pain. She could hear the voices behind her, most loudly Rennin. She thought, *He doesn't like to lose.*

Unexpectedly, she found herself walking on a path, which headed toward two openings. One was well lit and inviting. The other was cold and dark. The path became slippery, and Casey knew she had to tread carefully so she would not slip into the dark opening and a sure abyss.

Then somewhere to the side, she heard a strange flapping of wings and a voice calling her name. "Casey, last year I would not have spoken to you, but you have changed. At last you understand what love means." Casey sought the voice for it comforted her. At last she glimpsed a massive pearly white beast hovering above the light. The beast continued to talk to her. "Hello, Casey. I'm Draco. You need not fear me. You have a choice to make. You may continue on the path to the juncture in the road. The darkness will pull heavily on you. It is much harder to walk into the light. But that is not your choice. You must decide whether it is time to choose death or to stay and fight the battle. Very soon, Rennin will have to make a choice—whether to fight a battle with us against his own kind. He will need all those he holds dear. If you decide to leave him now, he will be weaker. You showed today that you have strength of character. I know asking you to stay and fight will be hard. You will suffer. Rennin is the last of his line. Without you, he could fail to come to us; then, we shall cease to be also. Only he can restore what once was."

Casey questioned the creature. "Renée is Rennin's wife. Why are you not talking to her?"

"Renée will remain his wife. We need her too, and she made her decision to follow Rennin to the ends of the world. You are d'Aubigné's mother. She must come to us as well. Besides, there is another that needs you that you do not yet know about—the soul mate you doubted you have. He must accompany Rennin. Now, you must decide. Will you follow the easy path or stay and fight for justice?"

The noises swirled around Casey. She was in a state of limbo.

Dr. Jamison managed to clear the room and disconnect Casey from all the apparatuses. As Renée started to walk out the door, she paused with a nagging thought in the back of her mind. Without explanation she said, "I need a few minutes alone with my sister."

"Of course," said Dr. Jamison. "I'll send someone for the body a little later."

Unknown to Renée, Rennin had stepped back to walk with her, and he watched in hypnotic silence. Renée spoke to herself, "I might be crazy, but I have to try this."

She stretched herself over her dead sister and said some ancient Gaelic words: "Mar a tha fuil agus beòthalachd an anam, Dia deònach," (As is blood and the enchantment of the soul, God willing.) before she spoke the incantation, "Blood of my blood; breath of my breath; restore sweet Casey from the brink of death." Renée placed her mouth on Casey's and then it appeared as if blood passed from one woman to the next. Renée gasped and fell to the floor.

Still not believing what he had just witnessed, Rennin knelt beside his wife. A thousand words floated back to his memory…"I am magic…I will show you magic…She is of Celtic blood…Renée will guide you…I put a spell on it…Only a priestess of Druid descent…the blood which flows in your true love's veins…"

Renée regained consciousness quickly. Seeing her husband beside her she asked, "Did it work?"

"Let's find out together," Rennin replied as Renée stood.

Casey stared at both of them in bewilderment and spoke one word. "Draco."

38
Cleansing, Emptying, Filling

Dr. Jamison came back into Casey's room in order to retrieve her charts and stopped dead in his tracks. "What the?"

Casey calmly said in a voice as one with laryngitis, "I decided to stay and fight."

"I signed your time of death twenty minutes ago." He stammered pointing at the chart, "H-h-how?"

"Don't you believe in miracles?" Casey growled in a low whisper.

"I have to now."

Optimistically, Casey asked a bit louder, but still in a voice much deeper than normal, "So, when's my first surgery?"

Gathering Casey's family around her, Dr. Jamison told them he could not explain Casey's revival. Neither Renée nor Rennin said a word. Dr. Jamison laid out eighteen months of surgical plans. Casey needed numerous skin grafts. He asked both Renée and Gerald to be tested for compatibility and if they would donate skin to be grafted. He refused to ask Rennin saying he would require at least eight weeks of recovery time himself.

"Eight weeks!" exclaimed Rennin. "Jacques could be dead by then."

Zane steadied Rennin's reaction. "Rennin, you can't just barge into Wilburn's compound anyway. You have to plan this to the last detail."

Still bewildered by the entire scenario, Dr. Jamison asked, "Will someone please explain to me the whole story surrounding what happened to Casey? The emotional impact could have a bearing on her recovery. I need to know."

"Why?" asked Rennin guardedly.

"I'm her doctor."

"No, there's more. You're hiding something. What are you afraid to tell us, Dr. Jamison?"

Jamison showed some agitation before he exploded, displaying he had the temperament associated with his flaming red head and eyes the color of the early morning sky. "When I left that room, Casey was dead, not in a coma. She was *dead.* When she flatlined, I felt the coldest, iciest, emptiest feeling I've ever known. It was as if something inside me died, like I had failed miserably. I can't explain it, but, Rennin, you're not the only person to have descended from O'Rourke blood. Just because my last name is Jamison, doesn't mean I don't know where my ancestors came from. Duncan Paul O'Rourke was my great-times-fifteen grandfather. His brother was Cameron, and his father was Rennin. Just because I came from one of Duncan's daughters doesn't mean I can't share the same heritage. I have diluted Iroquois blood as well, though you can't tell from my coloring."

Dr. Jamison barely took a breath as he continued his tirade. "Guess where I grew up, Rennin—Mom's Trading Post. I fished on the banks of Beaver Creek and listened to the tall-tales Shane O'Rourke used to tell us kids. I always thought they were just that, tall-tales like Paul Bunyan or embellished legends like Daniel Boone and Davey Crocket, until what happened last night with Casey. Guess what else—whatever happened last night had nothing to do with you, a true O'Rourke. It was Renée. Whatever occurred in there, Renée did it. She only has the name O'Rourke because she married you and chose to take it. O'Rourke blood does not necessarily mean O'Rourke name. That's where your James Wilburn really messed up. He can never eradicate the spirit displayed by our common ancestors. There will always be men and women who stand and fight for what's right. Lord! I never thought I would have to take a stand like that. I have always put my confidence in what I can see and prove scientifically. After Casey, I can't deny there's more, whether you call it faith, miracles, or magic. Casey has made me a part of whatever you're planning.

I will not fail her. So, you might as well tell me the full story. After all, we're kin."

Nobody spoke after Craig Jamison's diatribe for several minutes. Finally, Rennin asked a simple question using a familiar name rather than a formal one. "Craig, have you ever soared on the back of a dragon?"

"Excuse me?"

"Have you ever soared on the back of a dragon?"

Craig laughed heartily. "Often after an afternoon of fishing with old Shane, I've dreamed of dragons, one in particular whose name was Brindle. He often told me I was his Colin come back to him at last. I haven't seen Brindle in my dreams for a long time."

Rennin smiled. "I've seen Brindle, though he rarely speaks to me. Smoke talks to me most often although occasionally Draco finds it necessary to speak to me. Yes, I think you are meant to be a part of whatever unfolds, Craig. Over the next several weeks, I think you will understand the complete story of what has happened. Your job right now is to restore Casey. My immediate responsibility is in Haiti. Zane and I have some planning to do. Lives depend on what I must do, and"—He looked around at the group—"I must do it alone. Gerald, you must stay with Casey and watch over my family. Renée, don't even think about it. Your responsibility must be Caitlin and Morgan. Don't argue. I don't have the energy to argue. I know whom I need with me. I'll take care of it."

Craig performed his first skin graft on Casey's face, using skin from the insides of Renée's forearms two weeks after the incident. Where he could, he used Casey's own skin and grafted skin from her back to her front, but it was necessary to use donor skin because Casey had sustained so many burns. Rennin begged to be tested as a match, and Craig gave in when Rennin had healed sufficiently himself. However, neither Rennin nor Gerald matched

Casey's needs. The one other person besides d'Aubigné, and Craig would not consider using the child's skin at all, who matched well enough for a graft proved to be Jennifer Polson, who insisted she be allowed to help Casey because she was responsible for what had occurred. Her parents granted her permission to donate skin for Casey, reminding her all this was her fault.

Jennifer, herself, seemed to have recovered fully from the mental torment she had undergone. She no longer heard voices and was completely cognizant of what she had done under the influence of some supernatural force. She told Rennin the voices left her when he threatened to have a priest exorcise her. She said the only voice that still haunted her was her mother's.

During his recovery time, Rennin and Harvey Zane put a plan into action. Rennin placed a call to retired Lt. Col. Clifton Spell, a former Delta Force commander and Troy Tomerson's sensei for eighteen years. Unable to believe his ears as he listened to the saga of Rennin O'Rourke, Cliff Spell took the next available flight to meet a challenge beyond anything he had ever encountered.

The first observation Spell made when he walked into the house on the banks of Beaver Creek was Rennin was out of shape. To the untrained eye, the man would have appeared in perfect physical condition, but Spell recognized the loss of reflex time and precision timing, no matter how minute. The basement of the house was instantly transformed into a dojo where Rennin trained once again under a master black belt and military commando officer. Renée asked if she could train as well and Rennin asked why. Spell retorted, "Why not? Are you afraid she'll kick your ass, boy?" Rennin rubbed his nose, remembering her back fist the previous Halloween.

Spell also trained Renée and d'Aubigné in basic self-defense techniques. He was most impressed with the spirit in the child and commented, "She definitely belongs to you, Rennin. It's like having Troy Tomerson in my dojo all over again. That child has the eye of the tiger and the heart of a dragon and something else that I sense. Just what it is, I don't know."

Rennin replied, "She never wants to be a victim again."

Spell argued, "That might be part of it, but it's something deeper, supernatural."

Shane's words and the old wives' tale popped to the front of Rennin's mind again, causing him to contemplate his daughter's abilities deeply.

The day came when Spell announced that Rennin's training needed to transfer locations. "I can't teach you what you need to learn here inside these walls, Rennin."

"Where are we going, Sensei?" asked Rennin. "What do I do about my family while we're away?"

"Your family will be fine, son. I've trained them well. Gerald has become a bulldog when it comes to their safety. Renée, my boy, could snap an intruder's neck in seconds. I won't even begin to tell you what your daughter's capable of. You wouldn't believe me if I did. She's the best student I've ever had, even better than you. We're headed to a place for you to get your head together and then, some aquatic and stealth training. The terrain in Haiti is a great deal different than here."

"How will Renée get in touch with us?"

"She won't for a while. If you're intent on taking on the Wilburn fellow and his goons, you have to trust me."

"What about the school and the team?"

"This is why you must leave here for a time. Your thoughts are too divided. Gerald can coach the boys without you for a while. You must concentrate on your goal."

Renée understood what was needed. She had found an inner strength and encouraged her husband to focus on the task at hand. "We'll be just fine. You must do what you must do." Renée O'Rourke made love to her husband once again and sent him away to an unknown destination and mission with only two other people, Clifton Spell and Harvey Zane who had also been training although he, too, had served in the military.

Cliff landed his small, private aircraft on a camouflaged runway in a quaint nomadic Tibetan tent village. A wizened, toothless, old Tibetan hobbled out leaning heavily on a cane to meet Clifton Spell. Spell bowed low in great reverence of the old man, as did Rennin and Zane by example. The old man then hugged Spell as a father would his long-lost son. The two jabbered for some time in a tongue neither Rennin nor Zane could comprehend. Spell turned to Rennin, "He says you're too old and stubborn to learn his ways, yet because I ask it, he will teach you. Master Xing Tzu, I give to you Rennin O'Rourke, who, until I met his daughter, was the brightest, most promising student I ever had."

"Why did you not bring the daughter?" asked the old master in perfect English.

"She doesn't have to accomplish a mission any time soon, and she's only five years old."

"The perfect age to learn," argued the old man. "But we will see what the man offers." Master Xing turned his attention to his new protégé. "Can you climb?"

"Sir?" Rennin responded with deference.

Master Xing pointed his cane toward a peak in the distance. "Can you climb?"

Rennin felt immediately daunted by the task because rock climbing with Jake had never been on the magnitude of a mountain in the Himalayas. He inclined his head in a bow, whispered a quiet prayer, and responded, "With your guidance, I will succeed."

"Ah," the old master's eyes widened. "He seeks strength beyond himself. There may be hope for you yet, my son. Come. Tonight, you must feast for tomorrow you fast and climb."

The feast was bountiful and the wine potent. As Rennin drifted off to sleep, a young woman came to him, apparently to be his companion for the night. She apparently did not speak a word of English for she seemed not to understand the man did not desire her. Rennin took her by the hand and led her out of the tent in which he was to sleep. Spell and Xing still stood around the open village fire, so Rennin brought the girl to them and bowed. "Master Xing, at the risk of offending you, I cannot accept the gift this woman offers."

The old man raised an eyebrow. "My granddaughter does not please you?"

"She's very beautiful, Master, but I have a wife. I choose not to betray the vows I made to her."

Xing babbled to Spell in his native tongue before he jabbered to the girl, who took her leave, and returned his attention to the young man he was to apprentice. "You have done well tonight. You have sought enlightenment from a Power greater than yourself, and you have resisted the most primal need of a man. The wine you consumed should have lowered your inhibitions enough to succumb to that need. Your heart is true. Cliff has found a prize, and if your daughter is better than you, I would covet the chance to teach her. Sleep now. No one else will disturb you."

In Pittsburgh, Casey healed rapidly under the watchful eye of Craig Jamison. Her face, neck, shoulders, and arms sported new tender skin, delicate as a baby's bottom, but perfect; both knew though there would always be some scarring, which made the doctor focus on the parts most visible. Craig optimistically suggested Casey go home between surgeries. He told her the next surgery would be extensive. "Casey," he said, "I've found a donor that can give you the rest of your skin at one sitting. A young woman that matches you perfectly was killed two days ago in an auto accident in Philadelphia. She was an organ donor. They're shipping her out here day after tomorrow. We have several patients here who will be receiving some of her organs. Let me take you home for those two days. Visit with your family before we come back for extensive grafting."

"What about germs, Craig?" Casey asked seriously, her voice sill raspier than it had been before her incident. "You said I need a sterile environment."

"You do, but you also need to have your spirits lifted. I've made arrangements for a sterile room at Renée's house. Everyone will have to wear sterile clothing to visit you, but they can have some time with you away from this place, which can become depressing. You've been a real trooper through all of this. I'll be frank with you. The last graft will be tricky. I'll be replacing intimate tissue with that of another woman. I've had patients have very poor reactions to that surgery purely on emotional bases. I want you to be your strongest emotionally when we do the surgery."

"I see," said Casey. "Craig, how do you see it?"

"What do you mean?" he asked in a quandary.

"You've grafted skin on me several times now. Is it my skin, or does it belong to the person who donated it? Am I now part Renée, part Jennifer, and part Casey?"

"That's silly. Your body accepted the grafts and began regenerating its own skin."

"Then, what's the difference with this graft? Is it the area you'll be grafting? Does it bother you that you're repairing me with parts from another woman?"

"Why would that bother me, Casey? I'm your doctor."

She smiled a truly radiant smile. "Craig, at what stage of denial are you? Dare I be frank with you?"

"You've lost me. Please explain what you mean," he responded, vexed he had allowed the conversation to take this turn.

"All right," she said, with her old fire coming to the surface. "How many patients call you by your first name? Craig, how many patients do you spend the night with after their grafts? How many do you take home? How many do you worry about replacing private parts on? Stop hem-hawing and be honest."

"Casey, I think…um…I should finish my rounds. Think about going home for a day or two. I'll check on you later."

"No!" said Casey as she pulled herself painfully to a sitting position. "Stop avoiding the question. Is it that you're worried about the surgery or *me* in particular? I need to know."

He kept his back to her as he said softly, "Casey, doctors aren't supposed to become emotionally involved with their patients."

"I see," she said, still asserting herself. "Is that the problem? Have you become emotionally involved with this patient? Look at me, Craig."

He turned slowly from the door and looked her in the eye. "No, Casey. It's far worse than being emotionally involved with you. I've fallen desperately in love with you. Is that what you want me to say?"

She relaxed. "Only if you mean it."

"What does that mean?"

"Do you mean it?"

He walked back to Casey's bedside and took her hand. He looked into her dark-brown eyes for what seemed an eternity before he spoke. "Casey, I have never felt for anyone what I feel for you. It scares me to death. I'm terrified if I go home, you'll be gone when I come back. The night you died, before I even knew you, something inside me died with you. I was empty. Suddenly, there you were again, and I felt filled to overflowing. Every day I spend with you is better than the last. Is that love, Casey? I can't think of anything else to call it. By the same token, I'm afraid if you know, you'll reject me. I'm not the world's most handsome man. I have a terrible temper. I'm impatient. But, God help me, I love you, Casey."

She closed her eyes to try and keep tears from escaping, to no avail. The little secret-tellers would have their way. Craig was distraught. "Casey, I'm sorry. I didn't mean to make you cry. Forgive me."

"For what?" She laughed nervously. "Forgive you for loving me? Not on your life. Don't you understand? I couldn't be happier. I was so afraid all you felt for me was *pity*. I have felt like Frankenstein's monster, and you're Victor himself. I don't want to disappoint you. I've always been a hellion and a troublemaker. Craig, I was pregnant before I turned sixteen after I seduced a drunken man and lied to him for five years. I haven't thought I was worthy to be loved by any descent, respectable man. Just say it again so I know I'm not imagining it."

He lifted her hand to his lips and gently kissed the new baby skin. "Casey McClarty, I love you."

She laughed and cried at the same time. "Dr. Jamison, I bet you say that to all your patients."

Craig found some boldness and tipped Casey's chin upward as he brushed his lips across hers and whispered, "Only if they're named Casey McClarty and say it back to me."

Casey slipped her arms around Craig's neck and cried softly on his shoulder. "I love you, Craig. Please don't let me wake up if this is a dream."

He smoothed Casey's hair that had been cut short for it to grow back. He kissed the top of her head and laid her back on her pillow. "It's not a dream. Nonetheless, I am *still* your doctor, and we have a decision to make. Do you want to go home for a couple of days while we prepare for, hopefully, your last surgery?"

"Will you be there or here?"

"I'll come home with you and get you situated. I'll stay the night and come back here to get everything ready. Then I'll come back and get you. What do you say?"

"I *would* like to see d'Aubigné. I miss her."

"Then, let's take you home. I'll call Renée."

"Is it all right for me to tell my sister that I'm in love with my doctor? Worse—that my doctor's in love with me?"

"I hope you do. I would feel that this isn't real if you keep it a secret."

"Well, what about you, Dr. Jamison? Are you going to keep it a secret?"

"Only until after your last surgery. I would kind of like to keep my job. It's kind of hard to support a family without a job."

"Support a family? Craig, was that a very awkward proposal?"

Craig blushed as red as his hair. "I promise I'll do better when it's an official proposal. Casey, I do have a question for you though. What about Jacques? What's the story there?"

"Jacques is my best friend. Even less than a year ago, I was still such a child that I wanted to shock my father by telling him I was engaged to a Haitian. I owe Jacques a great deal. He really helped me to understand myself and to start thinking like an adult. If he's still alive, he's a prisoner being held by some insane maniac and being tortured. When he came to Columbia to work on his Master's, he also tried to gain asylum. I want to help him come to this country to stay. We are not in love with each other. He would be overjoyed to know someone loves me. Jacques's the one person who consistently tried to convince me I was worthy to be loved. He will adore you."

"That's a load off my mind." Craig grinned. "I think I could be jealous of any man that looks at you."

"Why? He would just be admiring your handiwork. Just remember, I'm not a piece of marble, and I have imperfections."

Craig laughed. "Yes, there's this little mole…"

She squealed, "Craig! Oh my God! That mole survived, and you noticed it?"

He laughed louder as he kissed her hand again. "Don't worry. Pygmalion I am not. I plan to leave that mole right where it is."

Casey spent a couple of days with her family, and Craig asked Gerald for permission to officially date his daughter before he took her back to the hospital for one more complicated surgery.

In Tibet, Rennin awoke to a toothless old man staring at him. For a brief moment he forgot where he was. Then he groggily remembered the day before and stammered, "Good morning, Master Xing."

"Good morning, my son. Rise. You must be on your way."

Rennin washed his face in the icy water in the basin that Xing handed him. He was wide awake. He left his tent prepared to travel. Xing handed him climbing gear and said, "Come."

Rennin walked half a day with the old man without a word. Finally, he broke the silence, "Master Xing, how are you going to climb the mountain?"

Xing laughed. "You Americans. You must talk. I am not climbing a mountain. I did my climbing long ago. I am too old to climb mountains. *You* are climbing the mountain."

"Am I climbing alone?" Rennin asked.

"Yes, my son. This is what your Native Americans would call a vision quest. It is nothing more than a time to find yourself. You must empty yourself in order to be filled. And you must do it alone."

Xing said nothing else until they made camp at the base of the mountain. Rennin was starving and thirsty for they had not stopped all day. Xing offered nothing in the way of repast. It dawned on Rennin that when Xing had said he would fast, it was literal. He hardly slept that night for the rumblings in his stomach.

The next morning, Xing pointed up the mountain. "Do you see the spot that appears discolored?"

"Yes, Master Xing."

"That is where you are going. Once inside you will have all you need. Drink the beverage you will find there. Relax and meditate in the way that suits you best. In a while, you will be outside yourself. Do not fear. Follow your quest to the end. You will find a guide to take you on your way. I will be here when you return."

Rennin harnessed himself to begin his climb. "I think I already know what my guide will be."

"Your dragon?"

"How did you know?"

"I have heard your dragon's voice. He told me you would come. I thought it would be years ago. He may, indeed, be your guide. I cannot tell. I thought mine would be some majestic beast as well. I have never told anyone what mine was. It turned out to be a silver fox. Ah, but the cunning of a fox... Your Rennin of old, which Cliff told me about, what was his guide?"

Rennin smiled. "A butterfly, I suppose. At least, that's the creature that delivered a message to him from his wife. I guess the butterfly could have been Morgan's guide."

"Ah. Even the weakest of creatures can guide your heart. Now, go. I shall await your return."

Rennin had a million questions he wanted to ask but knew he would receive no answers from the old man. He nodded and pulled himself up the first boulder toward the unknown.

As night fell, Rennin was twenty feet below the cave in the mountainside. Climbing in the dark could be treacherous. Neither could he hang on the side of the mountain until daylight. He thought to himself, *oh, for the eyes of a tiger now.* He dozed against the stone and jumped awake. The moon rose in a luminous silver orb, bathing the entire mountainside in a glistening radiance.

Rennin looked skyward and said aloud, "Thank You." He climbed the last twenty feet and pulled himself into the relative safety of the cave. He leaned against the wall and breathed for a while.

After a brief rest he stared into the darkness and focused on what appeared to be a lantern. He felt it and beside it found a box of matches. He lit the lantern, which cast an ominous glow throughout the cave. A pit for a fire lay at the center of the cave. Since the air was nearly frigid, Rennin built a fire in the pit. As Master Xing had said, he had everything he needed to survive for a short time in the cave, except food. There was a flask of some sort of drink beside the lantern and the matches. Master Xing had said to drink and then, to relax and meditate. Rennin's experience with meditation had always resulted in sleep. Nonetheless, he did as he had been told. He took several draughts of the liquid in the flask to quench his thirst after two days without water. It had a sweet, pleasant taste. Then he tried several different positions in order to meditate and not fall asleep. Master Xing had said to do what worked best for him. Finally, he leaned his back against the cave wall and hugged his knees to his chest and started to think.

His first thought he asked himself if this was meditation. *Is this all meditation really is—relaxing and thinking?* Rennin's thoughts drifted to other things. Faces swam before his eyes. The first face he saw to his surprise was d'Aubigné's with her saucer-like eyes staring at him. Immediately followed Caitlin and Morgan and the blurred face of a blond-haired boy. Then, Renée floated past and changed from a little pixie to a magnificently arrayed queen with a golden scepter. Casey and Craig floated into his mind together. He vaguely thought, *That would be nice.* He saw the faces of Jennifer Polson and Bobby Willis and the handsome face of an unknown boy. Gerald, Zane, and Cliff Spell went by. Eva Tomerson graced him with her mother's smile.

For a while, all thoughts brought comfort and assurance. Then, bizarre and gruesome pictures came to mind. He saw Skyelar lying in a pool of blood and guts. He saw charred bodies all around him. He heard himself crying. He watched his aunt Corrine as a blade ripped across her throat. He witnessed Jacques chained and beaten to unconsciousness and himself shooting Constable Dubois. A red Ferrari exploded, and Jake's dismembered head raced toward him with flames trailing behind. He envisioned James Wilburn's laughing, taunting head in his face. Rennin shivered.

He realized the fire was almost out and threw on more wood from the pile conveniently stacked in the cave. He glanced out the cave entrance. The moon hung like a silver Christmas ornament high in the sky. Not knowing what he should do next, Rennin took another swig of the liquid in the flask. He sat back against the wall of the cave and stared at the flames and spoke aloud, "Smoke, aren't you going to talk to me?"

Rennin heard Smoke's distinct reply. "It's not my turn. You must do what you must do before I'll be free to come to you. Soon, you will be screaming in fury at me, for I, too, must do what I must do."

Rennin kicked at the dust. "Riddles!" he fumed. "Why must everything always be in riddles? Why can't things be clear? Why can't I see exactly what I need to do?"

A woman's voice replied, "Because you're not looking in the right direction. Look up, Rennin. Look up." He vaguely recalled his mother, Denise, on an Easter egg hunt telling him to look up. The voice sounded like hers.

Rennin walked to the opening of the cave and gazed at the crystal-clear night sky. He had never seen the stars shine so brightly. The constellations were easily distinguished in the mountain sky. Prominently blinking in glory was the constellation Leo.

Rennin breathed deeply of the crisp cold air and asked, "What was I supposed to gain from that?"

He turned back inside to see a golden lion with a walnut mane licking his paw. "Whoa," he whispered in awe. Rennin suddenly found himself running through the African plains taking down and devouring a gazelle. He was confronted by a would-be master with a whip. He released a mighty roar as he pounced upon the faceless fool and ripped into his throat. He padded proudly through his pride and sat regally whisking his tail to and fro. He watched as the herds paraded before him unharmed and safe under his watchful eye. He listened to the sounds of the jungle where he ruled in majesty and honor. He roared again and the sounds that came from the roar were, "Serviendo guberno."

Rennin awoke with a start. He lay again in the cave, but he was stark naked, and the fire was completely out. He could feel abrasions all over his body, and he had the taste of blood in his mouth. Words floated through his memory, "Do what you must do…no regrets…in ruling I serve…the Lion of the tribe of Judah…vengeance is justice in some cases…not human…pure evil…make him suffer…I promise…" The faceless fool suddenly had a face. It belonged to James Wilburn.

Rennin dressed himself and repelled down the mountainside. He felt clean. The emptiness was gone and replaced with a fullness of purpose.

39
Vengeance Is Justice

As he had promised, Xing Tzu waited at the foot of the mountain. A fire roared, offering comfort and warmth, and the wafting smell of food brought Rennin to reality. Xing indicated a spot on the spread blanket. "Sit. Finally, you have returned. Your journey was long and took you far. Now, it is time for nourishment. Eat. Restore your strength. Then, prepare for your destiny."

Rennin seemed confused as he ate as if he had never tasted food. Even in the face of no silverware, the young man picked the pieces of meat up with his fingers and sopped the gravy-like substance with the tough bread the old man gave to him. "Master Xing, how long was I away?"

"A week."

"I've been gone an entire week?"

"Do not be amazed. During your quest, you have no concept of time. I can tell by your appearance you battled great demons. I would venture to say your greatest fear has been if you can consciously kill your enemy."

"I've already taken a life, Master Xing."

"Yes, but it was not a conscious act. It was instinct. You did what any good father would have done to protect those he loves."

"How do you know this?"

"Your dragon, Smoke, I believe he is called, spoke to me while you were away."

Rennin stretched his eyes wide, and his mouth fell open.

The old man laughed. "Do not be so amazed. You have been asking yourself if you can seek vengeance and keep your own soul intact. You have also been justifying your decision by assuming the creature you seek is inhuman."

"You didn't see what I saw, Master. That thing wasn't human."

"Yes, he was, Rennin. He was a human who has allowed himself to be corrupted by greed and hatred. What you saw was his inner being, something twisted and grotesque. Nonetheless, James Wilburn is a man, just as Quazel was a woman whose soul had become evil and ugly."

"You don't believe in the spirit world, Master?"

"I believe very much in the spirit world." The master sopped bread across the tin plate he used and ate the soaked food before he continued. "Yes, the spirits of greed and hatred have consumed James Wilburn. His soul is black as night. Yet, it is his soul. The spirits of evil will always plague mankind until the world is made new. Your task is to free the soul of a man you hate. Are you up to that task? What did you see in your quest?"

"I was a lion. I relished the kill, but only in the face of survival. When all was well, I ruled as the king of beasts, and those that would be prey were safe under my hand. I was a lion being threatened by a man who turned into James Wilburn. I tore out his throat without hesitation or regret. Does that mean that I'm as ruthless as James? Am I seeking vengeance or justice?" He held out his plate for more, and the old master spooned another helping of the mutton and mush he had prepared onto the plate.

"That is a philosophical debate, my son." Xing licked his fingers clean. "Justice is the prescribed punishment mandated by governments and laws for specific crimes. Vengeance is personal. It is retribution for some offense. In many cases, justice will never be meted out until the afterlife. In those cases, it is arguable that vengeance and justice are the same. What are the chances James Wilburn will ever be tried and convicted for the offenses he has perpetrated?"

"None," said Rennin sorrowfully.

"What are the probabilities he will continue to terrorize your family?"

The lion reared its protective head. "I will not allow that to happen."

The gnarled hand patted the young man's shoulder. "You have solved your own riddle. You must do what you must do without hesitation or regret."

Rennin gasped, "That is exactly what both Casey and Smoke said to me."

Xing smiled. "Listen to their wisdom." He stood and hobbled to his bed roll. "Now, rest."

The next morning Rennin and Xing started the trek back to the hamlet hidden in the mountains. Once again, there was no conversation. From out of nowhere, appeared a half dozen masked bandits, apparently bent on thievery. Xing and Rennin stood back to back and the old man remarked, "I am not as agile as I once was, my son."

Contrary to popular movie misconceptions, the bandits did not graciously attack one at a time, but as a vicious pack. Rennin could hear the old master using his cane like a bo. The only weapon Rennin had was a mountain climbing pack. He found that ropes with belay hooks attached made formidable weapons when swung with force. A rasping sound behind him told Rennin that Master Xing was in trouble. He forcefully pulled the would-be assassin off the old man and spun him around with his hand poised for a palm heel blow. The face that greeted Rennin was none other than James Wilburn.

A split second's hesitation had Rennin pinned beneath a force that must have been superhuman. Reaching inside for his strength, Rennin kicked his attacker off. One-on-one, hand-to-hand combat ensued. The struggle lasted for several minutes until Rennin pinned his foe around the neck to a tree using his right hand with his left hand poised to strike with a move that could have and would have torn the man's heart from his chest.

Master Xing's voice resounded with authority. "Rennin, stop."

Rennin looked again at their assailant, who was not at all James Wilburn, but one of Xing's own villagers. The other five men knelt in deference to the old man. Rennin loosened his grip on the man he held, who in turn knelt with his cohorts.

Xing spoke in his native tongue to the men, and they left him and Rennin alone. Xing commented as if the incident were an everyday occurrence. "You have the skill and the will to defeat your opponent. You have done well."

Rennin stammered, "Was that a...a test?"

"Of sorts," responded Xing.

"What if I had not heeded your voice?" asked Rennin.

"Then, I would have killed you," replied Xing displaying the dagger that he pulled from the top of his cane. "Or at least disabled you."

"How did I see Wilburn?"

"The hallucinogen I put in your food."

"You drugged me?"

"I did. I coated the bottom of your plate. You would have fought valiantly to defend an old man, but you would not have killed any but your enemy. Your heart is good, Rennin. You are not an evil man. However, you do have the will to eliminate your enemy. This you must do. It is, I believe, justice."

"Master Xing, what about the drug?"

"Not to worry. It only made you susceptible to my suggestion. It will have worn off by the time we arrive at the village. And I promise not to play any more tricks on you. So, if we are attacked again, I am a frail old man."

"Not so frail as you would have me believe," countered Rennin.

Xing laughed. "True. I told you my guide was a silver fox, a most cunning and brutal animal."

Xing and Rennin made camp for the night. Rennin hesitated to eat. Xing laughed again. "It is not drugged tonight. You have my word. You may relax."

Reclined against a tree, Xing, for the first time, chatted amiably with the younger man who accompanied him. "Tell me about your family. You have more than one child, yes?"

Rennin relaxed as he thought about how outnumbered he was. "Yes, I have three daughters. I'm not married to d'Aubigné's mother, Casey. My firstborn was an unexpected result of heavy alcohol consumption, but I love her, and I'd be lost without her. Renée, my wife, and I have twins, Caitlin and Morgan. They're babies, but from what I can tell so far, they look just like their mother, blonde-haired, blue-eyed pixies. What about you, Master Xing? Do you have family?"

"Yes. Living here hidden away, we get away from following the letter of Chinese rule. The authorities would have a difficult time finding us, and if we were bothered here, the bodies of those who came for us would never be discovered. And if I truly needed the help, Cliff would smuggle the whole village into America. I know too much about his nonexistent missions. Yes, Rennin, I have family. My wife has passed on, but she gave me two sons and one daughter. You met my granddaughter already."

"Yes, my first test. What if I had succumbed to the wine?"

Xing grinned a toothless grin. "Our tribal customs are polygamous. You would have a Tibetan wife."

Rennin choked on the bite he had in his mouth. After a fit of coughing he said honestly, "Renée would not have liked that."

Xing asked, "Your Renée, does she accept your child by the other woman? How does she feel about that woman?"

"That's a little complicated. Yes, she accepts d'Aubigné. Casey? That took some Divine Intervention. You see, Casey is Renée's younger sister."

"Hmm," grunted Xing. "But you never married Casey. What is your relationship with her now?"

"I suppose we're friends. We understand each other, as do Renée and Casey."

"You consider her family, a sister?"

"I suppose. I want only good things for Casey. I just am not the man for her."

"It is good you did not establish a relationship here with my granddaughter. You are a good man, but it would not have been a good match. Your heart belongs only to one, as mine did. I chose not to have multiple wives. Cliff, too, chose only one wife, my daughter."

"Why doesn't he bring her to America?"

"She died in childbirth—the granddaughter you met—Ming. I have a favor to ask of you, Rennin."

"How may I serve you, Master Xing?"

"Convince Cliff to take Ming back with him. As long as I live, the village is safe from government interference, but I am an old man. When I pass, the village will scatter. There will be no unity, for the men will not follow Ming's wisdom, though she is wise. She would be better off in America with her father. I am afraid Ming has very rebellious thoughts and would fall under Chinese injustice eventually. It is most likely the result of her American education."

"Then, she speaks English and pretended not to know what I was saying to her?"

"Yes, she did as I asked her to do, but she does not think I am right about our marriage rituals, and she is an American citizen already—her father is, after all, an American war hero. Will you convince Cliff it is time for her to be an American completely?"

"I'll speak to him, Master."

"You will succeed. You have a gift."

"To sway the mind?"

"You have heard that before?"

"Yes, sir."

"You can sway the weak-minded easily, but you have the gift of logic. You can present practical arguments. I have faith Cliff will do what you ask of him, but Cliff is not weak minded. Now, we should sleep. I confess—I am tired."

While Rennin faced demons in the mountains of Tibet, Craig Jamison battled another foe in Pittsburgh. During a tedious twelve-hour procedure, Craig painstakingly grafted skin from a tragically deceased young mother of two onto the disfigured breasts, abdomen, thighs, and pelvic area of Casey McClarty. Every stitch, every drop of surgical glue, he applied meticulously with love.

Angie Reid, Craig's longtime nurse, noticed the deep, dark circles beneath the young surgeon's eyes as he moved one chair into Casey's sterile recovery room. She tapped him on the shoulder as he collapsed into that chair. "Dr. Jamison, you need to go home and rest."

He shook his head. "I can't."

Less formally, Angie said, "Craig, you're not God. You need to give this one over to Him. Let the Great Physician heal her. You weren't supposed to fall in love with her."

Craig patted his friend's hand. "I couldn't help it. I've never known anyone like her. I suppose even I had to fall into the snare sooner or later. How many blind dates have you arranged for me?"

"None of them were twelve years younger than you or a patient."

Dreamily Craig yawned, "None of them were Casey."

Angie squeezed Craig's shoulder. "I just hope this is not heartache waiting to happen. I'll admit that I like her, too. There's something special about her. Good night, Craig."

Craig drifted into a restless sleep with thoughts of holding Casey McClarty in his arms and making love to the perfect woman who lay beneath new skin and old scars.

In the early morning hours before dawn, Casey called Craig's name, and he sprang to his feet. "Craig!" Casey's hysterical voice called out to him.

He clasped the hand that reached out for him. "Craig, I'm freezing."

Craig touched Casey's face. "No! No! No!" he muttered angrily as he measured an amount of strong antibiotic and anti-rejection formula and injected it into the I.V. in Casey's arm. He took Casey's hand again. "It's gonna be all right, baby. I promise you."

Through chattering teeth, she asked, "Craig, what's wrong?"

"You have a fever. You must have an infection. I need to draw some blood."

"Am I rejecting the graft, Craig?"

"I don't know yet," he replied wearily.

Craig rushed the lab work on Casey's blood and began an aggressive treatment to keep her body from rejecting the skin graft. Still, Casey's fever climbed. Craig called Casey's family, who arrived within an hour. He also called an older colleague who had performed extensive grafts before. Dr. Simeon Rosenthal showed up and took control. Both doctors met with Casey's family.

Craig began an explanation and Renée stopped him. "Craig, shut up. It's time for you to let another doctor handle Casey's case. You're too close. You look like hell. If you continue like this, you'll be useless to Casey, and if it progresses badly, you'll blame yourself."

"She's right," agreed Dr. Rosenthal. "Craig, you're obviously in love with this woman. You should've called me sooner. Let me take over."

Craig nodded and walked away into the surgeons' lounge. Renée wanted to go after him, but Rosenthal advised her to let Craig be alone for a while. Meanwhile, Rosenthal ran more tests and reported back. At that point Casey was, indeed, rejecting the graft although the donor had been the closest match of any transplant she had received. "If she rejects this graft, it could be forever before we get that much tissue from one donor again. The best bet she has for continued donations is from a d'Aubigné O'Rourke. Is she available to donate?"

"No," said Renée decisively. She pointed to the little dark-haired angel that slept in the waiting room chair. "That's d'Aubigné, Dr. Rosenthal. She's Casey's daughter."

"Good, Lord!" exclaimed Rosenthal. "Casey's barely more than a child herself. Mrs. O'Rourke, both you and Jennifer Polson have already donated."

"You don't have to ask, Dr. Rosenthal. Of course, I'll give more to my sister, but is there anything to stop the rejection? Casey has been through hell for almost a year. Christmas is next week. Please tell us there's something."

Rosenthal nodded thoughtfully. "There is a new drug going through clinical trials. We've used it sparingly in extreme cases. It's still experimental, and the family must consent and release us from any recourse. Mr. McClarty, you're Casey's father. You'll have to sign some papers for us to try it."

Though still protective, Gerald McClarty had become an old man in the last two years. He looked worn and thin. Not having lost confidence in the young doctor who loved his daughter, Gerald asked, "What does Craig think about it?"

Acknowledging Craig was a huge part of this family now, Rosenthal said, "I'll ask him."

In the surgeon's quarters, Craig Jamison battled some demons even as Rennin did in the cave. Although he had witnessed Casey's miracle, he had not let go of his unbelief. He stared at his reflection in the mirror as Angie's words came back to him, "Craig, you're not God."

Craig spoke to the man in the mirror. "Of all the surgeries I've performed, why must this be my failure? Why this one? Why Casey?" He clutched the sides of the sink and sobbed, finally reaching for something outside himself. "Oh, God, I don't think

I've ever talked to You. I have tried to believe You don't even exist. Forgive me. Please, please, take care of Casey. I can't do anything else for her. I-I-I give her to You." As he looked into the mirror again, he could have sworn his reflection talked to him. "No, you're not God, Jamison." In his frustration, Craig punched the mirror, sending shards all over the floor and into his hand.

"You young fool!" snapped Rosenthal as he entered the rest area and grabbed Craig's hand. "I don't have time to worry about you," he grumbled as he picked glass from Craig's hand and washed it in the sink. Rosenthal gruffly poured iodine all over Craig's hand, and Craig hollered. "Oh, shut up!" snapped Rosenthal. "You did it to yourself. You'll live. Your hand will hurt for a few days, and you won't do surgery for a couple of weeks, but you'll live. I think you need to take a few weeks off anyway. Get your head together. As for Casey, you *can* do something for her. I want to use the new drug—make Casey a part of the case studies. Her father won't consent unless you approve. Craig, it's her best shot." Rosenthal bandaged Craig's hand. "Well, what will you say to Gerald McClarty?"

Craig relented, "I'll tell him to do it. It had better work, Simeon."

"Come on, Craig. It's time for you to be part of the family and let me be the doctor. She must be something to have captured your heart. I was beginning to think the day would never come."

"She's amazing," said Craig as they walked out to Casey's family.

Renée took one look at Craig's bandaged hand. "Oh, yeah," she said sarcastically. "There's definitely O'Rourke blood in your veins."

Craig turned to Gerald. "Gerald, sign the consent forms. Right now, it's Casey's best shot."

Gerald signed the forms, and the wait began. Renée forced Craig into a chair between her and Gerald. Some eighteen hours later, Simeon Rosenthal breathed a sigh of relief. He optimistically announced that Casey's temperature was normal. "Who gets the first five-minute visit?"

Nobody responded for fear of upsetting another. A haughty, "Humph!" jerked three adults to their senses, and all eyes turned to a little girl with her arms akimbo. "Am I the only one around here that has a clue? If Craig doesn't go in first, he'll have a stroke. He's as bad as my daddy. He can't live without my mommy just like Daddy can't live without Aunt Renée. Come on people!" She stomped her foot. "Move! I want to see my mommy sometime today."

Walking backward into a sterile robe and mask Craig pointed at d'Aubigné. "That, Simeon, is just a little piece of Casey."

Gerald chuckled. "Oh, no. That's Casey's poetic justice."

Rennin yawned widely. He opened his eyes and was surprised the sun was so high in the sky and Xing had not urged him to be on their way. He stretched and yawned again. Xing appeared to be sleeping soundly. Rennin amused himself with the thought of rousting the old master to get a move on. He stretched and yawned again before he strode to Xing Tzu and gently shook him. "Master, we should be going. It's time to wake up. Master Xing?" The realization the old master had passed to the next world in his sleep struck like a red wasp lying in wait. Rennin wrapped him tightly in the blanket which covered him and draped the surprisingly light weight over his shoulders. He walked into the village bearing its dead patriarch.

Rennin could see instantly Xing had been right. The villagers prepared to send the old soul on its way and then to move out quickly. They, indeed, feared the Chinese government now that Xing Tzu was dead.

Cliff Spell also prepared to leave. Rennin detained him. "Sensei, would you call me a man of honor?"

"Of course, I would."

"Would a man of honor grant the last request of a dying friend?"

"No doubt. What are you trying to say?"

"Master Xing made a request of me last night before we slept. I feel honor-bound to abide by it."

"Naturally. What is it?"

"He wanted you to take Ming to America with you. She is your daughter, after all."

"Xing told you?"

"You seem surprised, Sensei."

"I am. When she was born, we thought it best the government not know she was the daughter of a black-ops officer."

"Does she know?"

"Yes. I've visited her often over the years, and she was educated in America. Xing wants her out of the country. She must be a rabble-rouser."

"It would appear so."

Spell rubbed his stubbly beard. "I had wanted to go to our next training stop. You have to have some aquatic and stealth training before you go into Wilburn's camp. We'll need to make a slight detour. Do you mind seeing your family for a few days? Do you think Renée can handle another troublemaker?"

Rennin shook his head. "I'm dying to hold my wife and hug my girls. I don't think Ming will be much of a troublemaker in America. She does speak English."

"Fluently."

"Do you have papers for her?"

"I do. She is, after all, an American citizen already. She has a passport."

"I think she'll be much more than that for me. I don't think Renée will have to worry about her at all. Sensei, I never asked how you got us into Tibet without clearance. How are you gonna get us out?"

Spell smirked. "Some secrets I will have to take to my grave, like where her two uncles are. Trust me, my boy."

Spell approached Ming who was sullenly packing her belongings and spoke with her. From the reaction he witnessed and the snippet of conversation he heard, Rennin assumed she was pleased with the arrangement. Ming flung her arms around Spell's neck and cried gleefully, "Oh, Papa!"

Spell's Lincoln Town Car meandered up the driveway to the house on the banks of Beaver Creek and encountered a house ablaze with lights and sounds. A soft snow fell as the passengers alighted. There were a couple of cars Rennin didn't recognize in the driveway, a light-blue Porsche and a small, older Toyota pickup. Rennin closed his eyes and listened to the joyful noises coming from inside his home. His eyes popped open as he exclaimed, "Good grief! It's Christmas Eve. I haven't bought a single gift."

Zane clapped him on his shoulder. "Never fear. Your pal here took care of everything. I just hope I read you well enough. However, I think your presence might be all that's required tonight. Shall we spring a surprise on the unsuspecting? Besides, I need to at least call my boys for Christmas. It's obvious I won't make it back to Puma Pass."

Ming hesitated. Rennin assured her, "Ming, you are a welcome guest in my home."

As Rennin opened the door to his house, he didn't recognize it. The normally organized-for-the-holidays was in disarray as the family was just trimming the tree, and it was apparent Renée's eggnog was being well consumed. Rennin listened attentively for the voices. It was well past eight, yet he heard d'Aubigné's squeals of laughter. Gerald sounded exuberant, and Renée giggled with intoxication. He heard other voices. *Yes, it's Casey, and is that Craig Jamison?* He also heard the sometimes still cracking voice of Bobby Willis and the subdued voice of Jennifer Polson, as if she felt out of place.

Rennin walked into the boisterous living room unnoticed as Renée, Gerald, and Bobby, hung ornaments on the tree, and the "baby" Satin that had turned into a mini panther batted the ones on the lower branches. D'Aubigné crawled around the floor with her two little sisters. Jennifer sat quietly on the sofa, and Craig dangled mistletoe above Casey's head just to have an excuse to kiss her, which he did soundly to Rennin's amazement. Finally, d'Aubigné bounced onto the sofa and screamed over all the chaos, "Daddy!" In two seconds, she was in her father's arms. She was closely followed by a blonde pixie.

Rennin whispered to Renée, "Do we have enough room and food for a few more guests?"

Renée welcomed her company graciously. Rennin introduced Ming all around. The others had at least met before. Rennin held Caitlin and Morgan and marveled at their growth. Another hour of merrymaking and Renée scooted d'Aubigné off to her bath and put two other little joys to bed as Bobby and Jennifer wished everyone a Merry Christmas and took their leave.

Rennin knelt by Casey. "You look great. Is there something you'd like to tell me?"

"Like what?" Casey teased as Craig sat on the arm of the chair where he had ensconced her.

"Like, since when do doctors plant lip locks on their patients? I witnessed that little pretend-the-mistletoe-is-over-your-head incident."

Craig said jauntily, "I've resigned as Casey's doctor. I'd rather be her lover and her husband, but we haven't made that official yet. Do we have your approval?"

"I'm not her father," laughed Rennin. "But are you sure about this, Craig? I swear as God is my witness—she is a pain in the ass."

"I know," said Craig with a wink. "She has already made me punch a mirror and swear vengeance on her behalf. Do you need a partner, long-lost cousin?"

Rennin caressed Casey's cheek and glanced at the three people he had brought home with him. "I already have three partners in crime. They're well-trained in combat and fighting techniques. You're a doctor. You took an oath to do no harm. Craig, I plan to do a great deal of harm. James Wilburn is a dead man. I can't ask you to be a party to that. I *can* ask you to be the guard on the home front. Take care of my family, all of them. But that will be another day. It's Christmas, and I plan to celebrate the birth of our Savior. I say that with renewed assurance. And, Craig, Casey, you have more than my approval. You had better ask me to be your best man."

Rennin suddenly felt himself being pulled. "Daddy, tuck me in. Hurry so Santa Claus can come."

When all was settled, Rennin tiptoed behind Renée and held the mischievous mistletoe over her head. "You don't need mistletoe." She smiled as she kissed her husband hungrily.

40
Necessary Preparation

Christmas morning bustled with activity. Caitlin and Morgan squealed in delight at the sounds and sights and smells and surprises that greeted them when they touched the right buttons on the toys Santa had brought them while d'Aubigné chomped at the bit to try out her ice skates and changed into her warm-ups and chandelier earrings. The combination brought tears of laughter to all the adults in her life. D'Aubigné finally conceded ice-skating on Christmas Day when the ponds were not frozen enough, and the ice rink was closed, in lieu of using her new paints and canvases. However, she refused to change her fashion statement of the day. Nonetheless, her father was destined to take her ice skating the day after Christmas and spent more time on his butt than on his feet. Rennin swore Renée and Casey conspired to give d'Aubigné ice skates just to humiliate him.

Zane had read his friend well and bought especially appropriated gifts. For Casey there was a jade lotus incense burner with a matching holder and an assortment of natural incense. For Gerald, Zane had chosen a gold-and-silver-on copper kapala. Craig had a jade-and-copper Medicine Buddha. For Jennifer, Zane had found an amethyst mala, and for Bobby, there was an antique Tibetan sword. The teenagers had taken their gifts home the night before. D'Aubigné received a white gold dragonfly pendant set with rubies; and for the twins, Zane had chosen sweaters of the finest Tibetan wool. Just for fun, Zane had thrown in a dragon door handle and an exquisite filigree dragon for Renée, but Renée's real gift turned out to be a full-length silver-fox coat. Not knowing what Zane had purchased on his behalf, Rennin had the strangest feeling Master Xing somehow resided somewhere within the folds of Renée's coat. He would never voice that thought because only to Rennin had Master Xing ever revealed what guided him during his quest.

The week between Christmas and the New Year sped by, and Caitlin and Morgan celebrated their first birthday. Having missed the birth of his daughters, Rennin basked in the experience of being covered in cake frosting. Reluctantly, the day came for his departure with Cliff Spell. However, added to the mercenary group of O'Rourke, Spell, and Zane was another Spell. Ming's agility and stealth ability rivaled her father's, and she would not be left behind in a place where she knew no one.

Once again, Rennin bade his family good-bye in an endeavor to ensure their safety. After driving back to Miami, the small company of warriors sailed into the Atlantic in Cliff 's world-class sailboat. After several weeks at sea, they dropped anchor off the coast of a small, lush, tropical island. Rennin asked Spell, "Where are we?"

Spell answered candidly, "We are nowhere. This place does not exist. Do you see it on any of the maps?"

Careful perusal of the nautical maps showed no sign of the island. Rennin acknowledged, "Okay, Sensei, the island is uncharted, but how do you hide an island?"

"Spells and enchantments," laughed Cliff.

Rennin gave his teacher a look that said, "Be real."

Spell said seriously, "If any of you get on to that island without dying, you'll understand. And when we leave, if you ever tell anyone where it is, you'll be dead."

It didn't take long for the other three members of Spell's crew to understand what he had meant by getting to the island alive. A large ship could not sail in the shallow waters, and a life raft ran amok in an electrically charged mine field. Rennin, Zane, and Ming found themselves burned and singed on repeated failed attempts.

Rennin suggested to the other two that they dive—use the scuba gear aboard ship to swim under the minefield. Spell watched as they geared up for the attempt and tossed each one a canister. "What's this?" asked Rennin.

"You'll see," Spell answered mysteriously.

Five minutes in the water found three scuba divers back aboard the sailboat. It was not Rennin who flew into a rage as they re-boarded the boat, but Ming, "Papa! The water is infested with sharks!"

Rennin assisted her. "And if the sharks don't get us, the damned jellyfish will."

"I gave you shark repellant," stated Spell as if it were obvious.

Rennin stayed awake that night racking his brain. Near dawn, the ship's sonar pinged loudly enough to alert him that something large was on the side of the ship away from the shore. He watched contemplatively as a school of dolphins danced across the ocean. "Smart creatures," he said to himself. "Stay over there, or you will singe your hide. You already know that though. That's why you're so far away. The sharks would disperse if you came closer. If we could push them and the jellyfish away, we could swim beneath the charges." He shouted to the school of sleek silvery mammals, "I'm naming one of you Danielle. Thank you!"

For the rest of the day, Rennin disappeared below deck. Spell called to him, "Are you ill?"

"No!"

"What are you doing?"

"Using my gift."

"What?"

"Don't worry about it, Sensei. I'm doing what I must do."

Rennin went to bed early that evening. After Spell and the others had gone to sleep, he donned scuba gear, gathered an underwater flashlight and a few provisions in a waterproof pouch, and flipped the switch on the sonar. "This had better work," he muttered. He slipped quietly into the water and plunged beneath the surface with the light in front of him.

To Rennin's satisfaction, the path before him was clear of both sharks and jellyfish. He swam ahead. Shining the light above him, he could see the thin electrical netting glistening as it skimmed the water just inches below the surface. He pulled himself onto the beach. Inwardly, he gloated that his marine biology classes had paid off, and he had used his gift of logic to circumvent nature—or at least, his Sensei.

Rennin considered briefly searching for the generator that must control the electrical netting, but his logic warned him to wait for daylight. He figured if there was a generator, there had to be at least one person making sure it kept running, and there were probably obstacles and barriers inland. He stretched out on the sand and slept.

As the sun warmed the earth, Rennin awoke. He sat on the beach and ate the fruit and cereal bars he had dropped in the pouch the night before and waited for those aboard the boat to realize he was missing. It did not take long for Spell to note that his star pupil had disappeared. He scanned the beach from which Rennin waved triumphantly. "What the devil did he do?" Spell asked aloud.

Spell noted the wetsuit, so Rennin had obviously swum ashore. He hollered, "Ming, suit up. See if our little aquatic friends are down there."

"Papa?"

"If you don't trust me, trust him." He pointed to the shore. "The little shit did something. He made it to shore."

Ming, seeing the sharks and jellyfish had disbursed, decided to join Rennin on the beach.

Spell snapped at Zane, "Aren't you going?"

Zane shook his head. "I don't trust you. I'm waiting for something to come out of the jungle and carry them away."

Spell grinned. "So is Rennin. That's why he didn't venture further in. He's still a kid at heart. He wanted to gloat that he passed my first test."

Zane said truthfully, "Maybe he still craves that fatherly approval. That's why he was such a great quarterback—he always wanted McClarty's approval."

Spell scrutinized Zane. "You're worried about him."

"You bet."

"Me, too. Troy was a great kid—easy to love. I don't care that he has a new name. I'm here to make sure he stays alive. There's not a truly mean bone in the man's body although he can display a killer instinct. I'm worried that he won't be able to kill James Wilburn."

Zane said, "That's not what I worry about. I have no doubt he'll kill that scum. I'm worried about what he'll do afterward. I worry about how it'll change him."

Spell clapped Zane on the shoulder. "That's why he has us around—to watch his back in more ways than one. Suit up. I'm dying to know what he did."

Zane and Spell came ashore with no provisions except bottled water, one of which Zane tossed Rennin. Spell demanded, "What did you do?"

After several swigs, Rennin said cryptically, "The dolphins told me what to do. I just listened."

"All right, smartass!" snapped Spell. "So, now you're Dr. Doolittle? What did you do?"

Rennin gloried in the fact that he had outwitted the master. "I reprogrammed your sonar. It no longer picks up incoming movement. It sends out sound waves that annoy the sharks and jellyfish. They moved on to other parts for their own comfort. Step one is complete." He flicked his thumb over his shoulder. "God only knows what you have in store for us in there."

Spell grunted, "Well, now that you can get ashore, you have to decide what to do next. You didn't come prepared. So, I guess you have to go back to the boat and make some decisions."

Rennin asked, "Are you gonna undo my handiwork and bring the sharks back?"

"Nope. You solved that problem fair and square. But the next time you solve step one, you should have some tentative plan about step two to preclude all the swimming back and forth."

"I had to be sure the reprogrammed sonar worked."

"You've had all night to know it worked. By now, the three of you should be somewhere in the heart of the island. You wasted valuable time to gloat and receive praise. Rennin, this isn't karate class where I give you a pat on the back for a job well done or a football field where you win a nice ring. These exercises are designed to help you get into Wilburn's compound. There will be no one there waiting to give you a reward. Ming, I'm disappointed you swam ashore without supplying yourself. You should've known better. And Zane, even after saying you didn't trust me, you did nothing but bring water to the two waifs. Now, get your asses back to the boat and think about what to do next."

Sufficiently chastised, Rennin, Ming, and Zane met in Rennin's quarters to discuss their next move. Rennin spoke quietly, "All right. I think we can safely surmise that this is a special-forces training area Cliff still has some connection with. Frankly, I'm not sure he's retired. To be able to get here, he has some strings to pull somewhere. We'll be facing thinking humans now. There must be some sort of compound in there where the electrical netting is controlled. We have to secure that compound."

He gazed out the porthole. "Somehow, I don't think Cliff would let any of us actually get killed out here, unless he would like Renée to slit his throat or poison his tea." Rennin made eye contact with the other two. "Yes, I think she could do it, too. Nonetheless, he's not above having some real hurt put on us. This is where he wants us to learn stealth. We can't just go barging through the jungle. And, seeing as how Wilburn's compound isn't in a jungle, I think our foliage on the island is just thick enough to form a barrier to hide the compound. He has wanted to make it as closely simulated as possible.

"So, what do we need to take with us on shore besides some water and fruit and cereal bars? What are your thoughts?"

Ming said, "Camouflage and weapons, but no guns without silencers. We need stealth weapons. And if Papa isn't equipped with real guns and bullets, maybe Rennin's correct about not letting us die."

"Master Xing was not willing to let his pupils die when we were together. I can't believe Cliff would be different."

"Rennin, Papa is a trained assassin. That's what he does. True, he has done extraction missions, but his forté is quiet death. You didn't know, did you?"

Rennin shook his head as Ming continued, "He's teaching you to kill quietly and without detection. Your primary goal is to kill James Wilburn. You'll have to eliminate others before you get to him. Yes, you hope your friend, Jacques, is still alive, and you want to rescue him, but that's a secondary goal, probably one you should leave to me. That's my forté, rescue. I have rescued a number of political prisoners, among them my uncles, but that doesn't mean I can't or won't eliminate any sentries or guards that stand in my way."

Rennin said, "Zane?"

Zane said, "I guess my forté is gathering information, but I do it with parabolic microphones and telephoto lenses. I have no idea what I'll be good for here except to have your back. I *am* an excellent marksman. Give me my nine-millimeter."

Ming said, "How are you with a sniper rifle?"

"I can do that. It's what I did in Desert Storm," replied Zane.

Ming suggested, "Then, let's see what my father has aboard this barge."

The three headed to the supply hold. Spell asked as they trooped by, "What are you doing now?"

"Supplies," said Rennin.

"Really?" quipped Spell as he started to follow his charges.

Rennin held up his hand. "No, Sensei. If we succeed or fail, let us do it without your scowls or grunts, which could mean anything. You can see what we've taken after we leave and worry and fret without our knowing."

The supply hold contained a myriad of weaponry. All the guns, however, were supplied with tranquilizer darts, not bullets. Ming commented, "Well, at least we really don't have to worry about dying here. When we get to Haiti, the guns and bullets will be real." She tried a different locker with a combination. Biting her lip, she said, "They're in there." Ming examined the darts. "Sleeping compound. Anyone we hit with these will be out for hours. You can bet they're supplied likewise."

They outfitted Zane with an easily assembled, lightweight sniper rifle with ammunition and the equivalent to a nine-millimeter with three fifteen-round clips.

Ming chose two nine-millimeter approximations with several clips, a variety of shurikens, a couple of sets of neko, and a kama set. She thrust a set of neko at Zane. To his unasked question, she replied, "For scaling walls." She looked at Rennin. "You take a set, too."

Rennin took a set of neko, a whip, and a garrote. He examined various guns and remarked, "They're so impersonal. James is very personal."

Ming took Rennin's hands in hers. "For James, all you'll need are these; however, getting to James can't be so personal. You must be practical. The garrote is excellent for Haiti, not here. Take a nine-millimeter with clips and kamas. Please, don't kill these men who are apparently working with my father. I don't think he wishes for any of them to die either. But he is looking to see what you choose for your real enemy. Put your deadly weapons on the table, so he knows you considered them."

Ming handed each man binoculars, a measure of rope, a harness with climbing and belay equipment, and a grappling gun. "Trust me," she assured them. "I think we may be traveling above the ground as much as possible. The ground will be strewn with traps."

They examined the various items of camouflage. "What color do we take?" asked Zane.

Their choices included classic black spandex, tawny and black, and a gray mixture for urban assault. "Take one of each," said Rennin. "They're very light and take up very little space. We can change as needed."

They decided to pack only energy bars and water until Ming opened a bottle of capsules. "Ah," she mused. "Take several of these. They're the antidote to the sleeping compound. If you're hit, you will have about thirty seconds to bite into one of these. It'll counter the sleeping compound."

Ming turned toward Rennin. "Do you feel I'm assuming too much control?"

"No," said Rennin. "You know more about this than I do."

"Then, may I suggest that we go in at first light? Papa expects you to go in by cover of darkness. And we should approach so that they must look east into the rising sun."

The three conspirators ate dinner and went to bed without answering any of Spell's questions, which aggravated him. As they slept, he took inventory of what was missing from the stores with some measure of approval. He picked up the garrote and chuckled.

Before dawn, Spell heard the minutest splash as Rennin, Ming, and Zane headed to the shore. He awoke and watched through binoculars as the three appeared on shore and stowed their wet suits in lieu of, for the time being, the tawny and black camouflage of a tiger. What surprised him was Rennin did not take the lead, and neither did the group walk into the jungle. Rather, Ming was on point, and they scaled the palms to work their way through the branches rather than the undergrowth. He had to admit to himself that he had underestimated his longtime pupil. Troy Tomerson would never have relinquished command even when he was not the best for the job, and Spell had assumed the man who now called himself Rennin O'Rourke would be the same. He had also assumed that Troy's idea of stealth would have included cover of darkness, not blinding sunlight in his enemies' eyes, and the man's quarterback mentality would have been a frontal assault. In many ways, still the boy Spell had taught as Troy Tomerson, the man, Rennin O'Rourke had become a formidable opponent. He saw Zane's concerns for the man had foundation. Rennin had already shown that he could take a life when pushed to his limit, but calculated vengeance and deliberate assassination were different matters. Spell no longer doubted James Wilburn would die. He now worried what part of a boy turned man that he cared for would die in the process. Over the years in his profession, Spell had allowed few to capture his heart. The man he saw swing out of sight through the treetops was one of them.

As Rennin, Ming, and Zane made their way through the trees by various techniques, from jumping from trunk to trunk to swinging on the vines that were naturally available, several camouflaged guards found themselves sleeping soundly from the silent nine-millimeter darts fired by the climbers. Half a mile in thickness, just enough to conceal a compound from the beach, the jungle growth ended and gave way to what could be a small town surrounded by a stone fort.

In the trees, the three placed themselves so their approach would be with the sunrise. Then, Rennin and Ming changed into camouflage that would best hide them against the grayness of concrete.

There were four guard towers situated at the corners of the compound. It appeared two men guarded each tower. Zane positioned himself in the branches of a palm to pick off the guards methodically. He planned to take out the rear guards first, just the way Gary Cooper as Sergeant York had described a turkey shoot so many years before. "If you take out the back, the front ones don't have a clue they're in danger." Zane grinned.

Ming and Rennin descended the trees and slithered to the point they were against the wall of the fortress and awaited a brilliant sunrise.

"Damn!" whispered Rennin as two of the jungle guards came out of the wooded area. Rennin hoped Zane saw the two men. Zane had seen them and thought momentarily about taking them out, but it would be too obvious to the front guard towers if two of theirs dropped before their eyes. Zane thought, *Sorry, Rennin, these are yours.* However, he began his mission a little early as he took aim at the farthest tower and fired two rapid shots into the backs of two unsuspecting guards. Rennin saw the glint of steel and instantly understood.

Ming and Rennin seemed to read each other's thoughts as they flattened themselves to the ground and waited. Zane took aim again at the second back tower. One...and the other pulled out a radio...two. Zane could only hope there had been no communication time.

The sun popped over the treetops. Zane fired into one of the front towers, rapidly twice, but not rapidly enough for the two on foot patrol not to see something. He had no time to worry about the jungle guards as he fired again into the last tower. A shuriken caught one of the walking guards in the side. Obviously, the shurikens were also dipped in sleeping compound as the man fell into a slump. The second guard fired his weapon in the direction of the thrown shuriken before Rennin's shot found its mark.

Breathlessly, Rennin and Ming hugged the wall, unsure if one shot would rouse the compound. When nothing stirred on the other side, they nodded in unison to scale the wall. Rennin pulled his grappling gun. Ming stayed his hand, "Too loud." She indicated the neko, and Rennin followed her example.

As thoughts of Spiderman played through Rennin's mind, he and Ming dropped noiselessly to the ground on the other side of the wall. Each took a row of buildings to the outside of the four rows inside the compound. Armed with a nine-millimeter in each hand they made their way up the outside row of buildings, met in the middle and came down the center line together.

By the time they reached the center line, Zane had made his way into the nearest guard tower and picked off four skulking recruits. Within an hour, the three had managed to capture the generator, and on the boat, Spell became keenly aware of the lack of the distinctive buzz he knew to be the electrical netting. "I'll be damned!" he uttered as he dropped a motorized dinghy and went ashore.

Spell quickly made his way to the compound, unhindered by sleeping trainees. He was greeted at the gate by three nine-millimeter dart guns pointed at him. "So, shoot already," he growled, miffed by the ineptitude of the young mercenaries in training on the island.

Several hours later in the briefing room of the compound, supposedly retired Lt. Col. Clifton Spell glared at two dozen young recruits and snarled, "You let three civilians take this compound."

One young recruit ventured, "Sir, they were three civilians trained by you."

Spell was in the young man's face. "I guess we know the first one off the island."

"Why?" asked Rennin in the man's defense. "Because he said what all the others are thinking? He happens to be the only one who even got off a shot. How long have they even been training, Sensei? And their intel was just a little off, wasn't it?"

Chagrinned, Spell gave the men a night off to relax and talked with his three immediate protégés. "All right, Rennin, so you used the sun as cover and the treetops as a pathway. And you used my assumptions about you against these kids. Nice work."

"All the credit goes to Ming."

"Traitor," moaned Spell.

"I thought the purpose of this mission was to help Rennin, Papa."

"And so, it is. Well done."

"Sensei?" said Rennin with a question weighing in the air.

"What?"

"I thought you were retired."

Spell grunted. "I'm officially retired from Uncle Sam, but I'm mercenary enough to work on commission. All I do is train babies to kill or die these days. After this little escapade with you, I *am* retiring. Every one of these kids would be dead if this had been real. I really have had enough of that on my conscience. I'm ready to teach simple martial arts, find Ming a husband, and be a grandfather."

"Papa!" Ming said in embarrassment.

"It's true," insisted Spell, "but," flicking his thumb toward Rennin he finished, "he's already taken."

"So am I," said Zane, feigning hurt feelings. "But Nicole couldn't care less what I'm up to. What do you say, Ming? Wanna go for it?"

"No!"

"Speaking of going for it," said Spell, "we need to get some rest. Tomorrow we sail for Haiti."

The next morning, Spell made sure each member of the group headed for Haiti was outfitted appropriately with the weapons suited to skill and preference. He left his trainees with specifics to address and two scenarios to expect within the next few weeks although he stated emphatically, he was retiring.

Once aboard the boat, Rennin switched the sonar to its original settings and the tell-tale buzz of the electrified netting resumed. Travel was easy for the next several days, and the sailboat glided safely into harbor on a once magnificent island.

As always, Rennin was anxious to act. Spell reminded him a great deal could have changed since Zane was last there. Spell also insisted that he and Ming do the reconnaissance because neither of them had been there before and would not be recognized. They returned with a layout of the compound and a guard count. It was similar to the training compound, except James Wilburn also had some underground containment facilities, apparently where his prisoners were held and a villa where he housed himself in luxury. Ming claimed the underground area as her primary responsibility.

She planned to free anyone she found there, but specifically she was to locate and rescue Jacques Picard if he were alive.

As had been his assignment during the training mission, Zane located a small stand of trees in which to hide and armed his M40 to its fullest. Rennin's only concern, according to Spell, was Wilburn. He instructed his protégé not to engage anyone else unless there was no choice. "The others belong to me," he informed Rennin.

The next decision was harder—when to go in. The lack of natural cover made the dawn approach moot. They considered a broad daylight method, but the civilian interference was too risky; however, Spell felt certain that Wilburn would have heightened security measures at night. Therefore, the final decision was dusk and early evening when there would still be a great many tourists, relief organizations, and other activity for distraction, yet not the hustle and bustle of the full day.

The decision having been made, Spell insisted Rennin practice some form of relaxation because he was wound too tightly. Rennin argued it was hard to relax when he considered what he was about to do. "What would relax you?" Spell inquired seriously of the young man.

Rennin smiled half to himself as he answered, "Renée. Making love to Renée."

"Hell," snapped Spell, "use your imagination, boy."

Rennin laughed, "It's hardly the same, Sensei."

"It is if you get yourself to that level of deep meditation. Find something you can focus on that is only about your wife. Focus until all you see is Renée. Put yourself there."

In the solitude of his room, the only thing Rennin had that was completely about Renée was the loop from an antique watch chain he wore as a wedding ring. He sat with his back against the wall as he twisted the loop and thought about his wife. After what must have been an eternity, it was as if Rennin could feel the love of his life holding him, and before he was aware time had passed, Cliff Spell pulled him to reality. The appointed time had arrived.

41
Retribution, Restoration, and Release

Men wearing military fatigues was commonplace in the streets of Port-au-Prince. After the earthquake, there was a constant military presence. No one paid any attention to the three men as they walked to their destination. The unassuming petite Asian woman wearing black spandex and carrying a large straw purse and chatting in broken English to various people drew no more attention than any other relief worker. Ming meandered unnoticed to the backside of the compound. Zane peeled off from his comrades and vanished into a small stand of trees.

What must have served as a dinner bell and shift-change warning sounded within the compound as Rennin and Spell blended into the exterior wall. Fifteen minutes after the bell, Spell recognized the glint of steel, and Zane picked off the first of the rear guards. The second glint followed rapidly. A few seconds and the third and fourth flashes occurred to Spell's expectant eye. A furtive, silent, black-clad figure dropped inside the rear wall of the compound just as the evening shadows gathered.

Spell watched soundlessly as the fifth and sixth flashes indicated two guards left in the front towers. He timed Zane from the previous shots as the sun sank, prohibiting further refractions of steel. A nod from the master sent two men with neko up the front wall of the compound. Just as noiselessly as the black-clad figure earlier, the two men landed inside the compound.

Knowing the mess hall would be crowded with unarmed men who left their weapons outside in the vestibule of the facility, but James Wilburn never graced his employees with his presence in such a modest setting with scanty, by his terms, provisions, Spell and Rennin hit the diners with grenades composed of a heavy herbal sleeping compound as they, themselves, bit into a capsule of antidote.

With two dozen sleeping men disposed, Rennin and Spell made their way toward the area that served as Wilburn's residence. Two men kept the dinner watch outside the front gate of the main house. Simultaneously, two shurikens caught the unwary guards in the neck.

As darkness fell, Rennin and Spell shed their military camouflage for the black spandex they wore beneath. Light from within the villa declared Wilburn entertained a low-level government official for dinner. Indicating the corrupt official would not be missed, Spell drew a finger across his throat.

Through the garden toward the dining room, the two men crept undetected. From beneath the windowsill, only one guard could be seen in the dining room where two wicked men planned how to maneuver illicit drugs through the country for great personal profit while its citizenry suffered poverty and neglect. Spell tried the window and found it unlocked. He indicated to Rennin this was the one situation where he would have to eliminate more than his main objective. He also indicated for Rennin to give him fifteen minutes to secure the hallway and disappeared around the corner of the building.

Rennin viewed his watch anxiously. The minutes became eons before he saw a crack in the dining room door. In perfect synchronization, Rennin drew aim on the guard as Spell targeted the government official. As if by one shot, both men collapsed, and Wilburn jumped to his feet. Rennin slipped through the window as Spell entered through the door to Wilburn's utter amazement. In fluid motion, Rennin holstered his gun, slid off his weapons' belt, removed the black knit mask, and pushed the dining table against the wall. Spell bolted the door and leaned against it with his arms folded across his chest.

Wilburn spat, "You really are not the nice little boy you pretend to be, are you, O'Rourke?"

Rennin said calmly, "I don't pretend to be anything. I am Rennin Duncan O'Rourke, and, as I promised, you are a dead man. It's you and me, right here, right now. There's nowhere left to run or to hide. I'm not armed, and I don't have curare with which to inject you. I want to see your eyes grow cold and dim when I kill you. I want to see the fear in your face as the flames of Hell engulf your miserable soul."

Rennin assumed a front stance, and, reminiscent of Bruce Lee, slightly flicked four fingers for James Wilburn to make a move toward him. When Wilburn did not move, Rennin taunted him, "Oh, come on, James. You can beat and rape a defenseless, untrained woman. You can manipulate the mind of a vulnerable teenager to kidnap three innocent children in order to sacrifice them for some bizarre religious ceremony, in addition to raping that fourteen-year-old child. You can hire a fat asshole to gut a harmless gay man. You can slit the throat of a woman who actually *loved* you. You can plant bombs on trains and in cars. But you can't fight me one-on one, man-to-man. You pathetic pussy."

James glanced toward Cliff Spell. "Don't worry about him," egged Rennin. "The only reason you'll have to worry about him is *if* you kill me." Once again, Rennin urged James forward with a hand motion. "Come on. I have promises to keep."

James stepped to his right, away from Cliff Spell. It appeared he would prefer to employ diplomacy as he spoke calmly and took a couple of steps toward his adversary. "You know, O'Rourke, you have the advantage of your youth."

"That's a joke. The only advantage I have is a few inches."

Before Rennin knew James had moved, a shuriken ripped across the outside of his left shoulder. Rennin glanced at the wound and chuckled as he swiped his right hand across the blood and touched his fingers to his mouth. "I can play that game if you would like, but that puts you too far away." Rennin charged James with a flying kick that sent the man crashing into the wall and onto the floor. Rennin shouted, "Get up!"

Rather than stand, James went for a sweep, which Rennin dodged easily. Rennin pulled the other man to his feet. "I said, 'Get up!'"

James threw a punch, which Rennin blocked and countered with his own. Despite, the age difference, James Wilburn was agile and superbly skilled in martial arts. In addition, James fought underhandedly as a blade appeared from his wrist and slashed across Rennin's abdomen.

Rennin laughed mockingly, "Looks as if I might need a few stitches. I'm tired of dancing with you." He grabbed James's wrist that sported the concealed blade. James uttered a dreadful cry of pain as Rennin snapped his radius and ulna. Rennin's next move put James on the ground and a foot into his chest, cracking his sternum.

James screamed, "Jesus!"

"Was that a prayer, James?" asked Rennin sarcastically while he picked up his nine-millimeter and shot James's left kneecap. "You should make it a prayer before you meet your Maker."

"You sadistic bastard!" screamed James

"Me? Sadistic? You must be looking in the mirror. There's no way I can mete out enough pain to ensure the retribution you deserve, but I promised Casey I would make you suffer." Rennin shot James's other kneecap before he retrieved the carving knife from the dining table. "Maybe I can disembowel you so that you can lie in your own filth and bleed to death like Skyelar." He pinned James's good hand to the floor with one thrust of the blade. Rennin continued in the vein of how to make James suffer. "Better yet, maybe I should castrate you and choke you to death on your own cock, although I'm sure it's very small, for raping the love of my life. Choose your poison, James," he continued as he put his heel into the man's crotch. "One way or another, you will die tonight."

Meanwhile, Zane waited in the tree stand and watched the courtyard through his night scope while Ming scoured the underbelly of a palatial dwelling. Having disposed of the guards, she deftly picked the locks on several cells, asking each occupant, "Are you Jacques?" and gathering the prisoners she found to one place with instructions to wait for release together.

At the very end of a corridor of unoccupied cells, Ming found one last prisoner in a cubicle less than six-feet in height and barely five-feet by five-feet. The creature shackled to the wall by his wrists and left to dangle in stagnant, putrid water was little more than a skeleton.

As the door squeaked on its hinges, the wraith lifted its head and barely whispered, "What more can zhou do to me, Weelburn? I weell not geeve zhou zat child. I weel not help zhou destroy Renneen O'Rourke. Just keel me and put an end to my suffereeng. Please?"

Ming's sing-song voice asked with the last ray of hope, "Are you Jacques?"

Eyes that looked as if they could roll from their sockets desperately tried to focus on the melodic sound as the voice rasped, "I once knew zat name."

Ming skillfully picked the manacles around Jacques's wrists but thought the hands of the man so bony they could have slipped through with ease. As the resistance to the weight the man had left gave way, he collapsed into the rancid water. Ming draped one of his arms over her shoulders. "Can you stand?" she asked. "Must I carry you?"

"Who are zhou?" asked Jacques weakly.

"I'm Ming Spell. I'm here with my father, Harvey Zane, and Rennin O'Rourke."

Some spark of life remained in the walking corpse. "Renneen ees here?"

"Yes. He has come to kill his nemesis, James Wilburn. My assignment is to find you and rescue you. Now, can you stand? You weigh almost nothing if I must carry you, but you're almost a foot taller than I am."

Jacques pulled himself up with Ming's help and leaned heavily on her as he tried to put weight on feet that were half rotted away from the fungus caused by the water. He whispered to Ming, "I deed not zeenk to feel any more pain. I zought by now my nervous seestem would have shut down."

"If you feel pain, you're alive," assured Ming. "If you die now, I will have failed Rennin. Don't die on me."

A huddle of twelve men waited patiently near the door as their delivering angel approached dragging one more of their kind. Without hesitation, two of their rank, who had not yet been in James Wilburn's clutches long, ran forward to hold the shell of a man who had become legend. The stories they had heard about the resistance of Jacques Picard had made them believe he must be some kind of spirit. Seeing the frail body, dispelled that belief, but strengthened the resolve of the men to continue the fight for justice in a country rife with injustice.

Ming examined the lot she had discovered and realized the only way to take them out of the compound would be directly through the front gate. Very few of them could scale a wall, least of all her objective. Indicating the need for extreme quiet and caution, Ming led the way into the courtyard. Zane's eagle eye found the group in his scope. The silhouette of Ming's figure assured him he was responsible for making sure they made it to the gate. Hoping Zane had seen her, Ming indicated the same to him.

Two by two, Ming sent the men toward the front wall. As they hugged the wall and inched toward the main gate, a jeep came through the entrance. As if one body, the whole group flattened against the wall. Zane took aim at the occupants of the jeep, two guards and one supposed police officer.

Zane saw in his scope a small black-clad figure snake her way along the ground toward the newcomers. She obviously read his mind, that he could take out two quickly, but a third could be a serious problem. As Zane popped the driver, Ming rose up from the inkiness with one nine-millimeter in each hand and with one shot each, felled the other two.

In disbelief, Jacques watched the precision with which the angel of mercy worked. Ming rejoined the men in a full run. "Go!" she ordered. The prisoners disbanded into all directions once outside the gate. The two men supporting Jacques asked, "Où nous le prenons?"

Ming looked to the gaunt face for translation. "Where do we take heem?" Jacques barely whispered.

Ming draped Jacques's arm over her shoulders. "I'll take him from here. You go now to where you need to be." She jutted her chin toward the exit.

Although the woman's instructions were in English, the men needed no further encouragement as they took off into the darkness. Ming led Jacques to the stand of trees where they sat on the ground. Ming said guardedly, "Zane?"

Zane acknowledged their presence. "It's cool, Ming. I have the courtyard covered."

"Can you see Papa and Rennin?"

"Oh, yeah. I just wish Rennin would go ahead and kill the bastard, but he's a man of honor and did promise Casey to make him suffer."

Jacques asked, "What deed Weelburn do to Casey?"

"It's a long story," said Ming.

Jacques hacked a serious cough. "What else have I to do?"

As they waited, Ming, in hushed tones, told Jacques all that she knew. She finished by saying, "I hope you weren't planning a future with Casey. She's seriously involved with her doctor."

"Good," said Jacques. "Alzough now I have nozeeng keepeeng me here. I cannot stay now zat Weelburn has keelled my mozer. Even eef Renneen keells Weelburn, my government wants me dead. I cause too much trouble here."

Ming gently rubbed Jacques's thigh. "You sound like me. The Chinese government is rejoicing about my sudden disappearance. Since we're both in need of a new home, you'll come to America with me. In my part of the world, they say once you save a life, you're responsible for that life forever. I guess I'm stuck with you. I *did* save your life, such as it is."

"I can leeve wif zat," Jacques tried to laugh, but his body was racked with a fit of coughing.

Ming eyed the man. "You have pneumonia, dysentery, and trench foot, and you need tremendous amounts of food. You're a great challenge. Are you worth it?"

Jacques smiled. "Renneen zought so."

Ming noted, "You still have all your teeth. I'm surprised. We shall see if you're worth my effort. Zane, what's happening? I need to get my charge some medical attention."

"Not here," argued Jacques. "Do what zhou can for me, but no doctors here."

"Trust me. I'll restore you if Rennin ever gets his ass back out here."

"Well, James, how would you like to die?" Rennin asked again.

James spat, "If you have the balls to kill me, do it with your bare hands."

Another voice came from James's mouth. "Rennin, it doesn't matter how I die, just release me from the torment. You're the only one who can. I've been trapped in here for so long. Please, release me."

Rennin spoke to Spell, "Sensei, did you hear that?"

"Yes," replied Spell. "You have the balls. Just do it and let's get out of here. You can't make him suffer enough to make up for what Casey endured."

The voice came to Rennin again. It was obvious Spell didn't hear it. "Rennin, I have suffered for years. Release me. I was once called James Wilburn until this demon came along. I can't free myself, but you can."

Master Xing's words came back to Rennin. "You must release the soul of one you hate."

The voice that Rennin was used to hearing continued to hurl insults at him. "Just shoot me then. You don't have the balls to make it truly personal. I'll make it truly personal with that little green-eyed bastard of yours. Considering her mother's temperament, she'll be absolutely delicious."

"Contemno et Avaritia et Concupiscentiam Suam Terram afornicationem, iubeo vobis nomine tenus Patris et nomine tenus Redemptor Filius et nomine tenus Sanctus Spiritus, relinquo hic homo hominis. Adstringo vobis et repeto vobis fovea Damno oriundus numquam," ("Hate and Greed and Lustful Immorality, I command you in the Name of the Father and of the Son and of the Holy Ghost to leave this man. I bind you and vanquish you to the pit of Hell, never to return.") flowed from Rennin's lips before he was once again a lion running across an African plain when a would-be tamer came at him with a whip and a stool, intent upon forcing him into a cage. The lion leapt at the tormentor mauling the stool from his hand with one paw and tearing his throat out with the other.

"Oh, my God," gasped Cliff Spell.

"Oh, my God," gasped Harvey Zane.

"What happened?" asked Ming.

"You don't want to know," replied Zane

"Is Rennin all right?"

"I can't answer that, but James Wilburn is dead."

42
A Council Meeting

In his left hand, Rennin held James Wilburn's larynx dripping blood onto the man's corpse. Cliff Spell took hold of Rennin's wrist as he spoke commandingly, "Let it go."

Another voice echoed through the air, "Thank you." This time Spell heard it and looked around trying to find it.

Still another voice full of wisdom and comfort floated on the winds. "Do what you must do without hesitation or regret."

Spell shook the younger man. "Rennin, let it go. You did what you had to do. We need to leave now."

Coming back to himself, Rennin dropped James's voice box onto the body at his feet and stared momentarily at the blood on his hands. Methodically, he picked up his weapon's belt and snapped it around his waist, holstering his nine-millimeter. He pulled the black mask over his face and walked out the front door with Cliff by his side. Spell whispered as they walked, "You should've let me do it. It's nothing new to me. He's just one more piece of dead vermin."

Rennin shook his head. "He's free. It had to be me. Master Xing knew. Can we please leave it there? I don't want to talk about it—ever."

Outside the gate, Rennin and Spell slipped back into their fatigues and made their way to the stand of trees where Zane and Ming stood ready to leave with Jacques draped between them. Spell took one look at the apparition that had somehow survived Wilburn's dungeon and observed, "We won't look inconspicuous heading back to the boat."

He surveyed the motley crew around him. Zane and Ming supported a skin-covered skeleton that could not stand alone. Rennin held his middle where he was finally aware his own blood seeped from his knife wound. "What was I thinking?" Spell chastised himself. "Stay here."

With the agility of a cat, he raced back into the compound and returned with the commandeered jeep that had recently arrived. After all people climbed in, he took the most direct route back to where his sailboat was docked and loaded his precious human cargo. Ten minutes later, he boarded, having left the jeep on a side street. Zane and Spell weighed anchor and set sail while Ming attended the wounded and sick.

Ming steered Jacques onto a cot in the small cabin Spell had designated as his infirmary, where she deposited him with an explanation. "Since Rennin's bleeding, I need to take care of him first. I'll return to you shortly. Rest."

Jacques obeyed without argument. Ming examined Rennin's cuts. "You'll live," she assured him. "Here. Take this." Ming handed Rennin two capsules and a bottle of water.

"What is it?"

"Something to make you sleep."

"I don't need to sleep."

"I need for you to sleep. We're not having a council meeting to discuss it. This is an arbitrary, unilateral decision. Swallow. If you don't swallow, I'll shoot you with a dart."

Knowing the woman was serious, Rennin complied with Ming's request, and while he slept, she sutured his shoulder and his midsection. She admired her work for a moment. "Not bad," she commented to Jacques. "Dr. Jamison would be proud."

Jacques replied, "Jameeson. He ees Casey's doctor?"

"He was. He says he resigned as her doctor because he fell in love with her. Does that fact disturb you?"

"No."

"Good. You don't need anything to disturb you right now. You must concentrate on healing yourself. Let's see where to begin with you."

"Am I zat deesgusteeng?"

"Yes. So, since the stench from your body makes it difficult to care for you, we'll begin with a bath and some clean clothes."

Ming helped Jacques to the shower stall where she removed the tattered rags covering his emaciated body. She commanded him not to move as she left him sitting on the corner seat, walked on deck, and threw the revolting material into the ocean.

When she returned, Jacques had not budged but sat in the corner of the shower like a helpless child. She stepped into the stall with a pair of clippers and pushed the button. "I hope you aren't attached to this—do you call it hair?" Ming proceeded to shave Jacques's head without protest from him. His dreadlocks joined the habiliments of the dead that had covered his body. Ming came back and turned on the shower and adjusted the temperature. She undressed herself and stepped into the stall with a bar of Dial soap and a washcloth.

There was some life left in the young man, as he sat upright and murmured, "I am not completely dead. Zhou are naked."

Ming glanced unconcerned at her state of undress. "Did you expect me to get into the shower with my clothes on? Get a grip. You need my help." Ming gently bathed every inch of the neglected and wasted human. As she ended with the man's feet, pieces of flesh slid down the drain, and Jacques winced as the hot water and antibacterial soap burned the open sores on his feet. The hot steamy water sent him into a fit of coughing.

After Ming slipped into a robe, she helped Jacques into a clean set of pajamas and a clean bed, coated his feet in antifungal salve, and started a humidifier of eucalyptus oil. Offhandedly as Ming pulled covers over Jacques, she commented, "You're much lighter than I expected you to be."

"Not all Haitians are sharcoal black," Jacques replied weakly. "My great-great-grandmozer was a voodoo priestess, and she married a Frenchman. And zhou speak Engleesh better zan I do alzough zhou are Shinese."

"My father's American, and I am *not* Chinese. My mother was Tibetan. I was educated in America. Now, rest while I make you something to eat. You are far too skinny for my liking."

"Breeng me a steak, a filet mignon, medium rare and a baked potato wif butter, sour cream, sheese, and bacon. Zat ees what I have dreamed of for such a long time."

She patted his hand as she left. She returned a little later with a tray. "It's a little soon for you to eat steak. I've brought you scrumptious chicken soup, bread, apple sauce, milk, and some bayberry tea. I expect you to eat every bite." Ming placed the tray over Jacques's lap and gingerly sat on the edge of his bed.

Jacques's hand trembled as he lifted the spoon to his lips. Ming steadied his hand. She asked sympathetically, "Would you like me to do it?"

Jacques replied, "No, I would like to do eet myself, but I zeenk I need zhou to do eet for now. I do not see zhou as my mozer."

"How do you see me?" Ming asked as she scooped more soup for the man.

Jacques smiled. "Perhaps an angel."

"Careful," piped a voice from the other bed. "Angels can hold sway over your behavior. They must have powers like pixies. I remember seeing a pixie once. I married her. You're doomed, my friend."

"Renneen," said Jacques with genuine happiness. "Zank zhou for breengeeng an angel to me. Eet ees good to see zhou are well."

"It's good to see you're still alive. Ming, where's my food?"

Ming looked peeved. "You're capable of going to the galley."

"Man," complained Rennin. "Angels aren't supposed to have favorites, are they? I have stitches."

"Yes, I know. I gave them to you. Your wounds aren't deep. You'll live. Now, if you're hungry, you know where to find the food."

"Ming, we really need to work on your sense of humor." Rennin slid to his feet.

She countered, "I laugh when it's appropriate. I'd like to see you laugh right now." She grinned wickedly and winked at Jacques.

Rennin argued, "Ming, you're meaner than a sister. But..." he became serious. "You're one hell of fighter and a friend. Thank you, Ming. I think Jacques has a true angel in you." Rennin kissed Ming on the cheek. "I'm going to find something to eat."

Ming thumped Rennin's shoulder. "Ouch!" he grumbled.

She shrugged. "I didn't say you wouldn't be sore for several days, but you'll live. As will this one if you'll leave me alone and let me put some meat back on his bones."

"Do you think you can do it before we get back to Mom's Trading Post? No one will believe that's Jacques Picard. He's too skinny, and he has no hair. How did she talk you into losing the dreads?"

Jacques rubbed his hand across his smooth head. "I like eet, but I zeenk I would like a couple of eenches eef Meeng approves. She deed not geeve me an option on a haircut, but eet was time for a shange. I weell look more Amereecan zis way."

Ming shook her head and giggled. "Rennin, go. You, eat. I think you can handle the bread. I will be back in a moment."

Ming walked to the galley with Rennin. She asked honestly, "Are you all right?"

He nodded. "You don't have to nursemaid me. I was only teasing you."

"I know that, but you're my friend. What you did couldn't have been easy for you. If you ever need to talk, I'll listen, but I won't pry. I'm here when you're ready."

"Thanks." Rennin sat down in a galley chair. His stitches did hurt a great deal, and the exertion of walking seemed tremendous. Ming placed a sandwich and a glass of milk in front of him. Rennin nodded. "I thought I could do it myself."

"You can, but I'm a nice person." She squeezed his hand. "I thought Jacques might like some chocolate pudding." She set a Snak-Pak in front of Rennin. "Dessert." Ming started out the door.

"Do you like him?" asked Rennin.

"Excuse me?" she said in confusion.

"Jacques—do you like him?"

"He seems very nice. I think I already admire his loyalty and courage. When I went into the cell where he was, he didn't know who had come in. He informed whoever he thought it was, Wilburn I suppose, he wouldn't give you up before anyone even spoke to him. He's a man of honor, like you and my father—oh, and Zane. Do I like him? Yes, I like him. Why?"

"I was curious. You really seem to be taking care of him."

"Rennin, the man's half dead. If we had been a week later, he would've been dead. He can't care for himself at the moment."

"Yes, Nurse Ming. Ming Picard. It has a nice ring to it."

"What are you talking about? Don't let Papa hear you say something like that."

"Come on, Ming! Admit it. There's some chemistry there. I sensed it when I woke up and saw you feeding the man."

"Rennin, his hand was shaking so much that the soup wouldn't have made it to his mouth!"

"If you insist. By the way, how did he get so clean? Do you realize you're still wearing a bathrobe?"

"Rennin! You're misinterpreting everything. Stop it! I would've done the same thing for you."

"I know," he said with a rakish grin. "Now, whose tent was it you came into?"

She glared at him. He had hit a nerve. "Rennin, that was a test designed for you. I'll have you know, if you had responded differently, I would've cold-cocked you. I'm an American, Rennin. I've waited twenty-three years to fall in love. I can wait longer if need be. I will not be a wife or a concubine because some council deems it the way of life. Grandfather was a good man, but in that one area, he was wrong."

"I'm sorry, Ming," Rennin apologized. "I was only teasing you. You're a great lady, and you deserve someone to love you. You're no man's property. I have great respect for you. Truly, I meant no insult."

She nodded. "You're forgiven." She juggled the pudding cup in her hand and left the galley. As she walked back to the infirmary she thought, *Ming Picard? Where does Rennin get such silly notions?*

Jacques had managed to finish the meal Ming had brought him and put the tray on the floor. He slept soundly. She set the pudding on the small table by the cot and sat down in a chair to watch her patient sleep.

An iridescent silver slip of a winged creature called playfully, "Catch me if you can, Filigree!"

A gilded whelp, not much older than the silver slip took pursuit. "I'll catch you, Moonbeam. I'm bigger and older than you. And I'm a boy!"

"Oh, a whole twenty years," teased the young female dragon. "And like it makes a difference you're a boy. You'll only catch me when I slow down and let you catch me, but I think both our fathers would like that."

Filigree caught up to Moonbeam. "I told you I'd catch you."

"I slowed down. I wanted to talk to you."

"What about?"

"Do you think our fathers are arranging a marriage for us?"

"You're still too much of a baby."

"Humph!" snorted Moonbeam as she sailed away from her potential mate.

Suddenly, Moonbeam clutched at her chest and plummeted toward the ground. "Moonbeam!" called Filigree frantically as he raced toward the shining streak. Filigree caught hold of both of Moonbeam's wings in his talons and struggled to lower her to the beach below them. She lay there panting in pain as an arrow protruded from near the joint where her wing connected to her body.

Filigree comforted the terrified female as she wailed, "Filigree, a human! A human shot me!"

Filigree hated to leave the one he knew would one day be his mate on the shore, but he had no choice. "I'll be back as fast as I can. Let me get your father, Moonbeam."

"Filigree, I'm afraid. This could mean war. Father has said if the mediator and the governor don't come soon, there may be war between the dragons and the humans. Why did one of them shoot me?"

"I don't know, but I must get your father." Filigree zoomed away, and without the courtesy of asking admittance, soared into the cave, calling, "Smoke, sir!"

A gargantuan glistening gray dragon breathed fire toward the young golden whelp. "Whatever has possessed you to fly uninvited into my cave?"

"Sir, I'm sorry, but it's Moonbeam. Sir, she's hurt."

"How is my daughter hurt?"

"A human, sir." Filigree lowered his voice as if in conspiracy. "A human shot her, sir."

"Where is she?" roared Smoke.

"The beach, sir."

Smoke did not wait for the young suitor to keep up but soared to his daughter. Smoke landed with a thud. Without speaking, he broke the shaft of the arrow and pushed the weapon obviously intended for large prey through the delicate joint. Moonbeam whimpered. She looked imploringly at her father. "Father, please, don't start a war. The humans are frail. They can't survive a war with us."

Smoke breathed fire over the ocean as he thundered, "I will do what I must do without hesitation or regret."

Though to some it would not have made sense, Cliff Spell sailed first to Jamaica for a few days and then to Puerto Rico for a few days with a stop in the Bahamas before ever setting sail for Miami. He justified his meandering in two ways. First, if they were simply sailing for fun throughout the Caribbean the authorities would not suspect them of the massacre in Haiti. Second, he said he had to give Ming's two patients time to recuperate, especially Rennin so Renée wouldn't have his head on a platter. Rennin healed rapidly, and Jacques gained strength and weight to Ming's delight.

Finally, the sailboat docked in the marina in Miami where Cliff rented a slip for his vessel. The company stayed a few more days in Cliff's condominium. Ming insisted on shopping for Jacques, saying he couldn't wear pajamas all the time.

From the looks of the haul she brought in from the mall, Rennin felt certain she had maxed her father's credit card. Although she had mostly bought clothing for Jacques, she did not apologize for buying a few things for herself. Cliff seemed not to care.

Ming made Jacques try on the clothes she had bought. She told him, "I'd like to see you wearing real clothes."

He complied with her request, but he told her he was still much thinner than normal. She smiled at him radiantly. "That's why I bought some things larger. You'll fill out some more, but tonight you must wear this." She handed Jacques a navy-blue double-breasted suit with a starched, white, button-down shirt and a red silk tie and black dress shoes with navy blue socks.

"Why?" asked Jacques. "I would razer wear zee zheans and sneakers."

"Tomorrow. Tonight, you wear this."

"Why?"

"I'm taking you out for steak."

"You what?"

Ming clapped her hands in her way that meant for Jacques to hurry. "Don't argue. Chop, chop. I have reservations for us."

Jacques was left in the room with a smirking Rennin.

"What ees zat look for?" asked Jacques.

"You are doomed," Rennin replied. "I can hear the wedding bells now."

Jacques put on the suit, which fit perfectly. Rennin helped him because he fumbled so with the tie. He repeated, "Doomed."

Jacques previewed himself in the mirror and asked, "What should I do wif my hair?"

Rennin sprang from his bed as if he were in college again. "Oh, my God! You're absolutely, positively doomed. When is the date? I already have to be Craig's best man." Rennin continued to tease Jacques even as he helped him gel his now short hair. Rennin admired his handiwork. "There. Mr. GQ."

Ming knocked an hour later at the door. Jacques opened to see her in a red, satin, strapless cocktail dress. The dress hugged the few inches of her body that it covered. Short, the dress revealed most of her shapely, muscular legs. Her charcoal tresses tumbled over her shoulders in sleek smoothness. She asked simply, "Are you ready?"

Jacques asked nervously, "Zhust us?" as he pointed between the two of them.

"Yes," replied Ming as if there should not have been a question. She slipped her arm around Jacques's, and he allowed her to lead him away as he heard one word behind him when the door closed.

"Doomed."

Ming and Jacques were escorted to a prime table in one of the finest restaurants in Miami. Ming ordered a bottle of Cabernet Sauvignon produced at Bujold Vineyards from the vines planted in 1963 and produced in 1969. The waiter eyed the young Asian woman curiously. "That's an excellent year, miss."

Ming nodded her understanding that she had chosen a fine wine. The waiter realized he was not dealing with an amateur as he handed the couple menus and stepped away for the wine. Jacques whispered to Ming, "Zere are no prices on zis menu."

"Do you trust me, Jacques?" Ming asked.

"Of course."

"Then, let me do this."

The waiter returned with the house bread and the wine opened and breathing. He poured a bit into a glass and offered the cork to Jacques. Jacques passed the task to Ming by saying, "Zee lady ees zee wine connoisseur."

Ming inhaled the fragrance from the cork. She sipped the wine and let it play on her palette for a moment before she swallowed. "Excellent. Thank you."

The waiter poured two glasses of wine and asked, "Are you ready to order?"

Ming replied, "Yes. For starters, we'll have the sampler of fried crab claws, stuffed mushrooms, and calamari. We'll have two six-ounce filets, medium rare, two baked potatoes with butter, sour cream, cheese, and bacon, and two house salads with the house dressing on the side. For dessert, we'll have two blueberry cheesecakes and coffee."

"Very good, miss," the waiter acknowledged the order with a slight glance at the gentleman at the table. Jacques gave the contemptuous waiter a look that said, "You heard the lady," and nothing more.

Jacques commented to Ming after the waiter left, "He zeenks I am a zheegolo or somezeeng."

"Let him think what he pleases," replied Ming. "Or have I embarrassed you?"

Jacques said, "I am not embarrassed. I like to watch zhou make beegots feel uncomfortable. I zeenk zhou are..."

"I'm what?"

Jacques took a deep breath. "I zeenk zhou are very beauteeful when zhou take control of a seetuation."

Ming did not break eye contact with Jacques as many Asian women would have. "I've embarrassed you though. I apologize."

Jacques noticed several couples danced to the music the orchestra played. He grinned. "Zhou are forgeeven, eef zhou weell dance wif me."

Jacques stood, and Ming started to rise. He held up a subtle finger. Ming waited until Jacques pulled her chair out for her and offered her his hand. He walked her to the dance floor, and they slowly revolved with the music from the band. He whispered in her ear, "Zis place reeks of money. How deed zhou decide to come here?"

Ming sniggered. "I happen to know the owner very well. Let's see what the snobby little waiter does when he sees his boss's name on the credit card."

"Who owns zee restaurant?"

"I do. At least, my father and I do. My father bought the place years ago, but he has always had my name on the deed, so I would have income if something were to happen to him. It's my signature that appears on our waiter's paycheck. I've never been here though. My tastes don't usually run so formal, but I'm assured they make the best steak in town. I wanted you to have the best steak in town."

"Zank zhou," said Jacques as he escorted Ming back to their table.

The waiter served the salad and poured more wine. The steak was cooked to perfection and flavored well. Jacques and Ming ate and talked about the Himalayas and being a mistress of martial arts. They discussed Haitian politics with some sadness and the devastation of the earthquake. Ming was delighted to find Jacques was an architect by trade and had been working on his master's degree at Columbia.

The waiter served the cheesecake and coffee without comment. He returned a few minutes later and respectfully asked, "Will there be anything else for you this evening?"

"The check, please," replied Ming.

The waiter brought the check, which could easily have been a third of a year's salary for Jacques in Haiti. Ming handed the young waiter her credit card, which he took grudgingly. He ran the card and returned with the receipt. He was relieved the card was good. Ming signed her name with flair: *Ming Tai Spell.* She left the minimum gratuity expected and a little note.

The snobby young man opened the tab book. The note read:

You need to improve your attitude. The next time I come in here, you should be groveling at the feet of whomever you are serving, or you will be serving at McDonald's.

Ming Tai Spell

The young waiter recognized the familiar signature and mouthed the word, "Shit."

Jacques told Ming outside, "Zat was mean."

Ming defended her actions. "I didn't fire him. I gave him fair warning. Now, are you tired? Are you ready to go home?"

"No, I am not tired, but ees zat where I would be goeeng—home?"

Ming considered the question and answered, "I suppose that depends on you."

Jacques, too, had to consider the question, so he asked, "Are zhou ready to go home, or can I eenterest zhou een a walk along the beash?"

"I can walk a while," replied Ming. "But you'll ruin those shoes."

"May I tell zhou a secret?" asked Jacques. Ming nodded. "Zey are keeling my feet." Jacques sat on the curb and took off the costly dress shoes and stuffed his socks into them. Ming took off her slings. Both hooked the shoes on their fingers as they walked along the beach barefoot. Awkwardly, he took her hand as they continued to stroll.

"Look," said Jacques pointing upward. "A shooteeng star. Queeck, make a weesh."

Ming closed her eyes. Jacques looked down at the serene face and asked, "What deed zhou weesh?"

She looked up. "If I tell, then it won't come true." Ming continued to stare into Jacques's eyes. The man could not tear himself away from her gaze. Instead, he found his hands sliding up Ming's arms. He gently gripped her shoulders and pulled her toward him. As if steel drawn to a magnet, Jacques's mouth found Ming's. Her hands inched up his back. Jacques was loath to break the kiss that held him. He stared again into Ming's eyes. She whispered, "You see. If you don't tell, your wish comes true."

Jacques kissed Ming again as they meandered back to the car.

Back at the condo, Jacques plopped onto the bed next to Rennin's. Rennin queried, "How was the date?"

Jacques replied, "I am doomed."

Smoke slammed the broken arrow down in the midst of the council meeting. He bellowed, "We have no choice."

Draco's voice rumbled, "Smoke, it is not so easy for a dragon to enter that realm as it is for a human to disappear into this one. I don't know when it was last done, but it was long before our time when dragons frequently entered that world. And we were killed. They employed 'dragon slayers' who used weapons much like this one." He lifted the arrow in his talon. "Alexander and Duncan told me all about it. The weapons they have now are as powerful as dragon fire. I have seen the visions of destruction. The risk of entering that world is high."

"Draco, we have no choice. If he won't come of his own volition, it's time to take action. Moonbeam could have been

killed. We must act. I'm asking the council's permission to go."
Smoke pled his case.

Brindle intoned in his low whirr, "Smoke, he has to want to
come. If he doesn't want to come here, he can't govern. How do
we make him want to come?"

Smoke breathed a great sad sigh. "We take something he
would come for."

"Have we come to such tactics?" Draco closed his eyes and
groaned. "I see no alternative but to allow Smoke to make this
final attempt. What do you plan to take, Smoke?"

Smoke said, "Perhaps, it's better you not know."

Draco droned quietly, "We must vote. I regretfully vote yes.
Brindle?"

Brindle nodded. "Reluctantly, yes."

Draco turned to the council member who had said nothing.
"Char, it must be unanimous. What say you?"

Char's deep growl replied, "I will go with my son. He can't
accomplish this task alone."

Smoke looked at the quiet, but wise, dragon. "Father? I would
never ask you to go."

"You didn't ask."

"But you're a member of the council. What if something were
to happen to you?"

"You're my son. What if something were to happen to you? I
can be replaced as a council member. You cannot. None of us has
ever acted rashly except you. As I recall, you sneaked out at dusk
and returned at dawn in the early morning mist because you
blended perfectly with the colors of nature just to help a young
man see a young woman. The young man we must bring here is,
perhaps, more audacious than even that human was, but he is our
only hope. As you have said, 'We must do what we must do
without hesitation or regret.' The council has decided. We must
make preparations. What is your plan, my son?"

43
Trans-Atlantic Flight 777

Ming and Jacques reclined in the chaise lounges on the deck of Cliff's condominium as Cliff's voice resounded, "Ming, I need to talk to you."

Rennin and Zane tried to ease from the breakfast nook where they sat enjoying pastries and coffee. "Oh, stay there. This involves you too." Cliff snagged a pastry.

"Whew!" quipped Rennin. "I thought you were about to give Jacques the third degree."

"Why would I do that?" asked Spell in a surly mood before his morning coffee. One sip of the stout coffee Rennin had made snapped Cliff into the reality of what his young friend had said. Again, he inquired, "Why would I give Jacques the third degree? Is there something I should know?"

Rennin indicated his lips were zipped, and Zane just wagged his head. "My friend, that's what you get for keeping her hidden all these years."

Cliff argued, "Ming has never been hidden. She's had the best education and training I could possibly give her."

Zane refilled his cup and patted Cliff on the shoulder. "But you haven't watched her. You don't recognize the symptoms. I'm so glad I have two boys."

"They fall in love, too, Zane," said Rennin. He laughed outright. "I think we're worse than the women."

Cliff bellowed, "Ming!"

Once again Rennin and Zane tried to slip away. Spell pointed, still holding his pastry in his hand, and commanded, "Sit."

Ming and Jacques entered the kitchen from the deck chatting spiritedly. A pall fell over the entire room as Cliff pointed at Jacques and demanded, "Is there something you'd like to say to me this morning, Mr. Picard?"

Jacques displayed a terrified expression and blurted, "I only keessed her."

Rennin and Zane had to bite their lips to keep from laughing uncontrollably as Cliff crossed his arms over his chest. "It starts with kissing. And you must feel very guilty about the thoughts you had. You should see the look on your face." He pointed at Ming. "That's a prize above rubies or gold. I love her beyond anything else in this world. I will rip the heart out of any man who hurts her. Am I making myself clear to you?"

Jacques nodded as Ming yelled, "Papa, stop it!"

"What?" asked Cliff. "If this young fool is crazy enough to fall in love with the most stubborn, pigheaded, willful, and downright nasty sometimes woman on the face of the earth, then he should know what he's in for. Now, Mr. Picard, are you or are you not in love with my daughter? What are your intentions toward her?"

Jacques looked at Rennin imploringly. Rennin mouthed the word, "Doomed."

Jacques said aloud, "Doomed ees good."

"What?" said Ming.

Jacques met Cliff's eyes and never dithered after. "I am desteened. I am desteened to love Meeng. I have known eet seence zee moment I heard her voice een zee darkness of a cell een Haiti. She ees my light, my salvation. Yes, I love her. She loves me. Wif your permeession and her acceptance, I plan to marry her."

Jacques turned to Ming, took her hand, and dropped to his knees. "Meeng, I am a waif, deesplaced from all I have ever known. I have nozing to offer zhou but my heart. I love zhou. Zhour fazer says zhou are weellful and stubborn, but I see a strong, eendependent, self-assured woman who ees at zee same time loveeng, kind, and compassionate. Zhou are my beauteeful angel who holds sway over me. Een time, I weell again be able to properly care for zhou. Eef zhou weell haf me, zen, say zhou weell marry me. Be my angel for all eterneety."

"Oh, for God's sake," gagged Cliff. "Get up. If she doesn't marry you, I will."

"Hush, Papa," said Ming. She knelt in front of Jacques and took his face in her hands as tears fringed her eyelashes. She nodded and breathed, "Yes," as she kissed the young man who had captured her heart.

Cliff cleared his throat. "Just in case you're wondering, you have my blessing. And to think, I just wanted to know if Ming planned to go with us to Mom's Trading Post. I thought we would drive up tomorrow."

The trip to Mom's Trading Post was uneventful. Cliff traded his older Lincoln for a fully loaded Grand Caravan, and just before they left, Spell handed Jacques a dossier on a person saying, "There is someone you should meet. Read about him on the drive and tell me what you think of the man."

As they left Miami and entered the interstate, Jacques broke the seal on the portfolio and flipped it open. His own face and name stared back at him. He perused the documents. "Mr. Spell," Jacques said tentatively, "very leettle of zis ees true."

"What's not true?" asked Cliff.

"For example, I was not born een Miami."

Cliff argued, "Birth certificate says you were."

"What about my résumé? I have only worked for a brief time wif one company."

Spell argued again. "The president/CEO of O'Rourke Enterprises says you've been on his payroll since you graduated college three years ago. Ask him yourself."

Rennin piped, "It's true. He does say that. As a matter of fact, he'd like you to begin the startup of Dragon Builders with the slogan, 'Make your home legendary.' Of course, he'd really like it if you made your base of operation Mom's Trading Post."

Jacques continued, "Zee bankbook says I haf $85,000 een my checkeeng account and a saveengs account wif $150,000 as well as a sizeable eenvestment portfoleeo."

"Nice amount for such a young man," observed Cliff. "It's good to know my daughter won't be marrying a penniless bum with no job."

"But…"

Rennin pivoted toward the back seat where Ming and Jacques cuddled. "Jacques, there are only two words that need to escape your lips."

Jacques humbly whispered, "Merci."

Rennin chuckled. "Cheater. That's one word.

The Caravan pulled into the driveway of the house on the banks of Beaver Creek in the late afternoon of the next day. A little dark-haired girl played on the tire swing mounted on an old oak tree in the front yard. Not recognizing the vehicle, she ran inside to announce the arrival of strangers. "Aunt Renée, Mommy, we have company."

Casey McClarty, who was almost fully recovered from her encounter a little over a year before, and her sister, the mistress of the house, stepped onto the wide veranda of the old Victorian house to see who had arrived. Renée did not wait for the van to stop as she recognized the profile of her husband through the glass of the windshield. Rennin vaulted from the front seat and met Renée in the yard. After smothering her with kisses, he buried his face in her neck and through stifled sobs said, "It feels so good to be home."

The other passengers of the van unfurled themselves as Rennin picked up d'Aubigné who had waited patiently for her father. "I missed you," he said, planting a big kiss on her lips. "Where are my other two girls?"

"In the playpen inside."

On the way inside, with Renée under one arm and d'Aubigné on his hip and supported with the other arm, Rennin stopped and kissed Casey on the cheek. He whispered to her, "I kept my promise." They never spoke of the matter again.

As the other people walked toward the house, Casey slowly made her way to the group, looking for her dearest friend. She was within two feet of the man before she recognized him. Covering her mouth with her hands, she said, "Jacques?"

"Hello, l'enfant." They embraced each other, and Casey stood back from a man she had not seen in almost eighteen months.

"You look good," she said.

"Not too skeenny? Meeng says I am too skeenny."

Casey laughed. "You could use a few pounds, but I love the hair." She realized Jacques and Ming had been entwined in each other's arms. Casey said, "And a big question mark appeared above Casey's head."

Jacques grinned triumphantly. "We are engaged, l'enfant. Are zhou happy for me—us?"

"Yes!" cried Casey. "I am, too." She held her hand out to show off her one karat diamond solitaire.

Jacques said honestly, "I am threelled for zhou. I look forward to meeteeng your Dr. Jameeson. We do not haf a reeng yet, but we weell very soon."

Casey slipped one arm around Jacques's waist and one arm around Ming's waist and urged them toward the house as she chatted blithely. "Craig will be here for dinner. Now, you must tell me how this happened. When's the date? Craig and I dared not set a date until Rennin got home. Ming, I know you're not shy. Start talking, girl."

The next few weeks, the only topic of conversation in the house on the banks of Beaver Creek was weddings. Zane even moved Nicole and his two boys to Mom's Trading Post where he took over security for O'Rourke Enterprises, and his first assignment was to get back the money James Wilburn had pilfered. Nicole reluctantly left her home and was only cheered by the prospect of the weddings.

Jacques began Dragon Builders. His first assignment was a new gymnasium and field house for the high school. With Casey's advice, Jacques found the perfect engagement ring for Ming—a half karat tiffany solitaire with two smaller diamonds on each side. Casey also finagled Ming into having a double wedding.

Rennin even lost his fishing partner as d'Aubigné got caught up in the wedding plans as a junior bridesmaid and helped plan for her little sisters to be flower girls since they were walking. Rennin rudely interrupted the chattering females one afternoon as he bellowed, "Enough!"

The women became deadly silent. Rennin breathed. "I have the perfect plan for you. School will be out next week." Rennin handed each woman first-class plane tickets for her and her children. "There's a wonderful little church in Stonebridge, Ireland, and the inn there will make the perfect place for a reception. Your flight leaves in one week. I swear I will outfit the fellows with tuxes, and we'll join you at the end of the month. You can get married against the lushest backdrop on Earth. Renée, please tell them how wonderful this place is."

Renée agreed, "It *is* gorgeous there. But, Rennin, what about all our friends?"

"I'll charter a jet and fly them over. And Casey, Ming, I promise not to have a crazy bachelor party. We'll drink beer and talk about you. This is my gift to you. Please, accept it. I've already rented a house there for your convenience. If you don't go, I'll take the men, and we'll disappear there until the wedding day. Moreover, I *won't* promise not to have the most raucous shindig for the bachelors Ireland has ever seen. I might even fly in authentic Arabian belly dancers and a gifted Chinese masseuse."

Casey and Ming had a long talk with Craig and Jacques. They agreed to Rennin's proposal and the chatter turned to packing for a trip to Ireland. Rennin and the other men went upriver on a fishing expedition. Randall and Marshall Zane begged "Uncle"

Rennin and their father not to send them to Ireland with all the women. Compassionately, Rennin updated their tickets to go with the men.

June thirteenth arrived none too soon for Rennin's shattered nerves. He kissed Renée and explained to d'Aubigné that the cat had to ride in the cargo area of the plane. She was not happy that the mean airline wouldn't let her hold her baby on the plane. She told her daddy to buy the airline and change the rules. Gerald and Cliff flanked Rennin, and each put his arm around the young man and in unison they said, "Just wait until it's that one planning a wedding of her own."

Rennin growled, "I hope she elopes."

The flight took off from Pittsburgh to New York with a layover in New York until 4:00 A.M. The men stopped at a hot wing place where Rennin ordered Killian's and hot wings all around. Of course, the two boys had root beer, but even they sneaked sips of real beer from their dad and Rennin. All the men, having consumed far too much beer to drive back to Mom's Trading Post that evening, crashed at a nearby motel until morning.

In New York, the women settled into their first-class accommodations as the plane taxied down the runway shortly before dawn. With a long flight ahead, they dozed peacefully immediately after takeoff.

An hour over the Atlantic, gave way to one hellacious and unexpected storm. The pilot had no warning of any bad weather. Nonetheless, the passengers in first-class slept, all but one bright-green-eyed little girl who peered into the grayness. Outside her window, two large golden eyes blinked. D'Aubigné O'Rourke smiled and waved at the face in her window. One sharp talon scratched softly in response to the child's wave.

The pilot completely lost control of the aircraft as two massive winged beasts ripped engines from the plane and steered it toward the ocean. The pilot frantically radioed the predicament, without realizing the plane was being guided downward.

The temperature inside the plane rose rapidly as the winged creatures blew fire across the first-class section. When the metal gave way to the heat, the lighter of the two creatures used his razor-like talon to cut away the roof.

As the roof zipped away in the wind, the little green-eyed girl chirped, "Hi, Smoke. What are you doing here?"

The soot-black dragon demanded, "Which ones, Smoke? Quickly."

Smoke replied, "Her for sure," referring to the child who was not afraid. "And her." He pointed at Renée.

D'Aubigné said, "You can't leave my sisters and my mommy."

"Oh, hell," stammered the gray dragon, "take all of them."

Screams shattered the air as the plane hit the ocean with a thud and two winged creatures snatched the passengers in first class.

"Wait!" cried d'Aubigné. "You can't leave Satin."

"Satin?" inquired the black dragon.

"He's there in that part of the plane," said d'Aubigné pointing to the cargo hold. "Please, Smoke?"

Smoke whined, "Father, I can't stand it. Not when she uses those eyes just like Rennin used to."

Without further ado, the black dragon ripped the cargo hold open. "Where, child?" he demanded

"There in the little cage," replied d'Aubigné.

"A cat!" shrieked the dragon as he added a little cage to his load. "Oh, shut up!" he commanded the screaming women. "We are not going to eat you."

The two creatures rose above the clouds and blended into the storm. Peering from the cockpit the pilot said, "If I tell the authorities what I just saw, they'll think I have gone insane. I'll never fly again."

Rennin flipped on the television as the men bustled to head back home. A news report seemed to be on every channel. As the words of the reports filtered in, the men became completely quiet:

> *Once again, Trans-Atlantic Flight 777 has gone down over the Atlantic. Conflicting stories of a freak storm and dragons, yes, folks, <u>dragons</u> are abuzz. There appear to be no injuries to the passengers or crew; however, there was a great deal of damage, and every passenger in first-class is missing.*

A haunting refrain came to Rennin's mind. "You will be screaming in fury at me."

He stormed outside and raged, "Smoke! You bring my family back. What the hell are you doing? Have you gone crazy?"

Part Four

Serviendo Guberno

44
Mediation

Two immense winged creatures flew at break-neck speed with seven human females and one small black cat tucked carefully against their chests inside loosely clenched massive talons. The three children seemed unperturbed as they laughed and cooed during a wild ride. On the other hand, the women seemed incapable of being quiet as they screamed incessantly. The enormous black beast roared as he spat fire, "Please shut up!" He, then, turned a malevolent stare at the slightly smaller gray dragon. "Take *all* of them? Which ones can I drop? And you just had to give me the women. You get to carry the kids who love you. Let me see—I have to keep Renée. Which one of you is Renée?"

The gray dragon explained again, "The blonde one, Father."

"Very well. Then, I can drop the rest of you."

"You wouldn't dare!" shouted Renée.

"And why not? I am, as some of you have seen fit to call me, a vicious animal."

"Shut up!" commanded Renée. "You would not drop one of us because...because..."

"Yes?"

"Because dragons are not mean. They're meant to be our friends. You are a dragon, aren't you?"

"That I am. Now, that you've calmed yourself, let me introduce myself. I am Char, and this is..."

Renée whispered, "Rennin's Smoke. Is this real, or have I entered one of Rennin's dreams?"

"We're very real," assured Char.

D'Aubigné's voice chimed into the conversation. "Smoke, you're gonna be in *big* trouble. My daddy is gonna be so mad. Do you know what my daddy did to the last person who tried to hurt me?"

"He killed him," said Smoke matter-of-factly. "I know exactly what he did to that fat constable and to James Wilburn. The difference is, I'm not going to hurt you. We want your daddy to come after you. That's the whole point of this caper."

"Excuse me," snarled Renée. "How in the world did you know to come to that plane, and how do you know what happened with Dubois and James? *I* don't even know what happened with Dubois and James. Rennin never talks about it."

"That's because a part of Rennin he didn't know existed came to fruition that day. It's a part that frightens him, a part he can't control and had only glimpsed before, like at that beach party you went to years ago. It's the part that bonds him to me—the animal—the beast. Renée, do you really want to know what happened with Rennin that day? I can show you, but you must never tell him unless he finally tells you."

"I *have* to know. It's the only way I can help him heal."

"Father, put Renée on my back." Char carefully transferred Renée to Smoke's back and Smoke continued. "Renée, place your hand on the soft spot just above my eyes—either side will do. Now, relax and trust me."

As if watching a motion picture, Renée first saw flashes of many memories the dragon either cherished or abhorred: He sneaked off a breathtaking island in the middle of the night with a blond imp and interrupted the same imp on his honeymoon so Smoke could keep his promise to the human—He wailed with a broken heart as that human sailed from his life and rejoiced upon his return even though he was an old man—He frolicked with a satiny beige female whose name was Sand Dollar, the daughter of Brindle and Sandy, and mourned as the same female slipped into another world as she delivered an egg that Smoke incubated and hatched—He coddled and cuddled a shiny silvery slip he called Moonbeam—He removed an arrow from his daughter's wing and felt anger and hatred toward humans.

Then, Renée saw glimpses of a boy she once knew as he played with a girl she had forgotten, but she also saw the man she had wounded and the many things he would never have wanted her to see until the whole event with James Wilburn played before her eyes. She felt the rage and cold-blooded hatred that coursed through her husband at that moment, but also the compassion for the trapped soul. Renée let go of Smoke unable to breathe. Her heart broke for both the man she loved and the magnificent creature that now held her captive, for despite his deep desire to exact revenge he had come for her, not just Rennin, but *her* to mediate the turmoil and render a solution short of war and annihilation.

Sounding tired, Smoke said, "You pry too deeply. You know too much."

"On the contrary," argued Renée. "I don't know enough. If you want my help, I must know everything."

Char brightened. "Then you'll help us?"

"Yes," said Renée, "but I still don't understand how you knew about our flight."

"D'Aubigné told me," said Smoke. "Rennin isn't the only one with whom I have a connection, though my connection with d'Aubigné is sporadic. However, the storm was Divine Intervention. Even we dragons cannot control the weather."

"Do you...do you have a connection with Caitlin and Morgan?"

Smoke shook his head. "Talk to my father or Draco or one of the others. They were not given to me."

"Char?"

Char grinned. "All I'm going to say is I would suggest that you put a leash on Caitlin. If she's anything like her namesake..."

Suddenly, something whizzed past the dragon's head. "What was that?" asked Char in fright.

Renée also seemed alarmed. "Char, I have no idea where we are. I would guess you're over some country's airspace, and you didn't reply to their hails. That was a missile designed to shoot you down. You show up on radar. You have to fly low. Skim the ocean if you must, but the missile is coming back. It's tracking the heat you generate. I thought dragons were reptiles and cold-blooded."

"No, we aren't cold-blooded," corrected Char as the two creatures dove toward the earth. Char commanded, "Hold your breath," as they hit the ocean and plunged beneath the waves. The missile followed but continued downward. Thrown off course by the sea life, the missile detonated on the ocean floor. Nonetheless, the dragons felt its concussion before they emerged to fly only feet above the ocean. They checked their precious cargo, and all seemed unharmed except the cat yowled in terror. Gently, Char said, "D'Aubigné, take your pet," as he handed the terrified creature to its owner.

Then, Char growled, "You see, Smoke. We aren't safe in this world. They slew our kind years ago, knowing what we were. Now, they would kill us without even knowing who we are."

"You *are* a bit terrifying to some of us," said a shaky voice, but one that had never remained daunted. "What do you mean by saying d'Aubigné told you about our flight? How could my daughter tell you anything?"

"You haven't been listening, Miss Casey," Smoke said derisively. "We're connected in spirit. You might remember your fiancé is also connected to one of us—Brindle knows Craig well, although the lines of communication haven't been free lately. No doubt he'll accompany Rennin when he comes for Renée and his children, as will your father. How can you doubt that we're connected? Have you so soon forgotten your conversation with Draco? And before you two start, let me tell you of your husband's and fiancé's spirits." Flames flickered in the golden eyes. "Nicole, you're the only one who really doesn't belong here. You're here merely by association. You don't know your Zane or your boys at all. Perhaps, you don't know yourself. You must learn their hearts to find your own, or my father can drop you now. It's your decision. Ming, on the other hand, you know your father's heart and Jacques's. You know there's deep magic in them, as in you. Very few men and women have been welcomed to the shores of

Draconis in the last five hundred years because the hearts of men have grown dark and wicked. Cliff is very welcome here, but I fear once Rennin comes home, no more will be welcome. Even some of those already there should be banished. If another human tries to kill one of our kind, I will not hesitate to incinerate him."

"Is that why you so desperately want Rennin?" asked Renée. "Do you think he can stop the unrest between men and dragons?"

"No, Rennin is destined to govern and lead. You, my dear, are the mediator. I expect you to sort out who tried to kill my daughter and why. Rennin must return the leadership of the O'Rourke clan. Since the last in the O'Rourke line died, the men in our world have forsaken the code of friendship between us. They have blamed our kind for any and all of their misfortunes. Moreover, there is no magic left. Even the herbs once used for medicine no longer work. You know herbs. You studied them long ago when as a child you felt alone except for your *Troy*. If you don't help us, then our world will cease to exist. Men will hunt us to extinction even as they did in your world, so our ancestors fled persecution and eventual annihilation, or we will rid our world of man. We have nowhere left to flee. Neither outcome is what we want."

"You want me to mediate between you and the humans in your world?"

"We do, indeed."

Renée was awed to silence. No one else spoke or screamed.

The two dragons flew into the night and through the next day. In a voice of genuine concern, Casey tentatively asked, "Don't you need to rest? You must be exhausted."

Char's deep, throaty growl sounded fatigued. "There's no time to stop and relax. We'll rest when we get home. It's not much farther. Look ahead."

All eyes peered forward. Renée said, "It's a fogbank."

Char chuckled, "Is it?"

They flew into the vapor and for a moment, the humans almost could not breathe for the oppressive weight of the cloud. Instantly, the fog gave way to a crystal azure sky skimmed by wispy clouds.

"Welcome to Draconis," said Char cheerfully. "The fogbank was magically placed at the border of our realm a few centuries ago as a deterrent to unwanted men trying to find our world."

"Where?" asked Renée excitedly. "Where is it?"

"Well, we're over Draconian waters," explained Char. Both he and Smoke rose deftly into the sky and soared forward. "Look to your left. In a short time, you'll see the island called Isla Linda. Then, at our present speed, it will take about an hour to arrive on the main island of Draconis."

"But where are we? I mean on the map, where are we?" asked Renée

Ming said quietly, "It doesn't appear on any of our maps. Rennin once asked my father how to hide an island. My father replied, 'Spells and enchantments.' My father knows of this place, doesn't he, Char?"

Char cleared his throat. "Um, Cliff has been here and left. He had work he had to finish in the other world. It wasn't time for him to stay. He had to return for the sole purpose of training and guiding Rennin, although he didn't fully understand at the time. He was little more than a child himself when he came here—it was where his vision quest sent him. I'm certain if he ever discussed it with anyone, it was only your grandfather, Ming. Have you discussed your vision quest with anyone? Have you told anyone what your guide is?"

"No." admitted Ming.

"Not even Jacques?"

"No."

"Although at twelve, your quest took you to a dungeon and an eagle swooped in and rescued, not ate, the captive rabbit—a rabbit that took the face of an unknown young man, haggard and drawn and almost not human?"

"How do you know these things?" stammered Ming. "I've never had a visit from a dragon."

Char chortled, "Yes, you have. Don't you remember the scarlet dragon the first time you drank sake?"

"I thought I was hallucinating."

"No. That was Scarlet, my wife. Look! Isla Linda. We're almost home."

The conversation ceased as the humans viewed the prettiest scene they had ever beheld. Not long afterward, an island of sparkling white sand with a snow-capped mountain range in the background loomed ahead of them.

Even as they landed on the sand, a pearly white dragon greeted them. His voice was soft and kind without malice or threat except the disbelief he spoke toward Smoke. "Smoke! Oh, no." His massive head shook side-to-side. "You took his family. It's either a stroke of genius or the biggest mistake of your life. There's very little a man won't do for the woman he loves. There's nothing a good father won't do for his child." Draco stared at d'Aubigné. "Dear, God! She looks like Duncan. It's been far too long since I beheld eyes of that hue." Draco held out his massive talon for the child to climb onto as orange-yellow dragon tears welled in his eyes.

Without hesitation, d'Aubigné moved from Smoke's talon to Draco's. Draco winged skyward toward the mountains, Char and Smoke followed. As Draco loomed into her memory as the guide who sent her back to life, Casey returned the favor. When her eye caught a glint on the ground, Casey screamed in utter horror, "Draco, look out!"

In the nick of time, Draco rolled in the sky and caught the gargantuan arrow that had been aimed at his heart in his free talon. As Smoke had vowed, a stream of fire shot from his mouth, engulfing the two humans and the weapon they had created in their hiding place among the trees. Smoke raged, "Why would any human want to harm Draco, who has done nothing but love and protect them since the day he was born?"

The dragons swept into the mammoth cave that had served as their fortress and Alexander O'Rourke's home long ago. The dragon council met immediately, and within the week, representatives from each human town arrived, enraged two men had been killed.

Pandemonium ensued as humans raged and screamed and dragons followed suit. Renée stood between the groups and demanded they come to order and discuss the situation in a civilized manner. For a brief moment, both groups complied.

The humans hurled accusations: The dragons had burned their crops and stolen their flocks and their children.

The dragons denied the charges saying they knew which animals were designated for their use, and they had no reason to burn crops and would *never* harm a child. In turn the dragons charged the humans with two counts of attempted murder— Moonbeam and Draco.

The humans retaliated with the fact Smoke had incinerated two men. Smoke defended his action as a matter of necessity as the two had just tried to kill Draco, who happened to be holding a human child at the time.

The shouting match resumed.

Renée had no idea what to do. D'Aubigné tugged at Renée's arm. "Aunt Renée, what is mediation?"

Renée responded, "It's when one person tries to get two parties to state their complaints and work out a solution. I'm really trying here, d'Aubigné."

The little girl shook her head. "It isn't working."

"No, it's not. Rennin had better get here soon."

"We can't wait for Daddy. They'll kill one another." Before Renée could say another word, d'Aubigné's small voice magnified over the tumult. "Shut up!"

"Who are you?" asked one of the human representatives. "You're a little girl."

Sounding like a full-grown woman, but retaining the innocence that comes from pure love, d'Aubigné responded, "I am d'Aubigné Marie O'Rourke. My daddy is on his way here to take care of this mess. Until he gets here, I guess you'll have to deal with me. From this point forward, you will not speak unless my aunt Renée speaks to you. She'll ask the questions, and you'll answer one at a time. If you don't like that arrangement, I think I remember a story about a cave where a witch held people prisoner. If it still exists, I think I'll have you put in there—permanently. I am after all the great-great"—D'Aubigné paused and whispered to Renée—"How many greats are there, Aunt Renée?"

"I don't know, honey, but you're doing wonderfully. If you shoot fire from your fingertips, it would be impressive."

"Okay," said d'Aubigné as she continued. "I don't know how many greats there are, but my great-grand-somethings were Alexander and"—She raised her voice—"*Quazel*!" At which point, she shot lightning from her fingertips.

Nobody made a sound.

45
Into the Fog

There was no calming the ire that arose within Rennin O'Rourke. Even the tranquil coos from Cam and Tam did not relieve his tension. The other men, whose loved ones had also been on Flight 777, were as anxious as he. The mission they packed for was truly personal. Nonetheless, they did not seem to rage as Rennin did. Most of them were still unconvinced dragons had taken anyone. They felt it must have something to do with James Wilburn.

"No!" asserted Rennin. "It really was dragons. Come on! After everything we've encountered over the last few years, do you doubt their existence? Craig, Brindle has spoken to you. Please, say you believe. We can't get them back unless you do. I can't do this alone. I need your help. Casey needs you to believe. You said you had O'Rourke blood."

"I believe," said Jacques behind Rennin as he laid his packed duffle bag by the door. "When do we leave? Do zhou really understand what we are doeeng, Renneen? We weell not be getteeng zem back—at least, not to breeng home. Do zhou not see? Zis ploy or whatever eet ees, ees designed to breeng zhou zere. Have zhou not said zee dragons have told zhou zey need zhou? Zee only way to get zhou was to take somezeeng zhou weell go after. None of zem are een danger. Zey are zee carrot, zee bait, to draw zhou zere. When we go, we weell not be comeeng back. I am prepared to stay. Are zhou?"

Jacques's reasoning seemed to sooth Rennin's frenzied mind. "You're right," he agreed after a moment's consideration. "Smoke wouldn't hurt my family. But why did he take the rest of them?"

Jacques appeared to have the firmest grasp of the situation. "Because, Renneen, whezer by blood, marreeage, or choice, we are fameely. We have shosen to be a fameely. Where zhou go, we weell follow. We weell not desert zhou. Zhou might be zee only

412

one here wif zee last name of O'Rourke, but we are of one mind, one speereet."

"He's right," said Craig quietly. "I told you that the night Casey died. It's obvious Zane and Cliff feel the same. Gerald, Lord knows, that man loves you. We're in this together. It's just hard to overcome logic and admit there's a world beyond what I can comprehend. But I must."

"So," Cliff said as the others entered the room. "I guess we should decide what we want to take with us for a lifetime. It sounds as if we are moving away to God knows where. Am I correct? Rennin, what's your plan?"

Rennin sank onto the sofa in his family parlor. "I don't have a plan except to go to them."

"Very well, then," said Cliff. "All of you decide what you want to take with you. I assume the dragon pieces go, correct, Rennin? The rest of us have very little to consider. We'll ship everything to Miami and have it loaded onto my boat. Then, we'll sell the other things and have the currency turned into gold, silver, and any other precious metal or jewels you deem appropriate for the appreciation of dragons. After we've taken care of business, we'll set sail and follow that old map in the back of the old book. If this place is out there, we'll find it. Then, we'll confront whatever lies ahead. It's just as Jacques said. We're family. We stick together. Does my suggestion sit well with everyone else?"

There was some discussion as to the logistics of the plan, but no disagreement to the overall concept.

Nobody in Mom's Trading Post wanted to see the two coaches leave, especially Bobby Willis and Jennifer Polson, who had reunited after a trying time.

As Rennin and the others carefully packed the items for shipping, they had an unexpected visit from the two teenagers. Rennin had a great deal of affection for the two kids whose lives had been turned topsy-turvy in the wake of his arrival. He gladly took a break to visit with them one last time until he heard what they had to say. It seemed Jennifer must have been the mastermind behind the scheme. She did not hesitate with her request.

"Coach, we want to go with you."

"What?" Rennin shouted in amazement. "Are you crazy? You don't have the foggiest notion what you're even saying."

"Yes, we do, Coach," argued Bobby.

Rennin shook his head. "First of all, this isn't some little overnight expedition. We're never coming back. Second, you have your whole lives ahead of you. Third, your parents would kill all of us."

Jennifer snorted. "Coach, my parents act as if I don't exist anymore. They don't even notice when I don't come home for days at a time. Bobby's? Well, he's just about never existed for them. They've told him several times that they never wanted kids, and he was an accident. They've provided him with the necessities of life, but ask him how many times they've tucked him into bed or hugged and kissed him or even put a band-aid on his skinned knee. They leave him alone for weeks at a time. Coach O'Rourke, they beat the hell out of him for the least little thing. He didn't want me to tell you, but it might make you take us with you."

On a roll for venting, Jennifer persisted, "My folks still think I've gone insane and my mother constantly reminds me that I failed her. I don't know what she's talking about, but I'm a total disappointment to her. For God's sake, Coach! I really think she was there on Halloween. We don't belong here anymore, Coach. The only place we feel any acceptance or belonging is here with you."

Rennin tried to speak, but Jennifer held up her hand for him to wait.

"You think I don't know what I'm asking. I do. You think I don't believe there are dragons out there that have talked to you for a long time. I do. I can even name them if you would like since they've talked to me after I came under whatever influence that

was. Let's see; your favorite is Smoke—a big gray one. I
personally like the big black one with the gravelly voice—Char.
He's just so Goth. Then there's a gorgeous white one named Draco,
but my absolute favorite is the young golden one. His name is
Filigree. There are others. Shall I continue?"

"No!" said Rennin as his mind raced. "Neither are you going
off on this…this…this, I don't know what to call it." He put both
hands up sharply as if to ward off a blow. "You stay here. You be
here for each other. That's the last I want to hear of it. No more.
Now, go home. I love you both, and I will miss you. But you don't
belong with me."

Rennin hugged the two youngsters and kissed Jennifer on the
forehead. Once again, he assured them that they would be fine. As
the two were leaving, Cliff entered the room with one last large
crate to set on the porch until morning when the movers were
scheduled to arrive. Rennin gave his mentor a look that asked,
"How on Earth do I deal with that?"

Cliff grunted, "I heard. It's a terrible feeling to be unwanted,
but at least they have each other. You did the right thing. That's
what you wanted me to say, isn't it?"

"It *was* the right thing," insisted Rennin.

Cliff nodded as he set the last crate outside the door. Jennifer
and Bobby paused and turned back to wave to him. He bent his
back to the rear and groaned, "My back hurts. Let's see where we
stand. Zane has gone to Puma Pass to square everything there.
He'll be at the boat on Friday. Thank God, he's recovered about
ninety percent of what Wilburn stole. I think you can survive
without the rest, and you've given Peter Pryor power of attorney
to do business for O'Rourke Enterprises. I'm leaving in the
morning to tie up my affairs in Miami and get the boat ready. You,
Gerald, Jacques, Craig, and the boys will be there on Sunday. If
all goes well, we set sail bright and early on Monday morning.
You know, I was thinking about selling the sailboat and getting a
yacht though."

"Why?" asked Rennin. "The boat is huge, and we'll have more hands to sail this time."

"Yeah," Spell continued loudly, "but this time we'll have an old man and children with us. You know kids. They might want something to keep them occupied."

"They can read," said Rennin. "And why are you talking so damned loudly? Do you want Gerald to hear you call him old? He's not too much older than you."

"Ten years, but I was thinking more about the kids. They might want something like a TV or a gaming system to keep them occupied."

Rennin sniggered. "It won't do them much good once we get to Draconis. I bet they don't even have electricity. So, Sensei, just teach them to fight while we sail. Unless, you just want a yacht. The beds would be more comfortable."

"You talked me into it," said Spell as if it had not been his idea. "And you know that crate I brought down last; I think I'll load it in the van with the seats stored. It has something precious in it—something I think we should have with us. Well, good night. I have a long drive tomorrow."

Rennin stared after his friend, thinking that, perhaps, Cliff had lost his mind. He had behaved strangely. "Whatever," sighed Rennin as he locked the front door and went to bed.

With the seats down into their storage position, Cliff loaded the crate from the night before with Rennin's help. "Damn, that's heavy," commented Rennin. "What's in it?"

Cliff waved the younger man off. "Nothing for you to worry about—just something I think is important and nobody around here will miss. I'll see you on Sunday." Cliff drove down the driveway as the movers came to load the rest of the crates.

Rennin felt melancholy at the idea of leaving Mom's Trading Post. Although the two years he had lived there had been fraught with turmoil, he felt a love for the people. The last week he was there, Rennin finished painting a gray dragon on the side of the house. It was his way of leaving some form of protection on the community.

Having sold all the cars, Rennin, Gerald, Craig, Jacques, and Zane's two boys unfurled themselves from two taxis Sunday afternoon at the slip where Cliff Spell kept his sailboat. In its place floated a luxury yacht that could be sailed or run by engine. Painting in bold Old English lettering on the side read: 𝕯𝕽𝕬𝕲𝕺𝕹 𝕸𝕬𝕽𝕬. <u>Sea Dragon</u>. *How appropriate,* Rennin thought.

Randall and Marshall were in awe as they raced aboard to hugs from their father.

Harvey Zane greeted his friends and helped them load their bags. He commented to Rennin, "It was a good idea to get the yacht."

"Why?" Rennin asked.

"Man, can you imagine how low that sailboat would have ridden with almost a billion dollars in gold bullion, gems, and other precious items in the hold?"

"Jeez! I didn't even think about that," Rennin admitted. "Is it silly to take that gift to the dragons? What would they spend it on?"

Zane laughed. "I thought you knew dragons. I'm sure the ones that have been raised on Draconis aren't greedy. They'll enjoy just looking at it. To that small group of reptiles, I think you may be the treasure they want. You're the last of your line, after all."

"Here. I have no idea how many O'Rourkes are on Draconis."

"I think I do," replied Zane. "Three by birth and one by marriage. Think about it. That's why they so desperately need you there. Something must have gone terribly wrong, and they think that because you're descended from the savior of the island you can fix it. How often have you said the dragons have said they need you—not want—need? Use that logic now." Zane began to laugh. "I would love to see the look on Nicole's face."

Rennin gawked at the man. "Aren't you worried about her?"

"Rennin, you have a great lady. Nicole—well. Sometimes I don't even like her. If it weren't for the boys, I would probably have divorced her years ago, but I didn't want to do that to them. If she hadn't been pregnant with Randall, I would never have married her. She gave up her dreams to have my kid. I think she resents that fact. I will give her credit. She tried hard for a while. We had Marshall. Rennin, I haven't made love to my wife since before he was born. He's eight. Maybe, just maybe, something on Draconis will stir the passion again. I suppose I want that, if she'll just give me the chance. To be honest, I'm surprised the dragons took her. She seems empty."

"Have you talked to her about how you feel? Have you asked her how she feels?"

"We never talk. We just coexist."

"Harvey, have you been faithful to her?"

Looking embarrassed, Harvey Zane admitted to his friend, "I've found comfort from time to time. Rennin, I'm a man with needs."

Rennin nodded his understanding, but added, "Nicole is a woman with needs. How would you feel if you found out she had found comfort in the arms of another man?"

"I don't know."

"Maybe the emptiness is why the dragons took her. They want to give her and you the chance to be filled. From what I read in *Memoirs of Magic*, dragons are great big romantics. Read the book." Rennin placed a brotherly arm on a man who, until that moment, he had not known was hurting so much inside.

The yacht pulled easily into the Atlantic. Rennin had to admit not having to hoist sails was a much better way to travel. The group gathered every meal around the galley table like a family. They felt a closeness and camaraderie. They were a tight-knit group.

After a week at sea, the dinner table was set with two extra places. Rennin asked, "Did someone forget how to count? Sensei, what's up? You cooked tonight."

After receiving an encouraging nod from Harvey Zane, Cliff Spell sent everyone else from the galley as he sat down across from Rennin. "I have to tell you something. Remember that if you lose your temper with me, I'll kick your ass. I'm still the Master."

Rennin scowled as Cliff continued. "Rennin, it's a terrible feeling to be unloved and unwanted. When I was three, my mother, who was nothing more than a whore who supported her drug habit through prostitution, left me on the steps of a Catholic church in Boston. She never came back. I never knew my father. He was one of her johns. I suppose I should be thankful that abortions were still illegal when I was born. The nuns were good to me, but it's not being loved.

"I had a very misspent youth. I killed my first man when I was twelve."

Rennin started to speak, but Cliff held up his hand. "Let me finish. Only three other people know my whole story, Xing, Mai Tai, and Ming. I thought maybe being in a gang would give me the love and respect I so desperately wanted and needed. It didn't. At seventeen, I wandered into the Army recruiter's office. The man saw some potential in me. He helped me take my GED, and I joined the Army."

Cliff alternated between nodding and shaking his head. "No, the military isn't for everybody, but it was for me. Because of the military, I received a college degree and a sense of belonging, although my job was completely secret. You know that I was in black ops. I can never reveal some of the things I was involved in. I met Master Xing during one of those missions. For the first time in my life, I felt truly loved. Although the purpose of my being with Xing was my vision quest, we made a connection. He's the only father I ever knew. Then, I met Mai Tai. I dearly loved her, and when she died having Ming, I swore I would make sure my child knew I loved her. Yes, I left her with her grandfather for her own safety, but I visited her; and I loved her, and I took care of her. I meant what I said to Jacques—I would kill anyone who hurts her. There's one other person that I love almost as much as my own daughter."

He steepled his fingers and touched the tips to his lips. "I've allowed very few people to get close to me or to capture my heart over the years, partly to protect others and partly to protect myself. You are one of the few. I love you. You are like a son to me, although I'm not quite old enough to be your father. So, maybe you're like a little brother to me. When you're wrong, I'll tell you. You were wrong about Jennifer and Bobby." Cliff took a deep breath and said, "That's what was in the crate I brought with me."

The look of total shock on Rennin's face was indescribable. Spell continued. He flattened his hands on the tabletop.

"You know how early I get up. Do you know how many times I've found those two asleep on your front porch? Rennin, they really are unwanted. Hell, they left with me over two weeks ago. Was anyone been looking for them before you left? The only person that has shown them they were loved at all has been you. I couldn't let that love die. They're here, and they're staying. Search your heart and you'll understand their plight. Go outside yourself for few minutes, and you'll see. Now, if you want to throw a fit, go ahead. Just remember I can still kick your ass."

Rennin said nothing for quite some time. Finally, he stood and asked, "Where are they?"

"In the hold with the gold, like the treasures they are," Cliff responded sentimentally.

Rennin entered the hold where Jennifer and Bobby clasped hands and turned pale at the realization Cliff had finally revealed their secret. Rennin shook his head as tears stung his eyes. He searched his heart and the truth became evident. Bobby had been right—one of the women at the gristmill had been Jennifer's own mother. Rennin's heart broke as he considered the fact the woman was willing to sacrifice her only child to be used and abused by a man like James Wilburn. He took a moment to consider the gentle giant of a boy who would do anything to please him on the football field and realized it was the boy's cry for help. He thought about the times when he saw Bobby borrow lunch money or skip lunch because he had no money on him. He remembered the first time he saw the boy as he had shown up to earn some cash helping Rennin restore the house on the banks of Beaver Creek. Rennin was broken to realize how well the boy turned out when left to his own devices. He had often wondered if Bobby were colorblind with his mismatched clothing. Now he understood—the boy had done his own laundry. He finally understood why Bobby and Jennifer had gravitated toward each other. Rennin thought about the bruises he had seen on Bobby and had chalked up to aggressive play on the field. He could not believe the kids in front of him could have been so mistreated. He remembered his childhood and how much Eva had loved him. He couldn't speak. Rather, he held his arms open, and the two young people fell into them.

After holding on to them for several minutes, Rennin whispered, "I'm sorry. I really did not think your lives were so miserable. Forgive me for not seeing. Now, we have to come to an understanding. Sit down and let's talk."

The three sat on crates in the hold.

"If you come with me, then you'll have to think of me as your father, not your coach or your teacher. I have ideas of how I think a father should treat his kids. I expect you to obey me and respect me. I will love you, and I will always listen to what you have to say. I may not agree, but I'll listen. If I reach a decision, even if you disagree, I expect you to comply. I will never do anything to intentionally hurt you. If I'm wrong, I'll admit it. I expect the same from you. Speak now if you can't live with those conditions."

Both teenagers agreed, but Bobby made one point clear himself. "Sir, Jennifer is *not* my sister. I think you understand what

I'm saying without my going into details. If you can't live with that, tell us now."

Rennin looked from one to the other. "You're very young to make that kind of commitment. I think on Draconis they don't have a law about an age when you can get married. If you really want to be committed to each other, I ask you wait until we get there. If you still want to be together, then you can make that pledge. Bobby, Jennifer, I'll be honest. I do not want you sleeping together. This trip does not need the added burden of a pregnant teenager. I'm not trying to be mean. I'm asking that you wait."

Bobby and Jennifer exchanged looks and both nodded. Rennin let out a deep breath. "Well, if things are settled, then let's eat. Dinner's cold by now. Oh, and call me Rennin from now on. Since I'm not actually old enough to be your father, that's what my friends call me."

There seemed to be a number of surprises on the voyage. The weather turned nasty as a hurricane formed. The only thing they could do was to weather the storm and hope not to be thrown too far off course. After being slung across their rooms and being battered and bruised, the company came on deck to brilliant sunlight. The yacht had sustained little real damage, and Cliff Spell resumed course.

The days wore on, and nerves frayed. Randall and Marshall bickered constantly. Jennifer and Bobby had a fight, which ended with the girl declaring that there were lots of boys on Draconis and locking herself in her room. Even the nightly card and board games turned to accusations of cheating among the men.

After a week of squabbling, pouting, and raised voices, Rennin shouted above the din, "Stop it!" Cliff began to argue, but the gesture from the former student halted him and Rennin spoke, "If you say a word, we'll find out who the master really is today. The next person who opens his mouth, I will throw overboard."

Craig, who had said very little during the voyage, apparently did not believe Rennin's threat as he growled brusquely, "What's your problem?"

Being in as foul a mood as everyone else on board, Rennin lifted Craig bodily and threw him into the ocean and rounded on the rest. "Would anyone else like to go for a swim?"

All four kids answered in unison to Rennin's utter surprise, "Yes!" as they jumped over the side of the boat.

Cliff Spell and Gerald McClarty burst into laughter as the light dawned upon them—familiarity breeds contempt. They needed a short break from one another. They decided to join the kids.

Zane stopped the engine as he and Jacques looked at each other, "What the hell!" they chorused as they plunged into the waves.

The absurdity of the situation became clear. The laughter relieved the tension. As even the weight on his shoulders seemed to lift, Rennin muttered the old adage, "'If you can't beat 'em, join 'em.'" He at least had the good sense to strip to his boxers before he, too, dived into the mirth.

Taking the rest of the day off to just play and relax seemed to heal all the wounds, and all felt right aboard the yacht. The next day brought continued traveling. Bobby took his turn at the helm and began to worry he had done something wrong. He called, "Rennin, could you come here for a moment please?"

Rennin climbed the ladder to the helm and asked, "What's wrong?"

"None of the navigation equipment seems to be working." Bobby pointed at the needles that spun wildly.

Rennin examined the equipment, which appeared fine. "There's some kind of interference," he surmised. "It's not anything you did."

From the deck below, Spell hollered, "Yo! Stop the engines."

On a perfectly clear, sunshiny day, ahead of the yacht loomed a heavy fogbank. The small crew gathered on deck. Cliff whispered in astonishment, "I've been here."

"Where are we, Sensei?" asked Rennin. "When were you here?"

In a tone of solemn recollection, Cliff answered, "I was nineteen. It was just after I met Master Xing. It was my vision quest."

In a voice of conspiracy Rennin asked, "What's your guide? Mine is a lion."

"I know," confided Spell. "I saw it briefly in Haiti."

Rennin glanced at the man beside him. "You actually saw the manifestation of a lion?"

"Yes."

"Wow!" He stared over the gentle lapping waves. "I thought it was just spiritual."

"Me too until I saw yours. I suppose my guide is appropriate for a man who chose a life of stealth and death. I often wonder if my soul can ever be clean again. Mine is a glossy black king scorpion—quiet death. It even looks like me with my black hair, brown eyes, and olive skin, just dark."

Rennin placed a hand on his mentor's shoulder. "Your soul is not tarnished, Cliff. It's your conscience. Let it go, just as you told me. This is a time for you to renew yourself. Tell me something: Other than the man you told me about when you were twelve, were the others a part of your military responsibilities, at least until you helped me?"

"Yes, all but..."

"But what, Sensei?"

"I know exactly what you felt when it came to exacting revenge against Wilburn. I've been there, too. There was this one little Chinese Colonel who killed Mai Tai. He beat her so badly she went into premature labor and died. She bled to death, Rennin, before I could even get to her. With Wilburn, you didn't have the time to make him truly suffer. I did. By the time I finished with him, he begged to die. I didn't kill him. I left him in chains to starve. I hear starvation is the most excruciating death. Now,

Rennin, you know I can be vicious." He made eye contact with his former pupil. "Do you still think I can let it go?"

"Yep. Talk to Gerald. He has the perfect understanding of how to be forgiven. Now, where exactly are we?"

Cliff sighed. "You'll see. Sail into the fog."

Rennin took the helm and steered straight into the fogbank. For a moment, the weight of the cloud made breathing difficult. Then, the yacht eased into sunlight more brilliant than that which they had left. Looking behind them, there was no fog, only a smoky wisp here and there. Checking the gauges offered little in the way of direction as they spun uncontrollably. However, a sense of peace and purpose filled each person aboard the yacht.

Rennin called down, "Where to?"

Cliff inclined his head. "Follow your guide."

All eyes tracked Cliff's indication. What appeared to be a large gray bat could be seen in the distance. It grew ever larger as it flew directly toward the yacht while it treaded forward in the lowest speed.

Rennin's realization dawned like an electric bulb. The large gray bat was not a bat, but a dragon, and not just any dragon—it was Smoke. The shadow he caused above the yacht dropped the temperature ten degrees in a moment. As the creature hovered above the ship, a familiar voice said commandingly, "It took you long enough. What if I had really been in danger?"

Smoke unfurled his talon from which a blonde-haired, blue-eyed pixie emerged onto the deck of the yacht. Rennin pulled the craft to a full stop. Renée met him at the bottom of the ladder, and he drew her into his arms. He said, "I missed you, but I knew you were safe. Smoke would never hurt you. On the other hand..."

Rennin turned his attention to the gargantuan gray beast. "Smoke, you have a lot of explaining to do."

In a booming voice, the dragon responded, "Rennin Duncan O'Rourke, it is good to finally meet you in person, but as Renée said, it took you long enough. I regret having to stoop to human tactics to get your attention, but I did what I had to do. You're finally here. We need you to prevent a war. Of course, d'Aubigné might be able to do it. Between Renée's powers of persuasion and d'Aubigné's lighting, the humans are afraid to move. However, that is not what we dragons want. We want the balance and friendship we once shared with man."

"D'Aubigné's what?" asked Rennin.

"Oh, you'll see," assured Renée.

Smoke turned his attention to the other humans aboard the listing vessel. "Welcome to Draconis, all of you. Welcome back, Cliff. It's been far too long. If you'll be so kind as to bring this barge, as Ming calls it, along—it doesn't look like a barge to me— I would like to take Rennin on ahead. We'll see you in about a week. Pleasant sailing."

Smoke extended a massive talon. Rennin hesitated only long enough to say, "Put me on your back. I was meant to soar on the backs of dragons."

46
Upon This Rock

Smoke flew directly to Alexander's Cavern where the Dragon Council and the human representatives remained as they unyieldingly bickered. In Renée's absence, the arguments had begun again. As Smoke entered the mouth of the cave, Rennin saw d'Aubigné stomping around in one of her little tantrums when things did not go her way. She threw her hands into the air, and to her father's total astonishment, it appeared as if lightning shot from her fingertips. Rennin said, "What the..."

Renée calmly responded, "I told you that you would see."

Smoke gently picked Renée up and set her down in front of her niece. Renée scolded the child lightly. "D'Aubigné, I told you to learn to control that. You almost hit Smoke and me. And our...guest." Renée inclined her head toward the dragon who carefully set down his other passenger.

Seeing her father, d'Aubigné flew into his outstretched arms. "Daddy! Daddy! Please, make them stop fighting. Aunt Renée has talked herself blue in the face, and I'm tired of dusting myself with rocks just to make them shut up."

Rennin pouted for real. "What? No, 'Daddy, I missed you?' Where's my little sweetheart? What have you done with my daughter?"

In distress, d'Aubigné said, "Daddy, this is serious."

"So am I. You're my little girl, and this is not your responsibility. I promise to get to the bottom of the trouble and to put an end to the fighting. First, I want a hug from my daughter, not some perceived diplomat."

D'Aubigné blinked back tears as she clung tightly to Rennin's neck and whispered, "I did miss you, Daddy."

He kissed her cheek and whispered back, "And I missed you more than you will ever know. If Smoke had taken only you, I would've come. I can't imagine a life without you. I love you, darling. Now, what is this lightning? When did it start?"

The child explained, "When I got here. Aunt Renée told me it would be impressive, so I did it."

Renée shrugged. "I was joking. I had no idea it would actually happen."

Rennin asked, "What else can you do, d'Aubigné?"

Her eyes grew wide. "I don't know."

"Then, we'll talk about it later, okay?"

"Okay."

Rennin looked around at the dragons and the men who sat in stunned silence. "I suppose I should introduce myself. I am Rennin Duncan O'Rourke, and I have been summoned here to end this ridiculous feud."

Grievances came from every direction. "Stop!" Rennin shouted. "You," he pointed at the humans. "You put your complaints in writing, and I'll read them."

"In what?" asked a gray-haired representative.

"Writing."

The older man sounded grieved. "Mr. O'Rourke, I remember your last ancestor who governed this place from when I was a child. His name was also Rennin, and he came to us from outside nearly a hundred fifty years ago. After he died, it seems civilization left this rock. Very few of us can read or write. Many men behave as animals with less civility than the ancient ones. Many kill one another for the smallest offenses and mate in public like dogs in heat. Some of us attempt to keep a government and some semblance of order. It seems some have had their minds altered in some way. I, for one, am grateful you have arrived. Can you provide help for those of us who cannot put our grievances in writing?"

Rennin's voice caught as he spoke to the old man. "Yes, I'll provide help. I had no idea things were so bad. My idea of Draconis has been a utopia. I thought when I came here, I would be able to relax and put all care away. I see that is not the case. However, we will restore what once was. I give you my word."

Rennin requested Renée, Casey, Ming, and Nicole help the humans write out their complaints while he surveyed the area from the sky. When he read the complaints, most dealt with unexplained fires and missing farm animals. Rennin could understand why some of the humans would jump to the conclusion that, perhaps, a rogue dragon was behind the incidents; however, he did not say those words aloud. The one complaint that disturbed him most was the disappearance of several of the young boys and girls on the island. It seemed no girls had disappeared in twelve years, but a boy disappeared almost every month. Rather than speak or act immediately, he waited for Harvey Zane, so the detective could investigate the matter in detail.

Rennin rejoiced when the yacht finally docked. He felt he had been handed the fate of an entire world, and he could not make the decisions that needed to be made alone. He breathed relief to have his friends to help him with wise advice.

After Jacques, Craig, Gerald, and Cliff were showered with hugs and kisses, Nicole tentatively, as if she were terrified, hugged Zane and her two sons. Needless to say, Renée and Casey were shocked and apprehensive about the arrival of Jennifer and Bobby. They were not worried Rennin or any of the other men would be in trouble for having the children; they were concerned for the safety of their own children.

The only one who could calm either Renée or Casey regarding Jennifer's presence proved to be Draco. They worried the bizarre occurrences on the island could cause Jennifer to be influenced again by some sinister force. Draco decidedly told the two women to stop fretting about a child who had herself been used. He informed them it was his idea for both Jennifer and Bobby to be on the island. He had invited them to come and knew his connection to them was real because he had felt all the pain they had endured for years. He informed the mothers they had two more children to nurture and care for as they would their own, and those two children had a special place with him. He turned and walked away without further arguments or protests, leaving the two women to contemplate who held the real authority on Draconis.

After Rennin settled in, staying temporarily in the cave Alexander had once occupied, he showed Zane the reports the humans had made and asked him to investigate the incidents. Harvey Zane enlisted the help of the two teenagers that had embarked on this new life with the rest of them. He felt the kids might be able to snoop in areas where he would be too noticeable. His instincts proved to be right on the mark as Bobby provided information about a gang that had developed on the island over the last fifty years.

As with many gangs, the original formation of the group was not intent upon any form of mischief, but camaraderie and unity—a fraternity of sorts. However, the initiation practices had become increasingly violent and daring in nature. It had started with a dare for the new initiates to steal certain animals the farmers prized, but when the farmers blamed the dragons, the gang members did not return the animals as they had originally planned because some of them thought that it was even more audacious to see what would happen with the dragons.

This thought process backfired. The dragons did not take accusations against their character well and the arguing and bickering began. Some of the patrons of the gang at that time withdrew their support of the band of brothers. Theirs had been the first barns and crops burned as a warning to keep quiet. Bobby also reported somewhere in all this, the practice of old pagan religions requiring animal sacrifice reemerged. Bobby informed Zane and Rennin he was supposed to attend his first sacrifice the next week.

Rennin asked Bobby how he had come by all this information and where this ritual was to take place. Bobby laughed a little sarcastically.

"Rennin, it's a good thing these people aren't on the streets of Pittsburgh. They're so gullible. All I had to do was to let it be known I was lonely here in this new place because I had no friends my own age. They hold their meetings on the other island in that cave where the witch used to live."

Rennin rubbed his temples. "This could be more than ancient pagan religion. It could be a remnant of the evil that pervaded here once. How do I get into that meeting?"

"You don't," answered Bobby. "They only initiate kids—boys only—between the ages of twelve and eighteen. I'm supposed to find out what my initiation requirement will be after the sacrifice."

Rennin started to pace. "Bobby, I don't like letting you go alone into this thing. What if something happens to you? What if they discover you aren't truly interested in becoming a part of them?" He came to a dead stop. "You're not actually interested, are you?"

"Rennin! Maybe this is why Cliff felt I had to be here. Of this little group that has migrated here, I'm the only one the right age and gender to do this. Rennin, you'll have to trust me. You and Cliff have taught me well how to defend myself."

"Against a few, but not a gang," Rennin argued.

Cliff spoke his opinion. "Rennin, Bobby's right. We have to trust his judgment. He's a good kid."

"I don't doubt that, Sensei."

"Then, trust him. However, it might be a very good idea for Bobby to wear that amulet you told us about—the one that showed you Wilburn's soul."

Rennin nodded. "All right." Rennin opened a valet and pulled the emerald pendant from it. He held it up for all to see. "This scares the hell out of me, Sensei. I have this one, but where are the others? They should be here on the island. Who has them? Not *everyone* descended from either an O'Rourke or a Fitzpatrick or a Morales can be dead."

"I'll track them down," volunteered Zane. "Until then, I think Bobby needs to wear this thing, too, at least next week. I wish I had the technology here to wire you, Bobby. I'm worried about your safety as well. Don't do anything to draw undue attention to yourself. Promise that no matter what occurs, you'll play along."

"I promise," Bobby agreed.

A couple of days before the meeting, Bobby met his new friends on the beach. They had to leave early for the time it would take them to row to Isla Linda. It took a couple of days with rowers taking turns to row all the way to the second, smaller island. The men and boys stowed their boats out of sight, which Bobby found strange. If their practice was on the up-and-up, what need did they have to hide their boats?

They walked to a cave, which Bobby recognized from having read *Memoirs of Magic* on the trip to Draconis. The oldest man in the group, Igor Reinhardt, a long-haired and bearded man of about sixty-five, but who now looked much older to Bobby, touched the back wall of the cave and said, "*Iungo fratris honoris.*" The back of the cave gave way as if it vanished before their eyes.

Bobby's heart raced as the eerie glow from glowworms still illumined the hallway. Igor lit the two flambeaux on each side of the doorway that appeared. While the wall closed behind them upon their entry, Igor said in a distant voice, "Prepare yourselves." As he pointed at a couple of the younger boys, he commanded, "Take care of our young Mr. Willis." He ran a bony, icy finger along Bobby's jaw line, which although he was almost seventeen, had no reason to be shaved frequently. Involuntarily, Bobby shivered at the man's touch. The older man lifted the boy's chin and came precariously close to the boy's face. Bobby had the strangest sensation the old man might kiss him. Rather, Igor whispered almost imperceptibly in Bobby's ear. "There's more to you than meets the eye, but my eyes see very well." The hair on Bobby's neck stood on end as he felt the implied threat. Bobby thought to himself that the man's straight teeth had become crooked and pointed and his breath smelled like rancid meat. He had been in the old man's presence many times and had never noticed. Bobby touched his hand to his chest and felt Rennin's pendant. His thoughts raced, and he wondered if he was seeing Igor for what he really was. He was thankful for the pendant because he drew strength from its owner as he wore it.

Igor Reinhardt disappeared into one of the rooms along the hallway accompanied by only five other men. The others occupied various rooms it seemed according to age. Those who had not yet reached the age of eighteen all entered the same room where an assortment of robes in a spectrum of colors from stark white to sooty black hung. The two boys given charge over Bobby donned robes of a beige color. They eyed Bobby. One of them, Arlan Dover, placed his hand on a white robe. The other one shook his head and pointed to a slightly off-white robe.

"Are you sure?" asked Arlan as if the two boys read each other's thoughts.

"Ask him," replied the other boy, Tyler Bishop, who was about Bobby's age and about two years older than Arlan.

Arlan turned to Bobby and asked, "Bobby, are you a virgin?"

"What?" asked Bobby, shocked at the question.

Arlan repeated, "Are you a virgin? Have you ever been with a woman?"

Bobby stammered, "No. I mean yes." Bobby breathed deeply to calm his nerves as he read between the lines of the question. Obviously, the color robe one wore depended on his sexual exploits. "I mean, no, I'm not a virgin."

"How many?"

"Huh?"

Arlan seemed a little exasperated with the new initiate as he gave an irritated huff. Tyler intervened. "How many women have you been with, Bobby?"

Bobby did not know if this was a trap or test or what. He decided to be honest. If they were looking for a virgin, they were out of luck, but neither was he promiscuous. "Just one."

"Told you," said Tyler smugly to the youngest member of this strange group. Arlan handed Bobby the antique-white-colored robe. Bobby relaxed a bit, feeling he had passed at least the first test, until he heard Arlan whisper in Tyler's ear.

"The goddess is gonna be pissed. He's the only recruit this time, and he isn't a virgin. This is the third month without a virgin."

Tyler hissed back, "I'm glad he is not a virgin. I like him. I don't want him to disappear."

The men congregated in the hallway until Igor appeared from the room, which Bobby now realized was the one the witch, Quazel, had occupied, wearing a deep scarlet robe, like the ones the group at the gristmill had worn. Bobby noticed the men seemed to arrange themselves in a hierarchy first by the darkness of their robes, then age. Tyler whispered to him, "Just bring up the rear since we don't have any virgins this time around." Bobby looked around and noted that his robe was the lightest in color.

He whispered back, "They would wear real white, huh?"

Tyler merely nodded and put his finger to his lips. He flipped his hood over his head and folded his hands together, and they disappeared beneath the folds of his robe. Tyler took his place in the single file line that formed without oral command. Bobby followed suit.

The men filed into the room at the end of the corridor. They broke left and right as they entered the room and approached a long oval stone table with a bench that matched the shape around it. Igor Reinhardt occupied the seat at the head of the table. The men on either side of him ranked in degrees of lightness of their robes, with five men wearing cardinal. The boy in front of Bobby pealed left, so Bobby started to the right. Igor spoke to him, "Stop,

Mr. Willis. Take the seat at the end of the table. There's no need to be afraid. It's the seat where all initiates sit."

Bobby gave a furtive look at Tyler, who gave a quick nod. With this slight assurance, Bobby sat at the end of the table directly opposite the apparent leader of the group. Bobby noted his surroundings. The room hung heavily with a pungent aroma, and there seemed to be a fine yellow dust floating in the air. Bobby's eyes stung, and he felt lightheaded. Again, he was reminded of the gristmill.

Igor stood and walked around the table with a carafe of liquid from which he filled each man's goblet before he returned to his seat and filled his own. Igor raised his cup, and the others followed his example. Bobby's hand trembled slightly as he also raised his glass. He could see Igor watching him. The men chanted something in unison and drank deeply from their goblets. Bobby did not know what they had said or what he should do. Therefore, he looked directly at Igor for some form of instruction. With a slight incline of his head toward his goblet, Bobby asked nonverbally, "Do I drink?"

Seemingly impressed with the young man's composure, Igor nodded. Bobby drank from the goblet. Its contents were sweet and potent. After only a few swallows, he felt its effect. The other men had drained their goblets. Bobby knew if he did the same, he would not be able to function. He set the glass down. Igor smirked slightly as if he sensed Bobby wanted to be cognizant of what was about to take place.

Igor uncovered another jeweled grail set before him. Bobby recognized the baphomet engraved on its surface. His heart pounded. Igor held the chalice aloft while the others chanted once more. A sudden squealing startled Bobby so much he jumped in his seat. Being lowered from somewhere above was a pig, which Bobby realized was the Farmer Munro's prize hog, which had been reported missing a few days before.

The hog was lowered onto its back with its legs bound and sticking into the air. From beneath the folds of his robe, Igor pulled a wickedly curved blade and with more words Bobby did not understand, slit the throat of the screaming animal. Blood seeped onto the table while Igor caught some in the jeweled chalice from which he took a long thirsty draught, as if he had not drunk anything in ages. He refilled the grail and walked to the end of the table to one terrified teenager. Igor presented the goblet to Bobby. Bobby looked from the goblet to the man's face that no longer looked like the man he had met. His canine teeth extended over his bottom lip and his eyes glowed red. He spoke seductively, "Join us, Mr. Willis. Only one sip is required of you tonight if you wish to be a part of this organization."

Bobby quickly surveyed the table. All eyes were upon him. The look on Tyler's face told him if he did not drink, he would not leave the room alive. Bobby took the proffered cup and looked into the glowing red eyes. He did not want this creature to see fear or weakness in him. He thought to himself, *It's just pig's blood. I told Rennin when I met him I wasn't afraid, of anything. Well, I am now.* He took one swallow and handed the cup back.

Igor grinned wickedly as he asked, "Would you like more, Mr. Willis? You did not sip. Excellent. You may, indeed, move up quickly in this group." Igor walked back toward his seat.

Bobby's throat and chest felt as if they were on fire. He wanted to vomit profusely. He looked toward the one person present he felt any connection to. Tyler's eyes were closed as if in deep sorrow.

When Igor returned to his place, he said some more words, and it was as if a vicious pack of wolves had been unleashed as the men tore into the flesh of the dead animal and lapped the blood from the stone table. As Tyler looked toward Bobby, Bobby's hand was on his lips. Tyler mouthed the words, "I'm sorry," and joined the others.

After several minutes of feasting the others returned to their seats. Igor raised his hands as Bobby had often seen the minister at church do in order to pronounce a benediction. His voice was haunting. "Gentlemen, once again we have tasted the freshness of life. May it linger long upon our lips. Gentlemen, after many seasons, we have the opportunity to taste true freshness of life in its purest form. All of you have brought freshness to the table, but our newest member can bring something we have not had for a generation. Mr. Willis, you must bring something to the next feast. Bring us a virgin."

"A what?" asked Bobby, perplexed.

"A virgin," repeated Igor.

"Where do I get that?"

"What about that pretty little girlfriend of yours?"

Rather than the indignation Igor had expected, Bobby replied, "She's not a virgin."

"Ah, I see," said Igor. "Your one and only?"

Bobby nodded.

"Then, bring us that wonderful, tasty, little green-eyed witch."

"Witch?" Bobby was genuinely confused. "Do you mean d'Aubigné? She's a witch?"

Igor laughed viciously and ruthlessly. "And I thought you would be offended that I asked you to bring a child. Yes, she's a witch, sorceress, mage, whatever word you choose to use. She is the most powerful of her kind since Quazel herself. Bring her to the table at the next gathering. With her blood to fortify us, we will be invincible."

Bobby felt the room swirling before him. *Surely this is a horrible nightmare, and I will wake soon.* He tried to remain calm by asking, "When is the next meeting?"

"The next full moon."

No more words were spoken. Igor pronounced a benediction in the same strange tongue. Leaving the cave, Igor spoke the words, "*Rodeo portenis et fortis.*"

Loading into various boats, the men started toward the main island of Draconis. Bobby still felt as if he were walking in a dream. Tyler steered him by his elbow away from the beach and the boats. "We'll go tomorrow."

"What?" asked Bobby. "Won't they miss us?"

"No. They'll get home and sleep for days. I have to talk to you away from prying eyes and ears." Tyler maneuvered them to a small slit in the side of a hill. He lit one small candle which barely illuminated the grotto that had played such an important role in Draconian history, the place where Duncan O'Rourke had been restored to human form. "I cannot believe this!" he shouted. "What were you thinking?"

"I don't understand," said Bobby. "Please tell me this was all a dream. Please tell me I won't be like that." Bobby pointed out the entrance.

"Oh, my God!" bellowed Tyler. "Are you worried about yourself? Don't you realize Igor is planning to sacrifice that child and drink her blood? Haven't you figured out that he is some sort of vampire or *something*? I had hoped you would back out of coming. What do I do now?" He gripped his hair as if he wanted to pull it out.

"I had to come. I had to find out what's been going on?"

"Are you going to tell Rennin?"

"What?"

"Please tell me you're going to tell him. He has to put a stop to all of this. Once any of us drinks the blood of a human, we're damned. We can never be saved. You can't let that precious little girl die. I came out here to find out what was happening, too. I did just what you did because I was certain they were behind my sister's disappearance. Don't you see? She was my age and she disappeared when I was only five. She was the only girl in our family. I know she was a virgin. They killed her. My own father brought his daughter out here to die. They drank her blood. She was the last virgin sacrifice. Why do you think my robe is so much darker than yours? Do you think I just want to bed a bunch of girls? No, I've slept with a number of them and tricked Arlan into sleeping with a number of them so that they won't be sacrifices. How do we stop this?"

Another parent willing to sacrifice a child, just like Jen. Bobby tried to appraise his situation. He wasn't sure if Tyler was on the level with him or trying to trap him. Tyler's distress seemed real. Tyler's next two words convinced Bobby of what he had to do.

Through real tears, Tyler choked, "Help me."

Bobby nodded. "Yes, *we*, not I, go to Rennin."

"They'll kill me," said Tyler. "They killed my father and my mother when he tried to get out. I've been on my own for a very long time, living on the kindness of others."

"No, they won't. Rennin will protect you. But he might kill me if anything happens to d'Aubigné. Now, I'm going to ask you to help me." Bobby held out his hand. "Are we allies?"

Tyler grasped Bobby's hand as if he were a drowning man gripping a last-second life preserver. The two boys embraced stiffly. Bobby said, "We should get back."

"No. We have to wait for morning. The men will be passed out in the boats. At first light, you call one of the dragons to come for you. They'll come for you, but not for me."

Tyler doused the candle and the boys settled for the night. Still a bit apprehensive, Bobby lay in front of the entrance, so Tyler would have to step over him if he tried to leave. Bobby felt certain he would hear a splash if Tyler tried to swim out. He did not sleep all night and heard Tyler's fitful tossing and turning.

Before the sun streaked the sky, the two boys left the grotto, and Bobby called Smoke to come and get him. Smoke eyed the other human uncertainly. Bobby assured him, "Smoke, this is Tyler. He's an ally. He really needs to talk to Rennin, but I think all the other humans from Draconis should be gone."

Smoke growled, "Rennin sent them home already. He told them he would call them when he got to the bottom of their problems with us." Smoke sniffed the two boys. "You both smell of pig's blood. Why?"

"We'll tell Rennin," answered Bobby assertively.

Smoke agreed and flew both boys to Rennin in Alexander's Cavern. Together the boys told Rennin and his council about the night before and all that Tyler knew of the "brotherhood's" affairs.

Rennin looked around at the group of friends and family and devoted dragons. "I told you there was more to this than mischief. Now, what do we do?"

Casey shrieked from her mother's heart, "Just go and kill that monster just like you did James Wilburn."

"What about the rest of them?" asked Rennin. "If I kill Reinhardt, someone else could be worse." He spoke directly to Tyler. "Can you tell me who all is involved in the so-called brotherhood?"

"Yes, but I think you need to consider that some of us were either tricked or coerced into joining, especially those who were inducted after my sister's death. I chose to go thinking I could find out the truth. I found out, but I don't know how to get out alive now that I know. Will you please help me, Mr. O'Rourke? I'm really scared, but I couldn't let Igor kill your little girl."

Rennin put a hand on the boy's shoulder. "Yes, we'll help you. First, you'll stay here from now on. If they ask questions, you're hanging out with your newest best friend, Bobby. If you must say anything else, tell them you're doing your utmost to ensure Bobby fulfills his pledge."

"My only friend," Tyler muttered.

Rennin continued, "I have a plan in mind, but I might have to bind and gag Casey to implement it."

Casey glared at Rennin. "If it involves using d'Aubigné as bait, you're damned right."

"Do you think I would let anything happen to her, Casey?"

"Not intentionally, but some things are beyond your control."

"At least hear the plan."

Casey still glowered at Rennin as he talked. "In a couple of days so that it doesn't look suspicious, I'll fly to Isla Linda just to look around. I plan to go all over the island including Quazel's lair.

Tyler and Bobby have provided the passwords. Do they change, Tyler?"

"They never have since I've been going, sir."

"I want to figure out a way for us to hide in there and wait for them. I'll kill every last one of them if I have to. Yes, Casey, it involves letting d'Aubigné go with Bobby, but if Igor doesn't think he is getting what he wants, then, both these boys are as good as dead, plus many more. I would ask you to go with us, but you don't have a clue how to fight. I do want you involved in every other aspect of the plan. In addition to those of us who went after Wilburn, I think we need to add Jacques, Renée, and Craig."

"Craig can't fight either," stormed Casey.

"Cliff has one month to whip him into shape. And, Casey, if I still need to think about the prophecy of old, he's the only one with red hair besides Nicole. Zane, find those damned pendants before then. I think we also need to pay a real in-depth visit to King Satin's Realm.

Three days after the brotherhood's meeting, Rennin and his entourage paid a visit to Isla Linda as if they were on an outing. They went to Morgan's Meadow for a picnic. They visited the grotto. They walked in the villages. Last, they stopped in the cave where Satin had hidden and Quazel had lived behind the walls in the underbelly.

Leaving the teenagers as sentries, the rest of them went below. The rooms did, indeed, contain robes of various neutral shades from white to black. In the room where Igor had changed, there were vials of hallucinogenic herbs, poisons, and other magical things. There were bottles of nectar wine and the goblets and the scimitar that were used in the monthly ritual. There were books on black magic, and a rack of robes. There was one deep crimson robe, the scarlet robe Igor had worn, and several bright cardinal robes. The ceremony room was just as the boys had said except someone had cleaned the area. There was no evidence of the macabre scene the boys had described.

When Rennin returned to the outer cave, he questioned the boys again regarding the red robes. "Tyler, who besides Igor wears a red robe?"

"A few of the oldest men—there are five. I think they were there for the last human sacrifice. That's why they wear red."

"There's more than you know. That crimson robe smelled like a woman. Have you ever seen a woman at any of these rituals?"

"Never, sir. I'm not lying."

"I believe you," Rennin said to calm the boy's fear. "I just think there's something you don't know. Tell me about the missing boys and the goddess. Who or what is the goddess? What happens to the boys?"

"If the boys are young enough to be virgins, and I must tell you that on Draconis boys start young, sir..."

"All right. I understand." He held his hand up like a shield. "We'll discuss that later in detail, but just for the record, how old were you?"

"The first time?"

Rennin nodded.

Tyler said, "Fourteen."

"And when were you initiated?"

"A week later."

"Okay. Were there any other virgin boys initiated with you?"

"No. I also heard whispering about the fact that there were no virgins that month. There were three of us."

"And when there are virgin boys what happens at the initiation?"

"The same thing that happened with Bobby except when we leave, they're left behind with Igor. And if there happens to be more than one, which I've only seen twice, Igor chooses one. They're never seen again."

"I see. There's a stone altar behind where Igor sits. Have you ever seen any kind of ritual done there?"

"No, sir."

"Well, I think there's a woman behind the entire thing. She's the one that wears the crimson robe, and she does something to those boys. Tyler, do you know if Igor has always lived here?"

Tyler replied, "Legend says he washed ashore in a basket as an infant."

"And all the unrest, along with the formation of the brotherhood, occurred when he was about fifteen?"

"I think so, sir, but you might ask someone older about that."

"Tyler, I believe every word you've told me. I want you to know I'll do everything possible to get rid of this evil. One more question. Does Igor have a wife?"

"Yes, sir."

"Where do they live?"

"King Satin's Realm."

"Just where I plan to go tomorrow. Bobby, I think I need my pendant back now."

Bobby had forgotten he had not taken the necklace off. He touched the stone gingerly and pulled the chain over his head.

Rennin slipped it on and brought up the rear as the group left the cave. Rennin was surprised to see the one interloper in their midst waiting for him at the cave's mouth.

"Nicole, is something wrong?" he asked.

Without looking up from the ground, she asked, "May I please make a suggestion to you?"

"Of course."

"If you really stay here forever, don't live on the big island. Build your home here, and I mean right here on this rock. Make sure no one ever uses it for evil again." Nicole left without waiting for a reply.

She's scared for her boys. Rennin ran his hands over the surface of the rock face. "Maybe she has a good point. Upon this rock I will build a new world free of the evil that has plagued this land and stalked my family."

47
Guides

Bright and early the next morning, the wayfarers made a pilgrimage into the heart of the island of Draconis to the settlement known as King Satin's Realm. Many of the homes appeared to be unoccupied. Smoke explained that some of the native islanders were superstitious about living in the homes once occupied by Alexander, Duncan, or Aidan O'Rourke. However, Igor Reinhardt seemed unconcerned by the magical history of the village for he and his wife had chosen to live in the house built by Aidan O'Rourke. Rennin scowled slightly as he thought the place should be his home, but he also considered the suggestion Nicole had made to him on Isla Linda.

So as not to seem intrusive, Rennin and his companions visited several inhabitants and introduced themselves before they knocked on the door of the Reinhardt home. A startlingly exquisitely gorgeous woman about forty years old answered the door. The woman was about five-feet-ten inches tall. She had a Barbie-doll figure, long shimmering raven tresses, deep dark-chocolate eyes, and a creamy ivory complexion. A sharp breath of appreciation for the piece of human art from every man in the group, except Rennin and Bobby, echoed through the village. Rennin, too, breathed sharply, but for a different reason. Moreover, the intake of breath he perceived from the young man in their group boded fear, not reverence or awe.

Rennin calmly introduced the party, and Mrs. Reinhardt graciously invited them into her home and served them refreshments. Mrs. Victoria Reinhardt asked pointedly, "Mr. O'Rourke, will you want to move into this house?"

Rennin assured her that he had no intention of asking her to vacate the premises. He had simply wanted to visit the town his ancestors had established. As they left, Rennin asked Mrs.

Reinhardt, "I understand that some people are superstitious about living in the homes the O'Rourke family built."

She precluded the rest of his question, "I'm not superstitious, Mr. O'Rourke."

"I can see that," replied Rennin. "My question is about that house." He pointed to a house that was completely boarded up. "Whose was that, and why doesn't anyone live there? It's a magnificent house."

"Oh, that is the house built by the pirate, Ricardo. It seems bad things befell anyone who has lived there in the last fifty years or so. People say it has something to do with the pirate's curse or the fact Ricardo was related to Quazel. I think it's nonsense. I didn't choose that house because it needs many repairs." Although her words said she did not believe in the curse or was not superstitious, Victoria Reinhardt could not prevent the almost imperceptible shiver she displayed when she talked about Ricardo. Rennin noted both her words and her body language as they bade her good-bye. Igor had not chosen where they lived—Victoria had. And on the very spot Quazel had pitched her camp five hundred years before.

Upon their return to the cave, Rennin called a meeting. As everyone assembled, he said, "All right, I want to discuss what we saw when we met Victoria Reinhardt."

The looks on the women's faces were of open hostility. On the other hand, the men's faces showed rapt awe. Rennin decided to play teacher as he asked each one individually what he or she saw. He started with the one who should have been the wisest in the group, "Gerald what did you see?"

Gerald McClarty responded, "The most beautiful woman I've ever seen."

Rennin continued, "Cliff?"

Cliff breathed, "A goddess."

"Interesting comment," said Rennin. "Please, Craig, critique her from a doctor's perspective."

"She was an absolutely perfect physical specimen. Not a flaw anywhere."

"Hmmm," responded Rennin. "Jacques, be careful how you answer. You're sitting beside your intended."

Jacques said, "Eet was not so much what I saw as what I felt. I saw exactly what zese men saw. She ees gorgeous. What I felt was ice een my veins. I was terreefied, yet I could not take my eyes off her."

Rennin pursed his lips and nodded, "Zane, what about you?"

"Breathtaking. Fine as wine. I can't describe her, Rennin."

Rennin turned toward the ladies, "Okay, ladies, it's your turn."

"What about me?" asked Bobby, a bit offended.

Rennin pointed at the boy. "I'll get to you in a minute, Bobby. I think your take on this is just a little different. You might have something to add to what Jacques said. Let me start with you, Nicole, since you suggested I build my home on Isla Linda yesterday rather than take the home this woman lives in as my own. What did you see, or what do you think?"

Nicole spoke vehemently, with the most passion Rennin had ever seen in her. "I'm not surprised Harvey thinks she's beautiful. What was ugly about her? She's everything I'm not—tall, thin, pretty, well endowed. What man wouldn't want her? Nonetheless, there's something disconcerting about her. I think she would devour most men, especially men like Harvey—men with no passion in their souls."

"Whoa!" said Rennin. "I think it's time to move on. Casey?"

Casey was even nastier than Nicole. "She's a slut! She would do every man in this room in one sitting."

"Okay!" said Rennin. He had not expected the comments to run so deep. "Ming do you think you could say what you think with a little taste?"

"No," replied Ming. "I agree with Casey, but I dare her to come near Jacques. She'll be in much need of Craig's services if she does. I promise she will no longer be a perfect specimen."

"Very well. Let's see if the younger generation can be more discreet. Jennifer, what did you see?"

"My worst nightmare. I saw a woman who could be everything to all men, but I also saw the women who danced around me the night I was raped. I hope I never see her again."

Rennin looked at his wife and cocked his eyebrow. "Renée, darling, what did you see?"

"The one thing I fear the most, someone who could take you away from me."

"Really?" said Rennin. "That surprises me." He placed the copy of *Memoirs of Magic* on his wife's lap. "Renée, let me ask you again—what did you see?"

Renée looked at the old book. "I don't understand, Rennin."

"Think," said Rennin as he turned toward Bobby.

Renée blurted, "It's not possible, Rennin! She's dead—cremated."

Rennin said calmly, "Bobby, what did you see?"

Bobby shivered from head to foot. "I think I saw exactly what you saw. That's why you saved me for last, isn't it?"

Rennin nodded, "Tell them what you saw, and I'll tell you if it's the same thing I saw."

Bobby whispered in fear, "I saw something that had scraggly hair, red eyes, and long fangs as if it wanted to suck the blood from each of us. No, not each of us—just the men. I think it's that 'goddess' Arlan mentioned. I think it's the thing that has devoured the missing boys. God only knows what it did before it ate them. All I know is that thing scared me to death. Am I even close to what you saw, Rennin?"

"Very close, Bobby. I was wearing the emerald pendant, remember? You wore the pendant just a few days ago. Its effects haven't worn off yet."

Renée thumbed through the book again. "Rennin, do you really think Quazel has somehow been resurrected?"

"I don't know, but I do know that thing has to go. Zane, have you had any luck finding the other pendants?"

Zane shook his head. Nicole rubbed her head as if it were splitting as she spoke coldly. "Maybe I'm not so useless after all. I haven't read the damned book, but I have listened to every word I've heard since I got here. Nobody will live in the house the pirate built. The man was a *pirate*. What do pirates have? *Treasure*. What do they usually do with that treasure? *Bury* it. Where would this Ricardo person have buried the treasure? Could it be in that house somewhere or someplace he held dear?"

Rennin mused aloud, "Charlotte's grave."

"No," said Renée. "Draco told us Danielle died a year before Ricardo. They're in Danielle's grave. First, he would never have disturbed Charlotte's grave. Second, whom did he love more than he ever dreamed of loving Charlotte? Danielle. What would be more sacred and safe to him than the grave of his true love? Maybe Ricardo's spirit does haunt that house to keep its neighbors out. The bad things only started when she came along. Aidan's heirs would've known what was done with the amulets, but they've vanished. Perhaps they became lax in their vigilance. I bet if we search far enough back, we'll find the first missing boy was the last in the O'Rourke family line."

"Well," said Rennin. "I think it's time to exhume Danielle's body. If the amulets are there, we'll be one step closer to restoring the magic to this place. Let's take this step before we formulate more of a plan." He gave Nicole a genuine smile. "Very astute thinking, Nicole."

She blushed at the recognition.

Rennin continued, "Think of it like this: This is going for a first down long before we're in scoring position."

The exhumation of Danielle Martin Morales's body was a solemn affair and done discreetly on a rainy day when others would not be about. After such a long interment, there was nothing to be lifted from the grave, so with a feeling of desecration, but knowing Danielle would understand and approve if she knew the situation, Rennin climbed into the grave and took a deep steadying breath. He shivered as he recalled being buried alive. Gently moving the remains and rotted clothing of a long dead heroine of Draconian history, Rennin discovered a black silk pouch as perfect as the day it was buried. Inside the pouch were the other six pendants and the amulet Aidan O'Rourke had worn when he killed the witch, Quazel, along with a note which read:

If you have disturbed the resting place of my beloved Danielle, then you are a descendant of my dear friend, Aidan O'Rourke, and you have discovered the evil that once plagued Draconis has returned, perhaps, even stronger than before. You are in need of the contents of this pouch. Use them wisely, and this time banish the villainess to the pit of Hell with no return in any form if that is possible, for I know evil will remain until the world is made new. If you are any other than the one who rightly deserves these items, may the ground swallow you and consign you to an eternal damnation.

Ricardo Manuel Mendez Morales.

Back in the cave Alexander had once called home and in dry clothes, the small group of outsiders destined to reclaim the glory of Draconis met again to discuss the enchanted jewels. Looking at them spread upon a table, Renée asked reverently, "How do we know who gets which?"

"Faith," said Rennin. He picked up the ruby pendant and handed it to Craig. "I'm certain this one's yours. You're Brindle's Colin returned to him, remember?"

Craig caressed the jewel as if some part of his soul which had been lost was found before he said, "It's as if I can feel the strength and determination of Colin Fitzpatrick. All the doubts I've had seem to have vanished."

Rennin beheld the cobalt gaze of his wife's eyes and picked up the sapphire necklace. Slipping the stone over her head, he said, "There's no doubt where this one belongs. Only those eyes could command its power. It became obvious to me you truly are magic on Halloween night almost two years ago. Your Celtic blood, yea, Druidic blood, surfaced with a fury and a vengeance. You've never told me how you knew you could enter that pentagram unharmed. Neither have you ever explained how you were able to revive Casey. Now, might be a good time for all of us. I need to know."

Renée conceded to her husband's request. "You're not the only one who can trace a family lineage. When things were so bad for me as a teenager, I traced my lineage all the way back to Celtic Ireland where my ancestor was a Druid priestess. After reading about Druid practices, I knew that if I had continued in her practice, I would've been a priestess. I never thought I would even consider practicing any form of witchcraft, but when the lives of my daughters were at stake, nothing else mattered. It might interest you to know our family lines crossed paths long ago. I'm descended from Barbara Anne O'Rourke, daughter of Devlin Daniel O'Rourke and Melissa Beecham, whose mother and father were tried and hanged as witches during the Salem Witch Trials. So, you see, darling, there's a bit of actual O'Rourke blood flowing in my veins. The Druid line was passed through Melissa."

She smiled toward her sister. "The Druid line came from my father, that's why you couldn't enter the configuration although we're sisters." She took a deep breath and gazed back at Rennin. "As for Casey. I was selfish. I couldn't lose the sister I'd just found. I thought nobody was around to witness my triumph or failure. I analyzed the situation. If I failed, I was no worse off than I already was, and if I succeeded, I had my sister back. And if I succeeded, I wouldn't violate the DNR since it would be a supernatural occurrence—a legal loophole. Therefore, I performed the ritual Elizabeth used on Caitlin. It worked on Casey because, I think, she's my sister and I love her. The Gaelic says only blood and love can revive the spirit. Don't ask me to do it repeatedly. I don't think I can, except maybe for you or the girls. It drains some of the life of the giver. That much I do know. Now, I've told you my secret. Perhaps, you can tell me yours about James and Dubois."

Rennin scowled. "I never wanted to talk about it. The constable I shot from pure instinct, but I emptied his own gun into him. Casey knew because she was there. James. Whew! I broke his arm, shot both his kneecaps, pinned his hand with a carving knife, cracked his sternum, and stomped in his crotch to keep my promise to Casey." He made brief eye contact with his sister-in-law. "There was a supernatural occurrence as well. He asked me to free him in a voice that I had never heard."

"A gentle, kind voice," Renée interrupted. "I heard it only once—in Greece after he tried to destroy my dragon pendant and left bruises on me. It lasted about three minutes before the evil returned."

A nod showed Rennin understood. "I only heard it for a moment, too. Then, I ripped his throat out when he threatened to molest d'Aubigne. I'm not sorry I killed either of them. I feel absolutely no remorse. If that makes me evil, too, then, so be it. I will never speak of it again."

Rennin sighed as if he were fatigued, for he was, indeed, emotionally exhausted. *I do feel remorse for taking a life. That's why I can't talk about it. But it was necessary.*

A gentle thought came to his mind from Smoke. "I understand. You can always talk to me. I burned two humans, and I do feel sorry, but it was necessary." A sense of peace encompassed the man.

He surveyed the remaining pendants and focused on the task at hand. He held the onyx in his hand and weighed his thoughts before he presented it to Cliff Spell. "What could be more appropriate for a king scorpion?"

Cliff took the pendant without comment, but the look between the two men spoke volumes. Both knew the other had their regrets that each had to live with. A thought in Char's gravelly drawl entered Cliff's mind. "You told Rennin to let it go. Now, you let it go. You are not alone. I am here for you." A new bond between man and beast solidified. Cliff closed his eyes and nodded.

Rennin smiled at his next thought as he held the opal and appraised Ming. "As pure as the driven snow, you've waited for your one true love. Your heart, your mind, your soul are all unblemished as well. It only makes sense that you should have a symbol of innocence. That thing has no idea you're a virgin, my dear. In its mind, you're too old. Or if it does, it isn't so much the virgin it wants as my daughter. It has already tried twice and failed. Wear this knowing your innocence and purity might be the strongest weapons we have against this thing."

Ming held the opal and said, "Let me go with Bobby, Rennin."

He shook his head. "I need you to fight. Besides, it wouldn't work. Igor specifically asked for d'Aubigné. But thank you."

Rennin held the last two pendants and considered the last two men. "Master Xing said I had the gift of logic. Perhaps, this is the time that gift is truly being tested. Zane, you've said you don't feel a particular purpose being with me in all the things we've endured the last couple of years. What purpose does a topaz serve? What's so special about it? It doesn't jump out as a very valuable stone. Still, this is the stone Diggory Danaher wore. He brought Draconis its first hero. He, too, thought he was common, not valuable. However, you, my friend, are invaluable. You've always had my back when I needed you. We would be incomplete without you, just as the collection of stones would be incomplete without the topaz. It's yours." Rennin handed the topaz to Harvey Zane and turned toward the last member in the group of his choosing.

"Where do I begin?" Rennin shook his head and rubbed his chin. "The first time I met you, I didn't like or trust you. You were an ugly lump of coal. Just like that lump of coal, you have been pressed and tested and gone through the trials of fire and come out a diamond in the rough. You are strong and clear and good, just like this gem. You're a rare find. Jacques, you have proven you're a kindred spirit, a brother. I love you as such. I often wonder if you're as pure as Ming and that's what brought you together. I know your heart, soul, and mind are still untarnished. I won't ask you the rest. It's your business. Wear this flawless stone as my little brother."

Jacques's hand shook as he took the pendant from Rennin. Rennin pulled the younger, smaller man into a brotherly embrace. Words passed between them no one, but the dragons, could hear. Jacques whispered to Rennin, "Yes, I am. I never slept wif Casey. Zhou assumed I deed because of her heestory. And I never slept wif anyone een Haiti or New York. I was afraid of zee rampant disease een my country. I told zhou I was desteened to be wif Meeng and only Meeng. Eef zat ees being doomed, I am happy to be doomed."

Rennin laughed. "It's a good thing, Jacques. I wish I could go back in time and be with Renée, and only Renée. But I'm where I belong now, and if that's being doomed, then I'm happy to be doomed right beside you."

Having assigned the pendants, the next matter of concern was d'Aubigné. Rennin worried about his first born. It appeared that the magic lure of the island had freed her true gifts, but she had no idea how to control them. Rennin felt sure her abilities played some role in the fact the creature Victoria or Igor or both wanted her. He spoke with Cliff about the possibility of a vision quest, not only for d'Aubigné, but also for those in the party that had never experienced one. Cliff agreed to attempt it if he had a quiet place. Draco's knowledge and wisdom suggested the grotto on Isla Linda. Cliff began his work with the people who held enchanted pendants since they would be going into battle very soon.

Feeling that he would have an easier time with someone who already had some knowledge of the supernatural world, Cliff began with his future son-in-law. While he spent the time working on the people's spirits, hearts, and minds, Cliff insisted that Rennin continue the physical training, especially with Craig, whose idea of fighting was a drunken bar brawl in college.

In the grotto on Isla Linda, Cliff patiently worked with Jacques to calm his fears about an experience over which he had no control. Jacques trusted the man he already called "Papa" as Ming did. As Cliff assured the young man that Jacques would be completely safe, Jacques drank the beverage Cliff had prepared. Cliff hugged the nervous younger man and whispered, "Everything will be fine. I'll be right outside. Trust me. Relax and meditate. You'll find your way. I don't doubt you at all."

While Cliff waited expectantly and Rennin turned Craig's instincts into useful skills, Jacques eventually found himself flying unhindered through the air and devouring a multitude of insects. In the darkness as he flew, he was able to hear, rather than see dangers that approached. It was as if he had a sixth sense regarding events about to occur. He found himself whispering advice to a golden and walnut lion who listened to every word graciously and gratefully. As the sun rose, Jacques found himself in a cave and hanging from his feet as he fell asleep. He seemed to leave the creature and saw a large bat drifting off to slumber.

Jacques, himself, awoke inside the grotto, head down and back against one wall. He lowered himself, sat up, and laughed. "A bat? I should have known I would not be anyzeeng elegant or graceful. However, I am useful."

Jacques left the grotto to find Cliff sound asleep. He laughed aloud. "Eet Ees a good zeeng I was not een any danger. Wake up, old man!"

"Who's old," quipped Cliff? "I wasn't asleep. I was just resting my eyes."

"Eef zhou eenseest," Jacques complied good-naturedly. "Come on, Papa. Let's get zhour next veecteem."

"Well," demanded Cliff, "are you going to tell me?"

Jacques shook his head. "No. I am not very pretty, but I am very useful."

Cliff   sniggered. "Ming would disagree. She thinks you're what is known as a 'pretty boy.' I think I agree now that you're cleaned up and filled out. But you're still quite useful. You seem to sense things some of us miss. So, now what was your guide? We might need to know. It could be that somewhere in all this the guides can communicate when we cannot."

"Ees zat zhour way of tryeeng to coerce me eento telleeng zhou what zhou want to know?"

"No, I'm serious. I mean, I actually saw a visual manifestation of Rennin's in Haiti."

"All right, Papa. A bat. What deed zhou expect, another golden eagle like Meeng?"

"No. Mine is a king scorpion. What's so great about that except that it fits me? Think what the world would be like if there were no bats. We would be overrun with mosquitoes and such. Bats are very useful creatures. I think your guide suits your abilities quite well. I'm dying to see what the others might be."

As the two were ferried back to the main island, Harvey Zane prepared to accompany Cliff the next day. One after another the three remaining pendant owners took their turns. Zane's guide proved to be a ferret with the ability to get in and out of places unnoticed and to take things without detection. Zane felt good about the animal.

Craig took a few days from his training to go with Cliff. His loyalty and need to help others manifested itself as a faithful collie. Craig chuckled, "At the very least the coloring is right."

Cliff Spell was not in the least surprised that Renée's guide proved to be a polar bear. He had often compared her to a mother bear protecting her cubs. He felt that once he was able to work with Casey that she might prove to be a grizzly. However, before he would consent to doing a quest with Casey, Gerald, Jennifer, or Nicole, at which he just rolled his eyes because he felt it would be useless, he insisted that Bobby and d'Aubigné go through the ritual because they would be directly involved in the upcoming task.

Bobby's need and ability to lead and protect, as he had shown to his coach many times on the football field as a nose tackle and team captain even as a sophomore and junior, were displayed in the form of a magnificent silver-backed gorilla. Jennifer could not help but tease him that it was actually his ape-like mentality.

The highlight of this session of vision quests for Cliff was d'Aubigné. Casey argued until she was blue in the face d'Aubigné was too young. She lost the argument with everyone, including her six-year-old daughter. Cliff had intuitive inklings into at least the family of guides most of his other students would be, but he did not have a clue as to what animal might guide d'Aubigné.

Unlike the adults Cliff had handled, the child was not in the least apprehensive. She fell almost immediately into a state of deep meditation. It did not surprise Cliff when d'Aubigné emerged from her quest in less than twenty-four hours. She smiled gaily at "Uncle Cliff" and chirped, "I was a dolphin. I like that because they're pretty and smart. Uncle Cliff, why is Mommy so upset about me going with Bobby next week? Daddy says it's so we can stop some bad people who think they should hurt children. Is that true? Don't lie to me, or I'll know. And don't try to protect me. I need to know the truth. The dolphins told me to ask."

Cliff hesitated. "Maybe you should talk more to your mommy and daddy."

"No, Uncle Cliff. You have to tell me. Both of them are too scared to be completely honest. Am I in danger? Do these people want to hurt me? Is my daddy so upset because he thinks he's risking my life? Is that why Mommy's so mad at him? She's even mad at Craig. She says he should be supporting her, not Daddy. She made him sleep in another room. Now, am I right or wrong?"

"Come here," said Cliff as he picked up d'Aubigné as he had done Ming many times when she was a little girl. "You are exactly right. These very bad people are the ones causing all the trouble here. They told Bobby to bring you. Yes, d'Aubigné, their intention is to kill you. That's why your daddy and the rest of us are going to surprise them. Do you remember how your daddy had to go after the man named James Wilburn?"

She nodded.

"Well," Cliff continued, "that's exactly what we have to do now. We have to get rid of these people. Listen carefully. You do whatever your daddy or I tell you to do. Bobby has no intention of letting anyone hurt you, but you listen to Daddy or me. If anyone in our group tells you to do anything that sounds differently from what we say, don't do it. You find one of us or send your dolphin. Do you understand?"

"Yes, sir. I can always shoot lighting from my fingers if I have to."

"And you might. If for some reason we aren't around to protect you, shoot the lightning or whatever else you might be capable of doing. I mean it. You're a little girl, but if those people try to hurt you, kill them if you can. At least hurt them and run. We'll find you. You know I love you just like I love your daddy, don't you?"

"I love you, too, Uncle Cliff."

The duo returned to Draconis without discussing their talk with anyone else. Preparations began in earnest for the next full moon's ritual, and Cliff promised to do quests with the others after that time. However, two of those now residing in Alexander's Cavern would not wait until after the next full moon. First, Casey demanded that she have the opportunity to discover her guide for the sake of her child. Exhausted from his efforts, Cliff reluctantly gave in. Tyler stopped the two as they prepared to leave and asked, "Mr. Spell, is there any way you could do two of us at once?"

Cliff mussed the boy's hair and answered honestly, "No, Tyler. This is something that must be done in solitude. I wish I could, but I need time to prepare as well."

Tyler murmured with a deep frown on his face, "It's just as well. I probably don't have anything guiding my spirit anyway."

Cliff scowled. "I'm sure you do. I have an idea. Give me a few minutes."

Cliff found Rennin with his daughters and spoke conspiratorially with him. "Rennin, Tyler really needs this before we go out, but you know Casey will never shut up until she gets what she wants. I cannot do both of them. I need a few days to recuperate my own inner being before the full moon. Rennin, this boy is terrified he's somehow unsalvageable because he's a part of the so-called brotherhood. If he goes into the next meeting in this state of mind, he could easily betray the whole plan without meaning to. I have an idea. Isn't there the place the dragons gave to your ancestors as a sort of honeymoon suite? You take Tyler there and do his quest with him."

"Me? Sensei, I'm not ready for that. You're the master."

"Oh, for Heaven sake!" Cliff shouted. "Master is a title bestowed when you reach fifth degree black belt under a teacher, a master, from the original country. What do you think you did with Master Xing? You're as much a master martial artist as I am. I never told you, so I could hold my title over your head. The time has come for you to accept your position. Do this with Tyler. Besides, he feels safer and more confident with you. All you have to do is take him where he needs to be, tell him what to do and what to expect, and leave him to fulfill his quest alone. Take him in the morning when he begins fasting. We're running out of time."

Rennin agreed, and they told Tyler the plan. The boy seemed satisfied. So, Cliff and Casey went their way where Casey emerged feeling she should not have been so insistent since her guide proved to be a spider whose spun web was so strong her prey could not escape. Her prey turned out to be human beings. Cliff assured her being a spider was no worse than a scorpion. He encouraged her to think of her web as her ability to plan and stick to her plan and to convince others to follow.

While Casey overcame her repulsion to her guide, Rennin, on the ledge just outside the cave that had once served as a honeymoon suite, listened to a young man's horrific screams and had to fight the impulse to rescue the boy. After a time, the screams subsided. Rennin could not resist the urge to peek into the cave where Tyler was totally unaware of the man's presence as the sounds ensuing from within turned to a perfectly pitched tenor singing an operatic aria. Rennin stepped back onto the ledge and thought to himself. *And I thought my quest was weird. What in the hell is going on in that boy's mind?*

It was not too much longer before Rennin got the answer to his question. As Tyler tapped the dozing man on the shoulder, the boy grinned as if all was well with the world. He said, "That was amazing."

Rennin asked, "Is there anything you'd like to share?"

Tyler grinned more widely. "At least I wasn't a slug or a rat or a worm."

"Yes?" Rennin prompted.

Tyler said ecstatically, "Would you believe I was a mockingbird?"

"Yes." Rennin nodded energetically.

"Well, at first I was this ugly little featherless, helpless creature. The other baby mockingbird in the nest fell and was devoured by this serpent. The two adult mockingbirds attacked the serpent, and it ate them, too. Then, I fell from the nest, and the serpent tried to eat me. I got away and somehow learned to fly on my own. I kept pecking at the serpent, and then this lion came from nowhere and ripped the serpent to bits. Then, I just started singing while the lion walked around and let me sit on its shoulder. It was awesome!"

Rennin put his arm around the boy and roared. Tyler understood immediately and said excitedly, "Your guide is a lion, isn't it? You're king of beasts, but what good is a mockingbird?"

"Are you serious? Tyler, have you ever listened to a mockingbird sing? It's harmless. It doesn't eat crops, but bugs. But its song is incomparable. Why do you think it's called a mockingbird? It can imitate any bird's song. It adds joy and beauty to a dismal world. Tyler, have you ever listened to yourself sing? My boy, you have a gift. I heard you out here. If we were where I came from, you could be wealthy with that voice. When all this is settled, we have to do something about making sure other people hear you sing, just so you can add beauty to this world."

"But I don't know any music."

"You can learn. Obviously, you know some in your subconscious. In addition to the mockingbird's song, have you ever noticed the tenacity of the creature? A mockingbird will confront any other animal which threatens its nest. It truly protects those it loves. Now, let's get back and get ready to get rid of the serpent. This lion is ready to have a chance to relax and enjoy the mockingbird's song."

48
The Magic Returns

As the full moon approached, all nerves were on edge, not the least of which seemed to be the two people who usually remained calm in the worst circumstances. Both Ming and Jacques snapped at everyone, including each other, which escalated into a full-blown fight, sending Ming to her room in tears and Jacques to the beach where he kicked sand angrily. Ming would not talk to anyone, not even Casey who had become Ming's best friend, so Rennin followed Jacques to the beach.

Rennin demanded, "What in the devil is wrong with the two of you?"

Jacques stared at the man who had adopted him as a brother and blushed deep crimson. He answered shyly, "We are virgeens. Zhou zink eet ees zat pureety zat has some power over eveel. Boff of us feel zat we could endanger zee meession eef Igor or Veectoria can sense our presence. Meeng wants to shange zee seetuation eemmedeeately, but I want our union to be as husband and wife. She says eef I love her, zen, zat ees enough."

Rennin pursed his lips. "Do you love her?"

"Zhou know I do," said Jacques defensively.

"Then give her what she wants."

"But she has always wanted to be married unteel now."

"Like I said, give her what she wants. Marry her tonight and make love to your wife."

"How?"

Rennin put his arm around Jacques's shoulders. "I have a plan, so that everything is taken care of. You know, a captain can marry people if they're at sea. So, surprise Ming. Somehow get her onto the yacht. We'll all be there to support you. We'll put out for a couple of miles. Voila! Cliff can marry you as captain of the ship. It might not be exactly what was planned, but it works. I bet

Smoke can get that honeymoon cave fixed up in no time. Then, I just have to worry about the fallout from Casey. Oh, well, she'll have to wait. What do you say? Want to join the ranks of the doomed tonight?"

"Yes!"

"Okay, then. You work on Ming, and I'll take care of everything else."

The two conspirators went to work. Smoke arranged for the honeymoon suite to be decorated, and Nicole searched through the old clothes in the cave and found a feminine, frilly white dress that would be a perfect wedding gown. She also found a soft blue negligee that must have belonged to someone as petite as Ming. This she sent with Smoke to the honeymoon cave. Nicole seemed to have found something she was good at. She went aboard the yacht and decorated with the other women's help and unpacked her piano and a crate of sheet music, which were two things, along with a couple of guitars and a few other musical instruments, Zane had said Nicole would insist on having. Having heard Tyler had a wonderful voice, she worked for several hours with him to learn just one song to sing during the ceremony. Even she was enchanted by the resonance of the sounds Tyler could produce.

Contrary to Rennin's prediction, Casey enthusiastically joined the preparations. She appointed herself maid of honor and found an appropriate dress among the old clothing as well. She was overjoyed to find out Rennin had kept his word and brought tuxedoes for the men. She unpacked Rennin's, Cliff's, and Jacques's. She put d'Aubigné in a pretty little dress she found and gave her a basket of flower petals, creating a perfect flower girl. Jacques and Ming's friends boarded the yacht to await the groom's success in convincing the bride to talk to him.

Jacques knocked at the entrance to the chamber that served as Ming's quarters holding a cool cloth in his hand. Ming reluctantly opened the door displaying Jacques had judged her correctly. Her eyes were puffy and red. He held out his meager peace offering and said, "I am sorry."

Ming accepted the cool, damp cloth doused with herbs to reduce the swelling in her eyes. Jacques continued to create his surprise as he said, "I love zhou. Let's sneak out to sea a leettle way tonight on zee yacht and spend some time alone." He winked at Ming. "Eef zhou manage to seduce me, who am I to stop zhou?"

Ming laughed as all her anger was spent. "Is that really what you want?"

Jacques said, "I want to spend zee rest of my life loveeng zhou. Zee plans we made before we came here cannot be fulfeelled. I have to shange my way of zeenkeeng for our future. Weell you go sailing wif me tonight?"

Ming nodded. "We'll see what happens."

"Yes, we weell," replied Jacques mysteriously. He kissed Ming and left, saying, "Be ready to go at sundown."

Jacques called for Ming promptly at sundown. She wore cut offs and a t-shirt. Jacques wore his tux. He shook his head. "Zat weell never do." He handed Ming the dress Nicole had found. "Perhaps, vows made before God are all zat are required here. Weell zhou wear zis, please?"

Ming made as if to shut the door. "I am not leaveeng," Jacques informed her. "Eef zhou want to be wif me, zhou weell have to deal wif my watcheeng zhou. After all, I have seen zhou naked before."

"That was different," said Ming, her cheeks burning.

"Yes, eet was. I was not able to act on my eempulses, but eet was zee moment I knew for a fact zat I was 'doomed' as Renneen says."

Ming's hands shook as she tried to fasten the line of buttons up the back of the dress. A smirk played around Jacques's lips at Ming's discomfiture. He had never seen her so unsure of herself. The fact he had watched her dress made her nervous. He enjoyed having the upper hand for once in their relationship, but he was not patient at the moment. He walked boldly into the room from the doorway where Ming had told him to stay and finished buttoning the back of the dress. He kissed the nape of the neck and whispered, "Before zis night ees out, I weell unbutton every seengle one of zeese. I promeese."

As the couple left the entrance to the cave, Moonbeam waited for them. She gave what appeared to be a dragon's grin. "Zank zhou, Moonbeam," said Jacques pleasantly as he winked at a fellow conspirator. The young female dragon winked back.

The florescent glow from the dragon in the rising moonlight appeared ethereal as she hovered just above the helm of the yacht and lowered her two human passengers to the steering wheel of the ship. Jacques skillfully maneuvered the craft into the water as Moonbeam graciously flicked the mooring ropes on deck. She would be hovering above the ship very soon and was terribly excited to attend her first wedding.

Jacques watched as Ming felt the fresh sea air on her face. About three miles out, Jacques brought the engines to a stop. He invited Ming to take his arm to go on deck. As they rounded the turn, Casey, Rennin, and d'Aubigné met them and Nicole began to play "The Wedding March."

"What's going on?" asked Ming.

"We are getteeng married." Jacques grinned.

Almost speechless, Ming asked, "How?"

Rennin whispered, "We're at sea. Your father's captain of this ship. He can perform a wedding ceremony. Are you going to marry my little brother or what?"

Ming nodded. Rennin offered Casey his arm and they walked forward to serve as best man and maid of honor. D'Aubigné scattered her flower petals for the couple to walk upon behind her. Jacques kissed Ming's fingertips and asked, "Will zhou marry me right now, Meess Spell?"

"Yes," answered Ming. "This is the most wonderful surprise I've ever had. I love you, Jacques. Thank you."

Nicole changed the music to "The Bridal Chorus" as Jacques and Ming took their first step toward the prow of the ship where Cliff Spell waited with an impish grin on his face. Ming was overwhelmed at the outpouring of love from the people she had known for such a short time. She blinked very hard to keep joyful tears from staining her face. When they reached the very front of the bow, where Casey and Rennin stood on either side of the couple, Cliff began, "Well, this isn't exactly how I pictured giving my daughter in marriage, but it's perfect. Therefore, Jacques Picard, will you accept the gift of my daughter to be your wife?"

Jacques grinned like a little boy. "I weell."

Cliff turned to his daughter, "Ming, will you give yourself to this man unreservedly to be his wife?"

"I will," replied Ming.

Upon their agreeing to become husband and wife, Tyler sang "The Wedding Song" just as he and Nicole had practiced it all afternoon. Even the bride and groom were stunned to silence at the perfect voice.

Cliff performed a ceremony using tried, true, traditional wedding vows with the exception of asking Ming to obey anyone, for he knew she would never agree and that she took vows seriously. When he pronounced Jacques and Ming husband and wife, the entire group applauded and cheered.

Afterward, Nicole played some lively tunes and waltzes as the group celebrated. Harvey Zane quietly sat beside his wife and placed a glass of the island's nectar wine on the end of the piano for her. The expression on her face and the unasked question in her eyes brought tears to her husband's eyes. Zane took Nicole's hands from the piano keys and held them in his for a few moments before he said, "Shall we see if I still have it?" From memory, he began to play and sing to his wife "Sometimes When We Touch." Listening to the words, all but Rennin thought it just a love song for the newlyweds.

When he finished the song, Harvey Zane kissed his wife softly on the cheek and started to leave the piano stool. Nicole put a hand on his leg, "Stay," she said quietly.

After a short time of celebration by dragon standards, Ming threw the bouquet Nicole had made for her into the air. Thinking she would be the only one after it, Casey was surprised to battle Jennifer for the flowers. Only Casey's height prevailed in the skirmish. Rennin laughed so hard at the sight his sides hurt. Cliff took note and realized he would soon be performing another ceremony. Come Hell or high water, Casey McClarty would not be single much longer. Rennin wandered near Craig and Bobby who seemed to want to stay out of the fray, "You're both doomed," he informed them with a grin.

Bobby did not want to give his guardian the last word, so he retaliated, "You may be giving d'Aubigné away before Jennifer and I get married. You do realize she has a huge crush on Tyler."

"She's six," said Rennin seriously.

"So, maybe we'll wait at least ten years."

"Right," argued Rennin.

"You always have to have the last word, don't you?" Bobby laughed.

"With everyone except Renée. I gave that up a long time ago."

Moonbeam waited patiently while Jacques and Ming climbed onto her back. She was still excited as this was her first wedding and wedding trip. Ming asked as they passed Alexander's Cavern "Where are you taking us, Moonbeam?"

"You'll see," said the young dragon. After a few more minutes, Moonbeam deposited the couple outside another cave and called as she flew away, "Happy honeymoon."

Jacques scooped Ming into his arms and carried her into the cavern which had been decorated to the last detail from memory as it had been decorated for the first wedding the dragons could remember for Rennin and Morgan.

"This is gorgeous," said Ming. "How thoughtful."

Numerous candles illumined the room which was decorated with roses. The bed was strewn with rose petals, and the negligee Nicole had found lay on the bed. Ming touched the lacy garment. "I suppose I should put this on."

"Why?" asked Jacques.

"Because it…"

Jacques put his finger to Ming's lips, "Sh." He turned her around and kissed the back of her neck and unbuttoned the top button on her wedding dress. He kissed her neck again and unbuttoned the next button.

Ming said, "Jacques."

Again, Jacques whispered, "Sh. I have a promeese to keep." With each button he unfastened, Jacques preceded the action with a kiss to Ming's neck and back until he had kissed the entire length of her spine. Ming's heart raced.

She said again more nervously, "Jacques, what about the negligee?"

"Zhou can wear eet later," he replied as he slid the dress off Ming's shoulders and let it drop to the floor. Jacques unsnapped Ming's bra and slid it off her shoulders and let it drop to the floor. He kissed each shoulder and ran his fingers over Ming's skin. He turned his wife around and gently kissed her as he whispered, "I love zhou."

Jacques and Ming melted onto the bed and the entire island felt something move. It was as if the ground itself quivered as it felt magic infuse its every fiber. There was no loss of innocence for the couple, but coursing of magic between them. It spilled over to others on the island as well.

In the place that had come to be called Alexander's Cavern during the months Rennin O'Rourke had been on Draconis, Rennin and Renée found themselves completely alone for the first time since the man's arrival. The wine and romance of the evening still weighed powerfully on their hearts. They found every inch of each other and made love for the first time in the mystical place that had haunted their minds always.

Down the way in another small fissure that served as quarters for Casey McClarty and Craig Jamison, Craig held Casey close to his heart, but did not make love to her. Instead, he asked her to marry him once again and promised to make her his wife the day after the full moon. They drifted to sleep secure in each other's arms.

Across the way in yet another small room, Jennifer Polson cried softly on the shoulder of Bobby Willis. Bobby asked her what the matter was. Her reply almost tore out the boy's heart. "Ming wore a white dress honestly, Bobby. I'm a lot younger than she is, and I can't do that. What we witnessed tonight was real magic—love that's pure. We can never have that."

"Why?" asked Bobby. "You know I love you with all my heart."

Jennifer whispered, "I don't doubt that, but in our great need to feel loved, we already took the purity away. Neither of us can claim a true wedding night."

"I think I understand what you're saying. No, we can't undo what's been done, but we can start over." Bobby got out of the bed and gathered his things.

"Where are you going?" Jennifer asked, distressed. "I never meant to chase you away."

"You haven't. I'm not leaving you; I just am not going to sleep here for a while. I'm going to share a room with Tyler." Bobby sat on the edge of the bed. "Jen, I'm all male. I can't help wanting you, but I can put some space between temptation and us. I won't come to you again as a lover until Cliff pronounces us husband and wife. We really missed something by not waiting and by not dating properly. After I help Rennin with this thing he must do, I want to court you the old-fashioned way. Let's say, in six months, I'll ask you to marry me in a very romantic way. Then, we'll have a proper wedding and do things the right way. I love you, Jennifer. Believe me—this is harder for me than it is for you." Bobby grinned impishly. "Will you agree with my proposal?"

"Yes, but you don't necessarily have to wait six months if you get the urge before that to marry me. I love you, Bobby."

He kissed her. "Good night, then. You know where to find me if you need me."

Outside the entrance to the room Bobby sighed, "I think I'll be doing a lot of fishing for the next six months."

All the way at the end of this particular corridor, the cave ended in a large cavern that had three smaller rooms off it in a semicircular pattern. Harvey and Nicole Zane occupied this area, so their two boys could have some space. Ever since his arrival, Harvey had slept in the common room on an old-fashioned davenport while the boys shared the largest of the rooms off it and Nicole slept in one of the others. Harvey could not bring himself to go into the other room to sleep. It felt too permanent, and although he had told Rennin sometimes he did not even like Nicole, he had some remnant of feeling for her as he had shown at the wedding earlier. She was, after all, the mother of his two sons.

Randall and Marshall Zane snored peacefully as Harvey stared at the small stalactites above his head, and Nicole tossed and turned in the next room. Finally, the petite auburn-haired woman sat up in bed and said softly through clenched teeth, "Damn it, Harvey Zane. Why must you be so stubborn? Why can't you come to me? You sang that stupid song at the wedding. Do you feel anything for me?" Hot tears stung her eyes.

She lit one candle, got out of bed, and once again rummaged through clothes stored in the room where she slept. She found a deep-red satin negligee small enough to fit her. She put it on, brushed her hair, and appraised herself in the somewhat out-of-focus mirror. Again, she spoke aloud in quiet tones to the man in the other room. "I'm not ugly, Harvey. I don't want flares of passion from you. I want you to love me, not feel obligated to me. I would rather have constant, abiding embers than flares, but if I have to start the fire, I guess I will."

Taking the candle, Nicole marched into the outer room where Harvey hastily closed his eyes. She walked straight to her husband and demanded, "Open your eyes, Harvey. I know you're not asleep."

Guiltily, the man opened his eyes. However, he did not expect to see what he beheld standing before him. "You look very nice, Nicole," he stammered.

"Nice, Harvey? I don't want to look nice. Nice is wimpy. I want to look sexy. I want your heart to leap when you see me."

Nicole knelt beside the man who lay on the old couch. "Am I that repulsive to you, Harvey? Do you feel anything for me?" She caressed the almost smooth top of her husband's head. "Harvey, I was never shown how to love. My home was cold. You know that. I don't want to be cold."

Unwanted tears sprang to the woman's doe-like eyes. "Harvey, I do love you. I always have. I just don't know how to show it." Nicole closed her eyes as the tears dripped down her cheeks. She swallowed hard to gain control of her voice and whispered, "Harvey, give me the chance to love you. Show me what love is. Please, don't throw me away like everyone else in my life."

Nicole's last statement cut like a knife. Harvey knew how alone Nicole had been. He knew she had been left pretty much to fend for herself and her only solace and companion had been her music. He knew she had given up her career as a concert pianist when she became pregnant with Randall, and she was devoted to her children. Harvey sat up and gently brushed the tears from his wife's face.

"Nicole, do you really love me—someone who can never give you the things you have always wanted?"

"What have I always wanted, Harvey?"

"A comfortable life with beautiful things."

Nicole laughed a little bitterly. "Smoke told me that I didn't know you. Maybe it's the other way around. I know the kinds of things you've done. I know you haven't just followed some unfaithful spouse to take pictures. I know you've taken dangerous detective work like helping Rennin with James Wilburn because you thought you had to make more money for me. I don't want money, Harvey. I want you to love me, really love me—me, someone who has nothing to offer anyone except music. Your love and the love of my children and, yes, music, are the only beautiful things I need in my life. It's just, I've never had your love. You didn't marry me because you loved me, but because you felt obligated. I don't want you to be obligated to me. If that's all you feel for me, leave. You're free. I don't know what the customs are here, but I'm sure there is some way for me to release you from our marriage. But know this, Harvey David Zane—I love you. Yes, I love you."

Nicole stood and trooped back to the room where she slept, leaving her husband to contemplate her words and to feel completely desolate. Harvey watched her sashay away. He heard the slight rustle of the satin. It took him only a few seconds to realize what he had always wanted was walking away from him, and he was the only one who could stop its loss. Harvey leapt from the old couch and caught up to his wife, putting his hand on her shoulder, "Nicole?"

She turned around as real tears streamed down her cheeks. What Harvey saw was raw emotion, something Nicole had never shown him. He breathed in his disbelief, "Nicole."

She did not wait for him to speak another word. She wrapped her arms around Harvey's neck and pulled his face to hers. She kissed him with a deep lustful passion. When she released him from the embrace in which she held him, he could hardly breathe. Harvey stared into his wife's eyes for a brief moment before he lifted her into his arms and carried her to bed where they made love with a passion for each other neither had ever felt before.

Later, as Nicole lay in Harvey's arms and he gently caressed her hair he breathed, "I love you, Nicole, more than anything. I love you." They drifted to sleep as a new magic was born within them.

In the main room of Alexander's Cavern, two older men played chess. Gerald McClarty grumbled, "Where are you tonight, Cliff? You're playing like a beginner."

Cliff confessed, "I don't know. I was just thinking about someone I haven't seen in years. And it wasn't Mai Tai. It was Margaret Sanders, the woman I spent a great deal of time with after Mai Tai died. I haven't thought about her in years, not since she bade me farewell because, according to her, she couldn't compete with a ghost. Gerald, why did I let her get away? She was a great lady. And why did you not ever find someone else? Admit it. You had feelings for that real estate agent."

"Stephanie Pitts?"

"Yeah."

"Maybe, but she was so much younger than I was. It would just have been perverted."

"Well, we're sitting here two old widowers with only each other for company. Now, that's just sick. Neither of us is that old or ugly. We should do something about it."

Gerald McClarty laughed. "When you get back next week, we'll discuss finding some magic for ourselves. Right now, checkmate."

In the heart of the island of Draconis, Victoria Reinhardt awoke in a cold sweat and hit the man who lay beside her with force. "What?" screeched Igor Reinhardt.

"Don't you feel it?" demanded Victoria.

"Feel what?" asked Igor irritably, having been awakened from the first real sleep he had experienced in a long time. "I felt you hit me." He rubbed the spot on his back.

"The magic is back," snarled Victoria.

"What magic, dear?"

"Pure love. Pure, innocent, unadulterated love. Oh, it makes me sick."

49
Destiny

Ming and Jacques returned from a real honeymoon to find everyone in Alexander's Cavern to be renewed and energized. There seemed to be no explanation for the freshness, but it was a welcome change.

With only two days left before Bobby and d'Aubigné would have to go back to Isla Linda, Rennin took his group back to the island where they formulated a plan of concealment. The day before the full moon under the camouflage of predawn on the back of a misty dragon who had frequently sneaked to and from Isla Linda in his younger days, they went once more to lie in wait for those who would harm an innocent child.

As on the day of the last trip to Isla Linda, the brotherhood met early in order to row to the smaller island. This time d'Aubigné accompanied Bobby and Tyler. Each boy held one of her hands. She had to tell them on the way to the beach they were crushing her fingers. They told her they were scared.

The little girl gave them a withering look. "You two need to chill out before you give my daddy's plan away. He would never let anyone hurt me. I'll be fine. You can count on it." Then, so much like her mother, she kissed both boys on the cheek. "I love you for caring about me, but relax."

On the trip to the smaller island, Igor Reinhardt's nerves were frayed to the last neuron as d'Aubigné chatted blithely all the way there and expected the man to graciously carry on a conversation. Finally, he snapped, "Do you ever shut up?"

"Why?" asked d'Aubigné, innocently. "I'm trying to make new friends. I can't do that if I don't know anything about you."

Igor said desperately, "Please, be quiet. You're making this very difficult for me. You're too sweet."

Frowning, d'Aubigné said, "Humph!" as she laid her head on Bobby's shoulder. "He's mean," she whispered to Bobby.

Bobby whispered back, "Sh. Take a nap on my shoulder."

"I'm too nervous."

Bobby kissed the little girl on her head. "Who needs to chill out now?"

When they finally arrived on the second island that made up the land of Draconis, they stowed the boats again and the ritual began as usual except Igor took d'Aubigné's hand. "You need to come with me now."

"Why?" demanded d'Aubigné as she jerked her hand from Igor's. "I want to stay with Bobby, you mean old goat."

Igor was taken aback by the child's outburst. He said guardedly, "You can't go with Bobby because the boys will be changing clothes in there. I have something for you to wear down here."

The little girl folded her arms across her chest and glared at the old man. "I can walk by myself, thank you."

Igor relented. "Very well. Come along, then."

D'Aubigné followed the man down the corridor but glanced over her shoulder to see both Bobby and Tyler throw her little kisses. She also quietly scanned the walls and ceiling looking for some clue of her father's presence. She saw none.

The child entered the chamber with Igor to find Victoria Reinhardt waiting for them. Victoria smiled maliciously, but cooed, "Hello, child." She held out her hand to d'Aubigné, "Come with me. I have a special robe for you to wear."

Victoria handed d'Aubigné a white silk robe that reminded the girl of the costume she had worn one Halloween. The little girl grudgingly took the garment and changed her clothes while Victoria donned the deep crimson robe.

Once again Victoria offered d'Aubigné her hand and the girl repeated what she had said to Igor. "I can walk by myself, thank you."

The response rankled Victoria, but she remained calm. "Have it your way. Come with me."

The two entered the room where the stone table was set. D'Aubigné looked around her uncomfortably. "Over here, dear," Victoria coaxed the little girl.

D'Aubigné trudged near the woman and noted the stone altar. She said assertively, "Oh, no! Someone has already tried this. We are not going there again!"

"Oh, yes, we are," snarled Victoria as she grabbed d'Aubigné's wrist.

D'Aubigné bit the woman hard. "You leave me alone, you wicked old witch!" she shrieked as she ran toward the door.

Victoria caught d'Aubigné by the hair and pulled her back. Then, she pinned the child and forced her onto the altar, where she bound her swiftly. The child was a better actress than either her mother or her aunt Renée. She screamed frantically, but the only names she called were, "Bobby! Tyler! Help!"

Victoria laughed triumphantly. "Soon, dear. They'll help very soon. Soon they, along with me, will consume your blood and your flesh, restoring the spirit of Quazel to its rightful place—as the goddess she should have been revered as five hundred years ago!"

D'Aubigné spat, "You evil, vile, old woman! Quazel's dead. Aidan O'Rourke killed her."

Victoria laughed harder. "Her spirit lives in me. That stupid fool, Igor, helped me do what I could only dream of. Darling, when he first saw me, he lusted so deeply. I had him unearth the bones of a queen. From them, I formulated a potion to which I added the blood of the last O'Rourke boy on this chunk of land. As I drank, I became Quazel—alive and well. I forced Igor to drink with me, and he has been my dutiful slave ever since. When I begin to feel old, we sacrifice a virgin girl, whose blood I consume to renew my youth. In the interim I am fortified by the blood of virgin boys, but I have not had nourishment in three months. I've felt old lately. It's time to renew my vigor with you, my dear. And what makes you so much more delicious is you really do have the blood of Alexander O'Rourke and Quazel Rodriguez flowing through your veins."

D'Aubigné laughed in the woman's face. "You ugly old hag! You're right. I do have their blood in my veins. I swear, tonight, you will die. It's my destiny to make sure you never come back again."

Victoria stuffed a handkerchief into the child's mouth and flung open the doors to the chamber. "Let's begin!" she commanded the group of men waiting outside.

The ritual began as usual except Victoria took the seat of honor, and Igor sat beside her. She served the wine just as Igor had done at Bobby's first ceremony. Bobby felt the room spin after only one sip. He was being affected differently than before. There was no screaming pig, but a hissing little girl. He thought: *No! Rennin, where are you?*

Bobby felt himself becoming useless; he could not fight the effects of whatever was in that wine. He could not help d'Aubigné. He made eye contact with Tyler, who seemed to be having difficulty breathing. Bobby saw Tyler barely touch his lips to the goblet before him and discreetly dump the remainder onto the for while mouthing the words, "I won't do it."

D'Aubigné's continued vocalization gave the boys enough distraction from Victoria's gaze for Bobby to pour the rest of his wine onto the floor also.

Victoria spoke in a language Bobby could not understand. The next thing Bobby saw was Victoria with the sacrificial scimitar over d'Aubigné. Bobby heard himself shouting, "No! Rennin, where are you?"

It seemed as if the walls came to life. The men and boys in varying shades of neutral seemed unable to function as they moved against the walls. The men in cardinal sprang to life and fought with the creatures that appeared. To Bobby's eyes, he saw different animals emerge from the walls. After a few minutes of hard concentration, he realized he was seeing the guides of those who cared for him. The animals eventually became the people he knew.

Pandemonium reigned. Bobby felt himself become the giant protective ape as Victoria tried to escape the room. He yanked her back and flung her across the table. She lunged at the boy to plunge a dagger into his chest just as a harmless, gentle mockingbird flew in front of him. The instant the dagger struck the creature, it became another innocent child, another victim— Tyler Bishop.

Above all the noise, the shrillest screeches could be heard from one frantic, angry little girl who had managed to get the gag out of her mouth. The name that she screamed was, "Tyler!"

In a matter of moments, it seemed a great hush fell over all those present as five men in cardinal robes lay dead and the Reinhardts knelt before a tall, green-eyed, left-handed conqueror and a small female version of the same, who had been untied by a sneaky ferret during the fray.

Igor gazed up into the eyes of Rennin O'Rourke with a look of relief on his face. He spoke clearly and distinctly, "Mr. O'Rourke, how glad I am to see you. Please, kill me first and free me from this demon's clutches." Igor looked contemptuously at the woman who called herself his wife.

In a compassionate tone, Rennin said, "I've heard similar words before. Be free."

Rennin gave a nod, and Cliff snapped Igor Reinhardt's neck in one motion. The man lay dead beside an excessively wicked woman who spat, "Do you really think you can kill me? It has been tried and failed. I will not stay dead."

Rennin did not speak. He felt himself become a lion once more, and the next second, he held Victoria Reinhardt's still beating heart in his hand.

A small voice beside him said, "This time you will stay dead for there will be nothing left of you to turn into a potion." Even as

she spoke, something different from the lightning that usually shot
from her fingertips came from somewhere inside d'Aubigné
O'Rourke. As the stunned crowd looked on, a consuming blast of
energy akin to a small atomic bomb shot toward the two
Reinhardts, and there was nothing left. The remains were
completely vaporized. Rennin's hand was singed and blistered
since he had held Victoria's heart.

"Sorry, Daddy," said d'Aubigné as she ran to Bobby and Tyler.
Bobby held Tyler's head on his lap as Tyler gasped for breath with
a dagger protruding from his chest.

D'Aubigné reached for the blade and Tyler jerked in severe
pain. D'Aubigné shouted, "Daddy Craig, do something. You're a
doctor. Don't let him die." She stared at the gentle songbird whose
light brown hair and light blue eyes gave him an angelic
appearance. "Tyler, don't you die. You have to wait for me to grow
up. I've already decided that I'm gonna marry you some day. I
always get what I want. You're doomed."

Even in his agony, Tyler could not hold back a laugh. He
whispered as blood trickled from his mouth. "I'll make a deal with
you. If Craig keeps me alive, I'll marry you ten years from today."

Craig said, "Don't touch the blade. We need to get him back to
where I have some medical equipment."

The small group of warriors looked around at a larger group
of befuddled men who seemed not to have a clue where they were
or what had happened. Craig said again, "Don't worry about them
either. They'll make it home, and I don't think they'll remember a
thing now that the evil is gone."

Rennin lifted Tyler carefully into his arms. "So, you want to
marry my daughter in ten years, huh? You didn't ask me."

"It's her idea," moaned Tyler.

"Yes, I know. I heard. You think you're going to die so you
can get out of it. You're doomed."

50
The Next Generation

Back in Alexander's Cavern, the wait for news on Tyler's condition was long. Not having proper anesthesia, Craig enlisted Renée's help with some of the herbs she had said had medicinal uses. After several hours, Craig and Renée exited the room where they had secluded their patient.

"Well?" demanded d'Aubigné impatiently.

"D'Aubigné, that's enough," Rennin scolded. Then, just as impatiently, he demanded, "Well?"

Craig grinned. "I've still got it. Barring infection, he'll live. The dagger barely missed his heart and punctured his left lung, but with Renée's help we re-inflated it, and he's breathing on his own. He won't be singing at my wedding tonight, but he'll live."

D'Aubigné grinned triumphantly and asked, "May I see him now?"

"Oh, Jesus, please," groaned Rennin. "Yes, that's a prayer. Casey, you talk to her. Those are your genes speaking."

Casey guffawed. "Who fell in love with Renée when he was six? I at least waited until I was fifteen to have my first huge crush. I was twenty before I actually fell in love."

"It doesn't matter. She's six and she's talking about marrying the boy, whom she happened to have tricked into agreement because he thought he was going to die."

"All right," said Casey still giggling. "D'Aubigné, that was very wrong to do to Tyler. What if he never falls in love with you? He's a lot older than you are. He might not want to wait, what was it, ten years, to get married to someone he doesn't love."

D'Aubigné put her hands on her hips. "He's not as much older than me as Craig is than you. And he will too fall in love with me. Daddy already told him he was doomed. When Daddy tells a man he's doomed, he's doomed. Just ask Uncle Jacques."

"Oh, my God!" cried Rennin as Jacques tried to sneak away from the group. Rennin pled, with the man, "Jacques, help."

"What can I do?" asked Jacques, touching his chest. "Let her see Tyler. Ten years ees a long time. She just might get tired of Tyler before then. Right now, she needs to see heem."

"Thank you, Uncle Jacques." D'Aubigné gloated in her victory.

Craig told her she could see Tyler for five minutes, but then he needed to rest so he could get well. She tiptoed into the room and touched Tyler's hair, noticing he was pasty white. D'Aubigné whispered, "You will fall in love with me someday. One day you'll stand below my window and serenade me. You'll climb a trellis just to bring me flowers and proclaim your love to me. They all think I'm a foolish little girl, but about this, I know what will happen. For now, you sleep and get well. For now, it's enough that I love you." D'Aubigné kissed Tyler softly on the lips and tiptoed from the room.

He opened his eyes and watched the girl slip away. As she closed the door quietly behind her, the older boy mouthed the words to the air, "I'm doomed."

As he had promised, Craig married Casey that very night. They spent one night in the honeymoon suite because Craig was still a doctor. He was a man of his word, but he had a critically injured patient. Casey understood and made the most of her first night as Mrs. Jamison. Craig knew after that evening, he would never forget his wedding night.

During the next few weeks, the harmony between men and dragons was restored as the mayhem associated with the brotherhood's sacrifices stopped. Cliff kept his promises and performed the vision quests with Gerald, who was not surprised to find his guide to be a Pitbull, and Jennifer, who was shocked she was not an ugly despicable creature, but a sweet and gentle hummingbird. The surprise for Cliff proved to be Nicole Zane, whose wisdom had come to the forefront and was manifested as a pristine snow owl.

Rennin began a house on Isla Linda, connecting it to the mouth of the cave just as Nicole had suggested. It was d'Aubigné who convinced Craig and her mother to reclaim the house Aidan had built. Secretly, she wanted the house for the trellis beneath her window, the one the original O'Rourke twins had used as their secret passage centuries before. She sat on the seat connected to her window and fantasized about Tyler climbing the trellis. As she sat there, Tyler and Bobby tramped by. D'Aubigné waved and they waved back. Tyler gulped as he saw the trellis. He had heard every word the little girl had said to him.

"What's wrong with you?" asked Bobby.

"I'm doomed," whispered Tyler.

Bobby cackled. "You can't mean you have feelings for d'Aubigné?"

"That's not the point. She won't always be a little girl. I made a promise to her."

Bobby chortled again. "You have ten years to introduce her to someone else. She'll get over you. Just wait and see. It's just a crush. All little girls get them on somebody. On the other hand, I do have a promise to keep. Six months is a very long time. I only have three left. How would you feel about being my best man?"

"Yeah. I'd like that, but I'll bet you a week's chores d'Aubigné is Jennifer's maid of honor even if she is only seven.

"You're on. Jennifer will ask Renée."

During the three months before Bobby was to ask Jennifer to marry him, Craig found himself practicing a field of medicine that was not his forté. First, he had the pleasure of telling Nicole Zane she was pregnant. Harvey was ecstatic. Since Jacques and Ming's wedding, Harvey and Nicole had been acting like newlyweds themselves.

Not a week after Craig gave Nicole her news, he gave the same news to Ming. That night he confessed to his wife he was terrified to be the doctor responsible for delivering babies. Casey laughed and promised to help since she had some experience having delivered Caitlin and Morgan. She kissed Craig. "There's nothing to it if all goes well. You're a surgeon if someone must have a C-section like I did with d'Aubigné. Of course, I was only sixteen. Maybe there will not be any complications with this one."

"You're right," said Craig momentarily oblivious to what Casey had implied. She laughed softly as they turned over to go to sleep. She started counting to see how long it would take for her words to sink into Craig's consciousness.

At thirteen, Craig sat upright in bed and demanded, "What do you mean, 'this one'?"

Casey wiggled as close as she could get to her spouse. "I mean you're going to be the best father on this island even if you have to deliver the baby yourself in about seven months."

Craig sputtered, "Really? You and me? Really?"

"Yes, really."

The island was abuzz with the news that half its population seemed to be pregnant. Rennin really teased Renée asking, "What happened to you? Aren't you drinking the same water?"

Renée grinned in an offended way and retaliated, "Maybe it's the water fountain. Would you care to try again?"

"Yeah. Yeah, I would," said Rennin as he popped Renée with the hand towel he held and chased her into the cave on Isla Linda and pinned her against the wall.

Renée blushed. "Rennin, there are people out there working on our house."

"So?"

"You're scandalous."

He nodded. "I vaguely recall having my picture plastered on a few tabloids. I don't think there are any reporters here though," he said as he pressed himself against Renée.

"Rennin! Oh, my God!" She could feel he was ready to follow through with trying again.

"Are you saying no?"

Renée pulled her husband into the darkest recess of the cave. "When was the last time I told you no?"

The next morning, the O'Rourke entourage enthusiastically decorated the yacht for another wedding. Bobby had bided his time for six months before he took Jennifer on a picnic and proposed on one knee, presenting her with a diamond that had been among the trinkets in Alexander's Cavern. The ring proved to be the one Duncan had given Kieran to give to Miranda.

Cliff performed one more wedding as a sea captain, and able to sing once again, Tyler performed the music, a song called "Together as One," he had rehearsed with Nicole, who also played once again. Because Jennifer had once said her favorite dragon was the young golden one, Filigree flew her and Bobby to the honeymoon suite, where all their past seemed to vanish in the wake of a bright future. However, when Bobby returned from his honeymoon, he owed a week's chores to his good friend, Tyler, since d'Aubigné had, indeed, served as Jennifer's maid of honor.

The prevailing sense of amorousness on the island did not make Craig's job easier. Within two more months, both Jennifer and Renée announced they were also pregnant. Craig was swamped, especially the night he had to deal with three women in labor, including his own wife. He thought he would pull his hair out. Finally, just after dawn, Nicole delivered a baby girl that she and Harvey named Michelle Renée. Several hours later, Ming gave birth to Clifton Duncan.

At last, Craig was left with only Casey. After nearly a full day, she was exhausted. Craig told her he was ready to do another C-section because he was worried about her. Casey had the energy to argue, but Craig's wisdom prevailed. As Craig got Renée to help him, Casey released a blood curdling scream. Renée said, "I know that scream. It's the get-it-out-now scream."

Sure enough, in the twenty minutes it had taken Craig and Renée to prepare to perform a C-section, Colin Craig Jamison decided to cooperate and come the natural way.

The day after he became a grandfather, Cliff sat in the galley on the yacht alone. Rennin worried about his friend and sought him. When Rennin found Cliff, he was nursing a glass of scotch and turning a large manila envelope over in his hands. Rennin poured himself a glass of scotch and sat across from the pensive man. "What's that?" he asked.

"The last piece of mail I got before we left Miami."

"You haven't opened it yet? Why?"

"I was afraid to see what was inside. It's from Margaret Sanders. She's the only woman I even dated after Mai Tai died. She broke off our relationship because she felt she was competing with a ghost. I can't imagine why she would send me mail after twenty years, Rennin."

"You'll never know unless you open it."

Cliff downed the glass of scotch and opened the envelope. After several minutes, he handed the contents to the younger man. Inside was a letter which informed Cliff that he had another daughter and a granddaughter. Margaret had included pictures. With the good news, she also included bad news, informing Cliff she would never have bothered him except she had been diagnosed with colon cancer and the prognosis was not good. She wanted him to meet his newborn granddaughter because there was a good chance he might have to rear her if the chemotherapy did not work for Margaret. The young man, Conrad Moss, his daughter had married had been killed in action. He had been a Marine. In addition, his daughter, Cecily, had suffered a stroke during delivery and died. His granddaughter was healthy and named Laurel Elaine Moss.

After reading the material, Rennin could not decipher the look on Cliff's face. Finally, Cliff said, "I have to go back, Rennin. I have no choice. Why didn't I open this damned thing before we left? The baby would be a nearly two. What if Margaret? You understand, don't you?"

"Of course, I understand. I'll go with you. We'll bring them back here."

"You can't leave."

"Of course, I can. I'm not a prisoner here. I'll be back. Can you wait until the baby comes?"

"Rennin, you cannot go. You must stay here for Draconis. I'll get Zane and Ming to go with me. No. I guess Ming can't go either now. Zane won't want to go. I have to go alone. Don't worry. I'll come back. This is where I belong."

Rennin understood, but he did not want to see Cliff leave. Nonetheless, he saw his friend off a few days later and wished him all the luck in the world. Rennin turned his attention to the expectation of another child whose birth he would not miss.

Jennifer went into premature labor, but delivered a healthy, although small, baby boy that she and Bobby named Duncan Gerald Willis. A few weeks later, Renée got her opportunity to scream at Rennin as she much more swiftly delivered Aidan Alexander. Rennin thought back to his vision quest and remembered the blurred face of a blond-haired boy. He snuggled the baby to his chest and whispered, "It was you—the next generation of O'Rourkes.

As Rennin cuddled his son while Renée slept, Jacques popped his head in and announced, "Papa ees back."

Rennin furrowed his eyebrows. "So soon?"

51
In Ruling I Serve

A downhearted Clifton Spell greeted Rennin on the beach as Rennin demanded, "What's wrong? What happened?"

"I can't get through the barrier."

"What do you mean?"

Fists clenched tightly, Cliff repeated, "I cannot get through the barrier. I tried four different places. It appears that, perhaps, we *are* prisoners here. Something won't let me leave."

A long talk with the dragons did not shed any light on why the barrier was not open to leaving. According to them, the only purpose it had served before was to keep undesirables out. Over the years, many had left, but few had come.

During the next year, Cliff, along with others, tried several times to cross the plane into the outer realm, to no avail. Finally, after a long conversation with Draco, Cliff resigned himself that if he was to be with his granddaughter, she would one day come to Draconis. Draco felt the barrier had sealed to outward travel for the protection of the inhabitants of Draconis. His heart told him something was dreadfully wrong in the other world.

Time passed, and Rennin understood why the men and women who truly had served their states and country in government were called public servants. Helping to re-establish a workable form of government in the land of Draconis was the hardest job Rennin had ever done. He worked continuously to put the same kind of administration into place as Duncan had established so long before. However, against his protests, every person and dragon in the land from the lowliest farmer and fisherman to Draco insisted Rennin become the governor, and the position would not be determined by election, but by succession upon the death or disability of Rennin or any future governors. If Rennin or any governor afterward wanted to abdicate the position, it would pass to the next person in line, preferably the governor's eldest son. However, in the event no male heir had been born, then the governor's eldest daughter would rule.

Rennin argued the setup sounded too much like a monarchy. The dragons, especially, argued the difference was the governor would not be all powerful. The representative council could overrule his decision if the need arose. Moreover, the governor was expected to prepare his successor. The people and beasts did not want their world to fall prey to unscrupulous people again. They expected Rennin and his descendants to be upright and honest.

With a workable government in place, life became routine. The days passed, uncomplicated and uneventful. Gerald McClarty found his niche as he re-established an education system, which included instruction in the martial arts and football. Jacques insisted if they were going to play football, he be allowed to coach real football, so Draconian children also played soccer.

It seemed almost everyone from the world beyond taught something in Gerald's education system from Rennin teaching science and Renée teaching social studies to Nicole teaching music.

Rather than being annoyed the dragons and people wanted her little brother to one day replace Rennin, d'Aubigné contented herself with the development of her magical powers. The power that had lain dormant for centuries came to full bloom once again.

On numerous occasions Draconis felt tremors. Rennin chalked the events up to d'Aubigné, but she insisted she had not caused them. Still nothing seemed out of place, so life went on. The population grew, and the children grew. Little girls became young women right before their fathers' eyes, prompting the governor of the land to bring a proposal to the council—establish a legal marrying age. He told them to decide, but asked desperately, "Please, make it at least sixteen."

The discussion of the council turned to the fact Rennin, their beloved leader, was watching his eldest daughter bloom into a beautiful young woman. At fifteen, d'Aubigné turned heads everywhere she went. The twins were ten and Aidan was seven. Rennin was worried the children grew up too fast in this magnificent, mystical land. He remembered what Tyler had said to him years ago. Of course, the plaguing promiscuity vanished with Victoria and Igor. Nonetheless, Rennin saw the children who had come to Draconis with him, and they were no longer children. They were young men and women. Some even had children of their own.

In addition to seeing his children grow up, Rennin fretted about d'Aubigné's state of mind. Although dozens of young men sought her attention, she had never vacillated in her determination to marry Tyler Bishop, who had never married. On the contrary, during the last few months, the young man had been seen frequently visiting either the Jamison home or the home of Rennin O'Rourke. He expediently visited when d'Aubigné was at home. Rennin noted the stolen glances.

The week before d'Aubigné's sixteenth birthday, Tyler conveniently dropped by Rennin's house a few minutes before dinner. Naturally, the young man was summarily invited to stay for dinner since he had no real home of his own but spent most of his time in the home of his best friend, Bobby Willis. As a matter of fact, Tyler had his own room in the Willis home.

Throughout dinner, Rennin watched carefully, noting how Tyler looked at d'Aubigné when he thought nobody was looking at him, although Tyler found it difficult to ever sneak a peek at her because she never took her eyes off the young man. After dinner, Rennin told d'Aubigné to help with the dishes and challenged Tyler to a game of chess. Alone on the porch, Rennin came straight to the point. "We need to talk. You have seven months before the date will have been ten years. Are you lurking around d'Aubigné because you feel obligated to keep what you thought was a deathbed promise to a little girl? If so, leave. I'm her father, and I'll put a stop to the nonsense immediately. On the other hand, if you have feelings for my first born, then you need to do some serious courting. The Council has declared no one may marry before the age of sixteen. I signed the order. Let's face it—they passed the decree just for me because of my little green-eyed monster in there. This one time I was completely selfish. D'Aubigné is my baby. I love her. I will not allow anyone to hurt her. Now, it's your turn. Talk."

Tyler stared at the chessboard. "I think I'm doomed."

Rennin commanded, "Look at me when you talk. Never, and I mean never, lower your eyes from your opponent. Yes, at this moment I am your opponent. Now, look at me."

Tyler looked into the face of a man who had rescued, not only him, but his entire world. The look on Rennin's face was unfathomable. He was neither threatening nor encouraging. "I suppose it's some of both." Tyler explained, "I haven't found anyone in the last ten years I would want to spend my life with. There's nobody with the vibrancy and intelligence d'Aubigné possesses. I told Bobby a long time ago I was doomed. That is the word you've used often, isn't it? I told him d'Aubigné wouldn't be a little girl forever." He rubbed both hands down the sides of his face. "Rennin, she isn't a little girl anymore. She's the most beautiful woman I've ever seen. I know many of the men and boys on this island would give their right arm to woo her. She hasn't given them the time of day. If I wait too long, she might decide she really was a silly child and forget me. That would kill me." He shrugged and released a deep sigh. "Still, I have nothing. All I have is a singing voice. I fish all day and smell terrible at the end of the day. How someone as beautiful, elegant, and gifted as d'Aubigné could want me is mind-boggling. Yet, how do I look into those eyes and tell her no? When I look into her eyes, I don't want to tell her no. I want to..." Tyler shook his head. "Well, anyway, I suppose I'm doomed. So, I guess I'm asking your permission to date her." Tyler exhaled long as if he had been holding his breath.

Rennin went inside without a word. He returned with two glasses and a bottle of home-distilled whiskey. He poured two large glasses and handed one to Tyler. "You need this more than I do. First, I'll castrate you and hang your carcass from a tree for the entire island to see if you act upon what you want to do before your wedding night. Second, you've got to grow some backbone if you court d'Aubigné. You must learn to say no to her, or she will drive you mad. She's stubborn, strong-willed, independent, pig-headed, and downright nasty sometimes. At other times, she's loving, kind, compassionate, all those things you see. Third, take pride in what you do. Tyler, if Draconis didn't have men who fished for the whole domain, we would never eat fish. You help to keep this world alive. In addition, you do add beauty to the world when you sing, and you've taught other people to sing well. That's a gift. Use it. Fourth, I would say you're most definitely doomed. Here's a toast. To the doomed. May we wallow gleefully in our self-pity."

Rennin downed the entire glass of whiskey in one effort. Tyler tried to do the same and coughed uncontrollably. Rennin roared with laughter. "Now, I want to see you walk a straight line. If you date d'Aubigné, you'll have to learn to drink with me. She'll probably drive you to drink."

D'Aubigné came onto the porch drying her hands. She demanded, "Daddy, what did you do to Tyler?"

Rennin stood and gave his daughter his chair as he said, "I gave him a drink and my permission. Here, you play with the boy."

Smoke's voice sounded in his head. "He's a man, Rennin."

"Stop eavesdropping," Rennin sent back. He peered inside at the grandfather clock that bore the white dragon on its pendulum. He looked back at Tyler. "Midnight and you say good night. I won't be asleep."

D'Aubigné surveyed the chessboard, "You've only made two moves. What were you doing out here?"

Tyler grinned. "Keeping a promise."

"What?" said d'Aubigné as she made a calculated move on the board with her knight.

Tyler covered her hand with his, and she jumped and looked up from the board. He looked directly into her saucer-like emerald eyes and repeated, "I was keeping a promise and growing a backbone. I was asking your father for his permission to date you. That is, if you would consider someone of my humble position worthy of courting a princess. Will you go out with me?"

From the time she was six, d'Aubigné had fantasized about this young man asking her out, but when the moment came, she was speechless. Tyler prompted her, "The question does require an answer. Do I continue to hold your hand over this chessboard, or would you prefer I leave now?"

D'Aubigné came to her senses and realized Tyler was holding her hand. She gently withdrew her hand from his and asked, "Are you asking because you feel obligated to keep a promise to a silly little girl, or do you truly want to spend time with me? You should know I'm a royal pain in the ass. Just ask my daddy."

Tyler laughed. "I know what a pain you are, but you're the most gorgeous, vivacious pain I've ever seen. Do you really think I haven't even looked for a woman to be in my life during the last ten years? Do you think I just sat back and waited for you to grow up? I looked and found nothing I wanted. I watched you turn into a magnificent woman. Did you put a spell on me, or is this feeling truly from me?"

"No, I didn't put a spell on you."

"Then, I truly want to get to know you. Will you go out with me?"

"Daddy gave you his permission?"

"He did, um, with a few conditions. I can live with his conditions."

D'Aubigné laughed merrily. "I bet I know what his first condition was! Do you plan to hold to that condition?"

"Absolutely."

"Really?" D'Aubigné gave Tyler a look that would have brought him to his knees if he were not more afraid of her father.

He repeated, "Absolutely, so don't even look at me like that. It'll be hard enough without you making it harder, but I'm a man of my word. Besides, Rennin would kill me. You still haven't given me a straightforward answer. Are we dating officially or what?"

D'Aubigné nodded. "Oh, yeah. You're doomed."

Tyler took her hand again. "Good. Rennin and I already toasted our fate. In this case, doomed is good. So, will you walk with me on the beach for our first official date?"

"No. I will whip you in a game of chess. It's your turn."

The following Sunday, the day after a long sixteenth birthday celebration, Tyler took d'Aubigné on a picnic in Morgan's Meadow and returned her safely to her mother's house before dark. Over the next two months they swam together in the ocean, walked in the moonlight, played badminton in the meadow, and skied in the high mountains. Tyler always brought her home at a reasonable hour. After the annual harvest hayride, almost three months since their first date, Tyler deposited the lively young woman on her front porch on Draconis and turned to leave.

"This is ridiculous!" d'Aubigné said huffily.

"What is?" Tyler asked seriously.

She folded her arms and set her lips. "Do you ever even plan to kiss me?"

"Do you want me to kiss you?"

"What did my father threaten to do to you?" She dropped her arms to her sides, fingers on her hands splayed. "Did you believe him? I know he didn't tell you that you couldn't kiss me." D'Aubigné moved her hands to her hips and stomped her foot. "Yes, I want you to kiss me. I want you to kiss me right now."

Tyler felt as if he had been summoned before a high court. His first thought was he was glad this was Casey's porch and not Rennin's, although it seemed Rennin knew everything that happened on Draconis. Nonetheless, Tyler stepped back onto the porch and took the feisty imp into his arms, kissing her deeply and passionately.

When he released her, d'Aubigné took a small step back from the young man. Tyler smirked and asked, "Did that meet your expectations?"

She shook her head and replied absent-mindedly, "No, it surpassed them. Do it again."

Tyler kissed her softly and gently on the lips and said, "Good night, d'Aubigné." He walked down the steps.

"Tyler, wait."

"Good night," he said firmly and walked away to the Willis home, the house Duncan had built, where he slept.

Inside the house he called home, Tyler woke his friend. "Bobby, wake up. I need to talk to you."

Bobby Willis, who was only a year older than Tyler, but the father of three, dragged himself from bed with a yawn, "What's wrong?"

Cryptically Tyler replied, "Everything and nothing. Rennin's going to kill me."

"Why? Have you broken your agreement with him?"

"No, but oh, my God, Bobby, she's driving me insane. Four months is an eternity. I really am in love with her."

"Then, ask her to marry you. Plan a great big wedding. Planning a wedding will distract you from any other thoughts." Bobby laughed. "Oh, and make sure d'Aubigné does a lot of planning at Rennin's house. It'll drive him insane."

The next visit Tyler made was to Nicole Zane. She and Harvey had decided to live in the house built by Colin Fitzpatrick, which still housed the old harpsichord Colin and Ricardo had made for Mary Kate. Nicole welcomed the surprise visit. Tyler got straight to the point. "Nicole, I need your help."

"How can I help you?" she wanted to know.

"I need a song, but not just any song. Do you have a song for me to sing to the woman I love?"

"In love with d'Aubigné, are you?"

Tyler just grinned, shrugged, and said, "I'm doomed."

Nicole started looking through her sheet music. "When and where do you plan to sing this song?"

"Beneath her window in the moonlight as soon as I have it down. I might even use the guitar you taught me to play. I have to serenade her because she predicted it years ago."

"That's so sweet," sighed Nicole. "Harvey has actually sung to me in public, remember?"

"Yes, I do. That was your new beginning."

"How mushy do you want it to be?"

"That's why I came to you for help. I don't want to make her gag, and it should be something I can actually sing."

"Tyler, you can sing anything you want except for, maybe, extra low bass notes."

Nicole found several songs she thought might work and suggested they practice them and consider the words. After singing several songs and reading the words over and over, Tyler decided on "Bridge over Troubled Water." Nicole commented, "You had to choose the one with the hardest melody, didn't you?"

Tyler responded, "I chose the words. I can sing the tune."

They practiced more, and Tyler converted the chords for use on a guitar. Armed with timeless music, just after midnight the next evening, Tyler tossed tiny pebbles at d'Aubigné's window. Having already gone to sleep, the girl threw open the sash intent on screaming vehemently at her dream's intruder. When she poked her head out, Tyler plucked the first chord and said, "Hello, beautiful. This is for you." He serenaded the young woman just as she had said he would when she was six.

Enthralled, she listened to every note, every syllable. When he finished the song, Tyler threw her a kiss, slung the guitar onto his back, and started away. "You wait right there, Tyler Bishop," d'Aubigné commanded assertively. A minute later, the young woman threw her arms around her suitor. Tyler could not help but respond in kind. He held her warm, nightgown-clad body next to him and his heart skipped a beat. Tyler had not been with a woman since d'Aubigné had arrived on the island nearly eleven years earlier. However, he had not forgotten the carnal pleasure, and he had to breathe deeply and hold this new-bloomed woman at arms' length to steady himself.

He whispered, "I didn't intend for you to come out. You'll wake the entire house. Thank God it's your mother's house. Rennin would skin me alive."

"No, he wouldn't. You haven't done anything wrong, Tyler. Even my daddy wouldn't strangle you for your thoughts." D'Aubigné grinned knowingly. She surveyed the distance between them. "Now, do you really want me two feet from you?"

Tyler shook his head and admitted, "No," as he pulled the young woman into an embrace. He breathed her hair that smelled like sweet pea and lilacs. "No, I want you as close as you can possibly get—even closer than this, but that has to wait." He kissed her with a deep sensual kiss and whispered, "Go back to bed and think about me. I'll do the same. Who knows—maybe our mockingbird and dolphin can meet in secret? Now, isn't that a combination?"

As they walked entwined for a few feet Tyler whispered, "D'Aubigne, I…"

The girl's eyes widened expectantly. "Yes?"

He grinned mischievously. "I think I'll tell you with my next surprise."

"Tyler!" The girl stomped her foot.

"Good night," Tyler said as he walked away with great deliberation.

D'Aubigné slipped into the house right into her mother's wink and pop on the behind as she went back to bed. Casey watched the young man walk away, but she did not hear him say to himself, "Cold swim."

Rennin was called upon to attend a Council meeting as the tremors on the island became more frequent and intense. Nobody could explain them. Side-by-side after the meeting, Rennin and Draco looked toward the horizon. Once again Rennin saw himself as a lion surveying the creatures that came to him for safety. Rennin asked, "What do you see, Draco?"

"A very unhappy little redheaded girl living in impoverished conditions. Her grandmother tries hard to give her a good life, but it's a struggle. Although those conditions strengthened you and Renée, perhaps, Cliff should try to return for them again."

"Is it Margaret and Cliff's granddaughter that you see?"

"Yes."

"At least that means that Margaret's alive."

"This is true, but things are very bad out there, Rennin. I think the tremors are being caused by something out there. Cliff should try the barrier again. He should do it now, before he has to perform a wedding. I think he won't be able to get through, but we won't know unless he tries."

"Maybe one of you could fly him almost there in a fishing boat so that it won't take as long."

"Very well. I'll ask Char. He and Cliff have bonded."

Draco surveyed the docks where the fishing boats were arriving. "Yes, I'll ask Char, and I think I'll try to visit the child's dreams. Right now, you're wanted down there."

"Why? Nothing looks out of place."

"That's Tyler's boat."

Rennin squinted. "It's much larger than the others. It looks like an old sailing yacht."

"It is. It's the boat that brought Rennin and Rebekah here. It's the *Spirits' Desire.*"

Looking more closely, Rennin saw the name in beautiful script: *Spirits' Desire.*

"Tyler could have chosen to live on that vessel, just as his family before him, but his spirit's desire was to be close to your daughter, even before he realized it." Draco flipped up a small scale on his chest near his heart. "Give him this from me. It's for him to give to my girl."

Draco handed Rennin a diamond ring. Fashioning something so small had been a tedious task for the gargantuan creature. "I love her, Rennin. Something of Duncan lives boldly in her. Did you know Tyler is descended from Ricardo and Danielle?"

Rennin shook his head.

"Actually, Seamus and Danielle. He is a descendent of the last King Satin himself. Indeed, Tyler looks so much like Seamus O'Donnell, it's as if the man is reborn. He also has O'Rourke blood through Ginny." Draco continued, "No, the boy would never brag about his lineage. He's too self-deprecating, too modest. He doesn't understand why he felt the call to save this world so strongly. He does, however, know he loves your daughter. It's time for him to ask for her hand. Give it to him. Then, open the Morales house. We dragons boarded it up for the magic that's there should not be wielded by any other than d'Aubigné. It's for her and her children. Even as you serve the people of this world by ruling wisely and honestly, she and her descendants will serve by practicing magic wisely."

"Draco, why do you insist a man, a human, appear to be in control of this place when it's actually you?"

"Rennin, you understand perfectly well why a human must be the leader here. Men would never accept the rule of a beast—an animal. Even if I am as powerful as you believe, I would never act in defiance of your authority unless you had gone completely insane. We're a team. We work together. I need one of your kind,

498

who is wise and discerning, to help me as long as I live, which will be much longer than ten centuries more. I must suffer the loss of so many I love. I need one of your descendants, one of Duncan's descendants, for my spirit to survive. By now you understand that in ruling, we actually serve, but without each other, we could become too strong for the other."

"I do understand, Draco. So, why were you not my dragon? Why was it Smoke?"

"Your spirit is as adventurous as your namesake, just as Smoke's is. You fit each other. D'Aubigné is mine, and I am hers. We fit each other. I temper her tempestuousness. She lends me vitality." Draco inclined his head toward the deeply tanned young man who moored his boat for the night. "Tyler is meant for her, Rennin. You know that. You saw him, too, during your vision quest. Take care of my girl's future. I need to talk to Cliff and Char. It could impact Aidan's future." Draco dropped Rennin beside Tyler as he walked toward the home where he slept.

Tyler was surprised by the appearance. "Rennin! To what do I owe the honor of your company? The crew's taking care of the catch. I thought I might visit d'Aubigné tonight."

"That's what I would like to discuss with you—your future with my daughter. Is there something you'd like to ask me?"

Tyler laughed. "Do you mean it's time for me to make my intentions official?"

Rennin nodded. "Do you love her?"

"Yes, I do," Tyler answered seriously. "The funny thing is I think I knew I would love her the first time I met her. Do you think that's possible?"

"I do. I fell in love with Renée the day I saw her. I was five. Actually, I was six, but I thought I was five."

"What?"

Rennin waved his hand. "It's a long story. I'll tell you sometime when you visit your father-in-law."

"Does that mean I have your permission to marry your daughter?"

"It does. But you have to give her this. It's from Draco."
Rennin handed Tyler the ring.

As they spoke, they saw Char streaking over the ocean. Cliff
waved from a small boat.

Tyler asked, "What's going on?"

"We're checking the barrier again. Draco thinks the tremors
have something to do with the outside. Tyler, why didn't you tell
me that you were a descendant of Ricardo, actually Seamus, and
Danielle?"

"I don't want to be held to that standard. Seamus, Ricardo, and
Danielle were human, but they, as well as your ancestors, are often
seen as flawless. I'm not flawless. The three you named have
become legend. I don't want to be a legend. Does that make any
sense to you?"

"Yes. However, because of the Reinhardt incident, you, as all
of us, will one day be legend on Draconis. It's inevitable. In
addition, Ricardo was very much endowed with the gift of magic.
So is d'Aubigné. Ricardo trained his adopted son in the craft.
Young Seamus married an O'Rourke. Are you prepared for the
magical line when you marry my daughter?"

"It's a part of who she is. I might have to adjust, but I love all
of her, not just parts. It's my destiny."

"Good answer. One more question—are you willing to live in
the house Ricardo built for Danielle? Draco seems to think
d'Aubigné must live there."

"He's wise. Draco would never mislead one of us. I would live
in Alexander's Cavern if that's where d'Aubigné lived."

"Very well, then. D'Aubigné's coming out this Friday for the
weekend with us. I expect to see you at dinner. Let me know then
if I can throw an official engagement party, but don't feel rushed
to propose. Do that in your own time and way. Tyler, you're a good
man. I'm proud to claim you as my son. I still expect my daughter
to wear white on her wedding day, but, um, kiss the girl."

Tyler blushed. "I have kissed her. She wouldn't have let me
leave without it."

"I believe it. I'll see you for dinner Friday." Rennin turned his attention elsewhere as Tyler walked on toward home. Rennin called, "Smoke! I need a lift."

All the way home, Tyler stopped along the way and gathered various wildflowers. He grinned as he remembered a little girl telling him he would climb a trellis just to give her flowers. Looking once again at the ring an ancient being had made for one he loved, Tyler thought aloud, "I think I'll add a little something to the flowers." Then, he saw Rose flying overhead and asked if she'd take him the rest of the way home.

The young man practically skipped into the Willis home and went straight to bathe. Jennifer Willis gave her husband a questioning look. Bobby shrugged. "It probably has something to do with d'Aubigné."

When Tyler came from the bath, he hummed. He found a jar to hold his wildflowers temporarily. He pulled one stalk of something bright red and handed it to Jennifer. "Here you go, lovely lady. I thank you for all the hospitality you've shown me these many years, but if all goes as planned, I regretfully inform you I shall soon be living elsewhere."

"Did she say yes?" demanded Jennifer.

"I haven't asked yet."

"Ah," Bobby clued his wife, "Rennin gave his permission. When do you plan to ask?"

"Tonight. When I climb the trellis."

"You'll fall and kill yourself."

"Nope," Tyler argued. "This is how it has to be. I'm a mockingbird, remember? I can fly."

Jennifer gave the man a withering look, but nothing could deflate his mood.

Once again, Tyler waited for midnight. He tied the flowers with a ribbon provided by his gracious hostess for nearly ten years.

Jennifer and Bobby peered from their window in the house Duncan had built to see if the man made it to the top of the trellis. Jennifer thought it was romantic. Bobby told Tyler he had gone stark raving mad.

At the bottom of the trellis, Tyler nestled the bouquet inside his shirt. He tested the strength of the trellis with a good shake and started upward. At the top, he held tightly with one hand and tapped on d'Aubigné's window with the other. She awoke from a pleasant dream at the sound and wondered aloud with a grin, "What is that man up to now?"

D'Aubigné opened the window expecting to see Tyler below with a guitar. Instead he handed her a bunch of wildflowers through the window. She looked at him incredulously and asked point blank, "Did you hear what I said to you all those years ago?"

"Every word," Tyler answered. "Now, are you gonna leave me hanging precariously on a rickety wooden trellis, perchance, to fall to my death, or are you gonna invite me in?"

D'Aubigné gazed at the man holding tightly to the swaying trellis. She glanced at the flowers and back over her shoulder into the room. "This is my bedroom, Tyler. My father will skin you."

Tyler shook his head vehemently. "No, he won't. I'm not gonna break my word. Please let me in." The old trellis gave a slight cracking sound and Tyler grabbed the windowsill.

His pale blue eyes bored beseechingly into the green ones staring back at him. "I'll let go if you don't let me in."

"You would not," responded d'Aubigné.

For a split second, Tyler let go of the windowsill. D'Aubigné dropped the flowers, squealed, "Tyler, stop it," and grabbed the man's hands.

Tyler clasped the wood again. "Are you gonna let me in?"

"Yes," she said, flustered.

He hoisted himself through the window. He stared at the flowers on the floor and said, "You know, I picked every one of those just for you."

D'Aubigné snatched her flowers from the floor and argued, "I thought you were falling. I needed two hands."

Tyler smirked. "Thank you. My foothold really did break, but as little as you weigh, I would probably have pulled you out the window with me."

"I would've made you levitate."

Tyler conceded, "I missed that point. However, I got in here, didn't I?"

"Was that your plan, Mr. Bishop?" asked d'Aubigné as she stretched her eyes wide, and smiled, a dimple creasing her left cheek.

"It was," Tyler admitted. "I have something to ask you."

"And what might that be?" She pursed her lips and batted her eyes coquettishly.

"You know damned well what it might be, but I'll do it in a minute," Tyler said as he pulled d'Aubigné into his arms and kissed her commandingly. When he let her go, she felt lightheaded from the intensity of his kiss. She swooned, and he scooped her into his arms to keep her from falling. He set her on the bed and asked, "Are you all right?"

"I'm fine," d'Aubigné replied as if in a dream. "Continue. You have something to ask me."

Tyler knelt in front of the beauty who had stolen his heart and took her hands in his. He sighed deeply. "First, I should say I love you, but those three little words seem so trite. Yet, they speak the truth. I do love you, and I'm deeply, passionately, hopelessly in love with you. You're a spitfire that doesn't cow down to anyone. In addition to loving you, I admire you, and I like you. Almost ten years ago, I gave you my word that if I stayed alive, I would marry you. I really thought I was gonna die. But I'm still alive. Believe it or not, somewhere in the back of my mind I knew one day I would fall in love with you. You are the most special person I have ever known, and you're the most beautiful woman I've ever seen. Even as a little girl, you captured my heart. That affection has grown into a real, true, abiding love.

"You know I'm a simple man with a simple life. Yes, my ancestors helped to free this land from evil once, but I am not they. I am simply Tyler Ricardo Bishop—a man desperately in love with a woman. I've waited most of my life for you. Even before I knew you existed, I believed you were somewhere. At last, you came to me, not what I expected. Nonetheless, you are perfect for me. So, d'Aubigné Marie O'Rourke, will you marry me?"

Tyler loosened the ring Draco had made from the ribbon he had used and held it out, and d'Aubigné could not believe her eyes. She had seen Draco working on the trinket for days until he got it right. Seeing the ring in the man's hand, she knew Draco had given his approval, and her father must have done so as well. There was no doubt in her mind this was right. She answered the man without hesitation. "Yes, oh, yes."

Tyler slipped the ring onto her finger and sealed it with a kiss. Then, he kissed her again and started out the window.

"Don't be silly," said d'Aubigné. "Use the front door. The whole house is awake anyway. They heard me scream earlier."

D'Aubigné opened her bedroom door to see her mother, her stepfather, and her younger brother. To cover the uncomfortable moment, Craig grabbed the young man's hand. "Congratulations! Rennin and I thank you from the bottom of our hearts for taking her off our hands." Craig winked at his stepdaughter. "Let's all have a drink before you leave."

Cliff and Char returned bearing the news the barrier still did not give way for anyone to leave, but they had not expected any different result.

With Cliff's return, d'Aubigné prepared for an unusual wedding. She wanted the ceremony to be held at midnight because that is when Tyler had proposed. Rennin did not argue or throw anyone from his house. In the years on the island, weddings had become a lot less formal and complicated. Nevertheless, when

Rennin saw his little girl dressed in white with a crown of wildflowers in her hair, he had to pull her back into one of the cabins, hold her in his arms, and cry.

D'Aubigné felt his body shake with silent sobs and felt his warm tears in her hair. With tears of her own, she brushed the moisture from her father's face. "It's all right, Daddy. I'm not leaving you."

"I know, baby. I just didn't want everyone else to see me cry. Do you remember the day you got your ears pierced?"

She nodded. Then, she laughed. "I can't take you to lunch at McDonald's. I can only love you. That will never change. Sometimes—just sometimes, I miss McDonald's, Daddy. I miss fishing on the banks of Beaver Creek with you. I miss making 'hushdogs' with you and Grandpa. When I get back from my honeymoon, let's go fishing in the creek—just you and me."

Rennin nodded. Then, he asked, "Darling, do you realize just how big our responsibility is here?"

"Yes, Daddy, I do. I realize the awesome task we have before us. To lead a people is a daunting endeavor. When we undergo to rule, we must understand in doing so, we serve. But we'll never do it alone, Daddy. We have each other. We have Draco. You have Aunt Renée, and now, I have Tyler. We're never alone."

"I love you, my darling."

"I love you, Daddy. I also love Tyler. I would like to marry him now."

Rennin pulled his daughter's arm through his crooked elbow and walked her to meet a young man who was all smiles. Ten years to the day of making a promise, Tyler Bishop married d'Aubigné O'Rourke, joining two realms once more.

Epilogue

In the glow of a warm radiant sunrise, a golden-haired, emerald-eyed, shirtless, bronzed youth reminiscent of a Norse god of about seventeen bounded from the back of an equally youthful, iridescent, massive-winged beast of quicksilver. Breathlessly the young man approached an even larger shimmering slate-colored beast and an older man near fifty with mass of his own, standing well over six feet and having a well-preserved body and eyes that showed where the boy inherited his, as well as a head full of chestnut waves lightly streaked with ivory. "Daddy!" the boy called as he huffed. "Draco sent Moonbeam and me as fast as we could come. He says to hurry to the beach on the big island. Daddy, humans have washed ashore. Draco says the barrier must be open again."

The two men and beasts zoomed to their appointed destination as above them another even grander beast of glistening mother-of-pearl watched from a precipice far above as he did every morning and every evening.

A young man and a young woman lay motionless, yet breathing and clinging to what appeared to be pieces of an aircraft's fuselage and wing, on the gleaming sand of the beach as gentle aquamarine waves lapped at their feet, inching them further on shore. The older man pulled the unconscious man completely onto dry land as the young man reverently lifted the young woman, whose auburn hair was pulled into a bun, but had escaping wisps all around her face, and reflected the copper and gold of the early morning sun, into his arms. He breathed, "Daddy, she's exquisite, like the sunrise. She's a gift that's been sent to me."

"Aidan," his father warned gently, "you can't assume that. She's been sent here for safekeeping, but that she was sent for you—Don't let your imagination run wild."

The massive gray dragon finally spoke. "Rennin, I don't understand. I thought you were the last."

The man called Rennin smiled knowingly as he looked up at the white dragon who stood like a sentinel. "Draco understands, Smoke. That's why he watches the horizon every day. You see, Smoke, I may have been the last man who, at the time, was able to continue the bloodline of Alexander O'Rourke, but there is no way I could ever be the last exceptional man, if, indeed, I am exceptional."

"Oh, but you are, Rennin," argued the dragon.

"That's not the point, Smoke. Every generation will produce exceptional men and women, who will stand for what's right, just as every generation will produce wicked men and women who would destroy all that's good. The battle between good and evil will continue until the world is made new. That's why Draconis can never completely close its doors. There will always be those sent here for some reason—whether it's to be the sunrise in my son's life or not—like these two. Look at their clothing. Both wear a uniform bearing the insignia of the United States Navy. They are apparently Navy fliers from the indication of the debris. To be this far out, they must've been on an aircraft carrier or greatly off course, which tells me there must be tremendous unrest out there."

"Daddy," called the young man as the woman's voluminous dark-chocolate eyes flickered open.

The woman looked from the face of each man to the face of the enormous creatures that loomed behind them without reaction.

"Where am I?" her lark-like voice asked.

"Draconis," responded the young Norse god replica.

A slight ripple of a laugh escaped the woman's throat. "It's real. How's Stevens?"

"Alive."

"Who are you?"

"I am Aidan Alexander O'Rourke. And you are?"

"Captain Laurel Elaine Moss, United States Navy."

"You're very young to be a captain," said the older man inquiringly.

A weak, sad smile creased the woman's face. "We're all very young these days, sir." The wise older man and the too-wise-for-her-years young woman exchanged a look of understanding.

"There's a war?" asked the man.

"Yes, sir. I fear it will ultimately be called World War III or Armageddon itself, if anyone survives. How do Stevens and I get back to it?"

Rennin O'Rourke sat on the sand before he said, "Tell me about the war. How long has it raged? What started it?"

"Do you people live in the Dark Ages here? Is this some sort of third-world country?"

Rennin laughed loudly. "Perhaps we are by some standards. Suffice it to say our communication with the outside world is limited. So, please tell me about the war."

"We've been fighting ever since I can remember. Some say the war started with the attacks on 9/11 before I was ever born. It escalated as the Middle East grew increasingly volatile, and then the North Koreans finally developed a launching system that worked. Tedious alliances were formed and broken and reformed until some lunatic actually detonated atomic and bio-chem weapons. Yes, America retaliated because it was targeted at our west coast. California no longer has to worry about the San Andreas Fault. It's mostly unlivable. You speak perfect, even cultured, English, Mr. O'Rourke. Are you missionaries or something here? Are you going to join the fight? I ask again—how do I get back?"

Rennin doodled in the dirt as tears stung his eyes before he said thoughtfully, "Puma Pass? Peter? The Raiders? Gone? Destroyed?"

Captain Moss stared intently at the handsome older man. "You! I have your rookie football card. You were a football player. You're Troy Tomerson. You died. I must be dead."

"Captain Moss, you are, for all practical purposes, dead in that world. If you insist on going back, you most likely will never find your way here again. You must decide what's best for you. Your

Stevens must make his own decision. You cannot command him here. Do you want to go back or...?"

Aidan interrupted unthinkingly, "Stay and be my sunrise."

Finally, fully cognizant of her surroundings, the young woman commanded Aidan, "Put me down." Aidan complied as the woman continued to speak. "Just because I've suddenly been marooned on this God-forsaken place does not mean I intend to mate with the natives."

The barb struck home, but Aidan replied with a jerk of his head over his shoulder, "It sounds more like that's the God-forsaken world than this one." Aidan walked to the shimmering creature that had stood back from the crowd. Moonbeam lowered herself for him to climb upon her back.

The young captain, who could not be more than two years older than Aidan, took in her complete surroundings, including the golden native she had so coldly insulted. In an attempt to circumvent the comment without actually offering an apology, she said, "That's an interesting aircraft you have, Aidan Alexander O'Rourke. It appears to be low maintenance."

"Moonbeam needs food frequently, but she only eats bad humans," replied Aidan coldly. The young dragon giggled.

"Neither of these two nor that one"—Captain Moss pointed to the ridge above—"has had me for a snack yet."

Aidan extended a hand. "Would you care to try the aircraft, Captain Moss? Or are you, perhaps, afraid to fly with the natives?"

Laurel Elaine Moss extended her hand upward, and Aidan O'Rourke pulled her in front of him. She commented as the dragon lifted into the air, "The word fear does not exist in my vocabulary."

Rennin turned to the older dragon and said with a grin, "I think she looks more like an erupting volcano, and I think she has brought a little piece of war into one native's life. We had better take care of her copilot."

Smoke grunted, "Rennin, did you hear her name?"

Rennin nodded as a memory came back to him. "Smoke, do you think?"

"I do. She's the right age, and she's military just like her father and grandfather."

Rennin asked his reptilian friend, "Smoke, what if the war has come to us? What do we do?"

He climbed onto the dragon that had been in his dreams all his life, and Smoke guardedly scooped the young Stevens into a talon as he took flight to the heart of the island. Draco flew to meet them, and they disappeared into the foliage of the land. There were decisions to make.

Original completion date, July 28, 2006, Approximately 146,000 words.

Janet Taylor-Perry, B.S., M.A.T.
Author; Editor; Educator; Owner-Operator,
Dragon Breath Press

Like many of her characters, Janet is a history buff and loves anything of historical significance from old cars to old cemeteries. Get to know Janet and you'll see why she's been critically acclaimed at the Faulkner Wisdom Competition and won other awards and why her writing continues to receive 4 and 5-star reviews—It could be that readers see so much of her in her characters: mother, grandmother, educator, author, editor, entrepreneur, animal lover, and a person who has overcome great obstacles and still holds on to her faith.

janettaylorperry.com –For a reading experience
EXTRAORDINAIRE!

http://www.janettaylorperry.com/
http://janettaylor-perry.blogspot.com/
https://authorcentral.amazon.com/gp/profile
https://www.facebook.com/Author-Janet-Taylor-Perry-299698950061301/
janettaylorperry@gmail.com
https://www.facebook.com/janettaylorperrybooks/
Instagram: @janettaylorperry & @jtaylorperry
Twitter: Janet Taylor-Perry— @mom5kidz421
Goodreads:
https://www.goodreads.com/author/show/7376480.Janet_Taylor_Perry
Pinterest: https://www.pinterest.com/mumzy25/
YouTube: https://bit.ly/30hJsYg

The Legend of Draconis

Book IV

One World

No Longer Legend

Their idyllic life shattered by the arrival of two U.S. Navy fliers who washed ashore during a prolonged war, the inhabitants of Draconis must rise to the challenge to save a world that does not know dragons exist.

Captain Laurel Elaine Moss leads Aidan O'Rourke, the heir to the governorship of a mystical land, into a battle for the survival of mankind. But Aidan will never go alone. His bonded dragon, Moonbeam, will never desert him.

Humans and dragons from two realms must fight together to defeat what the outside world calls mutations from bio-chem weapons, but what Draconians dub "the evil gene."

Will the forces of good overcome a persistent evil that just will not die?

Are humans ready to become one world with creatures of lore?

www.ingramcontent.com/pod-product-compliance
Lightning Source LLC
Chambersburg PA
CBHW060211030726
47499CB00004B/997